The Medusa in the Shield contains stories to delight any reader. Those unfamiliar with the genre will discover a wide range of styles and subjects; the fan will encounter old favorites and new treasures.

Robert Aickman
Clive Barker
Michael Bishop
Ramsey Campbell
Thomas M. Disch
Dennis Etchison
William Faulkner
Charlotte Perkins Gilman
Robert Hichens
Henry James
Stephen King
D. H. Lawrence
Tanith Lee
J. Sheridan Le Fanu
H. P. Lovecraft
Richard Matheson
Flannery O'Connor
Edgar Allan Poe
Joanna Russ
Theodore Sturgeon

THE DARK DESCENT
edited by David G. Hartwell

The Color of Evil
The Medusa in the Shield
A Fabulous Formless Darkness

THE MEDUSA IN THE SHIELD

The Dark Descent Vol. 2

edited by David G. Hartwell

A TOM DOHERTY ASSOCIATES BOOK
NEW YORK

This is a work of fiction. All the characters and events portrayed in this book are fictitious, and any resemblance to real people or events is purely coincidental.

THE MEDUSA IN THE SHIELD

Copyright © 1987 by David G. Hartwell
Introduction to this volume copyright © 1991 by David G. Hartwell

This book first appeared as part of the Tor hardcover, THE DARK DESCENT.

A Tor Book
Published by Tom Doherty Associates, Inc.
49 West 24th Street
New York, N.Y. 10010

ISBN: 0-812-50966-8

First printing: November 1991

Printed in the United States of America

0 9 8 7 6 5 4 3 2 1

DEDICATION

To Tom Doherty and Harriet P. McDougal and the Tor Books Horror imprint, and especially Melissa Ann Singer, editor, for support and patience.

To Kathryn Cramer and Peter D. Pautz for their hard work and enthusiasm, as well as provocative discussion.

To Patricia W. Hartwell for letting the books pile up and the piles of paper fall over throughout the house and still loving me.

ACKNOWLEDGMENTS

This anthology grew out of three years of weekly discussions with Peter D. Pautz and Kathryn Cramer on the nature and virtues of horror literature, and its evolution. Peter's knowledge of the contemporary field and Kathryn's theoretical bent were seminal in the genesis of my own thoughts on what horror literature is and has become. Jack Sullivan, Kirby McCauley and Peter Straub were particularly helpful in discussing aspects of horror, and Samuel R. Delany contributed valuable insights, as well as the title for Part III. And I owe an incalculable debt to the great anthologists—from M. R. James and Dashiell Hammett, Elizabeth Bowen, Dorothy Sayers through Wise and Fraser, Boris Karloff and August Derleth to Kirby McCauley, Ramsey Campbell and Jack Sullivan—whose research and scholarship and taste guided my reading over the decades. Robert Hadji and Jessica Salmonson gave valuable support in late-night convention discussions, and the World Fantasy Convention provided an annual environment for advancing ideas in the context of the fine working writers and experts who make horror literature a vigorous and growing form in our time. Finally, my sincere thanks to Stephen King for *Danse Macabre*.

COPYRIGHT ACKNOWLEDGMENTS

CONTENTS

INTRODUCTION TO
THE MEDUSA IN THE SHIELD

This is the second volume of the three volume work, *The Dark Descent*, an anthology that examines the nature of horror literature and offers examples from Poe to the present. Together, the three volumes, *The Color of Evil*, *The Medusa in the Shield*, and *A Fabulous Formless Darkness*, cover the history and evolution of horror in fiction to our times. As is made clear in the general introduction, there are three currents or streams of horror that persist and intermingle throughout history. These streams are discernible in individual stories, in terms of what is more or less central to the aesthetic of an individual work.

I have chosen the pieces included in *The Medusa in the Shield* to represent literary investigations of horror based upon human psychology or psychological metaphor, especially abnormal psychology or psychological metaphors such as monsters, vampires, and ghosts. Some of these stories are supernatural, some are not, but all embody a transaction between the reader and the text that creates horrific sensations. These powerful feelings aroused are the point of horror in fiction, and these stories deliver.

As will be evident, my enterprise in *The Dark Descent* has been to redefine and clarify horror for our era, when it has become such a vital force in contemporary literature. Throughout history until today, the short story has been the form in which the evolution of horror has taken place. The classics of horror fiction are, for the most part, short stories and novellas, and this work represents the largest and most comprehensive collection of them in existence. It allows the contemporary reader access to the whole tradition of horror in the English language.

Each story in *The Medusa in the Shield* is an intense, often subtle laying bare of the human psyche, an experience

xiv   The Medusa in the Shield

in reading you will not soon forget. The power of horror, as one critic has suggested, is to bring to consciousness, if only for a moment, material we could otherwise not bear to look at. Thereby, it reawakens our emotions and strengthens us through awe and fear and wonder.

So, then, here is *The Medusa in the Shield*. . . .

David G. Hartwell

Introduction to
The Dark Descent

> To taste the full flavor of these stories you must bring
> an orderly mind to them, you must have a reasonable
> amount of confidence, if not in what used to be called
> the laws of nature, at least in the currently suspected
> habits of nature. . . . To the truly superstitious the
> "weird" has only its Scotch meaning: "Something
> which actually takes place."
>
> —Dashiell Hammett, *Creeps by Night*

> The appeal of the spectrally macabre is generally nar-
> row because it demands from the reader a certain de-
> gree of imagination and a capacity for detachment from
> everyday life. Relatively few are free enough from the
> spell of daily routine to respond. . . .
>
> —H. P. Lovecraft, *Supernatural Horror in
> Literature*

I

On a July Sunday morning, I was moderating a panel
discussion at Necon, a small New England convention
devoted to dark fantasy. The panelists included Alan Ryan,
Whitley Strieber, Peter Straub, Charles L. Grant and, I believe, Les Daniels, all of them horror novelists. The theme
of the discussion was literary influences, with each partici-
pant naming the horror writers he felt significant in the genesis of his career. As the minutes rolled by and the litany of
names, Poe and Bradbury and Leiber and Lovecraft and
Kafka and others, was uttered, I realized that except for a
ritual bow to Stephen King, every single influential writer

named had been a short story writer. So I interrupted the panel and asked them all to spend the last few minutes commenting on my observation. What they said amounted to this: the good stuff is pretty much all short fiction.

After a few months of thought, I spent a late Halloween night with Peter Straub at the World Fantasy Convention, getting his response to my developing ideas on the recent evolution of horror from a short story to a novel genre. My belief that the long-form horror story is avant-garde and experimental, an unsolved aesthetic problem being attacked with energy and determination by Straub and King and others in our time, solidified as a result of that conversation.

But it seemed to me too early to generalize as to the nature of the new horror novel form. What, then, I asked myself, has happened to the short story? The horror story has certainly not up and vanished after 160 years of development and popularity; far from it. As an administrator of the annual World Fantasy Awards since 1975, I was aware of significant growth in short fiction in the past decade. And so the idea of this book was conceived, to conclude the era of the dominance of short-form horror with a definitive anthology that attempts to represent the entire evolution of the form to date and to describe and point out the boundaries of horror as it has been redefined in our contemporary field. For it seemed apparent to me that the conventional approach to horror codified by the great anthologies of the 1940s is obsolete, was indeed becoming obsolete as those books were published, and has persisted to the detriment of a clearer understanding of the literature to the present. It has persisted to the point where fans of horror fiction most often restrict their reading to books and stories given the imprimatur of a horror category label, thus missing some of the finest pleasures of this century in that fictional mode. I have gathered as many as could be confined within one huge volume here in THE DARK DESCENT, with the intent of clearing the air and broadening future considerations of horror.

Fear has its own aesthetic—as Le Fanu, Henry James, Montagu James and Walter de la Mare have repeatedly shown—and also its own propriety. A story dealing in fear ought, ideally, to be kept at a certain pitch. And that austere other world, the world of the ghost, should inspire, when it impacts on our own, not so much revulsion or shock as a sort of awe.

—Elizabeth Bowen, *The Second Ghost Book*

The one test of the really weird is simply this—whether or not there be excited in the reader a profound sense of dread, and of contact with unknown spheres and powers.

—H. P. Lovecraft, *Supernatural Horror in Literature*

II The Evolution of Horror Fiction

For more than 150 years horror fiction has been a vital component of English and American literature, invented with the short story form itself and contributing intimately to the evolution of the short story. Until the last decade, the dominant literary form of horror fiction was the short story and novella. This is simply no longer the case. Shortly after the beginning of the 1970s, within a very few years, the novel form assumed the position of leadership. First came a scattering of exceptionally popular novels—*Rosemary's Baby, The Other, The Exorcist, The Mephisto Waltz,* with attendant film successes—then, in 1973, the deluge, with Stephen King on the crest of the wave, altering the nature of horror fiction for the foreseeable future and sweeping along with it all the living generations of short fiction writers. Very few writers of horror fiction, young or old, resisted the commercial or aesthetic temptation to expand into the novel form, leading to the creation of some of the best horror novels of all time as well as a large amount of popular trash rushed into print. The models for these works were the previous bestsellers, popular films and the short fiction masterpieces of previous decades.

When the tide ebbed in the 1980s, much of the trash was left dead in the backlists of paperback publishers, but the horror novel had become firmly established. This is significant from a number of perspectives. Rapid evolution and experimentation was encouraged. All kinds of horror literature benefited from the incorporation of every conceivable element of horrific effect and technique from other literature and film and video and comics.

The most useful and provocative view we can take on the horror novel in recent years is that it constitutes an avant-garde and experimental literary form which attempts to translate the horrific effects previously thought to be the nearly exclusive domain of the short forms into newly conceived long forms that maintain the proper atmosphere and effects. Certainly isolated examples of more or less successful novel-length horror fiction exist, from *Frankenstein* and *Dracula* to *The Haunting of Hill House*, but they are comparatively infrequent next to the constant, rich proliferation and development of horror in shorter forms in every decade from Poe to the present. The horror novels of the past do not in aggregate form a body of traditional literature and technique from which the present novels spring and upon which they depend.

It is evident both from the recent novels themselves and from the public statements of many of the writers that Stephen King, Peter Straub and Ramsey Campbell, and a number of other leading novelists, have been discussing among themselves—and trying to solve in their works—the perceived problems of developing the horror novel into a sophisticated and effective form. In so doing, they have highlighted the desirability of a volume such as THE DARK DESCENT, which represents the context from which the literature springs and attempts to elucidate the whole surround of horror today.

Horror novels grow to a very large extent out of the varied and highly evolved novellas and short stories exemplified in this book. Our perceptions of the nature of horror literature have been changing and evolving rapidly in recent decades, to the point where a compilation of the horror story, organized according to new principles, is needed to manifest the broadened nature of the literature.

Before proceeding in the next section to begin an anatomy of horror, it is interesting to note that there has been a renewed fashion for horror in every decade since the First World

War, but this is the first such "revival" that has produced numerous novels.

There was a general increase in horror, particularly the ghost story, in the 1920s under the influence of M. R. James, both a prominent writer and anthologist, and such masters as Algernon Blackwood, Walter de la Mare, Edith Wharton and others. At that time the great horror magazine, *Weird Tales*, was founded in the U.S. In the 1930s, the dark fantasy story or weird tale became prominent, influenced by the magazine mentioned above, the growth of the H. P. Lovecraft circle of writers, and a proliferation of anthologies, either in series or as huge compendiums celebrating the first century of horror fiction. After the films and books of the 1930s, the early 1940s produced the finest "great works" collections, epitomized by *And the Darkness Falls*, edited by Boris Karloff, and *Great Tales of Terror and the Supernatural*, edited by Herbert Wise and Phyllis Fraser; and Arkham House, the great specialty publisher devoted to this day to bringing into print collections by great horror authors, was founded by writer Donald Wandrei to print the collected works of H. P. Lovecraft. After the war came the science fiction horrors of the 1950s, in all those monster films and in the works of Richard Matheson, Jack Finney, Theodore Sturgeon and Ray Bradbury. In the early sixties we had the craze for "junk food" paperback horror anthologies and collections, under the advent of the midnight horror movie boom on TV. But as we remarked above, short fiction always remained at the forefront. Even the novelists were famous for their short stories.

A lot has changed.

Atmosphere is the all-important thing, for the final criterion of authenticity is not the dovetailing of a plot but the creation of a given sensation.

—H. P. Lovecraft, *Supernatural Horror in Literature*

Much as we ask for it, the *frisson* of horror, among the many oddities of our emotional life, is one of the oddest. For one thing, it is usually a response to something that is not there. Under normal circumstances, that is, it attends only such things as nightmares phobias and literature. In that respect it is unlike terror, which is extreme and sudden fear in the face of a material threat. . . . The terror can be dissipated by a round of buckshot. Horror, on the other hand, is fascinated dread in the presence of an immaterial cause. The frights of nightmares cannot be dissipated by a round of buckshot; to flee them is to run into them at every turn.

—Sigmund Freud, *The Uncanny*

III   What It Is

Sigmund Freud remarked that we immediately recognize scenes that are supposed to provoke horror, "even if they actually provoke titters." It seems to me, however, that horror fiction has usually been linked to or categorized by manifest signs in texts, and this has caused more than a little confusion among commentators over the years. Names such as weird tales, gothic tales, terror tales, ghost stories, supernatural tales, macabre stories—all clustered around the principle of a real or implied or fake intrusion of the supernatural into the natural world, an intrusion which arouses fear—have been used as appellations for the whole body of literature, sometimes interchangeably by the same writer. So often, and in so many of the best works, has the intrusion been a ghost, that nearly half the time you will find "horror story" and "ghost story" used interchangeably. And this is so in spite of the acknowledged fact that supernatural horror in literature embodies many manifestations (from demons to vampires to werewolves to pagan gods and more) and, further, that ghosts are recognizably not supposed to horrify in a fair number of ghost stories.

J. A. Cuddon, a thorough scholar, has traced the early connections between ghost and horror stories from the 1820s to the 1870s, viewing them as originally separable: "The growth of the ghost story and the horror story in this mid-century period tended to coalesce; indeed, it is difficult to establish objective criteria by which to distinguish between the two. A taxonomical approach invariably begins to break down at an early stage. . . . On balance, it is probable that a ghost story will contain an element of horror.'' Jack Sullivan, another distinguished scholar and anthologist, sums up the problems of definition and terminology thusly: "We find ourselves in a tangled morass of definitions and permutations that grows as relentlessly as the fungus in the House of Usher.'' Sullivan chooses "ghost story'' as generic, presumably to have one leg to stand on facing in each direction.

We choose "horror'' as our term, both in accordance with the usage of the marketplace (Tor Books has a Tor Horror line; horror is a label for the marketing category under which novels and collections appear), and because it points toward a transaction between the reader and the text that is the essence of the experience of reading horror fiction, and not anything contained within the text (such as a ghost, literal or implied). And moreover, H. P. Lovecraft, the theoretician and critic who most carefully described the literature in his *Supernatural Horror in Literature*, who was certainly the most important American writer of horror fiction in the first half of this century, has to the best of my memory not a single conventional ghost story in the corpus of his works.

It is Lovecraft's essay that provides the keystone upon which any architecture of horror must be built: atmosphere. And it seems to me that Freud is in accord. What this means is that you can experience true horror in, potentially, any work of fiction, be it a western, a contemporary gothic, science fiction, mystery, whatever category of content the writer may choose. A work may be a horror story (and indeed included in this anthology) no matter what, as long as the atmosphere allows. This means that horror is set free from the supernatural, that it is unnecessary for the story to contain any overt or implied device or manifestation whatsoever. The emotional transaction is paramount and definitive, and we recognize its presence even when it doesn't work as it is supposed to.

To them [people who don't read horror] it is a kind of
pornography, inducing horripilation instead of erection.
And the reader who appears to relish such sensations—
why he's an emotional masochist, the slave of an un-
holy drug, a decadent psychotic beast.

—David Aylward, *Revenge of the Past*

First, the longing for mystic experience which seems
always to manifest itself in periods of social confusion,
when political progress is blocked: as soon as we feel
that our own world has failed us, we try to find evidence for another world; second, the instinct to inocu-
late ourselves against panic at the real horrors loose on
the earth . . . by injections of imagery horror, which
soothe us with the momentary illusion that the forces
of madness and murder may be tamed and compelled
to provide us with a mere dramatic entertainment.

—Edmund Wilson, *A Literary Chronicle*

I used to read horror when I was depressed to jump-
start my emotions—but it only gave me temporary relief.

—Kathryn Cramer (personal correspondence)

It proves that the tale of horror and/or the supernatural
is serious, *is* important, *is* necessary . . . not only to
those human beings who read to think, but to those who
read to feel; the volume may even go a certain distance
toward proving the idea that, as this mad century races
toward its conclusion—a conclusion which seems ever
more ominous and ever more absurd—it may be the
most important and useful form of fiction which the
moral writer may command.

—Stephen King, Introduction to *The Arbor House
Treasury of Horror and the Supernatural*

IV The Death of Horror

The death of the novel and the death of the short story are literary topics we joke about, so it should come as no particular surprise that a recent, and otherwise excellent, collection of essays on supernatural fiction in America from 1820–1920 states that supernatural fiction died around 1920 ("dematerialized"), to be replaced by psychoanalysis, which took over its function. Now it seems to me surprising to maintain that fiction that embodies psychological truth in metaphor is replaceable by science—it sounds rather too much like replacing painting with photography. Yet this is only a recent example of the obituary approach, an effective gambit when dealing with material you wish to exterminate, and often used by self-appointed arbiters of taste.

Let's resurrect the great Modernist critic, Edmund Wilson, for a few minutes. Wilson wrote an essay on horror in the early 1940s that challenged the whole canon of significant works established by the anthologies of the 1930s and '40s, from Dorothy Sayers and M. R. James and Hugh Walpole and Marjorie Bowen to Wise and Fraser, and Karloff. Wilson proposed his own list of masterpieces, from Poe and Gogol ("the greatest master") and Melville and Turgenev through Hardy, Stevenson, Kipling, Conrad's *The Heart of Darkness* and Henry James' *The Turn of the Screw* to Walter de la Mare and, ultimately, Kafka ("he went straight for the morbidities of the psyche"). He, Wilson, seems to be reaching toward a redefinition of horror literature, but unfortunately his essay vibrates with the discomfort of the humanist and rationalist confronting the supernatural. He rejects nearly every classic story in the horror canon and every single writer principally known for work in the field, reserving particular antipathy for H. P. Lovecraft, the anti-Modernist (to whom he devoted a whole separate essay of demolition).

Wilson's comments on Kafka are instructive. Kafka's "visions of moral horror" are "narratives that compel our attention, and fantasies that generate more shudders than the whole of Algernon Blackwood or M. R. James combined." Kafka's characters "have turned into the enchanted denizens of a world in which, prosaic though it is, we can find no firm foothold in reality and in which we can never even be certain whether souls are being saved or damned . . . he went straight for the morbidities of the psyche with none of the puppetry of specters and devils that earlier writers still carried with them." Wilson's view of the evolution of horror is implicit in these comments. He sees the literature as evolving in a linear fashion into fantasies of the psyche removed entirely from supernatural trappings. Any audience interested in these trappings is regressive. He sees no value to a modern reader in obsolete fiction.

Since Wilson's presupposition is that the evolution of horror ended with Kafka, his theory of horror reading among his contemporaries—that they are indulging in a "revived" taste for an obsolete form—allows him to start from the premise that the ghost story is dead, that it died with the advent of the electric light, and to conclude immediately that contemporary versions are doomed attempts to revive the corpse of the form. Sound familiar? It's the familiar "death of literature" obituary approach. Well, back to the grave, Edmund. You're dead, and horror literature is alive and well, happily evolving and diversifying.

But Wilson's approach to the horror canon was and remains generally stimulating. For it appears that as horror has evolved in this century it has grown significantly in the areas of "the morbidities of the psyche" and fantasies of "a world in which, prosaic though it is, we can find no firm foothold in reality."

In order to achieve the fantastic, it is neither necessary nor sufficient to portray extraordinary things. The strangest event will enter into the order of the universe if it is alone in a world governed by laws. . . . You cannot impose limits on the fantastic; either it does not exist at all, or else it extends throughout the universe. It is an entire world in which things manifest a captive, tormented thought, a thought both whimsical and enchained, that gnaws away from below at the mechanism's links without ever managing to express itself. In this world, matter is never entirely matter, since it offers only a constantly frustrated attempt at determinism, and mind is never completely mind, because it has fallen into slavery and has been impregnated and dulled by matter. All is woe. Things suffer and tend towards inertia, without ever attaining it; the debased, enslaved mind unsuccessfully strives toward consciousness and freedom.

—Jean-Paul Sartre, *AMINADAB or The Fantastic Considered as a Language*

V The Three Streams

We return to the life and state of horror fiction in the present. Contemporary horror fiction occurs in three streams, in three principal modes or clusters of emphasis: 1. moral allegorical 2. psychological metaphor 3. fantastic. The stories in this anthology are separated according to these categories. These modes are not mutually exclusive, but usually a matter of emphasis along a spectrum from the overtly moral at one extreme to the nearly totally ambiguous at the other, with human psychology always a significant factor but only sometimes the principal focus. Perhaps we might usefully imagine them as three currents in the same ocean.

Stories that cluster at the first pole are characteristically supernatural fiction, most usually about the intrusion of supernatural evil into consensus reality, most often about the horrid and colorful special effects of evil. These are the stories of children possessed by demons, of hauntings by evil ghosts from the past (most ghost stories), stories of bad places (where evil persists from past times), of witchcraft and satanism. In our day they are often written and read by lapsed Christians, who have lost their firm belief in good but still have a discomforting belief in evil. Stories in this stream imply or state the Manichean universe that is so difficult to perceive in everyday life, wherein evil is so evident, horror so common that we are left with our sensitivities partly or fully deadened to it in our post-Holocaust, post-Vietnam, six-o'clock news era. A strong extra-literary appeal of such fiction, it seems to me, is to jump-start the readers' deadened emotional sensitivities.

And the moral allegory has its significant extra-literary appeal in itself to that large audience that desires the attribution of a moral calculus (usually teleological) deriving from ultimate and metaphysical forms of good and evil behind events in an everyday reality. Ginjer Buchanan says that "all the best horror is written by lapsed Catholics."

In speaking of stories and novels in this first stream, we are speaking of the most popular form of horror fiction today, the commercial bestseller lineage of *Rosemary's Baby* and *The Exorcist*, and a majority of the works of Stephen King. These stories are taken to the heart of the commercial-category audience that is characteristically style-deaf (regardless of the excellence of some of the works), the audience that requires repeated doses of such fiction for its emotional effect to persist. This stream is the center of category horror publishing.

The second group of horror stories, stories of aberrant human psychology embodied metaphorically, may be either purely supernatural, such as *Dracula*, or purely psychological, such as Robert Bloch's *Psycho*. What characterizes them as a group is the monster at the center, from the monster of Frankenstein, to Carmilla, to the chain-saw murderer—an overtly abnormal human or creature, from whose acts and on account of whose being the horror arises. D. H. Lawrence's little boy, Faulkner's Emily, and, more subtly, the New Yorker of Henry James' "The Jolly Corner" show the extent to which this stream interpenetrates and blends with the mainstream of psychological fiction in this century. Both Lovecraft and Edmund Wilson, from differing perspectives, see Joseph Conrad's *The Heart of Darkness* as essentially horror fiction. There has been strong resistance on the part of critics, from Wilson to the present, to admitting nonsupernatural psychological horror into consideration of the field, allowing many to declare the field a dead issue for contemporary literature, of antiquarian interest only since the 1930s. This trend was probably aided by the superficial examination of the antiquarianism of both M. R. James and H. P. Lovecraft.

But by 1939 an extremely significant transition is apparent, particularly in the U.S. *Weird Tales* and the Lovecraft circle of writers, as well as the popular films, had made horror a vigorous part of popular culture, had built a large audience among the generally nonliterary readership for pulp fiction, a "lower-class" audience. And in 1939 John W. Campbell, the famous science fiction editor, founded the revolutionary pulp fantasy magazine, *Unknown*. From 1923 to 1939, the leading source of horror and supernatural fiction in the English language was *Weird Tales*, publishing all traditional styles but tending toward the florid and antiquarian. *Unknown* was an aesthetic break with traditional horror fiction. Campbell demanded stories with contemporary, particularly urban, settings, told in clear, unornamented prose style. *Unknown* featured stories by all the young science fiction writers whose work was changing that genre in Campbell's *Astounding*: Alfred Bester, Eric Frank Russell, Robert A. Heinlein, A. E. Van Vogt, L. Ron Hubbard and others, particularly such fantasists as Theodore Sturgeon, Jane Rice, Anthony Boucher, Fredric Brown and Fritz Leiber.

The stories tended to focus equally on the supernatural and the psychological. Psychology was often quite overtly the underpinning for horror, as in, for example, Hubbard's "He Didn't Like Cats," in which there is an extended discussion between the two supporting characters as to whether the central character's problem is supernatural or psychological . . . and we never know, for either way he's doomed. *Unknown* broke the dominance of *Weird Tales* and influenced such significant young talents as Ray Bradbury and Shirley Jackson. The magazine encouraged the genrification of certain types of psychological fiction and, at the same time, crossbred a good bit of horror into the growing science fiction field. This reinforced a cultural trend apparent in the monster and mad scientist films of the 1930s, giving us the enormous spawn of SF/horror films of the 1950s and beyond.

It is interesting to note that as our perceptions of horror fiction and what the term includes change over the decades, differing works seem to fall naturally into or out of the category. The possibilities of psychological horror seem in the end to blur distinctions, and there is no question that horror is becoming ever more inclusive.

Stories of the third stream have at their center ambiguity as to the nature of reality, and it is this very ambiguity that generates the horrific effects. Often there is an overtly supernatural (or certainly abnormal) occurrence, but we know of it only by allusion. Often, essential elements are left undescribed so that, for instance, we do not know whether there was really a ghost or not. But the difference is not merely supernatural versus psychological explanation: third stream stories lack any explanation that makes sense in everyday reality—we don't know, and that doubt disturbs us, horrifies us. This is the fiction to which Sartre's analysis alludes, the fantastic. At its extreme, from Kafka to the present, it blends indistinguishably with magic realism, the surreal, the absurd, all the fictions that confront reality through paradoxical distance. It is the fiction of radical doubt. Thomas M. Disch once remarked that Poe can profitably be considered as a contemporary of Kierkegaard, and it is evident that this stream develops from the beginnings of horror fiction in the short story. In the contemporary field it is a major current.

Third stream stories tend to cross all category lines but usually they do not use the conventional supernatural as a distancing device. While most horror fiction declares itself at some point as violating the laws of nature, the fantastic worlds of third stream fiction use as a principal device what Sartre has called the language of the fantastic.

At the end of a horror story, the reader is left with a new perception of the nature of reality. In the moral allegory strain, the point seems to be that this is what reality was and has been all along (i.e., literally a world in which supernatural forces are at work) only you couldn't or wouldn't recognize it. Psychological metaphor stories basically use the intrusion of abnormality to release repressed or unarticulated psychological states. In her book, *Powers of Horror*, critic Julia Kristeva says that horror deals with material just on the edge of repression but not entirely repressed and inaccessible. Stories from our second stream use the heightening effect of the monstrously abnormal to achieve this release. Third stream stories maintain the pretense of everyday reality only to annihilate it, leaving us with another world entirely, one in which we are disturbingly imprisoned. It is in perceiving the changed reality and its nature that the pleasure and illumination of third stream stories lies, that raises this part of horror fiction above the literary level of most of its generic relations. So the transaction between the reader and the text that identifies all horror fiction is to an extent modified in third stream stories (there is rarely, if ever, any terror), making them more difficult to classify and identify than even the borderline cases in the psychological category. Gene Wolfe's "Seven American Nights" is, in my opinion, a story on the borderline of third stream, deeply disturbing but not conventionally horrifying. The mass horror audience is not much taken with third stream stories, regardless of craft or literary merit, because they modify the emotional jolt.

Although the manifest images of horror fiction are legion, their latent meanings are few. Readers and writers of horror fiction, like those of all the popular genres, seem under a compulsion to repeat. Certainly the needs satisfied by horror fiction are recurrent and ineradicable.

—George Stade, *The New York Times*,
　　Oct. 27, 1985

I recognize terror as the finest emotion and so I will try to terrorize the reader. But if I find that I cannot terrify, I will try to horrify, and if I find that I cannot horrify, I'll go for the gross-out.

—Stephen King, *Danse Macabre*

VI The Dark Descent

The descent of horror fiction from its origins in the nineteenth century to the many and sophisticated forms of the contemporary field has taken place in shorter stories. Now that the novel has taken over, the major writers are unlikely to devote their principal efforts to short fiction. So we have reached a point in the evolution of this literary mode at which we can take stock of its achievements in short fiction and assess its qualities and contributions to all of literature. The stories assembled in this book are divided according to the three streams we have identified, both to provide extended examples and to provoke further discussion. The short story is vigorously alive in horror today, in magazines, anthologies, and collections. Let it, for a moment, occupy the center of your attention. The best short fiction in modern horror is the equal of the best of all times and places.

Robert Aickman

THE SWORDS

Robert Aickman is surely one of the masters in this century of the ghost story and the horror story in the psychological metaphor strain. Characteristically Aickman uses not monstrosity but the fantastic to achieve his effects, as in "The Swords," a story of male sexual initiation in which the overt is transformed into the absurd and the surreal, a fantastic language. The effect is unusually powerful and horrifying, complex and devastating, and darkly humorous, because the reader is aware of so much more than the character. Aickman's work is perhaps best called symbolist. "The good ghost story gives form and symbol to themes from enormous areas of our own minds which we cannot directly discern, but which totally govern us," Aickman said. He categorized his own work as "strange stories," a general term that represents something close to Freud's "unheimlich." "Aickman's entire body of short fiction expresses a coherent vision," says the critic Gary Crawford. "Man is trapped in a vortex of subtle, symbolic terror, a victim of forces within himself over which he has no control." One might add that external reality is quite strange and literally, if not symbolically, uncontrollable. Aickman is, in Russell Kirk's opinion, "the greatest of all writers of the uncanny," and Fritz Leiber called him "a weatherman of the unconscious."

Corazón malherido
Por cinco espadas

FEDERICO GARCIA LORCA

My first experience?

My first experience was far more of a test than anything that has ever happened to me since in that line. Not more agreeable, but certainly more testing. I have noticed several times that it is to beginners that strange things happen, and often, I think, to beginners only. When you know about a thing, there's just nothing to it. This kind of thing included—anyway, in most cases. After the first six women, say, or seven, or eight, the rest come much of a muchness.

I was a beginner all right; raw as a spring onion. What's more, I was a real mother's boy: scared stiff of life, and crass ignorant. Not that I want to sound disrespectful to my old mother. She's as good as they come, and I still hit it off better with her than with most other females.

She had a brother, my Uncle Elias. I should have said that we're all supposed to be descended from one of the big pottery families, but I don't know how true it is. My gran had little bits of pot to prove it, but it's always hard to be sure. After my dad was killed in an accident, my mother asked my Uncle Elias to take me into his business. He was a grocery salesman in a moderate way—and nothing but cheap lines. He said I must first learn the ropes by going out on the road. My mother was thoroughly upset because of my dad having died in a smash, and because she thought I was bound to be in moral danger, but there was nothing she could do about it, and on the road I went.

It was true enough about the moral danger, but I was too simple and too scared to involve myself. As far as I could, I steered clear even of the other chaps I met who were on the road with me. I was pretty certain they would be bad influences, and I was always bound to be the baby of the party anyway. I was dead rotten at selling and I was utterly lonely—not just in a manner of speaking, but truly lonely. I hated the life but Uncle Elias had promised to see me all right and I couldn't think of what else to do. I stuck it on the road for more than two years, and then I heard of my present job with the building society—read about it, actually, in the local paper—so that I was able to tell Uncle Elias what he could do with his cheap groceries.

For most of the time we stopped in small hotels—some of them weren't bad either, both the room and the grub—but in a few towns there were special lodgings known to Uncle Elias, where I and Uncle Elias's regular traveller, a sad chap called Bantock, were ordered by Uncle Elias to go. To this day I don't know exactly why. At the time I was quite sure that there was some kickback for my uncle in it, which was the obvious thing to suppose, but I've come since to wonder if the old girls who kept the lodgings might not have been my uncle's fancy women in the more or less distant past. At least once, I got as far as asking Bantock about it, but he merely said he didn't know what the answer was. There was very little that Bantock admitted to knowing about anything beyond the current prices of soapflakes and Scotch. He had been 42 years on the road for my uncle when one day he dropped dead of a thrombosis in Rochdale. Mrs. Bantock, at least, had been one of my uncle's women off and on for years. That was something everyone knew.

These women who kept the lodgings certainly behaved as if what I've said was true. You've never seen or heard such dives. Noises all night so that it was impossible to sleep properly, and often half-dressed tarts beating on your door and screaming that they'd been swindled or strangled. Some of the travellers even brought in boys, which is something I have never been able to understand. You read about it and hear about it, and I've often seen it happen, as I say, but I still don't understand it. And there was I in the middle of it all, pure and unspotted. The woman who kept the place often cheeked me for it. I don't know how old Bantock got on. I never found myself in one of these places at the same time as he was there. But the funny part was that my mother thought I was extra safe in one of these special lodgings, because they were all particularly guaranteed by her brother, who made Bantock and me go to them for our own good.

Of course it was only on some of the nights on the road. But always it was when I was quite alone. I noticed that at

the time when Bantock was providing me with a few intro-
ductions and openings, they were always in towns where we
could stay in commercial hotels. All the same, Bantock had
to go to these special places when the need arose, just as
much as I did, even though he never would talk about them.

One of the towns where there was a place on Uncle Elias's
list was Wolverhampton. I fetched up there for the first time,
after I had been on the job for perhaps four or five months.
It was by no means my first of these lodgings, but for that
very reason my heart sank all the more as I set eyes on the
place and was let in by the usual bleary-eyed cow in curlers
and a dirty overall.

There was absolutely nothing to do. Nowhere even to sit and
watch the telly. All you could think of was to go out and get
drunk, or bring someone in with you from the pictures. Neither
idea appealed very much to me, and I found myself just wandering about the town. It must have been late spring or early
summer, because it was pleasantly warm, though not too hot,
and still only dusk when I had finished my tea, which I had to
find in a café, because the lodging did not even provide tea.

I was strolling about the streets of Wolverhampton, with
all the girls giggling at me, or so it seemed, when I came
upon a sort of small fair. Not knowing the town at all, I had
drifted into the rundown area up by the old canal. The main
streets were quite wide, but they had been laid out for daytime traffic to the different works and railway yards, and were
now quiet and empty, except for the occasional lorry and the
boys and girls playing around at some of the corners. The
narrow streets running off contained lines of small houses,
but a lot of the houses were empty, with windows broken or
boarded up, and holes in the roof. I should have turned back,
but for sound made by the fair; not pop songs on the ampli-
fiers, and not the pounding of the old steam organs, but more
a sort of high tinkling, which somehow fitted in with the
warm evening and the rosy twilight. I couldn't at first make
out what the noise was, but I had nothing else to do, very
much not, and I looked around the empty back streets, until
I could find what was going on.

It proved to be a very small fair indeed; just half a dozen
stalls, where a few kids were throwing rings or shooting off

toy rifles, two or three covered booths, and, in the middle, one very small roundabout. It was this that made the tinkling music. The roundabout *looked* pretty too; with snow-queen and icing sugar effects in the centre, and different coloured sleighs going round, each just big enough for two, and each, as I remember, with a coloured light high up at the peak. And in the middle was a very pretty, blonde girl dressed as some kind of pierrette. Anyway she seemed very pretty at that time to me. Her job was to collect the money from the people riding in the sleighs, but the trouble was that there weren't any. Not a single one. There weren't many people about at all, and inevitably the girl caught my eye. I felt I looked a Charley as I had no one to ride with, and I just turned away. I shouldn't have dared to ask the girl herself to ride with me, and I imagine she wouldn't have been allowed to in any case. Unless, perhaps, it was her roundabout.

The fair had been set up on a plot of land which was empty simply because the houses which had stood on it had been demolished or just fallen down. Tall, blank factory walls towered up on two sides of it, and the ground was so rough and uneven that it was like walking on lumpy rocks at the seaside. There was nothing in the least permanent about the fair. It was very much here today and gone tomorrow. I should not have wondered if it had had no real business to have set up there at all. I doubted very much if it had come to any kind of agreement for the use of the land. I thought at once that the life must be a hard one for those who owned the fair. You could see why fairs like that have so largely died out from what things used to be in my gran's day, who was always talking about the wonderful fairs and circuses when she was a girl. Such customers as there were, were almost all mere kids, even though kids do have most of the money nowadays. These kids were doing a lot of their spending at a tiny stall where a drab-looking woman was selling ice-cream and toffee-apples. I thought it would have been much simpler and more profitable to concentrate on that, and enter the catering business rather than trying to provide entertainment for people who prefer to get it in their houses. But very probably I was in a gloomy frame of mind that evening. The fair was pretty and old-fashioned, but no one could say it cheered you up.

The girl on the roundabout could still see me, and I was sure was looking at me reproachfully—and probably contemptuously as well. With that layout, she was in the middle of things and impossible to get away from. I should just have mooched off, especially since the people running the different stalls were all beginning to shout at me, as pretty well the only full adult in sight, when, going round, I saw a booth in more or less the farthest corner, where the high factory walls made an angle. It was a square tent of very dirty red and white striped canvas, and over the crumpled entrance flap was a rough-edged, dark painted, horizontal board, with written on it in faint gold capital letters THE SWORDS. That was all there was. Night was coming on fast, but there was no light outside the tent and none shining through from inside. You might have thought it was a store of some kind.

For some reason, I put out my hand and touched the hanging flap. I am sure I should never have dared actually to draw it aside and peep in. But a touch was enough. The flap was pulled back at once, and a young man stood there, sloping his head to one side so as to draw me in. I could see at once that some kind of show as going on. I did not really want to watch it, but felt that I should look a complete imbecile if I just ran away across the fairground, small though it was.

"Two bob," said the young man, dropping the dirty flap, and sticking out his other hand, which was equally dirty. He wore a green sweater, mended but still with holes, grimy grey trousers, and grimier sandshoes. Sheer dirt was so much my first impression of the place that I might well have fled after all, had I felt it possible. I had not noticed this kind of griminess about the rest of the fair.

Running away, however, wasn't on. There were so few people inside. Dotted about the bare, bumpy ground, with bricks and broken glass sticking out from the hard earth, were 20 or 30 wooden chairs, none of them seeming to match, most of them broken or defective in one way or another, all of them chipped and off-colour. Scattered among these hard chairs was an audience of seven. I know it as seven, because I had no difficulty in counting, and because soon it mattered.

I made the eighth. All of them were in single units and all were men: this time men and not boys. I think that I was the youngest among them, by quite a long way.

And the show was something I have never seen or heard of since. Nor even read of. Not exactly.

There was a sort of low platform of dark and discoloured wood up against the back of the tent—probably right on to the factory walls outside. There was a burly chap standing on it, giving the spiel, in a pretty rough delivery. He had tight yellow curls, the colour of cheap lemonade but turning grey, and a big red face, with a splay nose, and very dark red lips. He also had small eyes and ears. The ears didn't seem exactly opposite one another, if you know what I mean. He wasn't much to look at, though I felt he was very strong, and could probably have taken on all of us in the tent single-handed and come out well on top. I couldn't decide how old he was—either then or later. (Yes, I did see him again— twice.) I should imagine he was nearing 50, and he didn't look in particularly good condition, but it seemed as though he had just been made with more thew and muscle than most people are. He was dressed like the youth at the door, except that the sweater of the chap on the platform was not green but dark blue, as if he were a seaman, or perhaps acting one. He wore the same dirty grey trousers and sandshoes as the other man. You might almost have thought the place was some kind of boxing booth.

But it wasn't. On the chap's left (and straight ahead of where I sat at the edge of things and in the back row) a girl lay sprawled out facing us in an upright canvas chair, as faded and battered as everything else in the outfit. She was dressed up like a French chorus, in a tight and shiny black thing, cut low, and black fishnet stockings, and those shiny black shoes with super high heels that many men go for in such a big way. But the total effect was not particularly sexy, all the same. The different bits of costume had all seen better days, like everything else, and the girl herself looked more sick than spicy. Under other conditions, I thought to begin with, she might have been pretty enough, but she had made herself up with green powder, actually choosing it apparently, or having it chosen for her, and her hair, done in a tight bun,

like a ballet dancer's, was not so much mousy as plain colourless. On top of all this, she was lying over the chair, rather
than sitting in it, just as if she was feeling faint or about to
be ill. Certainly she was doing nothing at all to lead the chaps
on. Not that I myself should have wanted to be led. Or so I
thought at the start.

And in front of her, at the angle of the platform, was this
pile of swords. They were stacked criss-cross, like cheese-
straws, on top of a low stool, square and black, the sort of
thing they make in Sedgeley and Wednesfield and sell as Japanese, though this specimen was quite plain and undecorated,
even though more than a bit chipped. There must have been
30 or 40 swords, as the pile had four corners to it, where the
hilts of the swords were set diagonally above one another. It
struck me later that perhaps there was one sword for each
seat, in case there was ever a full house in the tent.

If I had not seen the notice outside, I might not have realized they *were* swords, or not at first. There was nothing
gleaming about them, and nothing decorative. The blades
were a dull grey, and the hilts were made of some black stuff,
possibly even plastic. They looked thoroughly mass-produced
and industrial, and I could not think where they might have
been got. They were not fencing foils but something much
solider, and the demand for real swords nowadays must be
mainly ceremonial, and less and less even of that. Possibly
these swords came from suppliers for the stage, though I
doubt that too. Anyway, they were thoroughly dingy swords,
no credit at all to the regiment.

I do not know how long the show had been going on before
I arrived, or if the man in the seaman's sweater had offered
any explanations. Almost the first thing I heard was him saying, ''And now, gentlemen, which of you is going to be the
first?''

There was no movement or response of any kind. Of course
there never is.

''Come *on*,'' said the seaman, not very politely. I felt that
he was so accustomed to the backwardness of his audiences
that he was no longer prepared to pander to it. He did not
strike me as a man of many words, even though speaking
appeared to be his job. He had a strong accent, which I took

to be Black Country, though I wasn't in a position properly to be sure at that time of my life, and being myself a Londoner.

Nothing happened.

"What you think you've paid your money for?" cried the seaman, more truculent, I thought, than sarcastic.

"You tell us," said one of the men on the chairs. He happened to be the man nearest to me, though in front of me.

It was not a very clever thing to say, and the seaman turned it to account.

"You," he shouted, sticking out his thick, red forefinger at the man who had cheeked him. "Come along up. We've got to start somewhere."

The man did not move. I became frightened by my own nearness to him. I might be picked on next, and I did not even know what was expected of me, if I responded.

The situation was saved by the appearance of a volunteer. At the other side of the tent, a man stood up and said, "I'll do it."

The only light in the tent came from a single Tilley lamp hissing away (none too safely, I thought) from the crosspiece of the roof, but the volunteer looked to me exactly like everyone else.

"At last," said the seaman, still rather rudely. "Come on then."

The volunteer stumbled across the rough ground, stepped on to my side of the small platform, and stood right in front of the girl. The girl seemed to make no movement. Her head was thrown so far back that, as she was some distance in front of me, I could not see her eyes at all clearly. I could not even be certain whether they were open or closed.

"Pick up a sword," said the seaman sharply.

The volunteer did so, in a rather gingerly way. It looked like the first time he had ever had his hand on such a thing, and, of course, I never had either. The volunteer stood there with the sword in his hand, looking an utter fool. His skin looked grey by the light of the Tilley, he was very thin, and his hair was failing badly.

The seaman seemed to let him stand there for quite a while, as if out of devilry, or perhaps resentment at the way he had to make a living. To me the atmosphere in the dirty tent seemed full of tension and unpleasantness, but the other men in the audience were still lying about on their hard chairs looking merely bored.

After quite a while, the seaman, who had been facing the audience, and speaking to the volunteer out of the corner of his mouth, half-turned on his heel, and still not looking right at the volunteer, snapped out: "What are you waiting for? There are others to come, though we could do with more."

At this, another member of the audience began to whistle, "Why are we waiting?" I felt he was getting at the seaman or showman, or whatever he should be called, rather than at the volunteer.

"Go on," shouted the seaman, almost in the tone of a drill instructor. "Stick it in."

And then it happened, this extraordinary thing.

The volunteer seemed to me to tremble for a moment, and then plunged the sword right into the girl on the chair. As he was standing between me and her, I could not see where the sword entered, but I could see that the man seemed to press it right in, because almost the whole length of it seemed to disappear. What I could have no doubt about at all was the noise the sword made. A curious thing was that we are so used to at least the idea of people being stuck through with swords, that, even though, naturally, I had never before seen anything of the kind, I had no doubt at all of what the man had done. The noise of the sword tearing through the flesh was only what I should have expected. But it was quite distinct even above the hissing of the Tilley. And quite long drawn out too. And horrible.

I could sense the other men in the audience gathering themselves together on the instant and suddenly coming to life. I could still see little of what precisely had happened.

"Pull it out," said the seaman, quite casually, but as if speaking to a moron. He was still only half-turned towards the volunteer, and still looking straight in front of him. He was not looking at anything; just holding himself in control while getting through a familiar routine.

The volunteer pulled out the sword. I could again hear that unmistakable sound.

The volunteer still stood facing the girl, but with the tip of the sword resting on the platform. I could see no blood. Of course I thought I had made some complete misinterpretation, been fooled like a kid. Obviously it was some kind of conjuring.

"Kiss her if you want to," said the seaman. "It's included in what you've paid."

And the man did, even though I could only see his back. With the sword drooping from his hand, he leaned forwards and downwards. I think it was a slow and loving kiss, not a smacking and public kiss, because this time I could hear nothing.

The seaman gave the volunteer all the time in the world for it, and, for some odd reason, there was no whistling or catcalling from the rest of us; but in the end, the volunteer slowly straightened up.

"Please put back the sword," said the seaman, sarcastically polite.

The volunteer carefully returned it to the heap, going to some trouble to make it lie as before.

I could now see the girl. She was sitting up. Her hands were pressed together against her left side, where, presumably, the sword had gone in. But there was still no sign of blood, though it was hard to be certain in the bad light. And the strangest thing was that she now looked not only happy, with her eyes very wide open and a little smile on her lips, but, in spite of that green powder, beautiful too, which I was far from having thought in the first place.

The volunteer passed between the girl and me in order to get back to his seat. Even though the tent was almost empty, he returned to his original place religiously. I got a slightly better look at him. He still looked just like everyone else.

"Next," said the seaman, again like a sergeant numbering off.

This time there was no hanging back. Three men rose to their feet immediately, and the seaman had to make a choice.

"You then," he said, jabbing out his thick finger towards the centre of the tent.

The man picked was elderly, bald, plump, respectable-looking, and wearing a dark suit. He might have been a retired railway foreman or electricity inspector. He had a slight limp, probably taken in the way of his work.

The course of events was very much the same, but the second comer was readier and in less need of prompting, including about the kiss. His kiss was as slow and quiet as the first man's had been: paternal perhaps. When the elderly man stepped away, I saw the girl was holding her two hands against the centre of her stomach. It made me squirm to look.

And then came the third man. When he went back to his seat, the girl's hands were to her throat.

The fourth man, on the face of it a rougher type, with a cloth cap (which, while on the platform, he never took off) and a sports jacket as filthy and worn out as the tent, apparently drove the sword into the girl's left thigh, straight through the fishnet stocking. When he stepped off the platform, she was clasping her leg, but looking so pleased that you'd have thought a great favour had been done her. And still I could see no blood.

I did not really know whether or not I wanted to see more of the details. Raw as I was, it would have been difficult for me to decide.

I didn't have to decide, because I dared not shift in any case to a seat with a better view. I considered that a move like that would quite probably result in my being the next man the seaman called up. And one thing I knew for certain was that whatever exactly was being done, I was not going to be one who did it. Whether it was conjuring, or something different that I knew nothing about, I was not going to get involved.

And, of course, if I stayed, my turn must be coming close in any case.

Still, the fifth man called was not me. He was a tall, lanky, perfectly black Negro. I had not especially spotted him as such before. He appeared to drive the sword in with all the force you might expect of a black man, even though he was so slight, then threw it on the floor of the platform with a clatter, which no one else had done before him, and actually drew the girl to her feet when kissing her. When he stepped back, his foot struck the sword. He paused for a second, gazing at the girl, then carefully put the sword back on the heap.

The girl was still standing, and it passed across my mind that the Negro might try to kiss her again. But he didn't. He went quietly back to his place. Behind the scenes of it all, there appeared to be some rules, which all the other men knew about. They behaved almost as though they came quite often to the show, if a show was what it was.

Sinking down once more into her dilapidated canvas chair, the girl kept her eyes fixed on mine. I could not even tell what colour her eyes were, but the fact of the matter is that they turned my heart right over. I was so simple and inexperienced that nothing like that had ever happened to me before in my whole life. The incredible green powder made no difference. I wanted that girl more than I had ever wanted anything. And I don't mean I just wanted her body. That comes later in life. I wanted to love her and tousle her and all the other, better things we want before the time comes when we know that however much we want them, we're not going to get them.

But, in justice to myself, I must say that I did not want to take my place in a queue for her.

That was about the last thing I wanted. And it was one chance in three that I should be next to be called. I drew a deep breath and managed to scuttle out. I can't pretend it was difficult. I was sitting near the back of the tent, as I've said, and no one tried to stop me. The lad at the entrance merely gaped at me like a fish. No doubt he was quite accustomed to the occasional patron leaving early. I fancied that the bruiser on the platform was in the act of turning to me at the very instant I got up, but I knew it was probably imagination on my part. I don't think he spoke, nor did any of the other men react. Most men at shows of that kind prefer to behave as if they were invisible. I did get mixed up in the greasy tent flap, and the lad in the green sweater did nothing to help, but that was all. I streaked across the fairground, still almost deserted, and still with the roundabout tinkling away, all for nothing, but very prettily. I tore back to my nasty bedroom, and locked myself in.

On and off, there was the usual fuss and schemozzle in the house, and right through the hours of darkness. I know, because I couldn't sleep. I couldn't have slept that night if I'd been lying between damask sheets in the Hilton Hotel. The girl on the platform had got deep under my skin, green face and all: the girl and the show too, of course. I think I can truly say that what I experienced that night altered my whole angle on life, and it had nothing to do with the rows that broke out in the other bedrooms, or the cackling and bashing on the staircase, or the constant pulling the plug, which must have been the noisiest in the Midlands, especially as it took six or seven pulls or more for each flush. That night I really grasped the fact that most of the time we have no notion of what we really want, or we lose sight of it. And the even more important fact that what we really want just doesn't fit in with life as a whole, or very seldom. Most folk learn slowly, and never altogether learn at all. I seemed to learn all at once.

Or perhaps not quite, because there was very much more to come.

The next morning I had calls to make, but well before the time arrived for the first of them I had sneaked back to that tiny, battered, little fairground. I even skipped breakfast, but breakfast in Uncle Elias's special lodging was very poor anyway, though a surprising number turned up for it each day. You wondered where so many had been hiding away all night. I don't know what I expected to find at the fair. Perhaps I wasn't sure I should find the fair there at all.

But I did. In full daylight, it looked smaller, sadder, and more utterly hopeless for making a living even than the night before. The weather was absolutely beautiful, and so many of the houses in the immediate area were empty, to say nothing of the factories, that there were very few people around. The fair itself was completely empty, which took me by surprise. I had expected some sort of gypsy scene and had failed to realize that there was nowhere on the lot for even gypsies to sleep. The people who worked the fair must have gone to bed at home, like the rest of the world. The plot of land was surrounded by a wire-mesh fence, put up by the owner to keep out tramps and meth-drinkers, but by now the fence wasn't up to much, as you would expect, and, after looking round, I had no difficulty in scrambling through a hole in it, which the lads of the village had carved out for fun and from having nothing better to do. I walked over to the dingy booth in the far corner, and tried to lift the flap.

It proved to have been tied up at several places and apparently from the inside. I could not see how the person doing the tying had got out of the tent when he had finished, but that was the sort of trick of the trade you would expect of fairground folk. I found it impossible to see inside the tent at all without using my pocketknife, which I should have hesitated to do at the best of times, but while I was fiddling around, I heard a voice just behind me.

"What's up with you?"

There was a very small, old man standing at my back. I had certainly not heard him come up, even though the ground was so rough and lumpy. He was hardly more than a dwarf, he was as brown as a horse-chestnut or very nearly, and there was not a hair on his head.

"I wondered what was inside," I said feebly.

"A great big python, two miles long, that don't even pay its rent," said the little man.

"How's that?" I asked. "Hasn't it a following?"

"Old-fashioned," said the little man. "Old-fashioned and out of date. Doesn't appeal to the women. The women don't like the big snakes. But the women have the money these times, *and* the power and the glory too." He changed his tone. "You're trespassing."

"Sorry, old man," I said. "I couldn't hold myself back on a lovely morning like this."

"I'm the watchman," said the little man. "I used to have snakes too. Little ones, dozens and dozens of them. All over me, and every one more poisonous than the next. Eyes darting, tongues flicking, scales shimmering: then *in*, right home, then back, then in again, then back. Still in the end, it wasn't a go. There's a time and a span for all things. But I like to keep around. So now I'm the watchman. While the job lasts. While anything lasts. Move on then. Move on."

I hesitated.

"This big snake you talk of," I began, "this python—"

But he interrupted quite shrilly.

"There's no more to be said. Not to the likes of you, any road. Off the ground you go, and sharply. Or I'll call the police constable. He and I work hand in glove. I take care to keep it that way. You may not have heard that trespass is a breach of the peace. Stay here and you'll be sorry for the rest of your life.''

The little man was actually squaring up to me, even though the top of his brown skull (not shiny, by the way, but matte and patchy, as if he had some trouble with it) rose hardly above my waist. Clearly, he was daft.

As I had every kind of reason for going, I went. I did not even ask the little man about the times of performances that evening, or if there were any. Inside myself, I had no idea whether I should be back, even if there were performances, as there probably were.

I set about my calls. I'd had no sleep, and, since last night's tea, no food, and my head was spinning like a top, but I won't say I did my business any worse than usual. I probably felt at the time that I did, but now I doubt it. Private troubles, I have since noticed, make very little difference to the way most of us meet the outside world, and as for food and sleep, they don't matter at all until weeks and months have passed.

I pushed on then, more or less in the customary way (though, in my case, the customary way, at that job, wasn't up to very much at the best of times), and all the while mulling over and around what had happened to me, until the time came for dinner. I had planned to eat in the café where I had eaten the night before, but I found myself in a different part of the city, which, of course, I didn't know at all, and, feeling rather faint and queer, fell instead into the first place there was.

And there, in the middle of the floor, believe it or not, sitting at a Formica-topped table, was my girl with the green powder, and, beside her, the seaman or showman, looking more than ever like a run-down boxer.

I had not seriously expected ever to set eyes on the girl again. It was not, I thought, the kind of thing that happens. At the very most I might have gone again to the queer show, but I don't think I really would have done, when I came to think out what it involved.

The girl had wiped off the green powder, and was wearing a black coat and skirt and a white blouse, a costume you might perhaps have thought rather too old for her, and the same fishnet stockings. The man was dressed exactly as he had been the night before, except that he wore heavy boots instead of dirty sandshoes, heavy and mud-caked, as if he had been walking through fields.

Although it was the dinner-hour, the place was almost empty, with a dozen unoccupied tables, and these two sitting in the centre. I must almost have passed out.

But I wasn't really given time. The man in the jersey recognized me at once. He stood up and beckoned to me with his thick arm. "Come and join us." The girl had stood up too.

There was nothing else I could do but what he said.

The man actually drew back a chair for me (they were all painted in different, bright colours, and had been reseated in new leatherette), and even the girl waited until I had sat down before sitting down herself.

"Sorry you missed the end of last night's show," said the man.

"I had to get back to my lodgings, I suddenly realized." I made it up quite swiftly. "I'm new to the town," I added.

"It can be difficult when you're new," said the man. "What'll you have?"

He spoke as if we were on licensed premises, but it was pretty obvious we weren't, and I hesitated.

"Tea or coffee?"

"Tea, please," I said.

"Another tea, Berth," called out the man. I saw that the two of them were both drinking coffee, but I didn't like the look of it, any more than I usually do.

"I'd like something to eat as well," I said, when the waitress brought the tea. "Thank you very much," I said to the man.

"Sandwiches: York ham, salt beef, or luncheon meat. Pies. Sausage rolls," said the waitress. She had a very bad stye on her left lower eyelid.

"I'll have a pie," I said, and, in due course, she brought one, with some salad on the plate, and the bottle of sauce. I really required something hot, but there it was.

"Come again tonight," said the man.

"I'm not sure I'll be able to."

I was finding it difficult even to drink my tea properly, as my hands were shaking so badly, and I couldn't think how I should cope with a cold pie.

"Come on the house, if you like. As you missed your turn last night."

The girl, who had so far left the talking to the other, smiled at me very sweetly and personally, as if there was something quite particular between us. Her white blouse was open very low, so that I saw more than I really should, even though things are quite different today from what they once were. Even without the green powder, she was a very pale girl, and her body looked as if it might be even whiter than her face, almost as white as her blouse. Also I could now see the colour of her eyes. They were green. Somehow I had known it all along.

"In any case," went on the man, "it won't make much difference with business like it is now."

The girl glanced at him as if she were surprised at his letting out something private, then looked at me again and said, "Do come." She said it in the friendliest, meltingest way, as if she really cared. What's more, she seemed to have some kind of foreign accent, which made her even more fascinating, if that were possible. She took a small sip of coffee.

"It's only that I might have another engagement that I couldn't get out of. I don't know right now."

"We mustn't make you break another engagement," said the girl, in her foreign accent, but sounding as if she meant just the opposite.

I managed a bit more candour. "I might get out of my engagement," I said, "but the truth is, if you don't mind my saying so, that I didn't greatly care for some of the others in the audience last night."

"I don't blame you," said the man very dryly, and rather to my relief, as you can imagine. "What would you say to a private show? A show just for you?" He spoke quite quietly, suggesting it as if it had been the most normal thing in the world, or as if I had been Charles Clore.

I was so taken by surprise that I blurted out, "What! Just me in the tent?"

"In your own home, I meant," said the man, still absolutely casually, and taking a noisy pull on his pink earthenware cup. As the man spoke, the girl shot a quick, devastating glance. It was exactly as if she softened everything inside me to water. And, absurdly enough, it was then that my silly pie arrived, with the bit of green salad, and the sauce. I had been a fool to ask for anything at all to eat, however much I might have needed it in theory.

"With or without the swords," continued the man, lighting a cheap-looking cigarette. "Madonna has been trained to do anything else you want. Anything you may happen to think of." The girl was gazing into her teacup.

I dared to speak directly to her. "Is your name really Madonna? It's nice."

"No," she said, speaking rather low. "Not really. It's my working name." She turned her head for a moment, and again our eyes met.

"There's no harm in it. We're not Catholics," said the man, "though Madonna was once."

"I like it," I said. I was wondering what to do about the pie. I could not possibly eat.

"Of course a private show would cost a bit more than two bob," said the man. "But it would be all to yourself, and, under those conditions, Madonna will do anything you feel like." I noticed that he was speaking just as he had spoken in the tent: looking not at me or at anyone else, but straight ahead into the distance, and as if he were repeating words he had used again and again and was fed up with but compelled to make use of.

I was about to tell him I had no money, which was more or less the case, but didn't.

"When could it be?" I said.

"Tonight, if you like," said the man. "Immediately after the regular show, and that won't be very late, as we don't do a ten or eleven o'clock house at a date like this. Madonna could be with you at a quarter to ten, easy. And she wouldn't necessarily have to hurry away either, not when there's no late-night matinée. There'd be time for her to do a lot of her novelties if you'd care to see them. Items from her repertoire, as we call them. Got a good place for it, by the way? Madonna doesn't need much. Just a room with a lock on the door to keep out the non-paying patrons, and somewhere to wash her hands.''

''Yes,'' I said. ''As a matter of fact, the place I'm stopping at should be quite suitable, though I wish it was brighter, and a bit quieter too.''

Madonna flashed another of her indescribably sweet glances at me. ''I shan't mind,'' she said softly.

I wrote down the address on the corner of a paper I had found on my seat, and tore it off.

''Shall we call it ten pounds?'' said the man, turning to look at me with his small eyes. ''I usually ask twenty and sometimes fifty, but this is Wolverhampton not the Costa Brava, and you belong to the refined type.''

''What makes you say that?'' I asked; mainly in order to gain time for thinking what I could do about the money.

''I could tell by where you sat last night. At pretty well every show there's someone who picks that seat. It's a special seat for the refined types. I've learnt better now than to call them up, because it's not what they want. They're too refined to be called up, and I respect them for it. They often leave before the end, as you did. But I'm glad to have them in at any time. They raise the standard. Besides, they're the ones who are often interested in a private show, as you are, and willing to pay for it. I have to watch the business of the thing too.''

''I haven't got ten pounds ready in spare cash,'' I said, ''but I expect I can find it even if I have to fiddle it.''

''It's what you often have to do in this world,'' said the man. ''Leastways if you like nice things.''

''You've still got most of the day,'' said the girl, smiling encouragingly.

''Have another cup of tea?'' said the man.

''No thanks very much.''

''Sure?''

''Sure.''

''Then we must move. We've an afternoon show, though it'll probably be only for a few kids. I'll tell Madonna to save herself as much as she can until the private affair tonight.''

As they were going through the door on to the street, the

girl looked back to throw me a glance over her shoulder, warm and secret. But when she was moving about, her clothes looked much too big for her, the skirt too long, the jacket and blouse too loose and droopy, as if they were not really her clothes at all. On top of everything else, I felt sorry for her. Whatever the explanation of last night, her life could not be an easy one.

They'd both been too polite to mention my pie. I stuffed it into my attaché case, of course without the salad, paid for it, and dragged off to my next call, which proved to be right across the town once more.

I didn't have to do anything dishonest to get the money.

It was hardly to be expected that my mind would be much on my work that afternoon, but I stuck to it as best I could, feeling that my life was getting into deep waters and that I had better keep land of some kind within sight, while it was still possible. It was as well that I did continue on my proper round of calls, because at one of the shops my immediate problem was solved for me without my having to lift a finger. The owner of the shop was a nice old gentleman with white hair, named Mr. Edis, who seemed to take to me immediately I went through the door. He said at one point that I made a change from old Bantock with his attacks of asthma (I don't think I've so far mentioned Bantock's asthma, but I knew all about it), and that I seemed a good lad, with a light in my eyes. Those were his words, and I'm not likely to make a mistake about them just yet, seeing what he went on to. He asked me if I had anything to do that evening. Rather pleased with myself, because it was not an answer I should have been able to make often before, not if I had been speaking the truth, I told him Yes, I had a date with a girl.

"Do you mean with a Wolverhampton girl?" asked Mr. Edis.

"Yes. I've only met her since I've been in the town." I shouldn't have admitted that to most people, but there was something about Mr. Edis that led me on and made me want to justify his good opinion of me.

"What's she like?" asked Mr. Edis, half closing his eyes, so that I could see the red all round the edges of them.

"Gorgeous." It was the sort of thing people said, and my real feelings couldn't possibly have been put into words.

"Got enough small change to treat her properly?"

I had to think quickly, being taken so much by surprise, but Mr. Edis went on before I had time to speak.

"So that you can cuddle her as you want?"

I could see that he was getting more and more excited.

"Well, Mr. Edis," I said, "as a matter of fact, not quite enough. I'm still a beginner in my job, as you know."

I thought I might get a pound out of him, and quite likely only as a loan, the Midlands people being what we all know they are.

But on the instant he produced a whole fiver. He flapped it in front of my nose like a kipper.

"It's yours on one condition."

"I'll fit in if I can, Mr. Edis."

"Come back tomorrow morning after my wife's gone out— she works as a traffic warden, and can't hardly get enough of it—come back here and tell me all about what happens."

I didn't care for the idea at all, but I supposed that I could make up some lies, or even break my word and not go back at all, and I didn't seem to have much alternative.

"Why, of course, Mr. Edis. Nothing to it."

He handed over the fiver at once.

"Good boy," he said. "Get what you're paying for out of her, and think of me while you're doing it, though I don't expect you will."

As for the other five pounds, I could probably manage to wangle it out of what I had, by scraping a bit over the next week or two, and cooking the cash book a trifle if necessary, as we all do. Anyway, and being the age I was, I hated all this talk about money. I hated the talk about it much more than I hated the job of having to find it. I did not see Madonna in that sort of way at all, and I should have despised myself if I had. Nor, to judge by how she spoke, did it seem the way in which she saw me. I could not really think of any other way in which she would be likely to see me, but I settled that one by trying not to think about the question at all.

My Uncle Elias's special lodging in Wolverhampton was not the kind of place where visitors just rang the bell and waited to be admitted by the footman. You had to know the form a bit, if you were to get in at all, not being a resident, and still more if, once inside, you were going to find the exact person you were looking for. At about half past nine I thought it best to start lounging around in the street outside. Not right on top of the house door, because that might have led to misunderstanding and trouble of some kind, but moving up and down the street, keeping both eyes open and an ear cocked for the patter of tiny feet on the pavement. It was almost dark, of course, but not quite. There weren't many people about but that was partly because it was raining gently, as it does in the Midlands: a soft, slow rain that you can hardly see, but extra wetting, or so it always feels. I am quite sure I should have taken up my position earlier if it hadn't been for the rain. Needless to say, I was like a cat on hot bricks. I had managed to get the pie inside me between calls during the afternoon. I struggled through it on a bench just as the rain was beginning. And at about half past six I'd had a cup of tea and some beans in the café I'd been to the night before. I didn't want any of it. I just felt that I ought to eat something in view of what lay ahead of me. Though, of course, I had precious little idea of what that was. When it's truly your first experience, you haven't; no matter how much you've been told and managed to pick up. I'd have been in a bad state if it had been any woman that was supposed to be coming, let alone my lovely Madonna.

And there she was, on the dot, or even a little early. She was dressed in the same clothes as she had worn that morning. Too big for her and too old for her; and she had no umbrella and no raincoat and no hat.

"You'll be wet," I said.

She didn't speak, but her eyes looked, I fancied, as if she were glad to see me. If she had set out in that green powder of hers, it had all washed off.

I thought she might be carrying something, but she wasn't, not even a handbag.

"Come in," I said.

Those staying in the house were lent a key (with a deposit to pay on it), and, thank God, we got through the hall and up the stairs without meeting anyone, or hearing anything out of the way, even though my room was at the top of the building.

She sat down on my bed and looked at the door. After what had been said, I knew what to do and turned the key. It came quite naturally. It was the sort of place where you turned the key as a matter of course. I took off my raincoat and let it lie in a corner. I had not turned on the light. I was not proud of my room.

"You must be soaked through," I said. The distance from the fairground was not all that great, but the rain was of the specially wetting kind, as I've remarked.

She got up and took off her outsize black jacket. She stood there holding it until I took it and hung it on the door. I can't say it actually dripped, but it was saturated, and I could see a wet patch on the eiderdown where she had been sitting. She had still not spoken a word. I had to admit that there seemed to have been no call for her to do so.

The rain had soaked through to her white blouse. Even with almost no light in the room I could see that. The shoulders were sodden and clinging to her, one more than the other. Without the jacket, the blouse looked quainter than ever. Not only was it loose and shapeless, but it had sleeves that were so long as to droop down beyond her hands when her jacket was off. In my mind I had a glimpse of the sort of woman the blouse was made for, big and stout, not my type at all.

"Better take that off too," I said, though I don't know how I got the words out. I imagine that instinct looks after you even the first time, provided it is given a chance. Madonna did give me a chance, or I felt that she did. Life was sweeter for a minute or two than I had ever thought possible.

Without a word, she took off her blouse and I hung it over the back of the single bedroom chair.

I had seen in the café that under it she had been wearing something black, but I had not realized until now that it was the same tight, shiny sheath that she wore in the show, and that made her look so French.

She took off her wet skirt. The best I could do was to drape it over the seat of the chair. And there she was, super high heels and all. She looked ready to go on stage right away, but that I found rather disappointing.

She stood waiting, as if for me to tell her what to do.

I could see that the black sheath was soaking wet, anyway in patches, but this time I didn't dare to suggest that she take it off.

At last Madonna opened her mouth. "What would you like me to begin with?"

Her voice was so beautiful, and the question she asked so tempting, that something got hold of me and, before I could stop myself, I had put my arms round her. I had never done anything like it before in my whole life, whatever I might have felt.

She made no movement, so that I supposed at once I had done the wrong thing. After all, it was scarcely surprising, considering how inexperienced I was.

But I thought too that something else was wrong. As I say, I wasn't exactly accustomed to the feel of a half-naked woman, and I myself was still more or less fully dressed, but all the same I thought at once that the feel of her was disappointing. It came as a bit of a shock. Quite a bad one, in fact. As often, when facts replace fancies. Suddenly it had all become rather like a nightmare.

I stepped back.

"I'm sorry," I said.

She smiled in her same sweet way. "I don't mind," she said.

It was nice of her, but I no longer felt quite the same about her. You know how, at the best, a tiny thing can make all the difference in your feeling about a woman, and I was far from sure that this thing was tiny at all. What I was wondering was whether I wasn't proving not to be properly equipped for life. I had been called backward before now, and perhaps here was the reason.

Then I realized that it might all be something to do with the act she put on, the swords. She might be some kind of freak, or possibly the man in the blue jersey did something funny to her, hypnotized her, in some way.

"Tell me what you'd like," she said, looking down at the scruffy bit of rug on the floor.

I was a fool, I thought, and merely showing my ignorance. "Take that thing off," I replied. "It's wet. Get into bed. You'll be warmer there."

I began taking off my own clothes.

She did what I said, squirmed out of the black sheath, took her feet gently out of the sexy shoes, rolled off her long stockings. Before me for a moment was my first woman, even though I could hardly see her. I was still unable to face the idea of love by that single, dim electric light, which only made the draggled room looked more draggled.

Obediently, Madonna climbed into my bed and I joined her there as quickly as I could.

Obediently, she did everything I asked, just as the man in the blue sweater had promised. To me she still felt queer and disappointing—flabby might almost be the word—and certainly quite different from what I had always fancied a woman's body would feel like if ever I found myself close enough to it. But she gave me my first experience none the less, the thing we're concerned with now. I will say one thing for her: from first to last she never spoke an unnecessary word. It's not always like that, of course.

But everything had gone wrong. For example, we had not even started by kissing. I had been cram full of romantic ideas about Madonna, but I felt that she was not being much help in that direction, for all her sweet and beautiful smiles and her soft voice and the gentle things she said. She was making herself almost too available, and not bringing out the best in me. It was as if I had simply acquired new information, however important, but without any exertion of my feelings. You often feel like that, of course, about one thing or another, but it seemed dreadful to feel it about this particular thing, especially when I had felt so differently about it only a little while before.

"Come on," I said to her. "Wake up."

It wasn't fair, but I was bitterly disappointed, and all the more because I couldn't properly make out why. I only felt that everything in my life might be at stake.

She moaned a little.

I heaved up from on top of her in the bed and threw back the bedclothes behind me. She lay there flat in front of me, all grey—anyway in the dim twilight. Even her hair was colourless, in fact pretty well invisible.

I did what I suppose was rather a wretched thing. I caught hold of her left arm by putting both my hands around her wrist, and tried to lug her up towards me, so that I could feel her thrown against me, and could cover her neck and front with kisses, if only she would make me want to. I suppose I might under any circumstances have hurt her by dragging at her like that, and that I shouldn't have done it. Still no one could have said it was very terrible. It was quite a usual sort of thing to do, I should say.

But what actually happened was very terrible indeed. So simple and so terrible that people won't always believe me. I gave this great, bad-tempered, disappointed pull at Madonna. She came up towards me and then fell back again with a sort of wail. I was still holding on to her hand and wrist with my two hands, and it took me quite some time to realize what had happened. What had happened was that I had pulled her left hand and wrist right off.

On the instant, she twisted out of the bed and began to wriggle back into her clothes. I was aware that even in the most nonexistent light she was somehow managing to move very swiftly. I had a frightful sensation of her beating round in my room with only one hand, and wondered in terror how she could possibly manage. All the time, she was weeping to herself, or wailing might be the word. The noise she made was very soft, so soft that but for what was happening, I might have thought it was inside my own head.

I got my feet on to the floor with the notion of turning on the light. The only switch was of course by the door. I had the idea that with some light on the scene, there might be certain explanations. But I found that I couldn't get to the switch. In the first place, I couldn't bear the thought of touching Madonna, even accidentally. In the second place, I discovered that my legs would go no farther. I was too utterly scared to move at all. Scared, repelled, and that mixed-up something else connected with disappointed sex for which there is no exact word.

So I just sat there, on the edge of the bed, while Madonna got back into her things, crying all the while, in that awful, heart-breaking way which I shall never forget. Not that it went on for long. As I've said, Madonna was amazingly quick. I couldn't think of anything to say or do. Especially with so little time for it.

When she had put on her clothes, she made a single appallingly significant snatch in my direction, caught something up, almost as if she, at least, could see in the dark. Then she had unlocked the door and bolted.

She had left the door flapping open off the dark landing (we had time-switches, of course), and I could hear her pat-patting down the staircase, and so easily and quietly through the front door that you might have thought she lived in the place. It was still a little too early for the regulars to be much in evidence.

What I felt now was physically sick. But I had the use of my legs once more. I got off the bed, shut and locked the door, and turned on the light.

There was nothing in particular to be seen. Nothing but my own clothes lying about, my sodden-looking raincoat in the corner, and the upheaved bed. The bed looked as if some huge monster had risen through it, but nowhere in the room was there blood. It was all just like the swords.

As I thought about it, and about what I had done, I suddenly vomited. They were not rooms with hot and cold running water, and I half-filled the old-fashioned washbowl, with its faded flowers at the bottom and big thumbnail chippings round the rim, before I had finished.

I lay down on the crumpled bed, too fagged to empty the basin, to put out the light, even to draw something over me, though I was still naked and the night getting colder.

I heard the usual sounds beginning on the stairs and in the other rooms. Then, there was an unexpected, businesslike rapping at my own door.

It was not the sort of house where it was much use first asking who was there. I got to my feet again, this time frozen stiff, and, not having a dressing-gown with me, put on my wet raincoat, as I had to put on something and get the door open, or there would be more knocking, and then complaints, which could be most unpleasant.

It was the chap in the blue sweater; the seaman or show-man or whatever he was. Somehow I had known it might be.

I can't have looked up to much, as I stood there shaking, in only the wet raincoat, especially as all the time you could hear people yelling and beating it up generally in the other rooms. And of course I hadn't the slightest idea what line the chap might choose to take.

I needn't have worried. Not at least about that.

"Show pass off all right?" was all he asked; and looking straight into the distance as if he were on his platform, not at anyone or anything in particular, but sounding quite friendly notwithstanding, provided everyone responded in the right kind of way.

"I think so," I replied.

I daresay I didn't appear very cordial, but he seemed not to mind much.

"In that case, could I have the fee? I'm sorry to disturb your beauty sleep, but we're moving on early."

I had not known in what way I should be expected to pay, so had carefully got the ten pounds into a pile, Mr. Edis's fiver and five single pounds of my own, and put it into the corner of a drawer, before I had gone out into the rain to meet Madonna.

I gave it to him.

"Thanks," he said, counting it, and putting it into his trousers pocket. I noticed that even his trousers seemed to be seaman's trousers, now that I could see them close to, with him standing just in front of me. "Everything all right then?"

"I think so," I said again. I was taking care not to commit myself too far in any direction I could think of.

I saw that now he was looking at me, his small eyes deep-sunk.

At that exact moment, there was a wild shriek from one of the floors below. It was about the loudest human cry I had heard until then, even in one of those lodgings.

But the man took no notice.

"All right then," he said.

For some reason, he hesitated a moment, then he held out

his hand. I took it. He was very strong, but there was nothing else remarkable about his hand.

"We'll meet again." he said. "Don't worry."

Then he turned away and pressed the black time-switch for the staircase light. I did not stop to watch him go. I was sick and freezing.

And so far, despite what he said, our paths have not re-crossed.

Thomas M. Disch

THE ROACHES

Poet, reviewer and novelist, Thomas M. Disch has
produced a variety of short fiction of uniformly high
quality over three decades, often in the horror mode.
Like Shirley Jackson, Peter Straub, Joyce Carol Oates
and Theodore Sturgeon, his domain is literature in the
broadest sense and his works increase the cross-
fertilization of categories that has proven so broadening to horror literature since the 1930s. Telepathy
has ordinarily been the domain of science fiction—in
"The Roaches," it becomes the basis for a particularly ironic drama of abnormal psychology, one which
might be compared to Stephen King's *Carrie*, as an
example of horror in a science fiction frame. At the
same time the absurd humor of this piece helps to
give it its Dischean charm, just a few steps short of
parody.

M iss Marcia Kenwell had a perfect horror of cockroaches. It was an altogether different horror than the
one which she felt, for instance, toward the color puce. Marcia Kenwell loathed the little things. She couldn't see one
without wanting to scream. Her revulsion was so extreme that
she could not bear to crush them under the soles of her shoes.
No, that would be too awful. She would run, instead, for the
spray can of Black Flag and inundate the little beast with
poison until it ceased to move or got out of reach into one of
the cracks where they all seemed to live. It was horrible,
unspeakably horrible, to think of them nestling in the walls,

under the linoleum, only waiting for the lights to be turned off, and then . . . No, it was best not to think about it.

Every week she looked through the *Times* hoping to find another apartment, but either the rents were prohibitive (this *was* Manhattan, and Marcia's wage was a mere $62.50 a week, gross) or the building was obviously infested. She could always tell: there would be husks of dead roaches scattered about in the dust beneath the sink, stuck to the greasy backside of the stove, lining the out-of-reach cupboard shelves like the rice on the church steps after a wedding. She left such rooms in a passion of disgust, unable even to think till she reached her own apartment, where the air would be thick with the wholesome odors of Black Flag, Roach-It, and the toxic pastes that were spread on slices of potato and hidden in a hundred cracks which only she and the roaches knew about.

At least, she thought, *I keep my apartment clean.* And truly, the linoleum under the sink, the backside and underside of the stove, and the white contact paper lining her cupboards were immaculate. She could not understand how other people could let these matters get so entirely out-of-hand. *They must be Puerto Ricans,* she decided—and shivered again with horror, remembering that litter of empty husks, the filth and the disease.

Such extreme antipathy toward insects—toward one particular insect—may seem excessive, but Marcia Kenwell was not really exceptional in this. There are many women, bachelor women like Marcia chiefly, who share this feeling though one may hope, for sweet charity's sake, that they escape Marcia's peculiar fate.

Marcia's phobia was, as in most such cases, hereditary in origin. That is to say, she inherited it from her mother, who had a morbid fear of anything that crawled or skittered or lived in tiny holes. Mice, frogs, snakes, worms, bugs—all could send Mrs. Kenwell into hysterics, and it would indeed have been a wonder, if little Marcia had not taken after her. It was rather strange, though, that her fear had become so particular, and stranger still that it should particularly be cockroaches that captured her fancy, for Marcia had never seen a single cockroach, didn't know what they were. (The

Kenwells were a Minnesota family, and Minnesota families simply don't have cockroaches.) In fact, the subject did not arise until Marcia was nineteen and setting out (armed with nothing but a high school diploma and pluck, for she was not, you see, a very attractive girl) to conquer New York.

On the day of her departure, her favorite and only surviving aunt came with her to the Greyhound Terminal (her parents being deceased) and gave her this parting advice: "Watch out for the roaches, Marcia darling. New York City is full of cockroaches." At that time (at almost any time really) Marcia hardly paid attention to her aunt, who had opposed the trip from the start and given a hundred or more reasons why Marcia had better not go, not till she was older at least.

Her aunt had been proven right on all counts: Marcia after five years and fifteen employment agency fees could find nothing in New York but dull jobs at mediocre wages; she had no more friends than when she lived on West 16th; and, except for its view (the Chock Full O'Nuts warehouse and a patch of sky), her present apartment on lower Thompson Street was not a great improvement on its predecessor.

The city was full of promises, but they had all been pledged to other people. The city Marcia knew was sinful, indifferent, dirty, and dangerous. Every day she read accounts of women attacked in subway stations, raped in the streets, knifed in their own beds. A hundred people looked on curiously all the while and offered no assistance. And on top of everything else there were the roaches!

There were roaches everywhere, but Marcia didn't see them until she'd been in New York a month. They came to her— or she to them—at Silversmith's on Nassau Street, a stationery shop where she had been working for three days. It was the first job she'd been able to find. Alone or helped by a pimply stockboy (in all fairness it must be noted that Marcia was not without an acne problem of her own), she wandered down rows of rasp-edged metal shelves in the musty basement, making an inventory of the sheaves and piles and boxes of bond paper, leatherette-bound diaries, pins and clips, and carbon paper. The basement was dirty and so dim that she needed a flashlight for the lowest shelves. In the obscurest corner, a faucet leaked perpetually into a gray sink; she had been resting near this sink, sipping a cup of tepid coffee (saturated, in the New York manner, with sugar and drowned in milk), thinking, probably, of how she could afford several things she simply couldn't afford, when she noticed the dark spots moving on the side of the sink. At first she thought they might be no more than motes floating in the jelly of her eyes, or the giddy dots that one sees after over-exertion on a hot day. But they persisted too long to be illusory, and Marcia drew nearer, feeling compelled to bear witness. *How do I know they are insects?* she thought.

How are we to explain the fact that what repels us most can be at times—at the same time—inordinately attractive? Why is the cobra poised to strike so beautiful? The fascination of the abomination is something that . . . Something which we would rather not account for. The subject borders on the obscene, and there is no need to deal with it here, except to note the breathless wonder with which Marcia observed these first roaches of hers. Her chair was drawn so close to the sink that she could see the mottling of their oval, unsegmented bodies, the quick scuttering of their thin legs, and the quicker flutter of their antennae. They moved randomly, proceeding nowhere, centered nowhere. They seemed greatly disturbed over nothing. *Perhaps,* Marcia thought, *my presence has a morbid effect on them?*

Only then did she become aware, aware fully, that these were the cockroaches of which she had been warned. Repulsion took hold; her flesh curdled on her bones. She screamed and fell back in her chair, almost upsetting a shelf of oddlots. Simultaneously the roaches disappeared over the edge of the sink and into the drain.

Mr. Silversmith, coming downstairs to inquire the source of Marcia's alarm, found her supine and unconscious. He sprinkled her face with tapwater, and she awoke with a shudder of nausea. She refused to explain why she had screamed and insisted that she must leave Mr. Silversmith's employ immediately. He, supposing that the pimply stockboy (who was his son) had made a pass at Marcia, paid her for the three days she had worked and let her go without regrets. From that moment on, cockroaches were to be a regular feature of Marcia's existence.

* * *

On Thompson Street Marcia was able to reach a sort of stalemate with the cockroaches. She settled into a comfortable routine of pastes and powders, scrubbing and waxing, prevention (she never had even a cup of coffee without washing and drying cup and coffeepot immediately afterward) and ruthless extermination. The only roaches who trespassed upon her two cozy rooms came up from the apartment below, and they did not stay long, you may be sure. Marcia would have complained to the landlady, except that it was the landlady's apartment and her roaches. She had been inside, for a glass of wine on Christmas Eve, and she had to admit that it wasn't exceptionally dirty. It was, in fact, more than commonly clean—but *that* was not enough in New York. *If everyone,* Marcia thought, *took as much care as I, there would soon be no cockroaches in New York City.*

Then (it was March and Marcia was halfway through her sixth year in the city) the Shchapalovs moved in next door. There were three of them—two men and a woman—and they were old, though exactly how old it was hard to say: they had been aged by more than time. Perhaps they weren't more than forty. The woman, for instance, though she still had brown hair, had a face wrinkly as a prune and was missing several teeth. She would stop Marcia in the hallway or on the street, grabbing hold of her coatsleeve, and talk to her—always a simple lament about the weather, which was too hot or too cold or too wet or too dry. Marcia never knew half of what the old woman was saying, she mumbled so. Then she'd totter off to the grocery with her bagful of empties.

The Shchapalovs, you see, drank. Marcia, who had a rather exaggerated idea of the cost of alcohol (the cheapest thing she could imagine was vodka), wondered where they got the money for all the drinking they did. She knew they didn't work, for on days when Marcia was home with the flu she could hear the three Shchapalovs through the thin wall between their kitchen and hers screaming at each other to exercise their adrenal glands. *They're on welfare,* Marcia decided. Or perhaps the man with only one eye was a veteran on pension.

She didn't so much mind the noise of their arguments (she was seldom home in the afternoon), but she couldn't stand their singing. Early in the evening they'd start in, singing along with the radio stations. Everything they listened to sounded like Guy Lombardo. Later, about eight o'clock they sang *a cappella*. Strange, soulless noises rose and fell like Civil Defense sirens; there were bellowings, bayings, and cries. Marcia had heard something like it once on a Folkways record of Czechoslovakian wedding chants. She was quite beside herself whenever the awful noise started up and had to leave the house till they were done. A complaint would do no good: the Shchapalovs had a right to sing at that hour.

Besides, one of the men was said to be related by marriage to the landlady. That's how they got the apartment, which had been used as a storage space until they'd moved in. Marcia couldn't understand how the three of them could fit into such a little space—just a room-and-a-half with a narrow window opening onto the air shaft. (Marcia had discovered that she could see their entire living space through a hole that had been broken through the wall when the plumbers had installed a sink for the Shchapalovs.)

But if their singing distressed her, *what* was she to do about the roaches? The Shchapalov woman, who was the sister of one man and married to the other—or else the men were brothers and she was the wife of one of them (sometimes, it seemed to Marcia, from the words that came through the walls, that she was married to neither of them—or to both), was a bad housekeeper, and the Shchapalov apartment was soon swarming with roaches. Since Marcia's sink and the Shchapalovs' were fed by the same pipes and emptied into a common drain, a steady overflow of roaches was disgorged into Marcia's immaculate kitchen. She could spray and lay out more poisoned potatoes; she could scrub and dust and stuff Kleenex tissues into holes where the pipes passed through the wall: it was all to no avail. The Shchapalov roaches could always lay another million eggs in the garbage bags rotting beneath the Shchapalov sink. In a few days they would be swarming through the pipes and cracks and into Marcia's cupboards. She would lay in bed and watch them (this was possible because Marcia kept a night-light burning in each room) advancing across the floor and up the walls, trailing the Shchapalovs' filth and disease everywhere they went.

One such evening the roaches were especially bad, and Marcia was trying to muster the resolution to get out of her warm bed and attack them with Roach-It. She had left the windows open from the conviction that cockroaches do not like the cold, but she found that she liked it much less. When she swallowed, it hurt, and she knew she was coming down with a cold. And all because of *them*!

"Oh go away!" she begged. *"Go away! Go away! Get out of my apartment."*

She addressed the roaches with the same desperate intensity with which she sometimes (though not often in recent years) addressed prayers to the Almighty. Once she had prayed all night long to get rid of her acne, but in the morning it was worse than ever. People in intolerable circumstances will pray to anything. Truly, there are no atheists in foxholes: the men there pray to the bombs that they may land somewhere else.

The only strange thing in Marcia's case is that her prayers were answered. The cockroaches fled from her apartment as quickly as their little legs could carry them—and in straight lines, too. Had they heard her? Had they understood?

Marcia could still see one cockroach coming down from the cupboard. *"Stop!"* she commanded. And it stopped.

At Marcia's spoken command, the cockroach would march up and down, to the left and to the right. Suspecting that her phobia had matured into madness, Marcia left her warm bed, turned on the light, and cautiously approached the roach, which remained motionless, as she had bidden it. *"Wiggle your antennas,"* she commanded. The cockroach wiggled its antennae.

She wondered if they would *all* obey her and found, within the next few days, that they all would. They would do anything she told them to. They would eat poison out of her hand. Well, not exactly out of her hand, but it amounted to the same thing. They were devoted to her. Slavishly.

It is the end, she thought, *of my roach problem*. But of course it was only the beginning.

Marcia did not question too closely the *reason* the roaches obeyed her. She had never much troubled herself with abstract problems. After expending so much time and attention on them, it seemed only natural that she should exercise a certain power over them. However, she was wise enough never to speak of this power to anyone else—even to Miss Bismuth at the insurance office. Miss Bismuth read the horoscope magazines and claimed to be able to communicate with her mother, aged sixty-eight, telepathically. Her mother lived in Ohio. But what would Marcia have said: that *she* could communicate telepathically with cockroaches? Impossible.

Nor did Marcia use her power for any other purpose than keeping the cockroaches out of her own apartment. Whenever she saw one, she simply commanded it to go the Shchapalov apartment and stay there. It was surprising then that there were always more roaches coming back through the pipes. Marcia assumed that they were younger generations. Cockroaches are known to breed fast. But it was easy enough to send them to the Shchapalovs.

"Into their beds," she added as an afterthought. *"Go into their beds."* Disgusting as it was, the idea gave her a queer thrill of pleasure.

The next morning, the Shchapalov woman, smelling a little worse than usual (Whatever was it, Marcia wondered, that they drank?), was waiting at the open door of her apartment. She wanted to speak to Marcia before she left for work. Her housedress was mired from an attempt at scrubbing the floor, and while she sat there talking, she tried to wring out the scrubwater.

"No idea!" she exclaimed. "You ain't got no idea how bad! 'S terrible!"

"What?" Marcia asked, knowing perfectly well what.

"The boogs! Oh, the boogs are just everywhere. Don't you have 'em, sweetheart? I don't know what to do. I try to keep a decent house, God knows—" She lifted her rheumy eyes to heaven, testifying. "—but I don't know what to do." She leaned forward, confidingly. "You won't believe this, sweetheart, but last night . . ." A cockroach began to climb out of the limp strands of hair straggling down into the woman's eyes. ''. . . they got into bed with us! Would you believe it? There must have been a hundred of 'em. I said to Osip, I said—What's wrong sweetheart?''

Marcia, speechless with horror, pointed at the roach, which had almost reached the bridge of the woman's nose. ''Yech!'' the woman agreed, smashing it and wiping her dirtied thumb on her dirtied dress. ''Goddam boogs! I hate 'em, I swear to God. But what's a person gonna do? Now, what I wanted to ask, sweetheart, is do you have a problem with the boogs? Being as how you're right next door, I thought—'' She smiled a confidential smile, as though to say this is just between us ladies. Marcia almost expected a roach to skitter out between her gapped teeth.

''No,'' she said. ''No, I use Black Flag.'' She backed away from the doorway toward the safety of the stairwell. ''Black Flag,'' she said again, louder. ''Black Flag,'' she shouted from the foot of the stairs. Her knees trembled so, that she had to hold onto the metal banister for support.

At the insurance office that day, Marcia couldn't keep her mind on her work five minutes at a time. (Her work in the Actuarial Dividends department consisted of adding up long rows of two-digit numbers on a Burroughs adding machine and checking the similar addition of her co-workers for errors.) She kept thinking of the cockroaches in the tangled hair of the Shchapalov woman, of her bed teeming with roaches, and of other, less concrete horrors on the periphery of consciousness. The numbers swam and swarmed before her eyes, and twice she had to go to the Ladies' Room, but each time it was a false alarm. Nevertheless, lunchtime found her with no appetite. Instead of going down to the employee cafeteria she went out into the fresh April air and strolled along 23rd Street. Despite the spring, it all seemed to bespeak a sordidness, a festering corruption. The stones of the Flatiron Building oozed damp blackness; the gutters were heaped with soft decay; the smell of burning grease hung in the air outside the cheap restaurants like cigarette smoke in a close room.

The afternoon was worse. Her fingers would not touch the correct numbers on the machine unless she looked at them.

One silly phrase kept running through her head: "Something must be done. Something must be done." She had quite forgotten that she had sent the roaches into the Shchapalovs' bed in the first place.

That night, instead of going home immediately, she went to a double feature on 42nd Street. She couldn't afford the better movies. Susan Hayward's little boy almost drowned in quicksand. That was the only thing she remembered afterward.

She did something then that she had never done before. She had a drink in a bar. She had two drinks. Nobody bothered her; nobody even looked in her direction. She took a taxi to Thompson Street (the subways weren't safe at that hour) and arrived at her door by eleven o'clock. She didn't have anything left for a tip. The taxi driver said he understood.

There was a light on under the Shchapalovos' door, and they were singing. It was eleven o' clock. "Something must be done," Marcia whispered to herself earnestly. "Something must be *done*."

Without turning on her own light, without even taking off her new spring jacket from Ohrbach's, Marcia got down on her knees and crawled under the sink. She tore out the Kleenexes she had stuffed into the cracks around the pipes.

There they were, the three of them, the Shchapalovs, drinking, the woman plumped on the lap of the one-eyed man, and the other man, in a dirty undershirt, stamping his foot on the floor to accompany the loud discords of their song. Horrible. They were drinking of course, she might have known it, and now the woman pressed her roachy mouth against the mouth of the one-eyed man—kiss, kiss. Horrible, horrible. Marcia's hands knotted into her mouse-colored hair, and she thought: *The filth, the disease!* Why, they hadn't learned a thing from last night!

Some time later (Marcia had lost track of time) the overhead light in the Shchapalovs' apartment was turned off. Marcia waited till they made no more noise. "Now," Marcia said, "all of you.

"All of you in this building, all of you that can hear me, gather around the bed, but wait a little while yet. Patience.

All of you . . .'' The words of her command fell apart into little fragments, which she told like the beads of a rosary—little brown ovoid wooden beads. ''. . . gather round . . . wait a little while yet . . . all of you . . . patience . . . gather round . . .'' Her hand stroked the cold water pipes rhythmically, and it seemed that she could hear them—gathering, scuttering up through the walls, coming out of the cupboards, the garbage bags—a host, an army, and she was their absolute queen.

''Now!'' she said. ''Mount them! Cover them! Devour them!''

There was no doubt that she could hear them now. She heard them quite palpably. Their sound was like grass in the wind, like the first stirrings of gravel dumped from a truck. Then there was the Shchapalov woman's scream, and curses from the men, such terrible curses that Marcia could hardly bear to listen.

A light went on, and Marcia could see them, the roaches, everywhere. Every surface, the walls, the doors, the shabby sticks of furniture, was motley thick with *Blattelae Germanicae*. There was more than a single thickness.

The Shchapalov woman, standing up in her bed, screamed monotonously. Her pink rayon nightgown was speckled with brown-black dots. Her knobby fingers tried to brush bugs out of her hair, off her face. The man in the undershirt who a few minutes before had been stomping his feet to the music stomped now more urgently, one hand still holding onto the lightcord. Soon the floor was slimy with crushed roaches, and he slipped. The light went out. The woman's scream took on a rather choked quality, as though . . .

But Marcia wouldn't think of that. ''Enough,'' she whispered. ''No more. Stop.''

She crawled away from the sink, across the room on to her bed, which tried, with a few tawdry cushions, to dissemble itself as a couch for the daytime. Her breathing became hard, and there was a curious constriction in her throat. She was sweating incontinently.

From the Shchapalovs' room came scuffling sounds, a door banged, running feet, and then a louder, muffled noise, perhaps a body falling downstairs. The landlady's voice: ''What the hell do you think you're—'' Other voices overriding hers. Incoherences, and footsteps returning up the stairs. Once more, the landlady: "There ain't no *boogs* here, for heaven's sake. The boogs is in your heads. You've got the d.t.'s, that's what. And it wouldn't be any wonder, if there were boogs. The place is filthy. Look at that crap on the floor. Filth! I've stood just about enough from you. Tomorrow you move out, hear? This *used* to be a decent building."

The Shchapalovs did not protest their eviction. Indeed, they did not wait for the morrow to leave. They quitted their apartment with only a suitcase, a laundry bag, and an electric toaster. Marcia watched them go down the steps through her half-open door. *It's done,* she thought. It's all *over*.

With a sigh of almost sensual pleasure, she turned on the lamp beside the bed, then the other lamps. The room gleamed immaculately. Deciding to celebrate her victory, she went to the cupboard, where she kept a bottle of *crème de menthe*.

The cupboard was full of roaches.

She had not told them where to go, where *not* to go, when they left the Shchapalov apartment. It was her own fault.

The great silent mass of roaches regarded Marcia calmly, and it seemed to the distracted girl that she could read *their* thoughts, their thought rather, for they had but a single thought. She could read it as clearly as she could read the illuminated billboard for Chock Full O'Nuts outside her window. It was delicate music issuing from a thousand tiny pipes. It was an ancient music box open after centuries of silence: "We love you we love you we love you we love you."

Something strange happened inside Marcia then, something unprecedented: she responded.

"I love you too," she replied. "Oh, I love you. Come to me, all of you. Come to me. I love you. Come to me. I love you. Come to me."

From every corner of Manhattan, from the crumbling walls of Harlem, from restaurants on 56th Street, from warehouses along the river, from sewers and from orange peels moldering in garbage cans, the loving roaches came forth and began to crawl toward their mistress.

Theodore Sturgeon

BRIGHT SEGMENT

Theodore Sturgeon's fiction was published in the science fiction field throughout his distinguished career,
although it encompassed a wide variety of genres. He
was one of the American masters of the short story
form and generally considered the greatest conscious
artist working in the field of SF and fantasy from the
1940s to the 1970s. His early stories were published
in John W. Campbell's *Astounding* and *Unknown*
magazines, but his greatest impact was achieved in
the fantastic fictions in *Unknown*, a significant proportion of them horror. He was a model for the young
Ray Bradbury, who contributed an enthusiastic introduction to Sturgeon's first collection, *Without Sorcery*
(1949). But it was in the 1950s, especially in such
works as *Some of Your Blood* and "And Now the
News," that Sturgeon reached the heights of his powers. "Bright Segment" was published in 1955 and is
a classic of horror fiction representative of Sturgeon's
mastery of penetrating psychological insight. His contributions to fantasy and horror were recognized by a
Life Achievement award from the World Fantasy Convention.

He had never held a girl before. He was not terrified; he
had used that up earlier when he had carried her in and
kicked the door shut behind him and had heard the steady
drip of blood from her soaked skirt, and before that, when
he had thought her dead there on the curb, and again when

she made that sound, that sigh or whispered moan. He had brought her in and when he saw all that blood he had turned left, turned right, put her down on the floor, his brains all clabbered and churned and his temples athump with the un-accustomed exercise. All he could act on was *Don't get blood on the bedspread.* He turned on the overhead light and stood for a moment blinking and breathing hard; suddenly he leaped for the window to lower the blind against the street light staring in and all other eyes. He saw his hands reach for the blind and checked himself; they were red and ready to paint anything he touched. He made a sound, a detached part of his mind recognizing it as the exact duplicate of that agonized whisper she had uttered out there on the dark, wet street, and leapt to the light switch, seeing the one red smudge already there, knowing as he swept his hand over it he was leaving another. He stumbled to the sink in the corner and washed his hands, washed them again, every few seconds looking over his shoulder at the girl's body and the thick flat finger of blood which crept curling toward him over the linoleum.

He had his breath now, and moved more carefully to the window. He drew down the blind and pulled the curtains and looked at the sides and the bottom to see that there were no crevices. In pitch blackness he felt his way back to the op-posite wall, going around the edges of the linoleum, and turned on the light again. The finger of blood was a tentacle now, fumbling toward the soft, stain-starved floorboards. From the enamel table beside the stove he snatched a plastic sponge and dropped it on the tentacle's seeking tip and was pleased, it was a reaching thing no more, it was only some-thing spilled that could be mopped up.

He took off the bedspread and hung it over the brass head-rail. From the drawer of the china closet and from the gate leg table he took his two plastic tablecloths. He covered the bed with them, leaving plenty of overlap, then stood for a moment rocking with worry and pulling out his lower lip with a thumb and forefinger. *Fix it right,* he told himself firmly. So she'll die before you fix it, never mind, fix it, right.

He expelled air from his nostrils and got books from the shelf in the china closet—a six-year-old World Almanac, a half-dozen paperbacked novels, a heavy catalog of jewelry findings. He pulled the bed away from the wall and put books one by one under two of the legs so that the bed was tilted slightly down to the foot and slightly to one side. He got a blanket and rolled it and slipped it under the plastic so that it formed a sort of fence down the high side. He got a six-quart aluminum pot from under the sink and set it on the floor by the lowest corner of the bed and pushed the trailing end of plastic down into it. *So bleed now,* he told the girl silently, with satisfaction.

He bent over her and grunted, lifting her by the armpits. Her head fell back as if she had no bones in her neck and he almost dropped her. He dragged her to the bed, leaving a wide red swath as her skirt trailed through the scarlet puddle she had lain in. He lifted her clear of the floor, settled his feet, and leaned over the bed with her in his arms. It took an unexpected effort to do it. He realized only then how drained, how tired he was, and how old. He put her down clumsily, almost dropping her in an effort to leave the carefully arranged tablecloths undisturbed, and he very nearly fell into the bed with her. He levered himself away with rubbery arms and stood panting. Around the soggy hem of her skirt blood began to gather, and as he watched, began to find its way lazily to the low corner. *So much, so much blood in a person,* he marveled, and *stop it, how to make it stop if it won't stop?*

He glanced at the locked door, the blinded window, the clock. He listened. It was raining harder now, drumming and hissing in the darkest hours. Otherwise nothing; the house was asleep and the street, dead. He was alone with his problem.

He pulled at his lip, then snatched his hand away as he tasted her blood. He coughed and ran to the sink and spat, and washed his mouth and then his hands.

So all right, go call up. . . .

Call up? Call what, the hospital they should call the cops? Might as well call the cops altogether. *Stupid.* What could I tell them, she's my sister, she's hit by a car, they going to believe me? Tell them the truth, a block away I see somebody push her out of a car, drive off, no lights, I bring her in out of the rain, only inside I find she is bleeding like this, they believe me? *Stupid*. What's the matter with you, mind your own business why don't you.

He thought he would pick her up now and put her back in the rain. Yes and somebody sees you, *stupid*.

He saw that the wide, streaked patch of blood on the linoleum was losing gloss where it lay thin, drying and soaking in. He picked up the sponge, two-thirds red now and the rest its original baby-blue except at one end where it looked like bread drawn with a sharp red pencil. He turned it over so it wouldn't drip while he carried it and took it to the sink and rinsed it, wringing it over and over in the running water. *Stupid*, call up somebody and get help.

Call who?

He thought of the department store where for eighteen years he had waxed floors and vacuumed rugs at night. The neighborhood, where he knew the grocery and the butcher. Closed up, asleep, everybody gone; names, numbers he didn't know and anyway, who to trust? *My God in fifty-three years you haven't got a friend?*

He took the clean sponge and sank to his knees on the linoleum, and just then the band of blood creeping down the bed reached the corner and turned to a sharp streak; *ponk* it went into the pan, and *pitti-pittipitti* in a rush, then drip-drip-drip-drip, three to the second and not stopping. He knew then with absolute and belated certainty that this bleeding was not going to stop by itself. He whimpered softly and then got up and went to the bed. "*Don't be dead,*" he said aloud, and the way his voice sounded, it frightened him. He put out his hand to her chest, but drew it back when he saw her blouse was torn and blood came from there too.

He swallowed hard and then began fumbling with her clothes. Flat ballet slippers, worn, soggy, thin like paper and little silken things he had never seen before, like just the foot of a stocking. More blood on—but no, that was peeled and chipped enamel on her cold white toes. The skirt had a button at the side and a zipper which baffled him for a moment, but he got it down and tugged the skirt off in an interminable series of jerks from the hem, one side and the other, while she rolled slightly and limply to the motion. Small silken pants, completely soaked and so badly cut on the left side that he snapped them apart easily between his fingers; but the other side was surprisingly strong and he had to get his scissors to cut them away. The blouse buttoned up the front and was no problem; under it was a brassiere which was cut right in two near the front. He lifted it away but had to cut one of the straps with his scissors to free it altogether.

He ran to the sink with his sponge, washed it and wrung it out, filled a saucepan with warm water and ran back. He sponged the body down; it looked firm but too thin, with its shadow-ladder of ribs down each side and the sharp protrusions of the hip-bones. Under the left breast was a long cut, starting on the ribs in front and curving upward almost to the nipple. It seemed deep but the blood merely welled out. The other cut, though, in her groin, released blood brightly in regular gouts, one after the other, eager but weakly. He had seen the like before, the time Garber pinched his arm off in the elevator cable-room, but then the blood squirted a foot away. Maybe this did, too, he thought suddenly, but now it's slowing up, now it's going to stop, yes, and you, stupid, you have a dead body you can tell stories to the police.

He wrung out the sponge in the water and mopped the wound. Before it could fill up again he spread the sides of the cut and looked down into it. He could clearly see the femoral artery, looking like an end of spaghetti and cut almost through; and then there was nothing but blood again.

He squatted back on his heels, pulling heedlessly at his lip with his bloody hand and trying to think. *Pinch, shut, squeeze. Squeezers. Tweezers!* He ran to his toolbox and clawed it open. Years ago he had learned to make fine chains out of square silver wire, and he used to pass the time away by making link after tiny link, soldering each one closed with an alcohol torch and a needle-tipped iron. He picked up the tweezers and dropped them in favor of the small spring clamp which he used for holding the link while he worked on it. He ran to the sink and washed the clamp and came back to the bed. Again he sponged away the little lake of blood, and quickly reached down and got the fine jaws of the clamp on the artery near its cut. Immediately there was another gush of blood. Again he sponged it away, and in a blaze of inspiration, released the clamp, moved it to the other side of the cut, and clamped it again.

Blood still oozed from the inside of the wound, but that terrible pulsing gush was gone. He sat back on his heels and painfully released a breath he must have held for two minutes. His eyes ached from the strain, and his brain was still whirling, but with these was a feeling, a new feeling almost like an ache or a pain, but it was nowhere and everywhere inside him; it wanted him to laugh but at the same time his eyes stung and hot salt squeezed out through holes too small for it.

After a time he recovered, blinking away his exhaustion, and sprang up, overwhelmed by urgency. *Got to fix everything.* He went to the medicine cabinet over the sink. Adhesive tape, pack of gauze pads. Maybe not big enough; okay tape together, fix right. New tube this sulfa-thia-dia-whatchamacall-um, fix anything, time I got vacuum-cleaner grit in cut hand, infection. Fixed boils too.

He filled a kettle and his saucepan with clean water and put them on the stove. Sew up, yes. He found needles, white thread, dumped them into the water. He went back to the bed and stood musing for a long time, looking at the oozing gash under the girl's breast. He sponged out the femoral wound again and stared pensively into it until the blood slowly covered the clamped artery. He could not be positive, but he had a vague recollection of something about tourniquets, they should be opened up every once in a while or there is trouble; same for an artery, maybe? Better he should sew up the artery; it was only opened, not cut through. If he could find out how to do it and still let it be like a pipe, not like a darned sock.

So into the pot went the tweezers, a small pair of needle-nose pliers, and, after some more thought, a dozen silver broach-pins out of his jewelry kit. Waiting for the water to boil, he inspected the wounds again. He pulled on his lip, frowning, then got another fine needle, held it with pliers in the gas flame until it was red, and with another of his set of pliers bent it around in a small semi-circle and dropped it into the water. From the sponge he cut a number of small flat slabs and dropped them in too.

He glanced at the clock, and then for ten minutes he scrubbed the white enamel table-top with cleanser. He tipped it into the sink, rinsed it at the faucet, and then slowly poured the contents of the kettle over it. He took it to the stove, held it with one hand while he fished in the boiling saucepan with a silver knife until he had the pliers resting with their handles out of the water. He grasped them gingerly with a clean washcloth and carefully, one by one, transferred everything from saucepan to table. By the time he had found the last of the needles and the elusive silver pins, sweat was running into his eyes and the arm that held the table-top threatened to drop right off. But he set his stumpy yellow teeth and kept at it.

Carrying the table-top, he kicked a wooden chair bit by bit across the room until it rested by the bed, and set his burden down on its seat. *This no hospital,* he thought *but I fix everything.*

Hospital! Yes, in the movies—

He went to a drawer and got a clean white handkerchief and tried to tie it over his mouth and nose like in the movies. His knobby face and square head were too much for one handkerchief; it took three before he got it right, with a great white tassel handing down the back like in an airplane picture.

He looked helplessly at his hands, then shrugged; so no rubber gloves, what the hell. I wash good. His hands were already pink and wrinkled from his labors, but he went back to the sink and scratched a bar of soap until his horny nails were packed with it, then cleaned them with a file until they hurt, and washed and cleaned them again. And at last he knelt by the bed, holding his shriven hands up in a careful salaam. Almost, he reached for his lip to pull it, but not quite.

He squeezed out two globs of the sulfa ointment onto the table-top and, with the pliers, squashed two slabs of sponge until the creamy stuff was through and through them. He mopped out the femoral wound and placed a medicated sponge on each side of the wound, leaving the artery exposed at the bottom. Using tweezers and pliers, he laboriously threaded the curved needle while quelling the urge to stick the end of the thread into his mouth.

He managed to get four tiny stitches into the artery below the break, out of it above the break. Each one he knotted with exquisite care so that the thread would not cut the tissue but still would draw the severed edges together. Then he squatted back on his heels to rest, his shoulders afire with tension, his eyes misted. Then, taking a deep breath, he removed the clamp.

Blood filled the wound and soaked the sponges. But it came slowly, without spurting. He shrugged grimly. So what's to do, use a tire patch? He mopped the blood out once more, and quickly filled the incision with ointment, slapping a piece of gauze over it more to hide it than to help it.

He wiped his eyebrows first with one shoulder, then the other, and fixed his eyes on the opposite wall the way he used to do when he worked on his little silver chains. When the mist went away he turned his attention to the long cut on the underside of the breast. He didn't know how to stitch one this size, but he could cook and he knew how to skewer up a chicken. Biting his tongue, he stuck the first of his silver pins into the flesh at right angles to the cut, pressing it across the wound and out the other side. He started the next pin not quite an inch away, and the same with the third. The fourth grated on something in the wound; it startled him like a door slamming and he bit his tongue painfully. He backed the pin out and probed carefully with his tweezers. Yes, something hard in there. He probed deeper with both points of the tweezers, feeling them enter uncut tissue with a soft crunching that only a fearful fingertip could hear. He conquered a shudder and glanced up at the girl's face. He resolved not to look up there again. It was a very dead face.

Stupid! but the self-insult was lost in concentration even as it was born. The tweezers closed on something hard, slippery and stubborn. He worked it gently back and forth, feeling a puzzled annoyance at this unfamiliar flesh that yielded as he moved. Gradually, very gradually, a sharp angular corner of *something* appeared. He kept at it until there was enough to grasp with his fingers; then he set his tweezers aside and gently worked it loose. Blood began to flow freely before it was half out, but he did not stop until he could draw it free. The light glinted on the strip of hollow-ground steel and its shattered margins; he turned it over twice before it came to him that it was a piece of straight razor. He set it down on his enamel table, thinking of what the police might have said to him if he had turned her over to them with that story about a car accident.

He stanched the blood, pulled the wound as wide apart as he could. The nipple writhed under his fingers, its pink halo shrunken and wrinkled; he grunted, thinking that a bug had crawled under his hand, and then aware that whatever the thing meant, it couldn't mean death, not yet anyway. He had to go back and start over, stanching the cut and spreading it, and quickly squeezing in as much ointment as it would hold. Then he went on with his insertion of the silver pins, until there was a little ladder of twelve of them from one end of the wound to the other. He took his thread, doubled it, put the loop around the topmost pin and drew the two parts of the thread underneath. Holding them both in one hand, he gently pinched the edges of the wound together at the pin. Then he drew the loop tight without cutting, crossed the threads and put them under the next pin, and again closed the wound. He continued this all the way down, lacing the cut closed around the ladder of pins. At the bottom he tied the thread off and cut it. There was blood and ointment all over his handiwork, but when he mopped up it looked good to him.

He stood up and let sensation flow agonizingly into his numb feet. He was sopping wet; he could feel perspiration searching its way down through the hairs of his legs; like a migration of bedbugs. He looked down at himself; wrinkles and water and blood. He looked across at the wavery mirror, and saw a bandaged goblin with brow-ridges like a shelf and sunken eyes with a cast to them, with grizzled hair which could be scrubbed only to the color of grime, and with a great gout of blood where the mouth hid behind the bandage. He snatched it down and looked again. *More better you cover your face, no matter what.* He turned away, not from his face, but with it, in the pained patience of a burro with saddle sores.

Wearily he carried his enameled table-top to the sink. He washed his hands and forearms and took off the handkerchiefs from around his neck and washed his face. Then he got what was left of his sponge and a pan of warm soapy water and came back to the bed.

It took him hours. He sponged the tablecloths on which she lay, shifted her gently so as to put no strain on the wounds, and washed and dried where she had lain. He washed her from head to toe, going back for clean water, and then had to dry the bed again afterward. When he lifted her head he found her hair matted and tacky with rain and drying blood, and fresh blood with it, so he propped up her shoulders with a big pillow under the plastic and tipped her head back and washed and dried her hair, and found an ugly lump and a bleeding contusion on the back of her head. He combed the hair away from it on each side and put cold water on it, and it stopped bleeding, but there was a lump the size of a plum. He separated half a dozen of the gauze pads and packed them around the lump so that it need not take the pressure off her head; he dared not turn her over.

When her hair was wet and fouled it was only a dark mat, but cleaned and combed, it was the darkest of auburns, perfectly straight. There was a broad lustrous band of it on the bed on each side of her face, which was radiant with pallor, cold as a moon. He covered her with the bedspread, and for a long while stood over her, full of that strange nowhere-everywhere almost-pain, not liking it but afraid to turn away from it . . . maybe he would never have it again.

He sighed, a thing that came from his marrow and his years, and doggedly set to work scrubbing the floor. When he had finished, and the needles and thread were put away, the bit of tape which he had not used, the wrappers of the gauze pads and the pan of blood from the end of the bed disposed of, and all the tools cleaned and back in their box, the night was over and daylight pressed weakly against the drawn blind. He turned out the light and stood without breathing, listening with all his mind, wanting to know from where he stood if she still lived. To bend close and find out she was gone—oh no. He wanted to know from here.

But a truck went by, and a woman called a child, and

someone laughed; so he went and knelt by the bed and closed his eyes and slowly put his hand on her throat. It was cool—please, not cold!—and quiet as a lost glove.

Then the hairs on the back of his hand stirred to her breath, and again, the faintest of motions. The stinging came to his eyes and through and through him came the fiery urge to *do*: make some soup, buy some medicine, maybe, for her, a ribbon or a watch; clean the house, run to the store . . . and while doing all these things, all at once, to shout and shout great shaking wordless bellows to tell himself over and over again, so he could hear for sure, that she was alive. At the very peak of this explosion of urges, there was a funny little side-slip and he was fast asleep.

He dreamed someone was sewing his legs together with a big curved sail needle, and at the same time drawing the thread from his belly; he could feel the spool inside spinning and emptying. He groaned and opened his eyes, and knew instantly where he was and what had happened, and hated himself for the noise he made. He lifted his hand and churned his fingers to be sure they could feel, and lowered them gently to her throat. It was warm—no, hot, too hot. He pushed back from the bed and scrabbled half-across the floor on his knuckles and his numb, rubbery legs. Cursing silently he made a long lunge and caught the wooden chair to him, and used it to climb to his feet. He dared not let it go, so clumped softly with it over to the corner, where he twisted and hung gasping to the edge of the sink, while boiling acid ate downward through his legs. When he could, he splashed cold water on his face and neck and, still drying himself on a towel, stumbled across to the bed. He flung the bedspread off and *stupid!* he almost screamed as it plucked at his fingers on the way; it had adhered to the wound in her groin and he was sure it had ripped it to shreds, torn a whole section out of the clumsily patched artery. And he couldn't see; it must be getting dark outside; how long had he crouched there? He ran to the light switch, leaped back. Yes, bleeding, it was bleeding again—

But a little, only a very little. The gauze was turned up perhaps halfway, and though the exposed wound was wet with blood, blood was not running. It had, while he was asleep, but hardly enough to find its way to the mattress. He lifted the loose corner of the gauze very gently, and found it stuck fast. But the sponges, the little sponges to put on the sulfa-whatchama, they were still in the wound. He'd meant to take them out after a couple of hours, not let the whole clot form around them!

He ran for warm water, his big sponge. Soap in it, yes. He squatted beside the bed, though his legs still protested noisily, and began to bathe the gauze with tiny, gentle touches.

Something made him look up. She had her eyes open, and was looking down at him. Her face and her eyes were utterly without expression. He watched them close slowly and slowly open again, lackluster and uninterested. "All right, all right," he said harshly, "I fix everything." She just kept on looking. He nodded violently, it was all that soothes, all that encourages, hope for her and a total promise for her, but it was only a rapid bobbing of his big ugly head. Annoyed as he always was at his own speechlessness, he went back to work. He got the gauze off and began soaking the edge of one of the sponges. When he thought it was ready to come, he tugged gently at it.

In a high, whispery soprano, "Ho-o-o-o . . . ?" she said; it was like a question and a sob. Slowly she turned her head to the left. "Ho-o-o-o?" She turned her head again and slipped back to unconsciousness.

"I," he said loudly, excitedly, and "I—" and that was all; she wouldn't hear him anyway. He held still until his hands stopped trembling, and went on with the job.

The wound looked wonderfully clean, though the skin all around it was dry and hot.

Down inside the cut he could see the artery in a nest of wet jelly; that was probably right—he didn't know, but it looked all right, he wouldn't disturb it. He packed the opening full of ointment, pressed the edges gently together, and put on a piece of tape. It promptly came unstuck, so he discarded it and dried the flesh all around the wound, put on gauze first, then the tape, and this time it held.

The other cut was quite closed, though more so where the

pins were than between them. It too was surrounded by hot, dry, red flesh.

The scrape on the back of her head had not bled, but the lump was bigger than ever. Her face and neck were dry and very warm, though the rest of her body seemed cool. He went for a cold cloth and put it across her eyes and pressed it down on her cheeks, and she sighed. When he took it away she was looking at him again.

"You all right?" he asked her, and inanely, "You all right," he told her. A small frown flickered for a moment and then her eyes closed. He knew somehow that she was asleep. He touched her cheeks with the backs of his fingers. "Very hot," he muttered.

He turned out the light and in the dimness changed his clothes. From the bottom of a drawer he took a child's exercise book, and from it a piece of paper with a telephone number in large black penciled script. "I come back," he said to the darkness. She didn't say anything. He went out, locking the door behind him.

Laboriously he called the office from the big drugstore, referring to his paper for each digit and for each, holding the dial against the stop for a full three or four seconds as if to be sure the number would stick. He got the big boss Mr. Laddie first of all, which was acutely embarrassing; he had not spoken to him in a dozen years. At the top of his bull voice he collided with Laddie's third impatient "Hello?" with "Sick! I—uh, *sick*!" He heard the phone say "—in God's name . . . ?" and Mr. Wismer's laughter, and "Gimme the phone, that's got to be that orangutan of mine," and right in his ear, "Hello?"

"Sick tonight," he shouted.

"What's the matter with you?"

He swallowed. "I can't," he yelled.

"That just old age," said Mr. Wismer. He heard Mr. Laddie laughing too. Mr Wismer said, "How many nights you had off in the last fifteen years?"

He thought about it, "No!" he roared. Anyway, it was eighteen years.

"You know, that's right," said Mr. Wismer, speaking to

Mr. Laddie without trying to cover his phone, "fifteen years and never asked for a night off before."

"So who needs him? Give him all his nights off."

"Not at those prices," said Mr. Wismer, and to his phone, "Sure, dummy, take off. Don't work no con games." The phone clicked off on laughter, and he waited there in the booth until he was sure nothing else would be said. Then he hung up his receiver and emerged into the big drugstore where everyone all over was looking at him. Well, they always did. That didn't bother him. Only one thing bothered him, and that was Mr. Laddie's voice saying over and over in his head, "So who needs him?" He knew he would have to stop and face those words and let them and all that went with them go through his mind. But not now, please not now.

He kept them away by being busy; he bought tape and gauze and ointment and a canvas cot and three icebags and, after some thought, aspirin, because someone had told him once . . . and then to the supermarket where he bought enough to feed a family of nine for nine days. And for all his bundles, he still had a thick arm and a wide shoulder for a twenty-five-pound cake of ice.

He got the door open and the ice in the box, and went out in the hall and picked up the bundles and brought those in, and then went to her. She was burning up, and her breathing was like the way seabirds fly into the wind, a small beat, a small beat, and a long wait, balancing. He cracked a corner off the ice-cake, wrapped it in a dishtowel and whacked it angrily against the sink. He crowded the crushed ice into one of the bags and put it on her head. She sighed but did not open her eyes. He filled the other bags and put one on her breast and one on her groin. He wrung his hands uselessly over her until it came to him *she has to eat, losing blood like that*.

So he cooked, tremendously, watching her every second minute. He made minestrone and baked cabbage and mashed potatoes and veal cutlets. He cut a pie and warmed cinnamon buns, and he had hot coffee with ice cream ready to spoon into it. She didn't eat it, any of it, nor did she drink a drop. She lay there and occasionally let her head fall to one side, so he had to run and pick up the icebag and replace it. Once again she sighed, and once he thought she opened her eyes, but couldn't be sure.

On the second day she ate nothing and drank nothing, and her fever was unbelievable. During the night, crouched on the floor beside her, he awoke once with the echoes of weeping still in the room, but he may have dreamed it.

Once he cut the tenderest, juiciest piece of veal he could find on a cutlet, and put it between her lips. Three hours later he pressed them apart to put in another piece, but the first one was still there. The same thing happened with aspirin, little white crumbs on a dry tongue.

And the time soon came when he had busied himself out of things to do, and fretted himself into a worry-reflex that operated by itself, and the very act of thinking new thoughts trapped him into facing the old ones, and then of course there was nothing to do but let them run on through, with all the ache and humiliation they carried with them. He was trying to think a new thing about what would happen if he called a doctor, and the doctor would want to take her to a hospital; he would say, "She needs treatment, old man, she doesn't need you," and there it was in his mind, ready to run, so:

Be eleven years old, bulky and strong and shy, standing in the kitchen doorway, holding your wooden box by its string and trying to shape your mouth so that the reluctant words can press out properly; and there's Mama hunched over a gin bottle like a cat over a half-eaten bird, peering; watch her lipless wide mouth twitch and say, "Don't stand there clackin' and slurpin'! Speak up, boy! What are you tryin' to say, you're leaving?"

So nod, it's easier and she'll say, "Leave, then, leave, who needs you?" and you go:

And be a squat, powerful sixteen and go to the recruiting station and watch the sergeant with the presses and creases asking "Whadda *you* want?" and you try, you try and you can't say it so you nod your head at the poster with the pointing finger, UNCLE SAM NEEDS YOU; and the sergeant glances at it and at you, and suddenly his pointing finger is half an inch away from your nose; crosseyed you watch it while he barks, "Well, Uncle don't need *you*!" and you wait,

watching the finger that way, not moving until you understand; you understand things real good, it's just that you hear
slowly. So there you hang crosseyed and they all laugh.

Or 'way back, you're eight years old and in school, that
Phyllis with the row of springy brown sausage-curls flying
when she tosses her head, pink and clean and so pretty; you
have the chocolates wrapped in gold paper tied in gold-string
mesh; you go up the aisle to her desk and put the chocolates
down and run back; she comes down the aisle and throws
them so hard the mesh breaks on your desk and she says,
loud, "I don't need these and I don't need you, and you know
what, you got snot on your face," and you put up your hand
and sure enough you have.

That's all. Only every time anyone says "Who needs him?"
or the like, you have to go through all of them, every one.
Sooner or later, however much you put it off, you've got to
do it all.

I get doctor, you don't need me.

You die, you don't need me.

Please . . .

Far back in her throat, a scraping hiss, and her lips moved.
She held his eyes with hers, and her lips moved silently, and
a little late for the lips, the hiss came again. He didn't know
how he guessed right, but he did and brought water, dribbling
it slowly on her mouth. She licked at it greedily, lifting her
head up. He put a hand under it, being careful of the lump,
and helped her. After a while she slumped back and smiled
weakly at the cup. Then she looked up into his face and
though the smile disappeared, he felt much better. He ran to
the icebox and the stove, and got glasses and straws—one
each of orange juice, chocolate milk, plain milk, consommé
from a can, and ice water. He lined them up on the chair-
seat by the bed and watched them and her eagerly, like a
circus seal waiting to play "America" on the bulb-horns. She
did smile this time, faintly, briefly, but right at him, and he
tried the consommé. She drank almost half of it through the
straw without stopping and fell asleep.

Later, when he checked to see if there was any bleeding,

the plastic sheet was wet, but not with blood. *Stupid!* he raged at himself, and stamped out and bought a bedpan.

She slept a lot now, and ate often but lightly. She began to watch him as he moved about; sometimes when he thought she was asleep, he would turn and meet her eyes. Mostly, it was his hands she watched, those next two days. He washed and ironed her clothes, and sat and mended them with straight small stitches; he hung by his elbows to the edge of the enameled table and worked his silver wire, making her a broach like a flower on a fan, and a pendant on a silver chain, and a bracelet to match them. She watched his hands while he cooked; he made his own spaghetti—tagliatelli, really—rolling and rolling the dough until it was a huge tough sheet, winding it up like a jelly-roll only tight, slicing it in quick, accurate flickers of a paring-knife so it came out like yellow-white flat shoelaces. He had hands which had never learned their limitations, because he had never thought to limit them. Nothing else in life cared for this man but his hands, and since they did everything, they could do anything.

But when he changed her dressings or washed her, or helped with the bedpan, she never looked at his hands. She would lie perfectly still and watch his face.

She was very weak at first and could move nothing but her head. He was glad because her stitches were healing nicely. When he withdrew the pins it must have hurt, but she made not a sound; twelve flickers of her smooth brow, one for each pin as it came out.

"Hurts," he rumbled.

Faintly, she nodded. It was the first communication between them, except for those mute, crowded eyes following him about. She smiled too, as she nodded, and he turned his back and ground his knuckles into his eyes and felt wonderful.

He went back to work on the sixth night, having puttered and fussed over her all day to keep her from sleeping until he was ready to leave, then not leaving until he was sure she was fast asleep. He would lock her in and hurry to work, warm inside and ready to do three men's work; and home again in the dark early hours as fast as his bandy legs would carry him, bringing her a present—a little radio, a scarf, something special to eat—every single day. He would lock the door firmly and then hurry to her, touching her forehead and check to see what her temperature was, straightening the bed gently so she wouldn't wake. Then he would go out of her sight, away back by the sink, and undress and change to the long drawers he slept in, and come back and curl up on the camp cot. For perhaps an hour and a half he would sleep like a stone, but after that the slightest rustle of her sheet, the smallest catch of breath, would bring him to her in a bound, croaking, "You all right?" and hanging over her tensely, frantically trying to divine what she might need, what he might do or get for her.

And when the daylight came he would give her warm milk with an egg beaten in it, and then he would bathe her and change her dressings and comb her hair, and when there was nothing left to do for her he would clean the room, scrub the floor, wash clothes and dishes and, interminably, cook. In the afternoon he shopped, moving everywhere at a half-trot, running home again as soon as he could to show her what he had bought, what he had planned for her dinner. All these days, and then these weeks, he glowed inwardly, hugging the glow while he was away from her, fanning it with her presence when they were together.

He found her crying one afternoon late in the second week, staring at the little radio with the tears streaking her face. He made a harsh cooing syllable and wiped her cheeks with a dry washcloth and stood back with torture on his animal face. She patted his hand weakly, and made a series of faint gestures which utterly baffled him. He sat on the bedside chair and put his face close to hers as if he could tear the meaning out of her with his eyes. There was something different about her; she had watched him, up to now, with the fascinated, uncomprehending attention of a kitten watching a tankful of tropical fish; but now there was something more in her gaze, in the way she moved and in what she did.

"You hurt?" he rasped.

She shook her head. Her mouth moved, and she pointed to it and began to cry again.

"Oh, you hungry. I fix, fix good." He rose but she caught

his wrist, shaking her head and crying, but smiling too. He sat down, torn apart by his perplexity. Again she moved her mouth, pointing to it, shaking her head.

"No talk," he said. She was breathing so hard it frightened him, but when he said that she gasped and half sat up; he caught her shoulders and put her down, but she was nodding urgently. "You can't talk!" he said.

Yes, yes! she nodded.

He looked at her for a long time. The music on the radio stopped and someone began to sell used cars in a crackling baritone. She glanced at it and her eyes filled with tears again. He leaned across her and shut the set off. After a profound effort he formed his mouth in the right shape and released a disdainful snort: "Ha! What you want talk? Don't talk. I fix everything, no talk I—" He ran out of words, so instead slapped himself powerfully on the chest and nodded at her, the stove, the bedpan, the tray of bandages. He said again, "What you want talk?"

She looked up at him, overwhelmed by his violence, and shrank down. He tenderly wiped her cheeks again, mumbling, "I fix everything."

He came home in the dark one morning, and after seeing that she was comfortable according to his iron standards, went to bed. The smell of bacon and fresh coffee was, of course, part of a dream; what else could it be? And the faint sounds of movement around the room had to be his weary imagination.

He opened his eyes on the dream and closed them again, laughing at himself for a crazy stupid. Then he went still inside, and slowly opened his eyes again.

Beside his cot was the bedside chair, and on it was a plate of fried eggs and crisp bacon, a cup of strong black coffee, toast with the gold of butter disappearing into its older gold. He stared at these things in total disbelief, and then looked up.

She was sitting on the end of the bed, where it formed an eight-inch corridor between itself and the cot. She wore her pressed and mended blouse and her skirt. Her shoulders sagged with weariness and she seemed to have some difficulty in holding her head up; her hands hung limply between her knees. But her face was suffused with delight and antic- ipation as she watched him waking up to his breakfast.

His mouthed writhed and he bared his blunt yellow teeth, and ground them together while he uttered a howl of fury. It was a strangled, rasping sound and she scuttled away from it as if it had burned her, and crouched in the middle of the bed with her eyes huge and her mouth slack. He advanced on her with his arms raised and his big fists clenched; she dropped her face on the bed and covered the back of her neck with both hands and lay there trembling. For a long moment he hung over her, then slowly dropped his arms. He tugged at the skirt. "Take off," he grated. He tugged it again, harder.

She peeped up at him and then slowly turned over. She fumbled weakly at the button. He helped her. He pulled the skirt away and tossed it on the cot, and gestured sternly at the blouse. She unbuttoned it and he lifted it from her shoul- ders. He pulled down the sheet, taking it right out from under her. He took her ankles gently in his powerful hands and pulled them down until she was straightened out on the bed, and then covered her carefully. He was breathing hard. She watched him in terror.

In a frightening quiet he turned back to his cot and the laden chair beside it. Slowly he picked up the cup of coffee and smashed it on the floor. Steadily as the beat of a wood- man's axe the saucer followed, the plate of toast, the plate of eggs. China and yolk squirted and sprayed over the floor and on the walls. When he had finished he turned back to her. "I fix everything," he said hoarsely. He emphasized each syllable with a thick forefinger as he said again, "*I* fix every- thing."

She whipped over on her stomach and buried her face in the pillow, and began to sob so hard he could feel the bed shaking the floor through the soles of his feet. He turned angrily away from her and got a pan and a scrub-brush and a broom and dustpan, and laboriously, methodically, cleaned up the mess.

Two hours later he approached her where she lay, still on her stomach, stiff and motionless. He had had a long time to think of what to say: "Look, you see, you *sick* . . . you see?'' He said it, as gently as he could. He put his hand on her shoulder but she twitched violently, flinging it away. Hurt and baffled, he backed away and sat down on the couch, watching her miserably.

She wouldn't eat any lunch.

She wouldn't eat any dinner.

As the time approached for him to go to work, she turned over. He still sat on the cot in his long johns, utter misery on his face and in every line of his ugly body. She looked at him and her eyes filled with tears. He met her gaze but did not move. She sighed suddenly and held out her hand. He leaped to it and pulled it to his forehead, knelt, bowed over it and began to cry. She patted his wiry hair until the storm passed, which it did abruptly, at its height. He sprang away from her and clattered pans on the stove, and in a few minutes brought her some bread and gravy and a parboiled artichoke, rich with olive oil and basil. She smiled wanly and took the plate, and slowly ate while he watched each mouthful and radiated what could only be gratitude. Then he changed his clothes and went to work.

He brought her a red housecoat when she began to sit up, though he would not let her out of bed. He brought her a glass globe in which a flower would keep, submerged in water, for a week, and two live turtles in a plastic bowl and a pale-blue toy rabbit with a music box in it that played ''Rock-a-bye Baby'' and a blinding vermilion lipstick. She remained obedient and more watchful than ever; when his fussing and puttering were over and he took up his crouch on the cot, waiting for whatever need in her he could divine next, their eyes would meet, and increasingly, his would drop. She would hold the blue rabbit tight to her and watch him unblinkingly, or smile suddenly, parting her lips as if something vitally important and deeply happy was about to escape them. Sometimes she seemed inexpressibly sad, and sometimes she was so restless that he would go to her and stroke her hair until she fell asleep, or seemed to. It occurred to him that he had not seen her wounds for almost two days, and that perhaps they were bothering her during one of these restless spells, and so he pressed her gently down and uncovered her.

He touched the scar carefully and she suddenly thrust his hand away and grasped her own flesh firmly, kneading it, slapping it stingingly. Shocked, he looked at her face and saw she was smiling, nodding. "Hurt?" She shook her head. He said, proudly, as he covered her, "I fix. I fix good." She nodded and caught his hand briefly between her chin and her shoulder.

It was that night, after he had fallen into that heavy first sleep on his return from the store, that he felt the warm firm length of her tight up against him on the cot. He lay still for a moment, somnolent, uncomprehending, while quick fingers plucked at the buttons of his long johns. He brought his hands up and trapped her wrists. She was immediately still, though her breath came swiftly and her heart pounded his chest like an angry little knuckle. He made a labored, inquisitive syllable, "Wh-wha . . . ?" and she moved against him and then stopped, trembling. He held her wrists for more than a minute, trying to think this out, and at last sat up. He put one arm around her shoulders and the other under her knees. He stood up. She clung to him and the breath hissed in her nostrils. He moved to the side of her bed and bent slowly and put her down. He had to reach back and detach her arms from around his neck before he could straighten up. "You sleep," he said. He fumbled for the sheet and pulled it over her and tucked it around her. She lay absolutely motionless, and he touched her hair and went back to his cot. He lay down and after a long time fell into a troubled sleep. But something woke him; he lay and listened, hearing nothing. He remembered suddenly and vividly the night she had balanced between life and death, and he had awakened to the echo of a sob which was not repeated; in sudden fright he jumped and went to her, bent down and touched her head. She was lying face down. "You cry?" he whispered, and she shook her head rapidly. He grunted and went back to bed.

It was the ninth week and it was raining; he plodded homeward through the black, shining streets, and when he turned into his own block and saw the dead, slick river stretching between him and the streetlight in front of his house, he experienced a moment of fantasy, of dreamlike disorientation; it seemed to him for a second that none of this had happened, that in a moment the car would flash by him and dip toward the curb momentarily while a limp body tumbled out, and he must run to it and take it indoors, and it would bleed, it would bleed, it might die. . . . He shook himself like a big dog and put his head down against the rain, saying *Stupid!* to his inner self. Nothing could be wrong, now. He had found a way to live, and live that way he would, and he would abide no change in it.

But there was a change, and he knew it before he entered the house; his window, facing the street, had a dull orange glow which could not have been given it by the street light alone. But maybe she was reading one of those paperback novels he had inherited with the apartment; maybe she had to use the bedpan or was just looking at the clock . . . but the thoughts did not comfort him; he was sick with an unaccountable fear as he unlocked the hall door. His own entrance showed light through the crack at the bottom; he dropped his keys as he fumbled with them, and at last opened the door.

He gasped as if he had been struck in the solar plexus. The bed was made, flat, neat, and she was not in it. He spun around; his frantic gaze saw her and passed her before he could believe his eyes. Tall, queenly in her red housecoat, she stood at the other end of the room, by the sink.

He stared at her in amazement. She came to him, and as he filled his lungs for one of his grating yells, she put a finger on her lips and, lightly, her other hand across his mouth. Neither of these gestures, both even, would have been enough to quiet him ordinarily, but there was something else about her, something which did not wait for what he might do and would not quail before him if he did it. He was instantly confused, and silent. He stared after her as, without breaking stride, she passed him and gently closed the door. She took his hand, but the keys were in the way; she drew them from his fingers and tossed them on the table and then took his hand again, firmly. She was sure, decisive; she was one who had thought things out and weighed and discarded, and now knew what to do. But she was triumphant in some way, too; she had the poise of a victor and the radiance of the witness to a miracle. He could cope with her helplessness, of any kind, to any degree, but this—he had to think, and she gave him no time to think.

She led him to the bed and put her hands on his shoulders, turning him and making him sit down. She sat close to him, her face alight, and when again he filled his lungs, "Shh!" she hissed, sharply, and smilingly covered his mouth with her hand. She took his shoulders again and looked straight into his eyes, and said clearly, "I can talk now, I can talk!"

Numbly he gaped at her.

"Three days already, it was a secret, it was a surprise," Her voice was husky, hoarse even, but very clear and deeper than her slight body indicated. "I been practicing, to be sure. I'm all right again, I'm all right. You fix everything!" she said, and laughed.

Hearing that laugh, seeing the pride and joy in her face, he could take nothing away from her. "Ahh . . ." he said, wonderingly.

She laughed again. "I can go, I can go!" she sang. She leapt up suddenly and pirouetted, and leaned over him laughing. He gazed up at her and her flying hair, and squinted his eyes as he would looking into the sun. "Go?" he blared, the pressure of confusion forcing the syllable out as an explosive shout.

She sobered immediately, and sat down again close to him. "Oh, honey, don't, *don't* look as if you was knifed or something. You know I can't camp on you, live off you, just for*ever*!"

"No, no you stay," he blurted, anguish in his face.

"Now look," she said, speaking simply and slowly as to a child. "I'm all well again, I can talk now. It wouldn't be right, me staying, locked up here, that bedpan and all. Now wait, wait," she said quickly before he could form a word, "I don't mean I'm not grateful, you been . . . you been, well, I just can't tell you. Look, nobody in my life ever did anything like this, I mean, I had to run away when I was thirteen, I done all sorts of bad things. And I got treated . . . I mean, nobody else . . . look, here's what I mean, up to now I'd steal, I'd rob anybody, what the hell. What I mean, why not, you see?" She shook him gently to make him see;

then, recognizing the blankness and misery of his expression, she wet her lips and started over. "What I'm trying to say is, you been so kind, all this—" She waved her hand at the blue rabbit, the turtle tank, everything in the room— "I can't take any more. I mean, not a thing, not breakfast. If I could pay you back some way, no matter what, I would, you know I would." There was a tinge of bitterness in her husky voice. "Nobody can pay you anything. You don't need anything or anybody. I can't give you anything you need, or do anything for you that needs doing, you do it all yourself. If there was something you wanted from me—" She curled her hands inward and placed her fingertips between her breasts, inclining her head with a strange submissiveness that made him ache. "But no, you fix everything," she mimicked. There was no mockery in it.

"No, no, you don't go," he whispered harshly.

She patted his cheek, and her eyes loved him. "I do go," she said, smiling. Then the smile disappeared. "I got to explain to you, those hoods who cut me, I asked for that. I goofed. I was doing something real bad—well, I'll tell you. I was a runner, know what I mean? I mean dope, I was selling it."

He looked at her blankly. He was not catching one word in ten; he was biting and biting only on emptiness and uselessness, aloneness, and the terrible truth of this room without her or the blue rabbit or anything else but what it had contained all these years—linoleum with the design scrubbed off, six novels he couldn't read, a stove waiting for someone to cook for, grime and regularity and who needs you?

She misunderstood his expression. "Honey, honey, don't look at me like that, I'll never do it again. I only did it because I didn't care, I used to get glad when people hurt themselves; yeah, I mean that. I never knew someone could be kind, like you; I always thought that was sort of a lie, like the movies. Nice but not real, not for me.

"But I have to tell you, I swiped a cache, my God, twenty, twenty-two G's worth. I had it all of forty minutes, they caught up with me." Her eyes widened and saw things not in the room. "With a razor, he went to hit me with it so hard he broke it on top of the car door. He hit me here *down* and here *up*, I guess he was going to gut me but the razor was busted.'' She expelled air from her nostrils, and her gaze came back into the room. "I guess I got the lump on the head when they threw me out of the car. I guess that's why I couldn't talk, I heard of that. Oh *honey*! Don't look like that, you're tearing me apart!''

He looked at her dolefully and wagged his big head helplessly from side to side. She knelt before him suddenly and took both his hands. "Listen, you *got* to understand. I was going to slide out while you were working but I stayed just so I could make you understand. After all you done. . . . See, I'm well, I can't stay cooped up in one room forever. If I could, I'd get work some place near here and see you all the time, honest I would. But my life isn't worth a rubber dime in this town. I got to leave here and that means I got to leave town. I'll be all right, honey. I'll write to you; I'll never forget you, how could I?''

She was far ahead of him. He had grasped that she wanted to leave him; the next thing he understood was that she wanted to leave town too.

"You don't go," he choked. "You need me."

"You don't need me," she said fondly, "and I don't need you. It comes to that, honey; it's the way you fixed it. It's the right way; can't you see that?''

Right in there was the third thing he understood.

He stood up slowly, feeling her hands slide from his, from his knees to the floor as he stepped away from her. "Oh God!'' she cried from the floor where she knelt, "you're killing me, taking it this way! Can't you be happy for me?''

He stumbled across the room and caught himself on the lower shelf of the china closet. He looked back and forward along the dark, echoing corridor of his years, stretching so far and drearily, and he looked at this short bright segment slipping away from him. . . . He heard her quick footsteps behind him and when he turned he had the flatiron in his hand. She never saw it. She came to him bright-faced, pleading, and he put out his arms and she ran inside, and the iron curved around and crashed into the back of her head.

He lowered her gently down on the linoleum and stood for a long time over her, crying quietly.

Then he put the iron away and filled the kettle and sauce-pan with water, and in the saucepan he put needles and a clamp and thread and little slabs of sponge and a knife and pliers. From the gateleg table and from a drawer he got his two plastic tablecloths and began arranging them on the bed.

"I fix everything," he murmured as he worked, "fix it right."

Clive Barker

DREAD

Clive Barker is the only horror writer of the 1980s to catapult to prominence and popularity on the basis of his short fiction, the six stunning volumes called *The Books of Blood*. His work has been called the wave of the future in horror by Ramsey Campbell and Stephen King, among others. Nothing could illustrate the profound changes in horror fiction over the past decade more clearly than that Barker is the *only* major writer to emerge through short fiction, while others are primarily novelists. Fashion and economic pressure have moved him recently toward the novel form in *The Damnation Game* (1985), but his success in the short story form has created manifest excitement among other short story wirters and has pointed out new directions for a new generation in horror. Rarely fully polished, the stories in *The Books of Blood* have a raw power that is undeniable, especially for the audience built for horror by the generally crudely executed novels of the previous decade. And, significantly, Barker's influences do not include a majority of the classics of horror from the past except, perhaps, King and Ellison—but rather the graphic horror of the famous E.C. comics of the 1950s, horror films and those same novels of the seventies mentioned above. A new hybrid tradition seems in the process of formation. "Dread" is one of the best stories from the six collections, moving at first in the direction of an examination of the nature of reality, then turning toward psychological monstrosities and heightened *grand guignol* violence. For Barker, powerful impact is all.

There is no delight the equal of dread. If it were possible to sit, invisible, between two people on any train, in any waiting room or office, the conversation overheard would time and again circle on that subject. Certainly the debate might appear to be about something entirely different; the state of the nation, idle chat about death on the roads, the rising price of dental care; but strip away the metaphor, the innuendo, and there, nestling at the heart of the discourse, is dread. While the nature of God and the possibility of eternal life go undiscussed, we happily chew over the minutiae of misery. The syndrome recognizes no boundaries; in bath-house and seminar-room alike, the same ritual is repeated. With the inevitability of a tongue returning to probe a painful tooth, we come back and back and back again to our fears, sitting to talk them over with the eagerness of a hungry man before a full and steaming plate.

While he was still at university, and afraid to speak, Stephen Grace was taught to speak of why he was afraid. In fact not simply to talk about it, but to analyze and dissect his every nerve-ending, looking for tiny terrors.

In this investigation, he had a teacher: Quaid.

It was an age of gurus; it was their season. In universities up and down England young men and women were looking east and west for people to follow like lambs; Steve Grace was just one of many. It was his bad luck that Quaid was the Messiah he found.

They'd met in the Student Common Room.

"The name's Quaid," said the man at Steve's elbow at the bar.

"Oh."

"You're—?"

"Steve Grace."

"Yes. You're in the Ethics class, right?"

"Right."

"I don't see you in any of the other Philosophy seminars or lectures."

"It's my extra subject for the year. I'm on the English Literature course. I just couldn't bear the idea of a year in the Old Norse classes."

"So you plumped for Ethics."

"Yes."

Quaid ordered a double brandy. He didn't look that well off, and a double brandy would have just about crippled Steve's finances for the next week. Quaid downed it quickly, and ordered another.

"What are you having?"

Steve was nursing half a pint of luke-warm lager, determined to make it last an hour.

"Nothing for me."

"Yes you will."

"I'm fine."

"Another brandy and a pint of lager for my friend."

Steve didn't resist Quaid's generosity. A pint and a half of lager in his unfed system would help no end in dulling the tedium of his oncoming seminars on "Charles Dickens as a Social Analyst." He yawned just to think of it.

"Somebody ought to write a thesis on drinking as a social activity."

Quaid studied his brandy a moment, then downed it.

"Or as oblivion," he said.

Steve looked at the man. Perhaps five years older than Steve's twenty. The mixture of clothes he wore was confusing. Tattered running shoes, cords, a grey-white shirt that had seen better days; and over it a very expensive black leather jacket that hung badly on his tall, thin frame. The face was long and unremarkable; the eyes milky-blue, and so pale that the color seemed to seep into the whites, leaving just the pinpricks of his irises visible behind his heavy glasses. Lips full, like a Jagger, but pale, dry and unsensual. Hair, a dirty blond.

Quaid, Steve decided, could have passed for a Dutch dope-pusher.

He wore no badges. They were the common currency of a student's obsessions, and Quaid looked naked without something to imply how he took his pleasures. Was he a gay, feminist, save-the-whale campaigner; or a fascist vegetarian? What was he into, for God's sake?

"You should have been doing Old Norse," said Quaid.

"Why?"

"They don't even bother to mark the papers on that course," said Quaid.

Steve hadn't heard about this. Quaid droned on.

"They just throw them all up into the air. Face up, an A. Face down, a B."

Oh, it was a joke. Quaid was being witty. Steve attempted a laugh, but Quaid's face remained unmoved by his own attempt at humor.

"You should be in Old Norse," he said again. "Who needs Bishop Berkeley anyhow. Or Plato, Or—"

"Or?"

"It's all shit."

"Yes."

"I've watched you, in the Philosophy Class—"

Steve began to wonder about Quaid.

"—You never take notes, do you?"

"No."

"I thought you were either sublimely confident, or you simply couldn't care less."

"Neither. I'm just completely lost."

Quaid grunted, and pulled out a pack of cheap cigarettes. Again, that was not the done thing. You either smoked Gauloises, Camel or nothing at all.

"It's not true philosophy they teach you here," said Quaid, with unmistakable contempt.

"Oh?"

"We get spoonfed a bit of Plato, or a bit of Bentham—no real analysis. It's got all the right markings of course. It looks like the beast: it even smells a bit like the beast to the uninitiated."

"What beast?"

"Philosophy. *True* Philosophy. It's a beast, Stephen. Don't you think?"

"I hadn't—"

"It's wild. It bites."

He grinned, suddenly vulpine.

"Yes. It bites," he replied.

Oh, that pleased him. Again, for luck: "Bites."

Stephen nodded. The metaphor was beyond him.

"I think we should feel mauled by our subject." Quaid

was warming to the whole subject of mutilation by education. "We should be frightened to juggle the ideas we should talk about."

"Why?"

"Because if we were philosophers worth we wouldn't be exchanging academic pleasantries. We wouldn't be talking semantics; using linguistic trickery to cover the real concerns."

"What would we be doing?"

Steve was beginning to feel like Quaid's straight-man. Except that Quaid wasn't in a joking mood. His face was set: his pin-prick irises had closed down to tiny dots.

"We should be walking close to the beast, Steve, don't you think? Reaching out to stroke, pet it, milk it—"

"What . . . er . . . what is the beast?"

Quaid was clearly a little exasperated by the pragmatism of the enquiry.

"It's the subject of any worthwhile philosophy, Stephen. It's the things we fear, because we don't understand them. It's the dark behind the door."

Steve thought of a door. Thought of the dark. He began to see what Quaid was driving at in his labyrinthine fashion. Philosophy was a way to talk about fear.

"We should discuss what's intimate to our psyches," said Quaid. "If we don't . . . we risk . . ."

Quaid's loquaciousness deserted him suddenly.

"What?"

Quaid was staring at his empty brandy glass, seeming to will it to be full again.

"Want another?" said Steve, praying that the answer would be no.

"What do we risk?" Quaid repeated the question. "Well, I think if we don't go out and find the beast—"

Steve could see the punchline coming.

"—sooner or later the beast will come and find us."

There is no delight the equal of dread. As long as it's someone else's.

* * *

Casually, in the following week or two, Steve made some enquiries about the curious Mr. Quaid.

Nobody knew his first name.

Nobody was certain of his age; but one of the secretaries thought he was over thirty, which came as a surprise.

His parents, Cheryl had heard him say, were dead. Killed, she thought.

That appeared to be the sum of human knowledge where Quaid was concerned.

"I owe you a drink," said Steve, touching Quaid on the shoulder.

He looked as though he'd been bitten.

"Brandy?"

"Thank you."

Steve ordered the drinks.

"Did I startle you?"

"I was thinking."

"No philosopher should be without one."

"One what?"

"Brain."

They fell to talking. Steve didn't know why he'd approached Quaid again. The man was ten years his senior and in a different intellectual league. He probably intimidated Steve, if he was to be honest about it. Quaid's relentless talk of beasts confused him. Yet he wanted more of the same: more metaphors: more of that humorless voice telling him how useless the tutors were, how weak the students.

In Quaid's world there were no certainties. He had no secular gurus and certainly no religion. He seemed incapable of viewing any system, whether it was political or philosophical, without cynicism.

Though he seldom laughed out loud, Steve knew there was a bitter humor in his vision of the world. People were lambs and sheep, all looking for shepherds. Of course these shepherds were fictions, in Quaid's opinion. All that existed, in the darkness outside the sheep-fold, were the fears that fixed on the innocent mutton: waiting, patient as stone, for their moment.

Everything was to be doubted, but the fact that dread existed.

Quaid's intellectual arrogance was exhilarating. Steve soon came to love the iconoclastic ease with which he demolished belief after belief. Sometimes it was painful when Quaid formulated a water-tight argument against one of Steve's dogmas. But after a few weeks, even the sound of the demolition seemed to excite. Quaid was clearing the undergrowth, felling the trees, razing the stubble. Steve felt free.

Nation, family, Church, law. All ash. All useless. All cheats, and chains and suffocation.

There was only dread.

"I fear, you fear, we fear," Quaid was fond of saying. "He, she or it fears. There's no conscious thing on the face of the world that doesn't know dread more intimately than its own heartbeat."

One of Quaid's favorite baiting-victims was another Philosophy and Eng. Lit. student, Cheryl Fromm. She would rise to his more outrageous remarks like fish to rain, and while the two of them took knives to each other's arguments Steve would sit back and watch the spectacle. Cheryl was, in Quaid's phrase, a pathological optimist.

"And you're full of shit," she'd say when the debate had warmed up a little. "So who cares if you're afraid of your own shadow? I'm not. I feel fine."

She certainly looked it. Cheryl Fromm was wet dream material, but too bright for anyone to try making a move on her.

"We all taste dread once in a while," Quaid would reply to her, and his milky eyes would study her face intently, watching for her reaction, trying, Steve knew, to find a flaw in her conviction.

"I don't."

"No fears? No nightmares?"

"No way. I've got a good family; I don't have any skeletons in my closet. I don't even eat meat, so I don't feel bad when I drive past a slaughterhouse. I don't have any shit to put on show. Does that mean I'm not real?"

"It means," Quaid's eyes were snake-slits, "it means your confidence has something big to cover."

"Back to nightmares."

"Big nightmares."

"Be specific: define your terms."

"I can't tell you what you fear."

"Tell me what you fear then."

Quaid hesitated. "Finally," he said, "it's beyond analysis."

"Beyond analysis, my ass!"

That brought an involuntary smile to Steve's lips. Cheryl's ass was indeed beyond analysis. The only response was to kneel down and worship.

Quaid was back on his soap-box.

"What I fear is personal to me. It makes no sense in a larger context. The signs of my dread, the images my brain uses, if you like, to *illustrate* my fear, those signs are mild stuff by comparison with the real horror that's at the root of my personality."

"I've got images," said Steve. "Pictures from childhood that make me think of—" He stopped, regretting this confessional already.

"What?" said Cheryl. "You mean things to do with bad experiences? Falling off your bike, or something like that?"

"Perhaps," Steve said. "I find myself, sometimes, thinking of those pictures. Not deliberately, just when my concentration's idling. It's almost as though my mind went to them automatically."

Quaid gave a little grunt of satisfaction. "Precisely," he said.

"Freud writes on that," said Cheryl.

"What?"

"Freud," Cheryl repeated, this time making a performance of it, as though she were speaking to a child. "Sigmund Freud: you may have heard of him."

Quaid's lip curled with unrestrained contempt. "Mother fixations don't answer the problem. The real terrors in me, in all of us, are pre-personality. Dread's there before we have any notion of ourselves as individuals. The thumb-nail, curled up on itself in the womb, feels fear."

"You remember, do you?" said Cheryl.

"Maybe," Quaid replied, deadly serious.

"The womb?"

Quaid gave a sort of half-smile. Steve thought the smile said: "I have knowledge you don't."

It was a weird, unpleasant smile; one Steve wanted to wash off his eyes.

"You're a liar," said Cheryl, getting up from her seat, and looking down her nose at Quaid.

"Perhaps I am," he said, suddenly the perfect gentleman.

After that the debates stopped.

No more talking about nightmares, no more debating the things that go bump in the night. Steve saw Quaid irregularly for the next month, and when he did Quaid was invariably in the company of Cheryl Fromm. Quaid was polite with her, even deferential. He no longer wore his leather jacket, because she hated the smell of dead animal matter. This sudden change in their relationship confounded Stephen; but he put it down to his primitive understanding of sexual matters. He wasn't a virgin, but women were still a mystery to him: contradictory and puzzling.

He was also jealous, though he wouldn't entirely admit that to himself. He resented the fact that the wet dream genius was taking up so much of Quaid's time.

There was another feeling; a curious sense he had that Quaid was courting Cheryl for his own strange reasons. Sex was not Quaid's motive, he felt sure. Nor was it respect for Cheryl's intelligence that made him so attentive. No, he was cornering her somehow; that was Steve's instinct. Cheryl Fromm was being rounded up for the kill.

Then, after a month, Quaid let a remark about Cheryl drop in conversation.

"She's a vegetarian," he said.

"Cheryl?"

"Of course, Cheryl."

"I know. She mentioned it before."

"Yes, but it isn't a fad with her. She's passionate about it. Can't even bear to look in a butcher's window. She won't touch meat, smell meat—"

"Oh." Steve was stumped. Where was this leading?

"Dread, Steve."

"Of meat?"

"The signs are different from person to person. *She fears meat*. She says she's so healthy, so balanced. Shit! I'll find it—"

"Find what?"

"The fear, Steve."

"You're not going to . . . ?" Steve didn't know how to voice his anxiety without sounding accusatory.

"Harm her?" said Quaid. "No, I'm not going to harm her in any way. Any damage done to her will be strictly self-inflicted."

Quaid was staring at him almost hypnotically.

"It's about time we learn to trust one another," Quaid went on. He leaned closer. "Betwen the two of us—"

"Listen, I don't think I want to hear."

"We have to touch the beast, Stephen."

"Damn the beast! I don't want to hear!"

Steve got up, as much to break the oppression of Quaid's stare as to finish the conversation.

"We're friends, Stephen."

"Yes . . ."

"Then respect that."

"What?"

"Silence. Not a word."

Steve nodded. That wasn't a difficult promise to keep. There was nobody he could tell his anxieties to without being laughed at.

Quaid looked satisfied. He hurried away, leaving Steve feeling as though he had unwillingly joined some secret society, for what purpose he couldn't begin to tell. Quaid had made a pact with him and it was unnerving.

For the next week he cut all his lectures and most of his seminars. Notes went uncopied, books unread, essays unwritten. On the two occasions he actually went into the university building he crept around like a cautious mouse, praying he wouldn't collide with Quaid.

He needn't have feared. The one occasion he did see Quaid's stooping shoulders across the quadrangle he was involved in a smiling exchange with Cheryl Fromm. She laughed, musically, her pleasure echoing off the wall of the History Department. The jealousy had left Steve altogether.

He wouldn't have been paid to be so near to Quaid, so intimate with him.

The time he spent alone, away from the bustle of lectures and overfull corridors, gave Steve's mind time to idle. His thoughts returned, like tongue to tooth, like fingernail to scab, to his fears.

And so to his childhood.

At the age of six, Steve had been struck by a car. The injuries were not particularly bad, but concussion left him partially deaf. It was a profoundly distressing experience for him; not understanding why he was suddenly cut off from the world. It was an inexplicable torment, and the child assumed it was eternal.

One moment his life had been real, full of shouts and laughter. The next he was cut off from it, and the external world became an aquarium, full of gaping fish with grotesque smiles. Worse still, there were times when he suffered what the doctors called tinnitus, a roaring or ringing sound in the ears. His head would fill with the most outlandish noises, whoops and whistlings, that played like sound-effects to the flailings of the outside world. At those times his stomach would churn, and a band of iron would be wrapped around his forehead, crushing his thoughts into fragments, dissociating head from hand, intention from practice. He would be swept away in a tide of panic, completely unable to make sense of the world while his head sang and rattled.

But at night came the worst terrors. He would wake, sometimes, in what had been (before the accident) the reassuring womb of his bedroom, to find the ringing had begun in his sleep.

His eyes would jerk open. His body would be wet with sweat. His mind would be filled with the most raucous din, which he was locked in with, beyond hope of reprieve. Nothing could silence his head, and nothing, it seemed, could bring the world, the speaking, laughing, crying, world, back to him.

He was alone.

That was the beginning, middle and end of the dread. He was absolutely alone with his cacophony. Locked in this house, in this room, in this body, in this head, a prisoner of deaf, blind flesh.

It was almost unbearable. In the night the boy would sometimes cry out, not knowing he was making any sound, and the fish who had been his parents would turn on the light and come to try to help him, bending over his bed making faces, their soundless mouths forming ugly shapes in their attempts to help. Their touches would calm him at last; with time his mother learned the trick of soothing away the panic that swept over him.

A week before his seventh birthday his hearing returned, not perfectly, but well enough for it to seem like a miracle. The world snapped back into focus; and life began afresh.

It took several months for the boy to trust his senses again. He would still wake in the night, half-anticipating the head-noises.

But though his ears would ring at the slightest volume of sound, preventing Steve from going to rock concerts with the rest of the students, he now scarcely ever noticed his slight deafness.

He remembered, of course. Very well. He could bring back the taste of his panic; the feel of the iron band around his head. And there was a residue of fear there; of the dark, of being alone.

But then, wasn't everyone afraid to be alone? To be utterly alone.

Steve had another fear now, far more difficult to pin down. Quaid.

In a drunken revelation session he had told Quaid about his childhood, about the deafness, about the night terrors.

Quaid knew about his weakness: the clear route into the heart of Steve's dread. He had a weapon, a stick to beat Steve with, should it ever come to that. Maybe that was why he chose not to speak to Cheryl (warn her, was that what he wanted to do?) and certainly that was why he avoided Quaid.

The man had a look, in certain moods, of malice. Nothing more or less. He looked like a man with malice deep, deep in him.

Maybe those four months of watching people with the sound turned down had sensitized Steve to the tiny glances, sneers and smiles that flit across people's faces. He knew Quaid's life was a labyrinth; a map of its complexities was etched on his face in a thousand tiny expressions.

The next phase of Steve's initiation into Quaid's secret world didn't come for almost three and a half months. The university broke for the summer recess, and the students went their ways. Steve took his usual vacation job at his father's printing works; it was long hours, and physically exhausting, but an undeniable relief for him. Academe had overstuffed his mind, he felt force-fed with words and ideas. The print work sweated all of that out of him rapidly, sorting out the jumble in his mind.

It was a good time: he scarcely thought of Quaid at all.

He returned to campus in the late September. The students were still thin on the ground. Most of the courses didn't start for another week; and there was a melancholy air about the place without its usual mêlée of complaining, flirting, arguing kids.

Steve was in the library, cornering a few important books before others on his course had their hands on them. Books were pure gold at the beginning of term, with reading lists to be checked off, and the university book shop forever claiming the necessary titles were on order. They would invariably arrive, those vital books, two days after the seminar in which the author was to be discussed. This final year Steve was determined to be ahead of the rush for the few copies of seminal works the library possessed.

The familiar voice spoke.

"Early to work."

Steve looked up to meet Quaid's pin-prick eyes.

"I'm impressed, Steve."

"What with?"

"Your enthusiasm for the job."

"Oh."

Quaid smiled. "What are you looking for?"

"Something on Bentham."

"I've got 'Principles of Morals and Legislation.' Will that do?"

It was a trap. No: that was absurd. He was offering a book; how could that simple gesture be construed as a trap?

"Come to think of it," the smile broadened, "I think it's the library copy I've got. I'll give it to you."

"Thanks."

"Good holiday?"

"Yes. Thank you. You?"

"Very rewarding."

The smile had decayed into a thin line beneath his—

"You've grown a mustache."

It was an unhealthy example of the species. Thin, patchy, and dirty-blond, it wandered back and forth under Quaid's nose as if looking for a way off his face. Quaid looked faintly embarrassed.

"Was it for Cheryl?"

He was definitely embarrassed now.

"Well . . ."

"Sounds like you had a good vacation."

The embarrassment was surmounted by something else.

"I've got some wonderful photographs," Quaid said.

"What of?"

"Holiday snaps."

Steve couldn't believe his ears. Had C. Fromm tamed the Quaid? Holiday snaps?

"You won't believe some of them."

There was something of the Arab selling dirty postcards about Quaid's manner. What the hell were these photographs? Split beaver shots of Cheryl, caught reading Kant?

"I don't think of you as being a photographer."

"It's become a passion of mine."

He grinned as he said "passion." There was a barely-suppressed excitement in his manner. He was positively gleaming with pleasure.

"You've got to come and see them."

"I—"

"Tonight. And pick up the Bentham at the same time."

"Thanks."

"I've got a house for myself these days. Round the corner from the Maternity Hospital, in Pilgrim Street. Number sixty-four. Some time after nine?"

"Right. Thanks. Pilgrim Street."

Quaid nodded.

"I didn't know there were any inhabitable houses on Pilgrim Street."

"Number sixty-four."

Pilgrim Street was on its knees. Most of the houses were already rubble. A few were in the process of being knocked down. Their inside walls were unnaturally exposed; pink and pale green wallpapers, fireplaces on upper stories hanging over chasms of smoking brick. Stairs leading from nowhere to nowhere, and back again.

Number sixty-four stood on its own. The houses in the terrace to either side had been demolished and bulldozed away, leaving a desert of impacted brick-dust which a few hardy, and foolhardy, weeds had tried to populate.

A three-legged white dog was patrolling its territory along the side of sixty-four, leaving little piss-marks at regular intervals as signs of its ownership.

Quaid's house, though scarcely palatial, was more welcoming than the surrounding wasteland.

They drank some bad red wine together, which Steve had brought with him, and they smoked some grass. Quaid was far more mellow than Steve had ever seen him before, quite happy to talk trivia instead of dread; laughing occasionally; even telling a dirty joke. The interior of the house was bare to the point of being spartan. No pictures on the walls; no decoration of any kind. Quaid's books, and there were literally hundreds of them, were piled on the floor in no particular sequence that Steve could make out. The kitchen and bathroom were primitive. The whole atmosphere was almost monastic.

After a couple of easy hours, Steve's curiosity got the better of him.

"Where's the holiday snaps, then?" he said, aware that he was slurring his words a little, and no longer giving a shit.

"Oh yes. My experiment."

"Experiment?"

"Tell you the truth, Steve, I'm not so sure I should show them to you."

"Why not?"

"I'm into serious stuff, Steve."

"And I'm not ready for serious stuff, is that what you're saying?"

Steve could feel Quaid's technique working on him, even though it was transparently obvious what he was doing.

"I didn't say you weren't ready—"

"What the hell is this stuff?"

"Pictures."

"Of?"

"You remember Cheryl."

Pictures of Cheryl. Ha.

"How could I forget?"

"She won't be coming back this term."

"Oh."

"She had a revelation."

Quaid's stare was basilisk-like.

"What do you mean?"

"She was always so calm, wasn't she?" Quaid was talking about her as though she were dead. "Calm, cool, and collected."

"Yes, I suppose she was."

"Poor bitch. All she wanted was a good fuck."

Steve smirked like a kid at Quaid's dirty talk. It was a little shocking; like seeing teacher with his dick hanging out of his trousers.

"She spent some of the vacation here."

"Here?"

"In this house."

"You like her then?"

"She's an ignorant cow. She's pretentious, she's weak, she's stupid. But she wouldn't *give*, she wouldn't give a fucking thing."

"You mean she wouldn't screw?"

"Oh no, she'd strip off her knickers soon as look at you. It was her fears she wouldn't give—"

Same old song.

"But I persuaded her, in the fullness of time."

Quaid pulled out a box from behind a pile of philosophy books. In it was a sheaf of black and white photographs, blown up to twice postcard size. He passed the first one of the series over to Steve.

"I locked her away you see, Steve." Quaid was as unemotional as a newsreader. "To see if I could needle her into showing her dread a little bit."

"What do you mean, locked her away?"

"Upstairs."

Steve felt strange. He could hear his ears singing, very quietly. Bad wine always made his head ring.

"I locked her away upstairs," Quaid said again, "as an experiment. That's why I took this house. No neighbors to hear."

No neighbors to hear what?

Steve looked at the grainy image in his hand.

"Concealed camera," said Quaid, "she never knew I was photographing her."

Photograph One was of a small, featureless room. A little plain furniture.

"That's the room. Top of the house. Warm. A bit stuffy even. No noise."

No noise.

Quaid proffered Photograph Two.

Same room. Now most of the furniture had been removed. A sleeping bag was laid along one wall. A table. A chair. A bare light bulb.

"That's how I laid it out for her."

"It looks like a cell."

Quaid grunted.

Photograph Three. The same room. On the table a jug of water. In the corner of the room, a bucket, roughly covered with a towel.

"What's the bucket for?"

"She had to piss."

"Yes."

"All amenities provided," said Quaid. "I didn't intend to reduce her to an animal."

Even in his drunken state, Steve took Quaid's inference. He didn't *intend* to reduce her to an animal. However . . .

Photograph Four. On the table, on an unpatterned plate, a slab of meat. A bone sticks out from it.

"Beef," said Quaid.

"But she's a vegetarian."

"So she is. It's slightly salted, well-cooked, good beef."

Photograph Five. The same. Cheryl is in the room. The door is closed. She is kicking the door, her foot and fist and face a blur of fury.

"I put her in the room about five in the morning. She was sleeping: I carried her over the threshold myself. Very romantic. She didn't know what the hell was going on."

"You locked her in there?"

"Of course. An experiment."

"She knew nothing about it?"

"We'd talked about dread, you know me. She knew what I wanted to discover. Knew I wanted guinea-pigs. She soon caught on. Once she realized what I was up to she calmed down."

Photograph Six. Cheryl sits in the corner of the room, thinking.

"I think she believed she could out-wait me."

Photograph Seven. Cheryl looks at the leg of beef, glancing at it on the table.

"Nice photo, don't you think? Look at the expression of disgust on her face. She hated even the smell of cooked meat. She wasn't hungry then, of course."

Eight: she sleeps.

Nine: she pisses. Steve felt uncomfortable, watching the girl squatting on the bucket, knickers around her ankles. Tearstains on her face.

Ten: she drinks water from the jug.

Eleven: she sleeps again, back to the room, curled up like a fetus.

"How long has she been in the room?"

"This was only fourteen hours in. She lost orientation as to time very quickly. No light change, you see. Her body-clock was fucked up pretty soon."

"How long was she in here?"

"Till the point was proved."

Twelve: Awake, she cruises the meat on the table, caught surreptitiously glancing down at it.

"This was taken the following morning. I was asleep: the

camera just took pictures every quarter hour. Look at her eyes . . .''

Steve peered more closely at the photograph. There was a certain desperation on Cheryl's face: a haggard, wild look. The way she stared at the beef she could have been trying to hypnotize it.

''She looks sick.''

''She's tired, that's all. She slept a lot, as it happened, but it seemed just to make her more exhausted than ever. She doesn't know now if it's day or night. And she's hungry of course. It's been a day and a half. She's more than a little peckish.''

Thirteen: she sleeps again, curled into an even tighter ball, as though she wanted to swallow herself.

Fourteen: she drinks more water.

''I replaced the jug when she was asleep. She slept deeply: I could have done a jig in there and it wouldn't have woken her. Lost to the world.''

He grinned. Mad, thought Steve, the man's mad.

''God, it stank in there. You know how women smell sometimes; it's not sweat, it's something else. Heavy odor: meaty. Bloody. She came on towards the end of her time. Hadn't planned it that way.''

Fifteen: she touches the meat.

''This is where the cracks begin to show,'' said Quaid, with quiet triumph in his voice. ''This is where the dread begins.''

Steve studied the photograph closely. The grain of the print blurred the detail, but the cool mama was in pain, that was for sure. Her face was knotted up, half in desire, half in repulsion, as she touched the food.

Sixteen: she was at the door again, throwing herself at it, every part of her body flailing. Her mouth a black blur of angst, screaming at the blank door.

''She always ended up haranguing me, whenever she'd had a confrontation with the meat.''

''How long is this?''

''Coming up for three days. You're looking at a hungry woman.''

It wasn't difficult to see that. The next photo she stood still in the middle of the room, averting her eyes from the temptation of the food, her entire body tensed with the dilemma.

"You're starving her."

"She can go ten days without eating quite easily. Fasts are common in any civilized country, Steve. Sixty percent of the British population is clinically obese at any one time. She was too fat anyhow."

Eighteen: she sits, the fat girl, in her corner of the room, weeping.

"About now she began to hallucinate. Just little mental ticks. She thought she felt something in her hair, or on the back of her hand. I'd see her staring into mid-air sometimes watching nothing."

Nineteen: she washes herself. She is stripped to the waist, her breasts are heavy, her face is drained of expression. The meat is a darker tone than in the previous photographs.

"She washed herself regularly. Never let twelve hours go by without washing from head to toe."

"The meat looks . . ."

"Ripe?"

"Dark."

"It's quite warm in her little room; and there's a few flies in there with her. They've found the meat: laid their eggs. Yes, it's ripening up quite nicely."

"Is that part of the plan?"

"Sure. If the meat revolted when it was fresh, what about her disgust at rotted meat? That's the crux of her dilemma, isn't it? The longer she waits to eat, the more disgusted she becomes with what she's been given to feed on. She's trapped with her own horror of meat on the one hand, and her dread of dying on the other. Which is going to give first?"

Steve was no less trapped now.

On the one hand this joke had already gone too far, and Quaid's experiment had become an exercise in sadism. On the other hand he wanted to know how far this story ended. There was an undeniable fascination in watching the woman suffer.

The next seven photographs—twenty, twenty-one, -two, -three, -four, -five and -six—pictured the same circular routine. Sleeping, washing, pissing, meat-watching. Sleeping, washing, pissing—

Then twenty-seven.

"See?"

She picks up the meat.

Yes, she picks it up, her face full of horror. The haunch of the beef looks well-ripened now, speckled with flies' eggs. Gross.

"She bites it."

The next photograph, and her face is buried in the meat.

Steve seemed to taste the rotten flesh in the back of his throat. His mind found a stench to imagine, and created a gravy of putrescence to run over his tongue. How could she do it?

Twenty-nine: she is vomiting in the bucket in the corner of the room.

Thirty: she is sitting looking at the table. It is empty. The water-jug has been thrown against the wall. The plate has been smashed. The beef lies on the floor in a slime of degeneration.

Thirty-one: she sleeps. Her head is lost in a tangle of arms.

Thirty-two: she is standing up. She is looking at the meat again, defying it. The hunger she feels is plain on her face. So is the disgust.

Thirty-three. She sleeps.

"How long now?" asked Steve.

"Five days. No, six."

Six days.

Thirty-four. She is a blurred figure, apparently flinging herself against a wall. Perhaps beating her head against it, Steve couldn't be sure. He was past asking. Part of him didn't want to know.

Thirty-five: she is again sleeping, this time beneath the table. The sleeping bag has been torn to pieces, shredded cloth and pieces of stuffing littering the room.

Thirty-six: she speaks to the door, through the door, knowing she will get no answer.

Thirty-seven: she eats the rancid meat.

Calmly she sits under the table, like a primitive in her cave, and pulls at the meat with her incisors. Her face is again expressionless; all her energy is bent to the purpose of the moment. To eat. To eat 'til the hunger disappears, 'til the agony in her belly and the sickness in her head disappear.

Steve stared at the photograph.

"It startled me," said Quaid, "how suddenly she gave in. One moment she seemed to have as much resistance as ever. The monologue at the door was the same mixture of threats and apologies as she'd delivered day in, day out. Then she broke. Just 'like that. Squatted under the table and ate the beef down to the bone, as though it were a choice cut."

Thirty-eight: she sleeps. The door is open. Light pours in.

Thirty-nine: the room is empty.

"Where did she go?"

"She wandered downstairs. She came into the kitchen, drank several glasses of water, and sat in a chair for three or four hours without saying a word."

"Did you speak to her?"

"Eventually. When she started to come out of her fugue state. The experiment was over. I didn't want to hurt her."

"What did she say?"

"Nothing."

"Nothing?"

"Nothing at all. For a long time I don't believe she was even aware of my presence in the room. Then I cooked some potatoes, which she ate."

"She didn't try and call the police?"

"No."

"No violence?"

"No. She knew what I'd done, and why I'd done it. It wasn't pre-planned, but we'd talked about such experiments, in abstract conversations. She hadn't come to any harm, you see. She'd lost a bit of weight perhaps, but that was about all."

"Where is she now?"

"She left the day after. I don't know where she went."

"And what did it all prove?"

"Nothing at all, perhaps. But it made an interesting start to my investigations."

"Start? This was only a start?"

There was plain disgust for Quaid in Steve's voice.

"Stephen—"

"You could have killed her!"

"No."

"She could have lost her mind. Unbalanced her permanently."

"Possibly. But unlikely. She was a strong-willed woman."

"But you broke her."

"Yes. It was a journey she was ready to take. We'd talked of going to face her fear. So here was I, arranging for Cheryl to do just that. Nothing much really."

"You forced her to do it. She wouldn't have gone otherwise."

"True. It was an education for her."

"So now you're a teacher?"

Steve wished he'd been able to keep the sarcasm out of his voice. But it was there. Sarcasm; anger; and a little fear.

"Yes, I'm a teacher," Quaid replied, looking at Steve obliquely, his eyes not focussed. "I'm teaching people dread."

Steve stared at the floor. "Are you satisfied with what you've taught?"

"And learned, Steve. I've learned too. It's a very exciting prospect: a world of fears to investigate. Especially with intelligent subjects. Even in the face of rationalization—"

Steve stood up. "I don't want to hear any more."

"Oh? OK."

"I've got classes early tomorrow."

"No."

"What?"

A beat, faltering.

"No. Don't go yet."

"Why?" His heart was racing. He feared Quaid, he'd never realized how profoundly.

"I've got some more books to give you."

Steve felt his face flush. Slightly. What had he thought in that moment? That Quaid was going to bring him down with a rugby tackle and start experimenting on his fears?

No. Idiot thoughts.

"I've got a book on Kierkegaard you'll like. Upstairs. I'll be two minutes."

Smiling, Quaid left the room.

Steve squatted on his haunches and began to sheaf through the photographs again. It was the moment when Cheryl first picked up the rotting meat that fascinated him most. Her face wore an expression completely uncharacteristic of the woman he had known. Doubt was written there, and confusion, and deep—

"en."

Dread.

It was Quaid's word. A dirty word. An obscene word, associated from this night on with Quaid's torture of an innocent girl.

For a moment Steve thought of the expression on his own face, as he stared down at the photograph. Was there not some of the same confusion on his face? And perhaps some of the dread too, waiting for release.

He heard a sound behind him, too soft to be Quaid.

Unless he was creeping.

Oh, God, unless he was—

A pad of chloroformed cloth was clamped over Steve's mouth and his nostrils. Involuntarily, he inhaled and the vapors stung his sinuses, made his eyes water.

A blob of blackness appeared at the corner of the world, just out of sight, and it started to grow, this stain, pulsing to the rhythm of his quickening heart.

In the center of Steve's head he could see Quaid's voice as a veil. It said his name.

"Stephen."

Again.

"—ephen."

"—phen."

"—hen."

"en."

The stain was the world. The world was dark, gone away. Out of sight, out of mind.

Steve fell clumsily amongst the photographs.

When he woke up he was unaware of his consciousness. There was darkness everywhere, on all sides. He lay awake for an hour with his eyes wide before he realized they were open.

Experimentally, he moved first his arms and his legs, then his head. He wasn't bound as he'd expected, except by his ankle. There was definitely a chain or something similar around his left ankle. It chafed his skin when he tried to move too far.

The floor beneath him was very uncomfortable, and when he investigated it more closely with the palm of his hand he realized he was lying on a huge grille or grid of some kind. It was metal, and its regular surface spread in every direction as far as his arms would reach. When he poked his arm down through the holes in this lattice he touched nothing. Just empty air falling away beneath him.

The first infra-red photographs Quaid took of Stephen's confinement pictured his exploration. As Quaid had expected the subject was being quite rational about his situation. No hysterics. No curses. No tears. That was the challenge of this particular subject. He knew precisely what was going on; and he would respond logically to his fears. That would surely make a more difficult mind to break than Cheryl's.

But how much more rewarding the results would be when he did crack. Would his soul not open up then, for Quaid to see and touch? There was so much there, in the man's interior, he wanted to study.

Gradually Steve's eyes became accustomed to the darkness.

He was imprisoned in what appeared to be some kind of shaft. It was, he estimated, about twenty feet wide, and completely round. Was it some kind of air-shaft, for a tunnel, or an underground factory? Steve's mind mapped the area around Pilgrim Street, trying to pinpoint the most likely place for Quaid to have taken him. He could think of nowhere.

Nowhere.

He was lost in a place he couldn't fix or recognize. The shaft had no corners to focus his eyes on; and the walls offered no crack or hole to hide his consciousness in.

Worse, he was lying spreadeagled on a grid that hung over this shaft. His eyes could make no impression on the darkness beneath him: it seemed that the shaft might be bottomless. And there was only the thin network of the grille, and the fragile chain that shackled his ankle to it, between him and falling.

He pictured himself poised under an empty black sky, and over an infinite darkness. The air was warm and stale. It dried up the tears that had suddenly sprung into his eyes, leaving them gummy. When he began to shout for help, which he did after the tears had passed, the darkness ate his words easily.

Having yelled himself hoarse, he lay back on the lattice. He couldn't help but imagine that beyond his frail bed, the darkness went on forever. It was absurd, of course. Nothing goes on forever, he said aloud.

Nothing goes on forever.

And yet, he'd never know. If he fell in the absolute blackness beneath him, he'd fall and fall and fall and not see the bottom of the shaft coming. Though he tried to think of brighter, more positive, images, his mind conjured his body cascading down this horrible shaft, with the bottom a foot from his hurtling body and his eyes not seeing it, his brain not predicting it.

Until he hit.

Would he see light as his head was dashed open on impact? Would he understand, in the moment that his body became offal, why he'd lived and died?

Then he thought: Quaid wouldn't dare. "Wouldn't dare!" he screeched. "Wouldn't dare!"

The dark was a glutton for words. As soon as he'd yelled into it, it was as though he'd never made a sound.

And then another thought: a real baddie. Suppose Quaid had found this circular hell to put him in because he would *never* be found, *never* be investigated? Maybe he wanted to take his experiment to the limits.

To the limits. Death was at the limits. And wouldn't that be the ultimate experiment for Quaid? Watching a man die: watching the fear of death, the motherlode of dread, approach. Sartre had written that no man could ever know his own death. But to know the deaths of others, intimately—to watch the acrobatics that the mind would surely perform to avoid the bitter truth—that was a clue to death's nature, wasn't it? That might, in some small way, prepare a man for his own death. To live another's dread vicariously was the safest, cleverest way to touch the beast.

Yes, he thought, Quaid might kill me; out of his own terror.

Steve took a sour satisfaction in that thought. That Quaid, the impartial experimenter, the would-be educator, was obsessed with terrors because his own dread ran deepest.

That was why he had to watch others deal with their fears. He needed a solution, a way out for himself.

Thinking all this through took hours. In the darkness Steve's mind was quick-silver, but uncontrollable. He found it difficult to keep one train of argument for very long. His thoughts were like fish, small, fast fish, wriggling out of his grasp as soon as he took a hold of them.

But underlying every twist of thought was the knowledge that he must out-play Quaid. That was certain. He must be calm; prove himself a useless subject for Quaid's analysis.

The photographs of these hours showed Stephen lying with his eyes closed on the grid, with a slight frown on his face. Occasionally, paradoxically, a smile would flit across his lips. Sometimes it was impossible to know if he was sleeping or waking, thinking or dreaming.

Quaid waited.

Eventually Steve's eyes began to flicker under his lids, the unmistakable sign of dreaming. It was time, while the subject slept, to turn the wheel of the rack—

Steve woke with his hands cuffed together. He could see a bowl of water on a plate beside him; and a second bowl, full of luke-warm unsalted porridge, beside it. He ate and drank thankfully.

As he ate, two things registered. First, that the noise of his eating seemed very loud in his head; and second, that he felt a constriction, a tightness, around his temples.

The photographs show Stephen clumsily reaching up to his head. A harness is strapped on to him, and locked in place. It clamps plugs deep into his ears, preventing any sound from getting in.

The photographs show puzzlement. Then anger. Then fear.

Steve was deaf.

All he could hear were the noises in his head. The clicking

of his teeth. The slush and swallow of his palate. The sounds boomed between his ears like guns.

Tears sprang to his eyes. He kicked at the grid, not hearing the clatter of his heels on the metal bars. He screamed until his throat felt as if it was bleeding. He heard none of his cries.

Panic began in him.

The photographs showed its birth. His face was flushed. His eyes were wide, his teeth and gums exposed in a grimace.

He looked like a frightened monkey.

All the familiar, childhood feelings swept over him. He remembered them like the faces of old enemies; the chittering limbs, the sweat, the nausea. In desperation he picked up the bowl of water and upturned it over his face. The shock of the cold water diverted his mind momentarily from the panic-ladder it was climbing. He lay back down on the grid, his body a board, and told himself to breathe deeply and evenly.

Relax, relax, relax, he said aloud.

In his head, he could hear his tongue clicking. He could hear his mucus too, moving sluggishly in the panic-constricted passages of his nose, blocking and unblocking in his ears. Now he could detect the low, soft hiss that waited under all the other noises. The sound of his mind—

It was like the white noise between stations on the radio, this was the same whine that came to fetch him under anesthetic, the same noise that would sound in his ears on the borders of sleep.

His limbs still twitched nervously, and he was only half-aware of the way he wrestled with his handcuffs, indifferent to their edges scouring the skin at his wrists.

The photographs recorded all these reactions precisely. His war with hysteria: his pathetic attempts to keep the fears from resurfacing. His tears. His bloody wrists.

Eventually, exhaustion won over panic; as it had so often as a child. How many times had he fallen asleep with the salt-taste of tears in his nose and mouth, unable to fight any longer?

The exertion had heightened the pitch of his head-noises.

Now, instead of a lullaby, his brain whistled and whooped him to sleep.

Oblivion was good.

Quaid was disappointed. It was clear from the speed of his response that Stephen Grace was going to break very soon indeed. In fact, he was as good as broken, only a few hours into the experiment. And Quaid had been relying on Stephen. After months of preparing the ground, it seemed that this subject was going to lose his mind without giving up a single clue.

One word, one miserable word, was all Quaid needed. A little sign as to the nature of the experience. Or better still, something to suggest a solution, a healing totem, a prayer even. Surely some Savior comes to the lips, as the personality is swept away in madness? There must be *something*.

Quaid waited like a carrion bird at the site of some atrocity, counting the minutes left to the expiring soul, hoping for a morsel.

Steve woke face down on the grid. The air was much staler now, and the metal bars bit into the flesh of his cheek. He was hot and uncomfortable.

He lay still, letting his eyes become accustomed to his surroundings again. The lines of the grid ran off in perfect perspective to meet the wall of the shaft. The simple network of criss-crossed bars struck him as pretty. Yes, pretty. He traced the lines back and forth, 'til he tired of the game. Bored, he rolled over onto his back, feeling the grid vibrate under his body. Was it less stable now? It seemed to rock a little as he moved.

Hot and sweaty, Steve unbuttoned his shirt. There was sleep-spittle on his chin but he didn't care to wipe it off. What if he drooled? Who was to see?

He half pulled off his shirt, and using one foot, kicked his shoe off the other.

Shoe: lattice: fall. Sluggishly, his mind made the connection. He sat up. Oh poor shoe. His shoe would fall. It would slip between the bars and be lost. But no. It was finely balanced across two sides of a lattice-hole; he could still save it if he tried.

He reached for his poor, poor shoe, and his movement shifted the grid.

The shoe began to slip.

"Please," he begged it, "don't fall." He didn't want to lose his nice shoe, his pretty shoe. It mustn't fall. It mustn't fall.

As he stretched to snatch it, the shoe tipped, heel down, through the grid and fell into the darkness.

He let out a cry of loss that he couldn't hear.

Oh, if only he could listen to the shoe falling; to count the seconds of its descent. To hear it thud home at the bottom of the shaft. At least then he'd known how far he had to fall to his death.

He couldn't endure it any longer. He rolled over on to his stomach and thrust both arms through the grid, screaming:

"I'll go too! I'll go too!"

He couldn't bear waiting to fall, in the dark, in the whining silence, he just wanted to follow his shoe down, down, down the dark shaft to extinction, and have the whole game finished once and for all.

"I'll go! I'll go! I'll go!" he shrieked. He pleaded with gravity.

Beneath him, the grid moved.

Something had broken. A pin, a chain, a rope that held the grid in position had snapped. He was no longer horizontal; already he was sliding across the bars as they tipped him off into the dark.

With shock he realized his limbs were no longer chained.

He would fall.

The man wanted him to fall. The bad man—what was his name? Quake? Quail? Quarrel—

Automatically he seized the grid with both hands as it tipped even further over. Maybe he didn't want to fall after his shoe, after all? Maybe life, a little moment more of life, was worth holding on to—

The dark beyond the edge of the grid was so deep; and who could guess what lurked in it?

In his head the noises of his panic multiplied. The thumping of his bloody heart, the stutter of his mucus, the dry rasp of his palate. His palms, slick with sweat, were losing their grip. Gravity wanted him. It demanded its rights of his body's bulk: demanded that he fall. For a moment, glancing over his shoulder at the mouth that opened under him, he thought he saw monsters stirring below him. Ridiculous, loony things, crudely drawn, dark on dark. Vile graffiti leered up from his childhood and uncurled their claws to snatch at his legs.

"Mama," he said, as his hands failed him, and he was delivered into dread.

"*Mama.*"

That was the word. Quaid heard it plainly, in all its banality.

"Mama!"

By the time Steve hit the bottom of the shaft, he was past judging how far he'd fallen. The moment his hands let go of the grid, and he knew the dark would have him, his mind snapped. The animal self survived to relax his body, saving him all but minor injury on impact. The rest of his life, all but the simplest responses, were shattered, the pieces flung into the recesses of his memory.

When the light came, at last, he looked up at the person in the Mickey Mouse mask at the door, and smiled at him. It was a child's smile, one of thankfulness for his comical rescuer. He let the man take him by the ankles and haul him out of the big round room in which he was lying. His pants were wet, and he knew he'd dirtied himself in his sleep. Still, the Funny Mouse would kiss him better.

His head lolled on his shoulders as he was dragged out of the torture-chamber. On the floor beside his head was a shoe. And seven or eight feet above him was the grid from which he had fallen.

It meant nothing at all.

He let the Mouse sit him down in a bright room. He let the Mouse give him his ears back, though he didn't really want them. It was funny watching the world without sound, it made him laugh.

He drank some water, and ate some sweet cake.

He was tired. He wanted to sleep. He wanted his Mama. But the Mouse didn't seem to understand, so he cried, and kicked the table and threw the plates and cups on the floor. Then he ran into the next room, and threw all the papers he could find in the air. It was nice watching them flutter up and flutter down. Some of them fell face down, some face up. Some were covered with writing. Some were pictures. Horrid pictures. Pictures that made him feel very strange.

They were all pictures of dead people, every one of them. Some of the pictures were of little children, others were of grown-up children. They were lying down, or half-sitting, and there were big cuts in their faces and their bodies, cuts that showed a mess underneath, a mish-mash of shiny bits and oozy bits. And all around the dead people: black paint. Not in neat puddles, but splashed all around, and finger-marked, and hand-printed and very messy.

In three or four of the pictures the thing that made the cuts was still there. He knew the word for it.

Axe.

There was an axe in a lady's face buried almost to the handle. There was an axe in a man's leg, and another lying on the floor of a kitchen beside a dead baby.

This man collected pictures of dead people and axes, which Stevie thought was strange.

That was his last thought before the too-familiar scent of chloroform filled his head and he lost consciousness.

The sordid doorway smelt of old urine and fresh vomit. It was his own vomit; it was all over the front of his shirt. He tried to stand up, but his legs felt wobbly. It was very cold. His throat hurt.

Then he heard footsteps. It sounded like the Mouse was coming back. Maybe he'd take him home.

"Get up, son."

It wasn't the Mouse. It was a policeman.

"What are you doing down there? I said get up."

Bracing himself against the crumbling brick of the doorway Steve got to his feet. The policeman shone his torch at him.

"Jesus Christ," said the policeman, disgust written over his face. "You're in a right fucking state. Where do you live?"

Steve shook his head, staring down at his vomit-soaked shirt like a shamed schoolboy.

"What's your name?"

He couldn't quite remember.

"Name, lad?"

He was trying. If only the policeman wouldn't shout.

"Come on, take a hold of yourself."

The words didn't make much sense. Steve could feel tears pricking the backs of his eyes.

"Home."

Now he was blubbering, sniffling snot, feeling utterly forsaken. He wanted to die: he wanted to lie down and die.

The policeman shook him.

"You high on something?" he demanded, pulling Steve into the glare of the streetlights and staring at his tear-stained face.

"You'd better move on."

"Mama," said Steve. "I want my Mama."

The words changed the encounter entirely.

Suddenly the policeman found the spectacle more than disgusting; more than pitiful. This little bastard, with his blood-shot eyes and his dinner down his shirt, was really getting on his nerves. Too much money, too much dirt in his veins, too little discipline.

"Mama" was the last straw. He punched Steve in the stomach, a neat, sharp, functional blow. Steve doubled up, whimpering.

"Shut up, son."

Another blow finished the job of crippling the child, and then he took a fistful of Steve's hair and pulled the little drug-gy's face up to meet his.

"You want to be a derelict, is that it?"

"No. No."

Steve didn't know what a derelict was; he just wanted to make the policeman like him.

"Please," he said, tears coming again, "take me home."

The policeman seemed confused. The kid hadn't started fighting back and calling for civil rights, the way most of them did. That was the way they usually ended up: on the ground, bloody-nosed, calling for a social worker. This one just wept. The policeman began to get a bad feeling about the kid. Like he was mental or something. And he'd beaten the shit out of the little snot. Fuck it. Now he felt responsible. He took hold of Steve by the arm and bundled him across the road to his car.

"Get in."

"Take me—"

"I'll take you home, son. I'll take you home."

At the Night Hostel they searched Steve's clothes for some kind of identification, found none, then scoured his body for fleas, his hair for nits. The policeman left him then, which Steve was relieved about. He hadn't liked the man.

The people at the Hostel talked about him as though he wasn't in the room. Talked about how young he was; discussed his mental-age; his clothes; his appearance. Then they gave him a bar of soap and showed him the showers. He stood under the cold water for ten minutes and dried himself with a stained towel. He didn't shave, though they'd lent him a razor. He'd forgotten how to do it.

Then they gave him some old clothes, which he liked. They weren't such bad people, even if they did talk about him as though he wasn't there. One of them even smiled at him; a burly man with a grizzled beard. Smiled as he would at a dog.

They were odd clothes he was given. Either too big or too small. All colors: yellow socks, dirty white shirt, pin-stripe trousers that had been made for a glutton, a thread-bare sweater, heavy boots. He liked dressing up, putting on two vests and two pairs of socks when they weren't looking. He felt assured with several thicknesses of cotton and wool wrapped around him.

Then they left him with a ticket for his bed in his hand, to wait for the dormitories to be unlocked. He was not impatient, like some of the men in the corridors with him. They yelled incoherently, many of them, their accusations laced with obscenities, and they spat at each other. It frightened him. All he wanted was to sleep. To lie down and sleep.

At eleven o'clock one of the wardens unlocked the gate to the dormitory, and all the lost men filed through to find themselves an iron bed for the night. The dormitory, which was large and badly lit, stank of disinfectant and old people.

Avoiding the eyes and the flailing arms of the other dere-
licts, Steve found himself an ill-made bed, with one thin
blanket tossed across it, and lay down to sleep. All around
him men were coughing and muttering and weeping. One
was saying his prayers as he lay, staring at the ceiling, on his
grey pillow. Steve thought that was a good idea. So he said
his own child's prayer.

"Gentle Jesus, meek and mild,
Look upon this little child,
Pity my—
What was the word?
Pity my—*simplicity*,
Suffer me to come to thee."

That made him feel better; and the sleep, a balm, was blue
and deep.

Quaid sat in darkness. The terror was on him again, worse
than ever. His body was rigid with fear; so much so that he
couldn't even get out of bed and snap on the light. Besides,
what if this time, this time of all times, the terror was true?
What if the axe-man was at the door in flesh and blood?
Grinning like a loon at him, dancing like the devil at the top
of the stairs, as Quaid had seen him, in dreams, dancing and
grinning, grinning and dancing.

Nothing moved. No creak of the stair, no giggle in the
shadows. It wasn't him, after all. Quaid would live 'til morning.

His body had relaxed a little now. He swung his legs out
of bed and switched on the light. The room was indeed
empty. The house was silent. Through the open door he could
see the top of the stairs. There was no axe-man, of course.

Steve woke to shouting. It was still dark. He didn't know
how long he'd been asleep, but his limbs no longer ached so
badly. Elbows on his pillow, he half-sat up and stared down
the dormitory to see what all the commotion was about. Four
bed-rows down from his, two men were fighting. The bone
of contention was by no means clear. They just grappled with
each other like girls (it made Steve laugh to watch them),
screeching and pulling each other's hair. By moonlight the

blood on their faces and hands was black: One of them, the older of the two, was thrust back across his bed, screaming: "I will not go to the Finchley Road! You will not make me. Don't strike me! I'm not your man! I'm not!"

The other was beyond listening; he was too stupid, or too mad, to understand that the old man was begging to be left alone. Urged on by spectators on every side, the old man's assailant had taken off his shoe and was belaboring his victim with it. Steve could hear the crack, crack of his blows: heel on head. There were cheers accompanying each strike, and lessening cries from the old man.

Suddenly, the applause faltered, as somebody came into the dormitory. Steve couldn't see who it was; the mass of men crowded around the fight were between him and the door.

He did see the victor toss his shoe into the air however, with a final shout of "Fucker!"

The shoe.

Steve couldn't take his eyes off the shoe. It rose in the air, turning as it rose, then plummeted to the bare boards like a shot bird. Steve saw it clearly, more clearly than he'd seen anything in many days.

It landed not far from him.

It landed with a loud thud.

It landed on its side. As his shoe had landed. His shoe. The one he kicked off. On the grid. In the room. In the house. In Pilgrim Street.

Quaid woke with the same dream. Always the stairway. Always him looking down the tunnel of the stairs, while that ridiculous sight, half-joke, half-horror, tip-toed up towards him, a laugh on every step.

He'd never dreamt twice in one night before. He swung his hand out over the edge of the bed and fumbled for the bottle he kept there. In the dark he swigged from it, deeply.

Steve walked past the knot of angry men, not caring about their shouts or the old man's groans and curses. The wardens were having a hard time dealing with the disturbance. It was the last time Old Man Crowley would be let in: he always invited violence. This had all the marks of a near-riot; it would take hours to settle them down again.

Nobody questioned Steve as he wandered down the corridor, through the gate, and into the vestibule of the Night Hostel. The swing doors were closed, but the night air, bitter before dawn, smelt refreshing as it seeped in.

The pokey reception office was empty, and through the door Steve could see the fire-extinguisher hanging on the wall. It was red and bright. Beside it was a long black hose, curled up on a red drum like a sleeping snake. Beside that, sitting in two brackets on the wall, was an axe.

A very pretty axe.

Stephen walked into the office. A little distance away he heard running feet, shouts, a whistle. But nobody came to interrupt Steve, as he made friends with the axe.

First he smiled at it.

The curve of the blade of the axe smiled back.

Then he touched it.

The axe seemed to like being touched. It was dusty, and hadn't been used in a long while. Too long. It wanted to be picked up, and stroked, and smiled at. Steve took it out of its brackets very gently, and slid it under his jacket to keep warm. Then he walked back out of the reception office, through the swing-doors and out to find his other shoe.

Quaid woke again.

It took Steve a very short time to orient himself. There was a spring in his step as he began to make his way to Pilgrim Street. He felt like a clown, dressed in so many bright colors, in such floppy trousers, such silly boots. He was a comical fellow, wasn't he? He made himself laugh, he was so comical.

The wind began to get into him, whipping him up into a frenzy as it scooted through his hair and made his eyeballs as cold as two lumps of ice in his sockets.

He began to run, skip, dance, cavort through the streets, white under the lights, dark in between. Now you see me, now you don't. Now you see me, now you—

* * *

Quaid hadn't been woken by the dream this time. This time he had heard a noise. Definitely a noise.

The moon had risen high enough to throw its beams through the window, through the door and on to the top of the stairs. There was no need to put on the light. All he needed to see, he could see. The top of the stairs were empty, as ever.

Then the bottom stair creaked, a tiny noise as though a breath had landed on it.

Quaid knew dread then.

Another creak, as it came up the stairs towards him, the ridiculous dream. It had to be a dream. After all, he knew no clowns, no axe-killers. So how could that absurd image, the same image that woke him night after night, be anything but a dream?

Yet, perhaps there were some dreams so preposterous they could only be true.

No clowns, he said to himself, as he stood watching the door, and the stairway, and the spotlight of the moon. Quaid knew only fragile minds, so weak they couldn't give him a clue to the nature, to the origin, or to the cure for the panic that now held him in thrall. All they did was break, crumble into dust, when faced with the slightest sign of the dread at the heart of life.

He knew no clowns, never had, never would.

Then it appeared; the face of a fool. Pale to whiteness in the light of the moon, its young features bruised, unshaven and puffy, its smile open like a child's smile. It had bitten its lip in its excitement. Blood was smeared across its lower jaw, and its gums were almost black with blood. Still it was a clown. Indisputably a clown even to its ill-fitting clothes, so incongruous, so pathetic.

Only the axe didn't quite match the smile.

It caught the moonlight as the maniac made small, chopping motions with it, his tiny black eyes glinting with anticipation of the fun ahead.

Almost at the top of the stairs, he stopped, his smile not faltering for a moment as he gazed at Quaid's terror.

Quaid's legs gave out, and he stumbled to his knees.

The clown climbed another stair, skipping as he did so,

his glittering eyes fixed on Quaid, filled with a sort of benign malice. The axe rocked back and forth in his white hands, in a petite version of the killing stroke.

Quaid knew him.

It was his pupil: his guinea-pig, transformed into the image of his own dread.

Him. Of all men. Him. The deaf boy.

The skipping was bigger now, and the clown was making a deep-throated noise, like the call of some fantastical bird. The axe was describing wider and wider sweeps in the air, each more lethal than the last.

"Stephen," said Quaid.

The name meant nothing to Steve. All he saw was the mouth opening. The mouth closing. Perhaps a sound came out: perhaps not. It was irrelevant to him.

The throat of the clown gave out a screech, and the axe swung up over his head, two-handed. At the same moment the merry little dance became a run, as the axe-man leapt the last two stairs and ran into the bedroom, full into the spotlight.

Quaid's body half turned to avoid the killing blow, but not quickly or elegantly enough. The blade slit the air and sliced through the back of Quaid's arm, sheering off most of his triceps, shattering his humerus and opening the flesh of his lower arm in a gash that just missed his artery.

Quaid's scream could have been heard ten houses away, except that those houses were rubble. There was nobody to hear. Nobody to come and drag the clown off him.

The axe, eager to be about its business, was hacking at Quaid's thigh now, as though it was chopping a log. Yawning wounds four or five inches deep exposed the shiny steak of the philosopher's muscle, the bone, the marrow. With each stroke the clown would tug at the axe to pull it out, and Quaid's body would jerk like a puppet.

Quaid screamed. Quaid begged. Quaid cajoled.

The clown didn't hear a word.

All he heard was the noise in his head: the whistles, the whoops, the howls, the hums. He had taken refuge where no rational argument, no threat, would ever fetch him out again.

Where the thump of his heart was law, and the whine of his blood was music.

How he danced, this deaf-boy, danced like a loon to see his tormentor gaping like a fish, the depravity of his intellect silenced forever. How the blood spurted! How it gushed and fountained!

The little clown laughed to see such fun. There was a night's entertainment to be had here, he thought. The axe was his friend forever, keen and wise. It would cut, and cross-cut, it could slice and amputate, yet still they could keep this man alive, if they were cunning enough, alive for a long, long while.

Steve was happy as a lamb. They had the rest of the night ahead of them, and all the music he could possibly want was sounding in his head.

And Quaid knew, meeting the clown's vacant stare through an air turned bloody, that there was worse in the world than dread. Worse than death itself.

There was pain without hope of healing. There was life that refused to end, long after the mind had begged the body to cease. And worst, there were dreams come true.

Edgar Allan Poe

THE FALL OF THE HOUSE OF USHER

The greatest and most influential of all horror writers, Edgar Allan Poe is the primary transition figure between the Gothic and the modern. He is responsible for the transformation of Gothic paraphernalia into useful devices for the investigation of human psychology (used consciously) and for symbolism. He characteristically used abnormal situations and characters for dramatic effect and characteristically wrote horror. His critical writing, as well as his fiction, has given instruction to generations of short story writers ever since, and influenced the entire course of the development and evolution of the short story . . . including the entire genres of mystery fiction and science fiction, which grow significantly out of his stories. Nearly a dozen of his stories are classics of nineteenth-century literature and of these, half are horror. "The Fall of the House of Usher" is printed here as representative. It is one of the foundations of the haunted house story (prior to Poe it was usually the haunted castle of the Gothic), provocative, symbolic, psychologically intricate. "In Poe's work a thing is never merely a 'thing'; it is a language," says the Poe-scholar Benjamin Franklin Fisher IV. Poe's horror stories invent the language of horror, give meaning to the idea of the fantastic as a language.

Son coeur est un luth suspendu;
Sitôt qu'on le touche il résonne.

—*De Béranger*

During the whole of a dull, dark, and soundless day in the autumn of the year, when the clouds hung oppressively low in the heavens, I had been passing alone, on horseback, through a singularly dreary tract of country, and at length found myself, as the shades of the evening drew on, within view of the melancholy House of Usher. I know not how it was—but, with the first glimpse of the building, a sense of insufferable gloom pervaded my spirit. I say insufferable; for the feeling was unrelieved by any of that half-pleasurable, because poetic, sentiment with which the mind usually received even the sternest natural images of the desolate or terrible. I looked upon the scene before me—upon the mere house, and the simple landscape features of the domain—upon the bleak walls—upon the vacant eye-like windows—upon a few rank sedges—and upon a few white trunks of decayed trees—with an utter depression of soul which I can compare to no earthly sensation more properly than to the after-dream of the reveller upon opium—the bitter lapse into every-day life—the hideous dropping off of the veil. There was an iciness, a sinking, a sickening of the heart—an unredeemed dreariness of thought which no goading of the imagination could torture into aught of the sublime. What was it—I paused to think—what was it that so unnerved me in the contemplation of the House of Usher? It was a mystery all insoluble; nor could I grapple with the shadowy fancies that crowded upon me as I pondered. I was forced to fall back upon the unsatisfactory conclusion, that while, beyond doubt, there *are* combinations of very simple natural objects which have the power of thus affecting us, still the analysis of this power lies among considerations beyond our depth. It was possible, I reflected, that a mere different arrangement of the particulars of the scene, of the details of the picture, would be sufficient to modify, or perhaps to annihilate its capacity for sorrowful impression; and, acting upon this idea, I reined my horse to the precipitous brink of a black and lurid tarn that lay in unruffled lustre by the dwelling, and gazed down—but with a shudder even more thrilling than before— upon the remodelled and inverted images of the gray sedge, and the ghastly tree-stems, and the vacant and eye-like windows.

Nevertheless, in this mansion of gloom I now proposed to myself a sojourn of some weeks. Its proprietor, Roderick Usher, had been one of my boon companions in boyhood; but many years had elapsed since our last meeting. A letter, however, had lately reached me in a distant part of the country—a letter from him—which, in its wildly importunate nature, had admitted of no other than a personal reply. The MS. gave evidence of nervous agitation. The writer spoke of acute bodily illness—of a mental disorder which oppressed him—and of an earnest desire to see me, as his best and indeed his only personal friend, with a view of attempting, by the cheerfulness of my society, some alleviation of his malady. It was the manner in which all this, and much more, was said—it was the apparent *heart* that went with his request—which allowed me no room for hesitation; and I accordingly obeyed forthwith what I still considered a very singular summons.

Although, as boys, we had been even intimate associates, yet I really knew little of my friend. His reserve had been always excessive and habitual. I was aware, however, that his very ancient family had been noted, time out of mind, for a peculiar sensibility of temperament, displaying itself, through long ages, in many works of exalted art, and manifested, of late, in repeated deeds of munificent yet unobtrusive charity, as well as in a passionate devotion to the intricacies, perhaps even more than to the orthodox and easily recognizable beauties, of musical science. I had learned, too, the very remarkable fact, that the stem of the Usher race, all time-honored as it was, had put forth, at no period, any enduring branch; in other words, that the entire family lay in the direct line of descent, and had always, with very trifling and very temporary variation, so lain. It was this deficiency, I considered, while running over in thought the perfect keeping of the character of the premises with the accredited character of the people, and while speculating upon the possible influence which the one, in the long lapse of centuries, might have exercised upon the other—it was this deficiency, perhaps, of collateral issue, and the consequent undeviating transmission, from sire to son, of the patrimony with the name, which had, at length, so identified the two as to merge the original title of the estate in the quaint and equivocal appellation of the ''House of Usher''—an appellation which seemed to include, in the minds of the peasantry who used it, both the family and the family mansion.

I have said that the sole effect of my somewhat childish experiment—that of looking down within the tarn—had been to deepen the first singular impression. There can be no doubt that the consciousness of the rapid increase of my superstition—for why should I not so term it?—served mainly to accelerate the increase itself. Such, I have long known, is the paradoxical law of all sentiments having terror as a basis. And it might have been for this reason only, that, when I again uplifted my eyes to the house itself, from its image in the pool, there grew in my mind a strange fancy—a fancy so ridiculous, indeed, that I but mention it to show the vivid force of the sensations which oppressed me. I had so worked upon my imagination as really to believe that about the whole mansion and domain there hung an atmosphere peculiar to themselves and their immediate vicinity—an atmosphere which had no affinity with the air of heaven, but which had reeked up from the decayed trees, and the gray wall, and the silent tarn—a pestilent and mystic vapor, dull, sluggish, faintly discernible, and leaden-hued.

Shaking off from my spirit what *must* have been a dream, I scanned more narrowly the real aspect of the building. Its principal feature seemed to be that of an excessive antiquity. The discoloration of ages had been great. Minute fungi overspread the whole exterior, hanging in a fine tangled web-work from the eaves. Yet all this was apart from any extraordinary dilapidation. No portion of the masonry had fallen; and there appeared to be a wild inconsistency between its still perfect adaptation of parts, and the crumbling condition of the individual stones. In this there was much that reminded me of the specious totality of old wood-work which has rotted for long years in some neglected vault, with no disturbance from the breath of the external air. Beyond this indication of extensive decay, however, the fabric gave little token of instability. Perhaps the eye of a scrutinizing observer might have discovered a barely perceptible fissure, which, extending from the roof of the building in front, made its way down the wall in a zigzag direction, until it became lost in the sullen waters of the tarn.

Noticing these things, I rode over a short causeway to the house. A servant in waiting took my horse, and I entered the Gothic archway of the hall. A valet, of stealthy step, thence conducted me, in silence, through many dark and intricate passages in my progress to the *studio* of his master. Much that I encountered on the way contributed, I know not how, to heighten the vague sentiments of which I have already spoken. While the objects around me—while the carvings of the ceilings, the sombre tapestries of the walls, the ebon blackness of the floors, and the phantasmagoric armorial trophies which rattled as I strode, were but matters to which, or to such as which, I had been accustomed from my infancy—while I hesitated not to acknowledge how familiar was all this—I still wondered to find how unfamiliar were the fancies which ordinary images were stirring up. On one of the staircases, I met the physician of the family. His countenance, I thought, wore a mingled expression of low cunning and perplexity. He accosted me with trepidation and passed on. The valet now threw open a door and ushered me into the presence of his master.

The room in which I found myself was very large and lofty. The windows were long, narrow, and pointed, and at so vast a distance from the black oaken floor as to be altogether inaccessible from within. Feeble gleams of encrimsoned light made their way through the trellissed panes, and served to render sufficiently distinct the more prominent objects around; the eye, however, struggled in vain to reach the remoter angles of the chamber, or the recesses of the vaulted and fretted ceiling. Dark draperies hung upon the walls. The general furniture was profuse, comfortless, antique, and tattered. Many books and musical instruments lay scattered about, but failed to give any vitality to the scene. I felt that I breathed an atmosphere of sorrow. An air of stern, deep, and irredeemable gloom hung over and pervaded all.

Upon my entrance, Usher arose from a sofa on which he had been lying at full length, and greeted me with a vivacious warmth which had much in it, I at first thought, of an over-done cordiality—of the constrained effort of the *ennuyé* man of the world. A glance, however, at his countenance convinced me of his perfect sincerity. We sat down; and for some moments, while he spoke not, I gazed upon him with a feeling half of pity, half of awe. Surely, man had never before so terribly altered, in so brief a period, as had Roderick Usher! It was with difficulty that I could bring myself to admit the identity of the wan being before me with the companion of my early boyhood. Yet the character of his face had been at all times remarkable. A cadaverousness of complexion; an eye large, liquid, and luminous beyond comparison; lips somewhat thin and very pallid, but of a surpassingly beautiful curve; a nose of a delicate Hebrew model, but with a breadth of nostril unusual in similar formations; a finely moulded chin, speaking, in its want of prominence, of a want of moral energy; hair of a more than web-like softness and tenuity;—these features, with an inordinate expansion above the regions of the temple, made up altogether a countenance not easily to be forgotten. And now in the mere exaggeration of the prevailing character of these features, and of the expression they were wont to convey, lay so much of change that I doubted to whom I spoke. The now ghastly pallor of the skin, and the now miraculous lustre of the eye, above all things startled and even awed me. The silken hair, too, had been suffered to grow all unheeded, and as, in its wild gossamer texture, it floated rather than fell about the face, I could not, even with effort, connect its Arabesque expression with any idea of simple humanity.

In the manner of my friend I was at once struck with an incoherence—an inconsistency; and I soon found this to arise from a series of feeble and futile struggles to overcome an habitual trepidancy—an excessive nervous agitation. For something of this nature I had indeed been prepared, no less by his letter, than by reminiscences of certain boyish traits, and by conclusions deduced from his peculiar physical confirmation and temperament. His action was alternately vivacious and sullen. His voice varied rapidly from a tremulous indecision (when the animal spirits seemed utterly in abeyance) to that species of energetic concision—that abrupt, weighty, unhurried, and hollow-sounding enunciation—that leaden, self-balanced, and perfectly modulated guttural utterance, which may be observed in the lost drunkard, or the irreclaimable eater of opium, during the periods of his most intense excitement.

It was thus that he spoke of the object of my visit, of his earnest desire to see me, and of the solace he expected me to afford him. He entered, at some length, into what he conceived to be the nature of his malady. It was, he said, a constitutional and a family evil, and one for which he despaired to find a remedy—a mere nervous affection, he immediately added, which would undoubtedly soon pass off. It displayed itself in a host of unnatural sensations. Some of these, as he detailed them, interested and bewildered me; although, perhaps, the terms and the general manner of their narration had their weight. He suffered much from a morbid acuteness of the senses; the most insipid food was alone endurable; he could wear only garments of certain texture; the odors of all flowers were oppressive; his eyes were tortured by even a faint light; and there were but peculiar sounds, and these from stringed instruments, which did not inspire him with horror.

To an anomalous species of terror I found him a bounden slave. "I shall perish," said he, "I *must* perish in this deplorable folly. Thus, thus, and not otherwise, shall I be lost. I dread the events of the future, not in themselves, but in their results. I shudder at the thought of any, even the most trivial, incident, which may operate upon this intolerable agitation of soul. I have, indeed, no abhorrence of danger, except in its absolute effect—in terror. In this unnerved, in this pitiable, condition I feel that the period will sooner or later arrive when I must abandon life and reason together, in some struggle with the grim phantasm, FEAR."

I learned, moreover, at intervals, and through broken and equivocal hints, another singular feature of his mental condition. He was enchained by certain superstitious impressions in regard to the dwelling which he tenanted, and whence, for many years, he had never ventured forth—in regard to an influence whose suppositious force was conveyed in terms too shadowy here to be re-stated—an influence which some peculiarities in the mere form and substance of his family mansion had, by dint of long sufferance, he said, obtained over his spirit—an effect which the *physique* of the gray walls and turrets, and of the dim tarn into which they all looked down, had, at length, brought about upon the *morale* of his existence.

He admitted, however, although with hesitation, that much of the peculiar gloom which thus afflicted him could be traced to a more natural and far more palpable origin—to the severe and long-continued illness—indeed to the evidently approaching dissolution—of a tenderly beloved sister, his sole companion for long years, his last and only relative on earth. "Her decease," he said, with a bitterness which I can never forget, "would leave him (him, the hopeless and the frail) the last of the ancient race of the Ushers." While he spoke, the lady Madeline (for so was she called) passed through a remote portion of the apartment, and, without having noticed my presence, disappeared. I regarded her with an utter astonishment not unmingled with dread; and yet I found it impossible to account for such feelings. A sensation of stupor oppressed me as my eyes followed her retreating steps. When a door, at length, closed upon her, my glance sought instinctively and eagerly the countenance of the brother; but he had buried his face in his hands, and I could only perceive that a far more than ordinary wanness had overspread the emaciated fingers through which trickled many passionate tears.

The disease of the lady Madeline had long baffled the skill of her physicians. A settled apathy, a gradual wasting away of the person, and frequent although transient affections of a partially cataleptical character were the unusual diagnosis. Hitherto she had steadily borne up against the pressure of her malady, and had not betaken herself finally to bed; but on the closing in of the evening of my arrival at the house, she succumbed (as her brother told me at night with inexpressible agitation) to the prostrating power of the destroyer; and I learned that the glimpse I had obtained of her person would thus probably be the last I should obtain—that the lady, at least while living, would be seen by me no more.

For several days ensuing, her name was unmentioned by either Usher or myself; and during this period I was busied in earnest endeavors to alleviate the melancholy of my friend. We painted and read together, or I listened, as if in a dream, to the wild improvisations of his speaking guitar. And thus, as a closer and still closer intimacy admitted me more unreservedly into the recesses of his spirit, the more bitterly did I perceive the futility of all attempts at cheering a mind from which darkness, as if an inherent positive quality, poured forth upon all objects of the moral and physical universe in one unceasing radiation of gloom.

I shall ever bear about me a memory of the many solemn hours I thus spent alone with the master of the House of Usher. Yet I should fail in any attempt to convey an idea of the exact character of the studies, or of the occupations, in which he involved me, or led me the way. An excited and highly distempered ideality threw a sulphureous lustre over all. His long improvised dirges will ring forever in my ears. Among other things, I hold painfully in mind a certain singular perversion and amplification of the wild air of the last waltz of Von Weber. From the paintings over which his elaborate fancy brooded, and which grew, touch by touch, into vaguenesses at which I shuddered the more thrillingly, because I shuddered knowing not why—from these paintings (vivid as their images now are before me) I would in vain endeavor to educe more than a small portion which should lie within the compass of merely written words. By the utter simplicity, by the nakedness of his designs, he arrested and overawed attention. If ever mortal painted an idea, that mortal was Roderick Usher. For me at least, in the circumstances then surrounding me, there arose out of the pure abstractions which the hypochondriac contrived to throw upon his canvas, an intensity of intolerable awe, no shadow of which felt I ever yet in the contemplation of the certainly glowing yet too concrete reveries of Fuseli.

One of the phantasmagoric conceptions of my friend, partaking not so rigidly of the spirit of abstraction, may be shadowed forth, although feebly, in words. A small picture presented the interior of an immensely long and rectangular vault or tunnel, with low walls, smooth, white, and without interruption or device. Certain accessory points of the design served well to convey the idea that this excavation lay at an exceeding depth below the surface of the earth. No outlet was observed in any portion of its vast extent, and no torch or other artificial source of light was discernible; yet a flood of intense rays rolled throughout, and bathed the whole in a ghastly and inappropriate splendor.

I have just spoken of that morbid condition of the auditory nerve which rendered all music intolerable to the sufferer, with the exception of certain effects of stringed instruments. It was, perhaps, the narrow limits to which he thus confined himself upon the guitar which gave birth, in great measure, to the fantastic character of his performances. But the fervid *facility* of his *impromptus* could not be so accounted for. They must have been, and were, in the notes, as well as in the words of his wild fantasies (for he not unfrequently accompanied himself with rhymed verbal improvisations), the result of that intense mental collectedness and concentration to which I have previously alluded as observable only in particular moments of the highest artificial excitement. The words of one of these rhapsodies I have easily remembered. I was, perhaps, the more forcibly impressed with it as he gave it, because, in the under or mystic current of its meaning, I fancied that I perceived, and for the first time, a full consciousness on the part of Usher of the tottering of his lofty reason upon her throne. The verses, which were entitled "The Haunted Palace," ran very nearly, if not accurately, thus:—

I

In the greenest of our valleys,
   By good angels tenanted,
Once a fair and stately palace—
   Radiant palace—reared its head.
In the monarch Thought's dominion—
   It stood there!
Never seraph spread a pinion
   Over fabric half so fair.

II

Banners yellow, glorious, golden,
   On its roof did float and flow

(This—all this—was in the olden
    Time long ago);
And every gentle air that dallied,
    In that sweet day,
Along the ramparts plumed and pallid,
    A winged odor went away.

III

Wanderers in that happy valley
    Through two luminous windows saw
Spirits moving musically
    To a lute's well-tuned law;
Round about a throne, where sitting
    (Porphyrogene!)
In state his glory well befitting,
    The ruler of the realm was seen.

IV

And all with pearl and ruby glowing
    Was the fair palace door,
Through which came flowing, flowing, flowing
    And sparkling evermore,
A troop of Echoes whose sweet duty
    Was but to sing,
In voices of surpassing beauty,
    The wit and wisdom of their king.

V

But evil things, in robes of sorrow,
    Assailed the monarch's high estate;
(Ah, let us mourn, for never morrow
    Shall dawn upon him, desolate!)
And, round about his home, the glory
    That blushed and bloomed
Is but a dim-remembered story
    Of the old time entombed.

VI

And travellers now within that valley,
   Through the red-litten windows see
Vast forms that move fantastically
   To a discordant melody;
While, like a rapid ghastly river,
   Through the pale door;
A hideous throng rush out forever,
   And laugh—but smile no more.

I well remember that suggestions arising from this ballad
led us into a train of thought wherein there became manifest
an opinion of Usher's which I mention not so much on account of its novelty (for other men[1] have thought thus), as on
account of the pertinacity with which he maintained it. This
opinion, in its general form, was that of the sentience of all
vegetable things. But, in his disordered fancy, the idea had assumed a more daring character, and trespassed, under certain
conditions, upon the kingdom of inorganization. I lack words
to express the full extent, or the earnest *abandon* of his per-
suasion. The belief, however, was connected (as I have previously hinted) with the gray stones of the home of his
forefathers. The conditions of the sentence had been here, he
imagined, fulfilled in the method of collocation of these
stones—in the order of their arrangement, as well as in that
of the many *fungi* which overspread them, and of the decayed
trees which stood around—above all, in the long undisturbed
endurance of this arrangement, and in its reduplication in the
still waters of the tarn. Its evidence—the evidence of the sentience—was to be seen, he said (and I here started as he
spoke), in the gradual yet certain condensation of an atmosphere of their own about the waters and the walls. The result
was discoverable, he added, in that silent yet importunate and
terrible influence which for centuries had moulded the des-
tinies of his family, and which made *him* what I now saw

[1] Watson, Dr. Percival, Spallanzani, and especially the Bishop of Lan-
daff.—See "Chemical Essays," vol. v.

him—what he was. Such opinions need no comment, and I
will make none.

Our books—the books which, for years, had formed no
small portion of the mental existence of the invalid—were,
as might be supposed, in strict keeping with this character of
phantasm. We pored together over such works as the "Ver-
vert et Chartreuse" of Gresset; the "Belphegor" of Machi-
avelli; the "Heaven and Hell" of Swedenborg; the
"Subterranean Voyage of Nicholas Klimm" of Holberg; the
"Chiromancy" of Robert Flud, of Jean D'Indaginé, and of
Dela Chambre; the "Journey into the Blue Distance" of
Tieck; and the "City of the Sun" of Campanella. One favorite volume was a small octavo edition of the "Directorium
Inquisitorium," by the Dominican Eymeric de Gironne; and
there were passages in Pomponius Mela, about the old Af-
rican Satyrs and Œgipans, over which Usher would sit
dreaming for hours. His chief delight, however, was found
in the perusal of an exceedingly rare and curious book in
quarto Gothic—the manual of a forgotten church—the
Vigiliœ Mortuorum Secundum Chorum Ecclesiœ Maguntinœ.

I could not help thinking of the wild ritual of this work,
and of its probable influence upon the hypochondriac, when,
one evening, having informed me abruptly that the lady Madeline was no more, he stated his intention of preserving her
corpse for a fortnight (previously to its final interment), in
one of the numerous vaults within the main walls of the
building. The worldly reason, however, assigned for this singular proceeding, was one which I did not feel at liberty to
dispute. The brother had been led to his resolution (so he
told me) by consideration of the unusual character of the malady of the deceased, of certain obtrusive and eager inquiries
on the part of her medical men, and of the remote and exposed situation of the burial-ground of the family. I will not
deny that when I called to mind the sinister countenance of
the person whom I met upon the staircase, on the day of my
arrival at the house, I had no desire to oppose what I regarded
as at best but a harmless, and by no means an unnatural,
precaution.

At the request of Usher, I personally aided him in the arrangements for the temporary entombment. The body having

been encoffined, we two alone bore it to its rest. The vault in which we placed it (and which had been so long unopened that our torches, half smothered in its oppressive atmosphere, gave us little opportunity for investigation) was small, damp, and entirely without means of admission for light; lying, at great depth, immediately beneath that portion of the building in which was my own sleeping apartment. It had been used, apparently, in remote feudal times, for the worst purposes of a donjon-keep, and, in later days, as a place of deposit for powder, or some other highly combustible substance, as a portion of its floor, and the whole interior of a long archway through which we reached it, were carefully sheathed with copper. The door, of massive iron, had been, also, similarly protected. Its immense weight caused an unusually sharp, grating sound, as it moved upon its hinges.

Having deposited our mournful burden upon tressels within this region of horror, we partially turned aside the yet unscrewed lid of the coffin, and looked upon the face of the tenant. A striking similitude between the brother and sister now first arrested my attention; and Usher, divining, perhaps, my thoughts, murmured out some few words from which I learned that the deceased and himself had been twins, and that sympathies of a scarcely intelligible nature had always existed between them. Our glances, however, rested not long upon the dead—for we could not regard her unawed. The disease which had thus entombed the lady in the maturity of youth, had left, as usual in all maladies of a strictly cataleptical character, the mockery of a faint blush upon the bosom and the face, and that suspiciously lingering smile upon the lip which is so terrible in death. We replaced and screwed down the lid, and, having secured the door of iron, made our way, with toil, into the scarcely less gloomy apartments of the upper portion of the house.

And now, some days of bitter grief having elapsed, an observable change came over the features of the mental disorder of my friend. His ordinary manner had vanished. His ordinary occupations were neglected or forgotten. He roamed from chamber to chamber with hurried, unequal, and objectless step. The pallor of his countenance had assumed, if possible, a more ghastly hue—but the luminousness of his eye had utterly gone out. The once occasional huskiness of his tone was heard no more; and a tremendous quaver, as if of extreme terror, habitually characterized his utterance. There were times, indeed, when I thought his unceasingly agitated mind was laboring with some oppressive secret, to divulge which he struggled for the necessary courage. At times, again, I was obliged to resolve all into the mere inexplicable vagaries of madness, for I beheld him gazing upon vacancy for long hours, in an attitude of the profoundest attention, as if listening to some imaginary sound. It was no wonder that his condition terrified—that it infected me. I felt creeping upon me, by slow yet certain degrees, the wild influences of his own fantastic yet impressive superstitions.

It was, especially, upon retiring to bed late in the night of the seventh or eighth day after the placing of the lady Madeline within the donjon, that I experienced the full power of such feelings. Sleep came not near my couch—while the hours waned and waned away. I struggled to reason off the nervousness which had dominion over me. I endeavored to believe that much, if not all of what I felt, was due to the bewildering influence of the gloomy furniture of the room—of the dark and tattered draperies, which, tortured into motion by the breath of a rising tempest, swayed fitfully to and fro upon the walls, and rustled uneasily about the decorations of the bed. But my efforts were fruitless. An irrepressible tremor gradually pervaded my frame; and, at length, there sat upon my very heart an incubus of utterly causeless alarm. Shaking this off with a gasp and a struggle, I uplifted myself upon the pillows, and, peering earnestly within the intense darkness of the chamber, hearkened—I know not why, except that an instinctive spirit prompted me—to certain low and indefinite sounds which came, through the pauses of the storm, at long intervals, I knew not whence. Overpowered by an intense sentiment of horror, unaccountable yet unendurable, I threw on my clothes with haste (for I felt that I should sleep no more during the night), and endeavored to arouse myself from the pitiable condition into which I had fallen, by pacing rapidly to and fro through the apartment.

I had taken but few turns in this manner, when a light step on an adjoining staircase arrested my attention. I presently recognized it as that of Usher. In an instant afterward he rapped, with a gentle touch, at my door, and entered, bearing a lamp. His countenance was, as usual, cadaverously wan— but, moreover, there was a species of mad hilarity in his eyes—an evidently restrained *hysteria* in his whole demeanor. His air appalled me—but anything was preferable to the solitude which I had so long endured, and I even welcomed his presence as a relief.

"And you have not seen it?" he said abruptly, after having stared about him for some moments in silence—"you have not then seen it?—but, stay! you shall." Thus speaking, and having carefully shaded his lamp, he hurried to one of the casements, and threw it freely open to the storm.

The impetuous fury of the entering gust nearly lifted us from our feet. It was, indeed, a tempestuous yet sternly beautiful night, and one wildly singular in its terror and its beauty. A whirlwind had apparently collected its force in our vicinity; for there were frequent and violent alterations in the direction of the wind; and the exceeding density of the clouds (which hung so low as to press upon the turrets of the house) did not prevent our perceiving the life-like velocity with which they flew careering from all points against each other, without passing away into the distance. I say that even their exceeding density did not prevent our perceiving this—yet we had no glimpse of the moon or stars, nor was there any flashing forth of the lightning. But the under surfaces of the huge masses of agitated vapor, as well as all terrestrial objects immediately around us, were glowing in the unnatural light of a faintly luminous and distinctly visible gaseous exhalation which hung about and enshrouded the mansion.

"You must not—you shall not behold this!" said I, shuddering, to Usher, as I led him, with a gentle violence, from the window to a seat. "These appearances, which bewilder you, are merely electrical phenomena not uncommon—or it may be that they have their ghastly origin in the rank miasma of the tarn. Let us close this casement;—the air is chilling and dangerous to your frame. Here is one of your favorite romances. I will read, and you shall listen:—and so we will pass away this terrible night together."

The antique volume which I had taken up was the "Mad

Trist'' of Sir Launcelot Canning; but I had called it a favorite of Usher's more in sad jest than in earnest; for, in truth, there is little in its uncouth and unimaginative prolixity which could have had interest for the lofty and spiritual ideality of my friend. It was, however, the only book immediately at hand; and I indulged a vague hope that the excitement which now agitated the hypochondriac, might find relief (for the history of mental disorder is full of similar anomalies) even in the extremeness of the folly which I should read. Could I have judged, indeed, by the wildly overstrained air of vivacity with which he hearkened, or apparently hearkened, to the words of the tale, I might well have congratulated myself upon the success of my design.

I had arrived at that well-known portion of the story where Ethelred, the hero of the Trist, having sought in vain for peaceable admission into the dwelling of the hermit, proceeds to make good an entrance by force. Here, it will be remembered, the words of the narrative run thus:

''And Ethelred, who was by nature of a doughty heart, and who was now mighty withal, on account of the powerfulness of the wine which he had drunken, waited no longer to hold parley with the hermit, who, in sooth, was of an obstinate and maliceful turn, but, feeling the rain upon his shoulders, and fearing the rising of the tempest, uplifted his mace outright, and, with blows, made quickly room in the plankings of the door for his gauntleted hand; and now pulling therewith sturdily, he so cracked, and ripped, and tore all asunder, that the noise of the dry and hollow-sounding wood alarumed and reverberated throughout the forest.''

At the termination of this sentence I started and, for a moment, paused; for it appeared to me (although I at once concluded that my excited fancy had deceived me)—it appeared to me that, from some very remote portion of the mansion, there came, indistinctly to my ears, what might have been, in its exact similarity of character, the echo (but a stifled and dull one certainly) of the very cracking and ripping sound which Sir Launcelot had so particularly described. It was, beyond doubt, the coincidence alone which had arrested my attention; for, amid the rattling of the sashes of the casements, and the ordinary commingled noises of the still increasing storm, the sound, in itself, had nothing, surely, which should have interested or disturbed me. I continued the story:

"But the good champion Ethelred, now entering within the door, was sore enraged and amazed to perceive no signal of the maliceful hermit; but, in the stead thereof, a dragon of a scaly and prodigious demeanor, and of a fiery tongue, which sate in guard before a palace of gold, with a floor of silver; and upon the wall there hung a shield of shining brass with this legend enwritten—

Who entereth herein, a conqueror hath bin;
Who slayeth the dragon, the shield he shall win.

And Ethelred uplifted his mace, and struck upon the head of the dragon, which fell before him, and gave up his pesty breath, with a shriek so horrid and harsh, and withal so piercing, that Ethelred had fain to close his ears with his hands against the dreadful noise of it, the like whereof was never before heard."

Here again I paused abruptly, and now with a feeling of wild amazement—for there could be no doubt whatever that, in this instance, I did actually hear (although from what direction it proceeded I found it impossible to say) a low and apparently distant, but harsh, protracted, and most unusual screaming or grating sound—the exact counterpart of what my fancy had already conjured up for the dragon's unnatural shriek as described by the romancer.

Oppressed, as I certainly was, upon the occurrence of this second and most extraordinary coincidence, by a thousand conflicting sensations, in which wonder and extreme terror were predominant, I still retained sufficient presence of mind to avoid exciting, by any observation, the sensitive nervousness of my companion. I was by no means certain that he had noticed the sounds in question; although, assuredly, a strange alteration had, during the last few minutes, taken place in his demeanor. From a position fronting my own, he had gradually brought round his chair, so as to sit with his face to the door of the chamber; and thus I could but partially perceive his features, although I saw that his lips trembled as if he were murmuring inaudibly. His head had dropped upon his breast—yet I knew that he was not asleep, from the wide and rigid opening of the eye as I caught a glimpse of it in profile. The motion of his body, too, was at variance with this idea—for he rocked from side to side with a gentle yet constant and uniform sway. Having rapidly taken notice of all this, I resumed the narrative of Sir Launcelot, which thus proceeded:

"And now, the champion, having escaped from the terrible fury of the dragon, bethinking himself of the brazen shield, and of the breaking up of the enchantment which was upon it, removed the carcass from out of the way before him, and approached valorously over the silver pavement of the castle to where the shield was upon the wall; which in sooth tarried not for his full coming, but fell down at his feet upon the silver floor, with a mighty great and terrible ringing sound."

No sooner had these syllables passed my lips, than—as if a shield of brass had indeed, at the moment, fallen heavily upon a floor of silver—I became aware of a distinct, hollow, metallic, and clangorous, yet apparently muffled, reverberation. Completely unnerved, I leaped to my feet; but the measured rocking movement of Usher was undisturbed. I rushed to the chair in which he sat. His eyes were bent fixedly before him, and throughout his whole countenance there reigned a stony rigidity. But, as I placed my hand upon his shoulder, there came a strong shudder over his whole person; a sickly smile quivered about his lips; and I saw that he spoke in a low, hurried, and gibbering murmur, as if unconscious of my presence. Bending closely over him, I at length drank in the hideous import of his words.

"Now hear it?—yes, I hear it, and *have* heard it. Long—long—long—many minutes, many hours, many days, have I heard it—yet I dared not—oh, pity me, miserable wretch that I am!—I dared not—I *dared* not speak! *We have put her living in the tomb!* Said I not that my senses were acute? I *now* tell you that I heard her first feeble movements in the hollow coffin. I heard them—many, many days ago—yet I dared not—I *dared not speak*! And now—to-night—Ethelred—ha! ha!—the breaking of the hermit's door, and the death-cry of the dragon, and the clangor of the shield—say, rather, the rending of her coffin, and the grating of the iron hinges of her prison, and her struggles within the coppered archway of the vault! Oh! whither shall I fly? Will she not be here anon? Is she not hurrying to upbraid me for my haste? Have I not heard her footstep on the stair? Do I not distinguish that heavy and horrible beating of her heart? Madman!''—here he sprang furiously to his feet, and shrieked out his syllables, as if in the effort he were giving up his soul—*"Madman! I tell you that she now stands without the door!"*

As if in the superhuman energy of his utterance there had been found the potency of a spell, the huge antique panels to which the speaker pointed threw slowly back, upon the instant, their ponderous and ebony jaws. It was the work of the rushing gust—but then without those doors there *did* stand the lofty and enshrouded figure of the lady Madeline of Usher. There was blood upon her white robes, and the evidence of some bitter struggle upon every portion of her emaciated frame. For a moment she remained trembling and reeling to and fro upon the threshold—then, with a low moaning cry, fell heavily inward upon the person of her brother, and in her violent and now final death-agonies, bore him to the floor a corpse, and a victim to the terrors he had anticipated.

From that chamber, and from that mansion, I fled aghast. The storm was still abroad in all its wrath as I found myself crossing the old causeway. Suddenly there shot along the path a wild light, and I turned to see whence a gleam so unusual could have issued; for the vast house and its shadows were alone behind me. The radiance was that of the full, setting, and blood-red moon, which now shone vividly through that once barely discernible fissure, of which I have before spoken as extending from the roof of the building, in a zigzag direction, to the base. While I gazed, this fissure rapidly widened—there came a fierce breath of the whirlwind—the entire orb of the satellite burst at once upon my sight—my brain reeled as I saw the mighty walls rushing asunder—there was a long tumultuous shouting sound like the voice of a thousand waters—and the deep and dank tarn at my feet closed sullenly and silently over the fragments of the *"House of Usher."*

Stephen King

THE MONKEY

Stephen King often writes in the mode of psychological horror, most often in the monster story. "The
Raft" and "The Crate" come to mind, but particularly
"The Monkey." Using the forms of the story of gen-
erational haunting, King draws on the Ray Bradbury-
esque device of the evil toy, a moral symbol of some
complexity. Shadows of the dark ironies of Robert
Bloch and Richard Matheson, and the graphic depic-
tions of E. C. comics, make this one of King's most
successful stories at integrating and interweaving the
strands of contemporary horror. Yet in spite of its
central concern with psychological horror, the story
retains the characteristic moral concerns that elevate
King's major work. One of King's most salient influences on the horror story is the extent to which he is
synthesizing and mutating, from his voluminous reading in horror, the entire historical development of the
field. As Dickens regenerated the Christmas ghost
story, so King has accomplished a wholesale regen-
eration of horror traditions in the contemporary field.

When Hal Shelburn saw it, when his son Dennis pulled
it out of a mouldering Ralston-Purina carton that had
been pushed far back under one attic eave, such a feeling of
horror and dismay rose in him that for one moment he thought
he surely must scream. He put one fist to his mouth, as if to
cram it back . . . and then merely coughed into his fist. Neither Terry nor Dennis noticed, but Petey looked around, momentarily curious.

"Hey, neat," Dennis said respectfully. It was a tone Hal rarely got from the boy anymore himself. Dennis was twelve.

"What is it?" Petey asked. He glanced at his father again before his eyes were dragged back to the thing his big brother had found. "What is it, Daddy?"

"It's a monkey, fartbrains," Dennis said. "Haven't you ever seen a monkey before?"

"Don't call your brother fartbrains," Terry said automatically, and began to examine a box of curtains. The curtains were slimy with mildew and she dropped them quickly. "Uck."

"Can I have it, Daddy?" Petey asked. He was nine.

"What do you mean?" Dennis cried. "*I* found it!"

"Boys, please," Terry said. "I'm getting a headache."

Hal barely heard them—any of them. The monkey glimmered up at him from his older son's hands, grinning its old familiar grin. The same grin that had haunted his nightmares as a child, haunted them until he had——

Outside a cold gust of wind rose, and for a moment lips with no flesh blew a long note through the old, rusty gutter outside. Petey stepped closer to his father, eyes moving uneasily to the rough attic roof through which nailheads poked.

"What was that, Daddy?" he asked as the whistle died to a guttural buzz.

"Just the wind," Hal said, still looking at the monkey. Its cymbals, crescents of brass rather than full circles in the weak light of the one naked bulb, were moveless, perhaps a foot apart, and he added automatically, "Wind can whistle, but it can't carry a tune." Then he realized that was a saying of his Uncle Will's, and a goose ran over his grave.

The long note came again, the wind coming off Crystal Lake in a long, droning swoop and then wavering in the gutter. Half a dozen small drafts puffed cold October air into Hal's face—God, this place was so much like the back closet of the house in Hartford that they might all have been transported thirty years back in time.

I won't think about that.

But the thought wouldn't be denied.

In the back closet where I found that goddammed monkey in that same box.

Terry had moved away to examine a wooden crate filled with knick-knacks, duck-walking because of the pitch of the eaves was so sharp.

"I don't like it," Petey said, and felt for Hal's hand. "Dennis c'n have it if he wants. Can we go, Daddy?"

"Worried about ghosts, chickenguts?" Dennis inquired.

"Dennis, you stop it," Terry said absently. She picked up a wafer-thin cup with a Chinese pattern. "This is nice. This———"

Hal saw that Dennis had found the wind-up key in the monkey's back. Terror flew through him on dark wings.

"Don't do that!"

It came out more sharply than he had intended, and he had snatched the monkey out of Dennis's hands before he was really aware he had done it. Dennis looked around at him, startled. Terry had also glanced back over her shoulder, and Petey looked up. For a moment they were all silent, and the wind whistled again, very low this time, like an unpleasant invitation.

"I mean, it's probably broken," Hal said.

It used to be broken . . . except when it wanted to be fixed.

"Well you didn't have to *grab*," Dennis said.

"Dennis, shut up."

Dennis blinked at him and for a moment looked almost uneasy. Hal hadn't spoken to him so sharply in a long time. Not since he had lost his job with National Aerodyne in California two years before and they had moved to Texas. Dennis decided not to push it . . . for now. He turned back to the Ralston-Purina carton and began to root through it again, but the other stuff was nothing but shit. Broken toys bleeding springs and stuffings.

The wind was louder now, hooting instead of whistling. The attic began to creak softly, making a noise like footsteps.

"Please, Daddy?" Petey asked, only loud enough for his father to hear.

"Yeah," he said. "Terry, let's go."

"I'm not through with this———"

"I said let's *go*."

It was her turn to look startled.

* * *

They had taken two adjoining rooms in a motel. By ten that night the boys were asleep in their room and Terry was asleep in the adults' room. She had taken two Valium on the ride back from the home place in Casco. To keep her nerves from giving her a migraine. Just lately she took a lot of Valium. It had started around the time National Aerodyne had laid Hal off. For the last two years he had been working for Texas Instruments—it was $4,000 less a year, but it was work. He told Terry they were lucky. She agreed. There were plenty of software architects drawing unemployment, he said. She agreed. The company housing in Arnette was every bit as good as the place in Fresno, he said. She agreed, but he thought her agreement was a lie.

And he had been losing Dennis. He could feel the kid going, achieving a premature escape velocity, so long, Dennis, bye-bye stranger, it was nice sharing this train with you. Terry said she thought the boy was smoking reefer. She smelled it sometimes. You have to talk to him, Hal. And *he* agreed, but so far he had not.

The boys were asleep. Terry was asleep. Hal went into the bathroom and locked the door and sat down on the closed lid of the john and looked at the monkey.

He hated the way it felt, that soft brown nappy fur, worn bald in spots. He hated its grin—*that monkey grins just like a nigger,* Uncle Will had said once, but it didn't grin like a nigger, or like anything human. Its grin was all teeth, and if you wound up the key, the lips would move, the teeth would seem to get bigger, to become vampire teeth, the lips would writhe and the cymbals would bang, stupid monkey, stupid clockwork monkey, stupid, stupid——

He dropped it. His hands were shaking and he dropped it.

The key clicked on the bathroom tile as it struck the floor. The sound seemed very loud in the stillness. It grinned at him with its murky amber eyes, doll's eyes, filled with idiot glee, its brass cymbals poised as if to strike up a march for some black band from hell, and on the bottom the words MADE IN HONG KONG were stamped.

"You can't be here," he whispered. "I threw you down the well when I was nine."

The monkey grinned up at him.

Hal Shelburn shuddered.

Outside in the night, a black capful of wind shook the motel.

Hal's brother Bill and Bill's wife Collette met them at Uncle Will's and Aunt Ida's the next day. "Did it ever cross your mind that a death in the family is a really lousy way to renew the family connection?" Bill asked him with a bit of a grin. He had been named for Uncle Will. Will and Bill, champions of the rodayo, Uncle Will used to say, and ruffle Bill's hair. It was one of his sayings . . . like the wind can whistle but it can't carry a tune. Uncle Will had died six years before, and Aunt Ida had lived on here alone, until a stroke had taken her just the previous week. Very sudden, Bill had said when he called long distance to give Hal the news. As if he could know; as if anyone could know. She had died alone.

"Yeah," Hal said. "The thought crossed my mind."

They looked at the place together, the home place where they had finished growing up. Their father, a merchant mariner, had simply disappeared as if from the very face of the earth when they were young; Bill claimed to remember him vaguely, but Hal had no memories of him at all. Their mother had died when Bill was ten and Hal eight. They had come to Uncle Will's and Aunt Ida's from Hartford, and they had been raised here, and gone to college here. Bill had stayed and now had a healthy law practice in Portland.

Hal saw that Petey had wandered off toward the blackberry tangles that lay on the eastern side of the house in a mad jumble. "Stay away from there, Petey," he called.

Petey looked back, questioning. Hal felt simple love for the boy rush him . . . and he suddenly thought of the monkey again.

"Why, Dad?"

"The old well's in there someplace," Bill said. "But I'll be damned if I remember just where. Your dad's right, Petey—those blackberry tangles are a good place to stay away from. Thorns'll do a job on you. Right, Hal?"

"Right," Hal said automatically. Pete moved away, not looking back, and then started down the embankment toward the small shingle of beach where Dennis was skipping stones over the water. Hal felt something in his chest loosen a little.

* * *

Bill might have forgotten where the old well had been, but late that afternoon Hal went to it unerringly, shouldering his way through the brambles that tore at his old flannel jacket and hunted for his eyes. He reached it and stood there, breathing hard, looking at the rotted, warped boards that covered it. After a moment's debate, he knelt (his knees fired twin pistol shots) and moved two of the boards aside.

From the bottom of that wet, rock-lined throat a face stared up at him, wide eyes, grimacing mouth, and a moan escaped him. It was not loud, except in his heart. There it had been very loud.

It was his own face, reflected up from dark water.

Not the monkey's. For a moment he had thought it was the monkey's.

He was shaking. Shaking all over.

I threw it down the well. I threw it down the well, please God don't let me be crazy. I threw it down the well.

The well had gone dry the summer Johnny McCabe died, the year after Bill and Hal came to stay at the home place with Uncle Will and Aunt Ida. Uncle Will had borrowed money from the bank to have an artesian well sunk, and the blackberry tangles had grown up around the old dug well. The dry well.

Except the water had come back. Like the monkey.

This time the memory would not be denied. Hal sat there helplessly, letting it come, trying to do with it, to ride it like a surfer riding a monster wave that will crush him if he falls off his board, just trying to get through it so it would be gone again.

He had crept out here with the monkey late that summer, and the blackberries had been out, the smell of them thick and cloying. No one came in here to pick, although Aunt Ida would sometimes stand at the edge of the tangles and pick a cupful of berries into her apron. In here the blackberries had gone past ripe to overripe, some of them were rotting, sweating a thick white fluid like pus, and the crickets sang maddeningly in the high grass underfoot, their endless cry: *Reeeeeeee—*

The thorns tore at him, brought dots of blood onto his bare arms. He made no effort to avoid their sting. He had been blind with terror—so blind that he had come within inches of stumbling onto the boards that covered the well, perhaps within inches of crashing thirty feet to the well's muddy bottom. He had pinwheeled his arms for balance, and more thorns had branded his forearms. It was that memory that had caused him to call Petey back sharply.

That was the day Johnny McCabe had died—his best friend. Johnny had been climbing the rungs up to his treehouse in his back yard. The two of them had spent many hours up there that summer, playing pirate, seeing make-believe galleons out on the lake, unlimbering the cannons, preparing to board. Johnny had been climbing up to the treehouse as he had done a thousand times before, and the rung just below the trap door in the bottom of the treehouse had snapped off in his hands and Johnny had fallen thirty feet to the ground and had broken his neck and it was the monkey's fault, the monkey, the goddam hateful monkey. When the phone rang, when Aunt Ida's mouth dropped open and then formed an O of horror as her friend Milly from down the road told her the news, when Aunt Ida said, "Come out on the porch, Hal, I have to tell you some bad news—," he had thought with sick horror, *The monkey! What's the monkey done now?*

There had been no reflection of his face trapped at the bottom of the well that day, only the stone cobbles going down into the darkness and the smell of wet mud. He had looked at the monkey lying there on the wiry grass that grew between the blackberry tangles, its cymbals poised, its grinning teeth huge between its splayed lips, its fur, rubbed away in balding, mangy patches here and there, its glazed eyes.

"I hate you," he had hissed at it. He wrapped his hand around its loathsome body, feeling the nappy fur crinkle. It grinned at him as he held it up in front of his face. "Go on!" he dared it, beginning to cry for the first time that day. He shook it. The poised cymbals trembled minutely. It spoiled everything good. Everything. "Go on, clap them! Clap them!"

The monkey only grinned.

"Go on and clap them!" His voice rose hysterically.
"Fraidy-cat, fraidy-cat, go on and clap them! I dare you!"

Its brownish-yellow eyes. Its huge and gleeful teeth.

He threw it down the well then, mad with grief and terror.
He saw it turn over once on its way down, a simian acrobat
doing a trick, and the sun glinted one last time on those
cymbals. It struck the bottom with a thud, and that must have
jogged its clockwork, for suddenly the cymbals *did* begin to
beat. Their steady, deliberate, and tinny banging rose to his
ears, echoing and fey in the stone throat of the dead well:
jang-jang-jang-jang—

Hal clapped his hands over his mouth, and for a moment
he could see it down there, perhaps only in the eye of imagination . . . lying there in the mud, eyes glaring up at the
small circle of his boy's face peering over the lip of the well
(as if marking its shape forever), lips expanding and contracting around those grinning teeth, cymbals clapping, funny
wind-up monkey.

Jang-jang-jang-jang, who's dead? *Jang-jang-jang-jang*, is
it Johnny McCabe, falling with his eyes wide, doing his own
acrobatic somersault as he falls through the bright summer
vacation air with the splintered rung still held in his hands to
strike the ground with a single bitter snapping sound? Is it
Johnny, Hal? Or is it you?

Moaning, Hal had shoved the boards across the hole, getting splinters in his hands, not caring, not even aware of them
until later. And still he could hear it, even through the boards,
muffled now and somehow all the worse for that: it was down
there in stone-faced dark, clapping its cymbals and jerking
its repulsive body, the sounding coming up like the sound of
a prematurely buried man scrabbling for a way out.

Jang-jang-jang-jang, who's dead this time?

He fought and battered his way back through the blackberry creepers. Thorns stitched fresh lines of welling blood
briskly across his face and burdocks caught in the cuffs of
his jeans, and he fell full-length once, his ears still jangling,
as if it had followed him. Uncle Will found him later, sitting
on an old tire in the garage and sobbing, and he had thought
Hal was crying for his dead friend. So he had been; but he
had also cried in the aftermath of terror.

He had thrown the monkey down the well in the afternoon. That evening, as twilight crept in through a shimmering mantle of ground-fog, a car moving too fast for the reduced visibility had run down Aunt Ida's manx cat in the road and gone right on. There had been guts everywhere, Bill had thrown up, but Hal had only turned his face away, his pale, still face, hearing Aunt Ida's sobbing (this on top of the news about the McCabe boy had caused a fit of weeping that was almost hysterics, and it was almost two hours before Uncle Will could calm her completely) as if from miles away. In his heart there was a cold and exultant joy. It hadn't been his turn. It had been Aunt Ida's manx, not him, not his brother Bill or his Uncle Will (just two champions of the rodayo). And now the monkey was gone, it was down the well, and one scruffy manx cat with ear mites was not too great a price to pay. If the monkey wanted to clap its hellish cymbals now, let it. It could clap and clash them for the crawling bugs and beetles, the dark things that made their home in the well's stone gullet. It would rot down there in the darkness and its loathsome cogs and wheels and springs would rust in darkness. It would die down there. In the mud and the darkness. Spiders would spin it a shroud.

But . . . it had come back.

Slowly, Hal covered the well again, as he had on that day, and in his ears he heard the phantom echo of the monkey's cymbals: *Jang-jang-jang-jang, who's dead, Hal? Is it Terry? Dennis? Is it Petey, Hal? He's your favorite, isn't he? Is it him? Jang-jang-jang—*

"Put that *down*!"

Petey flinched and dropped the monkey, and for one nightmare moment Hal thought that would do it, that the jolt would jog its machinery and the cymbals would begin to beat and clash.

"Daddy, you scared me."

"I'm sorry. I just . . . I don't want you to play with that."

The others had gone to see a movie, and he had thought he would beat them back to the motel. But he had stayed at the home place longer than he would have guessed; the old, hateful memories seemed to move in their own eternal time zone.

Terry was sitting near Dennis, watching "The Beverly Hillbillies." She watched the old, grainy print with a steady, bemused concentration that spoke of a recent Valium pop. Dennis was reading a rock magazine with the group Styx on the cover. Petey had been sitting cross-legged on the carpet, goofing with the monkey.

"It doesn't work anyway," Petey said. *Which explains why Dennis let him have it,* Hal thought, and then felt ashamed and angry at himself. He seemed to have no control over the hostility he felt toward Dennis more and more often, but in the aftermath he felt demeaned and tacky . . . helpless.

"No," he said. "It's old. I'm going to throw it away. Give it to me."

He held out his hand and Petey, looking troubled, handed it over.

Dennis said to his mother, "Pop's turning into a friggin schizophrenic."

Hal was across the room even before he knew he was going, the monkey in one hand, grinning as if in approbation. He hauled Dennis out of his chair by the shirt. There was a purring sound as a seam came adrift somewhere. Dennis looked almost comically shocked. His copy of *Tiger Beat* fell to the floor.

"Hey!"

"You come with me," Hal said grimly, pulling his son toward the door to the connecting room.

"Hal!" Terry nearly screamed. Petey just goggled.

Hal pulled Dennis through. He slammed the door and then slammed Dennis against the door. Dennis was starting to look scared. "You're getting a mouth problem," Hal said.

"Let *go* of me! You tore my shirt, you——"

Hal slammed the boy against the door again. "Yes," he said. "A real mouth problem. Did you learn that in school? Or back in the smoking area?"

Dennis flushed, his face momentarily ugly with guilt. "I wouldn't be in that shitty school if you didn't get canned!" he burst out.

Hal slammed Dennis against the door again. "I didn't get

canned, I got laid off, you know it, and I don't need any of your shit about it. You have problems? Welcome to the world, Dennis. Just don't you lay off all your problems on me. You're eating. Your ass is covered. At eleven, I don't . . . need any . . . shit from you.'' He punctuated each phrase by pulling the boy forward until their noses were almost touching and then slamming him back into the door. It was not hard enough to hurt, but Dennis was scared—his father had not laid a hand on him since they moved to Texas—and now he began to cry with a young boy's loud, braying, healthy sobs.

''Go ahead, beat me up!'' he yelled at Hal, his face twisted and blotchy. ''Beat me up if you want, I know how much you fucking hate me!''

''I don't hate you. I love you a lot, Dennis. But I'm your dad and you're going to show me respect or I'm going to bust you for it.''

Dennis tried to pull away. Hal pulled the boy to him and hugged him. Dennis fought for a moment and then put his face against Hal's chest and wept as if exhausted. It was the sort of cry Hal hadn't heard from either of his children in years. He closed his eyes, realizing that he felt exhausted himself.

Terry began to hammer on the other side of the door. ''Stop it, Hal! Whatever you're doing to him, stop it!''

''I'm not killing him,'' Hal said. ''Go away, Terry.''

''Don't you———''

''It's all right, Mom,'' Dennis said, muffled against Hal's chest.

He could feel her perplexed silence for a moment, and then she went. Hal looked at his son again.

''I'm sorry I badmouthed you, Dad,'' Dennis said reluctantly.

''When we get home next week, I'm going to wait two or three days and then I'm going to go through all your drawers, Dennis. If there's something in them you don't want me to see, you better get rid of it.''

That flash of guilt again. Dennis lowered his eyes and wiped away snot with the back of his hand.

''Can I go now?'' He sounded sullen once more.

''Sure,'' Hal said, and let him go. *Got to take him camping in the spring, just the two of us. Do some fishing, like Uncle Will used to do with Bill and me. Got to get close to him. Got to try.*

He sat down on the bed in the empty room and looked at the monkey. *You'll never be close to him again, Hal,* its grin seemed to say. *Never again. Never again.*

Just looking at the monkey made him feel tired. He laid it aside and put a hand over his eyes.

That night Hal stood in the bathroom, brushing his teeth, and thought: *It was in the same box. How could it be in the same box?*

The toothbrush jabbed upward, hurting his gums. He winced.

He had been four, Bill six, the first time he saw the monkey. Their missing father had bought a house in Hartford, and it had been theirs, free and clear, before he died or disappeared or whatever it had been. Their mother worked as a secretary at Holmes Aircraft, the helicopter plant out in Westville, and a series of sitters came in to stay with the boys, except by then it was just Hal that the sitters had to mind through the day—Bill was in first grade, big school. None of the babysitters stayed for long. They got pregnant and married their boyfriends or got work at Holmes, or Mrs. Shelburn would discover they had been at the cooking sherry or her bottle of brandy which was kept in the sideboard for special occasions. Most of them were stupid girls who seemed only to want to eat or sleep. None of them wanted to read to Hal as his mother would do.

The sitter that long winter was a huge, sleek black girl named Beulah. She fawned over Hal when Hal's mother was around and sometimes pinched him when she wasn't. Still, Hal had some liking for Beulah, who once in awhile would read him a lurid tale from one of her confession or true-detective magazines ("Death Came for the Voluptuous Redhead," Beulah would intone ominously in the dozey daytime silence of the living room, and pop another Reese's Peanut Butter Cup into her mouth while Hal solemnly studied the grainy tabloid pictures and drank his milk from his Wish-Cup). And the liking made what happened worse.

He found the monkey on a cold, cloudy day in March. Sleet ticked sporadically off the windows, and Beulah was asleep on the couch, a copy of *My Story* tented open on her admirable bosom.

So Hal went into the back closet to look at his father's things.

The back closet was a storage space that ran the length of the second floor on the left side, extra space that had never been finished off. One got into the back closet by using a small door—a down-the-rabbit-hole sort of door—on Bill's side of the boy's bedroom. They both liked to go in there, even though it was chilly in winter and hot enough in summer to wring a bucketful of sweat out of your pores. Long and narrow and somehow snug, the back closet was full of fascinating junk. No matter how much stuff you looked at, you never seemed to be able to look at it all. He and Bill had spent whole Saturday afternoons up here, barely speaking to each other, taking things out of boxes, examining them, turning them over and over so their hands could absorb each unique reality, putting them back. Now Hal wondered if he and Bill hadn't been trying, as best they could, to somehow make contact with their vanished father.

He had been a merchant mariner with a navigator's certificate, and there were stacks of charts back there, some marked with neat circles (and the dimple of the compass' swing-point in the center of each). There were twenty volumes of something called *Barron's Guide to Navigation*. A set of cockeyed binoculars that made your eyes feel hot and funny if you looked through them too long. There were touristy things from a dozen ports of call—rubber hula-hula dolls, a black cardboard bowler with a torn band that said YOU PICK A GIRL AND I'LL PICCADILLY, a glass globe with a tiny Eiffel Tower inside—and there were also envelopes with foreign stamps tucked carefully away inside, and foreign coins; there were rock samples from the Hawaiian island of Maui, a glassy Black—heavy and somehow ominous, and funny records in foreign languages.

That day, with the sleet ticking hypnotically off the roof just above his head, Hal worked his way all the way down to the far end of the back closet, moved a box aside, and saw another box behind it—a Ralston-Purina box. Looking over the top was a pair of glassy hazel eyes. They gave him a start and he skittered back for a moment, heart thumping, as if he had discovered a deadly pygmy. Then he saw its silence, the glaze in those eyes, and realized it was some sort of toy. He moved forward again and lifted it carefully from the box.

It grinned its ageless, toothy grin in the yellow light, its cymbals held apart.

Delighted, Hal had turned it this way and that, feeling the crinkle of its nappy fur. Its funny grin pleased him. Yet hadn't there been something else? An almost instinctive feeling of disgust that had come and gone almost before he was aware of it? Perhaps it was so, but with an old, old memory like this one, you had to be careful not to believe too much. Old memories could lie. But . . . hadn't he seen that same expression on Petey's face, in the attic of the home place?

He had seen the key set into the small of its back, and turned it. It had turned far too easily; there were no winding-up clicks. Broken, then. Broken, but still neat.

He took it out to play with it.

"Whatchoo got, Hal?" Beulah asked, waking from her nap.

"Nothing," Hal said. "I found it."

He put it up on the shelf on his side of the bedroom. It stood atop his Lassie coloring books, grinning, staring into space, cymbals poised. It was broken, but it grinned nonetheless. That night Hal awakened from some uneasy dream, bladder full, and got up to use the bathroom in the hall. Bill was a breathing lump of covers across the room.

Hal came back, almost asleep again . . . and suddenly the monkey began to beat its cymbals together in the darkness.

Jang-jang-jang-jang—

He came fully awake, as if snapped in the face with a cold, wet towel. His heart gave a staggering leap of surprise, and a tiny, mouselike squeak escaped his throat. He stared at the monkey, eyes wide, lips trembling.

Jang-jang-jang-jang—

Its body rocked and humped on the shelf. Its lips spread and closed, spread and closed, hideously gleeful, revealing huge and carnivorous teeth.

"Stop," Hal whispered.

His brother turned over and uttered a loud, single snore. All else was silent . . . except for the monkey. The cymbals clapped and clashed, and surely it would wake his brother, his mother, the world. It would wake the dead.

Jang-jang-jang-jang—

Hal moved toward it, meaning to stop it somehow, perhaps put his hand between its cymbals until it ran down (*but it was broken, wasn't it?*), and then it stopped on its own. The cymbals came together one last time—*Jang!*—and then spread slowly apart to their original position. The brass glimmered in the shadows. The monkey's dirty yellowish teeth grinned their improbable grin.

The house was silent again. His mother turned over in her bed and echoed Bill's single snore. Hal got back into his bed and pulled the covers up, his heart still beating fast, and he thought: *I'll put it back in the closet again tomorrow. I don't want it.*

But the next morning he forgot all about putting the monkey back because his mother didn't go to work. Beulah was dead. Their mother wouldn't tell them exactly what happened. "It was an accident, just a terrible accident" was all she would say. But that afternoon Bill bought a newspaper on his way home from school and smuggled page four up to their room under his shirt (TWO KILLED IN APARTMENT SHOOT-OUT, the headline read) and read the article haltingly to Hal, following along with his finger, while their mother cooked supper in the kitchen. Beulah McCaffery, 19, and Sally Tremont, 20, had been shot by Miss McCaffery's boyfriend, Leonard White, 25, following an argument over who was to go out and pick up an order of Chinese food. Miss Tremont had expired at Hartford Receiving; Beulah McCaffery had been pronounced dead at the scene.

It was like Beulah just disappeared into one of her own detective magazines, Hal Shelburn thought, and felt a cold chill race up his spine and then circle his heart. And then he realized the shootings had occurred about the same time the monkey——

* * *

"Hal?" It was Terry's voice, sleepy. "Coming to bed?"

He spat toothpaste into the sink and rinsed his mouth. "Yes," he said.

He had put the monkey in his suitcase earlier, and locked it up. They were flying back to Texas in two or three days. But before they went, he would get rid of the damned thing for good.

Somehow.

"You were pretty rough on Dennis this afternoon," Terry said in the dark.

"Dennis has needed somebody to start being rough on him for quite a while now, I think. He's been drifting. I just don't want him to start falling."

"Psychologically, beating the boy isn't a very productive——"

"I didn't *beat* him, Terry—for Christ's sake!"

"——way to assert parental authority——"

"Oh, don't give me any of that encounter-group shit," Hal said angrily.

"I can see you don't want to discuss this." Her voice was cold.

"I told him to get the dope out of the house, too."

"You did?" Now she sounded apprehensive. "How did he take it? What did he say?"

"Come on, Terry! What *could* he say? 'You're fired'?"

"Hal, what's the *matter* with you? You're not like this—what's *wrong*?"

"Nothing," he said, thinking of the monkey locked away in his Samsonite. Would he hear it if it began to clap its cymbals? Yes, he surely would. Muffled, but audible. Clapping doom for someone, as it had for Beulah, Johnny McCabe, Uncle Will's dog Daisy. *Jang-jang-jang*, is it you, Hal? "I've just been under a strain."

"I *hope* that's all it is. Because I don't like you this way."

"No?" And the words escaped before he could stop them; he didn't even want to stop them. "So pop a few Valium and everything will look okay again, right?"

He heard her draw breath in and let it out shakily. She began to cry then. He could have comforted her (maybe), but there seemed to be no comfort in him. There was too much terror. It would be better when the monkey was gone again, gone for good. Please God, gone for good.

He lay wakeful until very late, until morning began to gray the air outside. But he thought he knew what to do.

Bill had found the monkey the second time.

That was about a year and a half after Beulah McCaffery had been pronounced dead at the scene. It was summer. Hal had just finished kindergarten.

He came in from playing with Stevie Arlingen and his mother called, "Wash you hands, Hal, you're filthy like a pig." She was on the porch, drinking an iced tea and reading a book. It was her vacation; she had two weeks.

Hal gave his hands a token pass under cold water and printed dirt on the hand-towel. "Where's Bill?"

"Upstairs. You tell him to clean his side of the room. It's a mess."

Hal, who enjoyed being the messenger of unpleasant news in such matters, rushed up. Bill was sitting on the floor. The small down-the-rabbit-hole door leading to the back closet was ajar. He had the monkey in his hands.

"That don't work," Hal said immediately. "It's busted."

He was apprehensive, although he barely remembered coming back from the bathroom that night, and the monkey suddenly beginning to clap its cymbals. A week or so after that, he had had a bad dream about the monkey and Beulah—he couldn't remember exactly what—and had awakened screaming, thinking for a moment that the soft weight on his chest was the monkey, that he would open his eyes and see it grinning down at him. But of course the soft weight had only been his pillow, clutched with panicky tightness. His mother came in to soothe him with a drink of water and two chalky-orange baby aspirins, those Valium for childhood's troubled times. She thought it was the fact of Beulah's death that had caused the nightmare. So it was, but not in the way she thought.

He barely remembered any of this now, but the monkey still scared him, particularly its cymbals. And its teeth.

"I know that," Bill said and tossed the monkey aside. "It's stupid." It landed on Bill's bed, staring up at the ceiling, cymbals poised. Hal did not like to see it there. "You want to go down to Teddy's and get Popsicles?"

"I spent my allowance already," Hal said. "Besides, Mom says you got to clean up your side of the room."

"I can do that later," Bill said. "And I'll loan you a nickel, if you want." Bill was not above giving Hal an Indian rope burn sometimes, and would occasionally trip him up or punch him for no particular reason, but mostly he was okay.

"Sure," Hal said gratefully. "I'll just put that busted monkey back in the closet first, okay?"

"Nah," Bill said, getting up. "Let's go-go-go."

Hal went. Bill's moods were changeable, and if he paused to put the monkey away, he might lose his Popsicle. They went down to Teddy's and got them, then down to the Rec where some kids were getting up a baseball game. Hal was too small to play, but he sat far out in foul territory, sucking his root beer Popsicle and chasing what the big kids called "Chinese home runs." They didn't get home until almost dark, and their mother whacked Hal for getting the hand-towel dirty and whacked Bill for not cleaning up his side of the room, and after supper there was TV, and by the time all of that had happened, Hal had forgotten all about the monkey. It somehow found its way up onto *Bill's* shelf, where it stood right next to Bill's autographed picture of Bill Boyd. And there it stayed for nearly two years.

By the time Hal was seven, babysitters had become an extravagance, and Mrs. Shelburn's last word to the two of them each morning was, "Bill, look after your brother."

That day, however, Bill had to stay after school for a Safety Patrol Boy meeting and Hal came home alone, stopping at each corner until he could see absolutely no traffic coming in either direction and then skittering across, shoulders hunched, like a doughboy crossing no man's land. He let himself into the house with the key under the mat and went immediately to the refrigerator for a glass of milk. He got the bottle, and then it slipped through his fingers and crashed to smithereens on the floor, the pieces of glass flying everywhere, as the monkey suddenly began to beat its cymbals together upstairs.

Jang-jang-jang-jang, on and on.

He stood there immobile, looking down at the broken glass

and the puddle of milk, full of a terror he could not name or understand. It was simply there, seeming to ooze from his pores.

He turned and rushed upstairs to their room. The monkey stood on Bill's shelf, seeming to stare at him. He had knocked the autographed picture of Bill Boyd face-down onto Bill's bed. The monkey rocked and grinned and beat its cymbals together. Hal approached it slowly, not wanting to, not able to stay away. Its cymbals jerked apart and crashed together and jerked apart again. As he got closer, he could hear the clockwork running in the monkey's guts.

Abruptly, uttering a cry of revulsion and terror, he swatted it from the shelf as one might swat a large, loathsome bug. It struck Bill's pillow and then fell on the floor, cymbals still beating together, *jang-jang-jang*, lips flexing and closing as it lay there on its back in a patch of late April sunshine.

Then, suddenly, he remembered Beulah. The monkey had clapped its cymbals that night, too.

Hal kicked it with one Buster Brown shoe, kicked it as hard as he could, and this time the cry that escaped him was one of fury. The clockwork monkey skittered across the floor, bounced off the wall, and lay still. Hal stood staring at it, fists bunched, heart pounding. It grinned saucily back at him, the sun a burning pinpoint in one glass eye. *Kick me all you want*, it seemed to tell him. *I'm nothing but cogs and clockwork and a worm-gear or two, kick me all you feel like, I'm not real, just a funny clockwork monkey is all I am, and who's dead? There's been an explosion at the helicopter plant! What's that rising up into the sky like a big bloody bowling ball with eyes where the finger-holes should be? Is it your mother's head, Hal? Down at Brook Street Corner! The car was going too fast! The driver was drunk! There's one Patrol Boy less! Could you hear the crunching sound when the wheels ran over Bill's skull and his brains squirted out of his ears? Yes? No? Maybe? Don't ask me, I don't know, I can't know, all I know how to do is beat these cymbals together jang-jang-jang, and who's dead, Hal? Your mother? Your brother? Or is it you, Hal? Is it you?*

He rushed at it again, meaning to stomp on it, smash its loathsome body, jump on it until cogs and gears flew and its horrible glass eyes rolled across the floor. But just as he reached it its cymbals came together once more, very softly . . . (*jang*) . . . as a spring somewhere inside expanded one final, minute notch . . . and a sliver of ice seemed to whisper its way through the walls of his heart, impaling it, stilling its fury and leaving him sick with terror again. The monkey almost seemed to know—how gleeful its grin seemed!

He picked it up, tweezing one of its arms between the thumb and first finger of his right hand, mouth drawn down in a bow of loathing, as if it were a corpse he held. Its mangy fake fur seemed hot and fevered against his skin. He fumbled open the tiny door that led to the back closet and turned on the bulb. The monkey grinned at him as he crawled down the length of the storage area between boxes piled on top of boxes, past the set of navigation books and the photograph albums with their fume of old chemicals and the souvenirs and the old clothes, and Hal thought: *If it begins to clap its cymbals together now and move in my hand, I'll scream, and if I scream, it'll do more than grin, it'll start to laugh, to laugh at me, and then I'll go crazy and they'll find me in here, drooling and laughing, crazy, I'll be crazy, oh please dear God, please dear Jesus, don't let me go crazy—*

He reached the far end and clawed two boxes aside, spilling one of them, and jammed the monkey back into the Ralston-Purina box in the farthest corner. And it leaned in there, comfortably, as if home at last, cymbals poised, grinning its simian grin, as if the joke were still on Hal. Hal crawled backward, sweating, hot and cold, all fire and ice, waiting for the cymbals to begin, and when they began, the monkey would leap from its box and scurry beetlelike toward him, clockwork whirring, cymbals clashing madly, and——

—and none of that happened. He turned off the light and slammed the small down-the-rabbit-hole door and leaned on it, panting. At last he began to feel a little better. He went downstairs on rubbery legs, got an empty bag, and began carefully to pick up the jagged shards and splinters of the broken milk bottle, wondering if he was going to cut himself and bleed to death, if that was what the clapping cymbals had meant. But that didn't happen, either. He got a towel and wiped up the milk and then sat down to see if his mother and brother would come home.

His mother came first, asking, "Where's Bill?"

In a low, colorless voice, now sure that Bill must be dead, Hal started to explain about the Patrol Boy meeting, knowing that, even given a very long meeting, Bill should have been home half an hour ago.

His mother looked at him curiously, started to ask what was wrong, and then the door opened and Bill came in—only it was not Bill at all, not really. This was a ghost-Bill, pale and silent.

"What's wrong?" Mrs. Shelburn exclaimed. "Bill, what's wrong?"

Bill began to cry and they got the story through his tears. There had been a car, he said. He and his friend Charlie Silverman were walking home together after the meeting and the car came around Brook Street Corner too fast and Charlie had frozen, Bill had tugged Charlie's hand once but had lost his grip and the car——

Bill began to bray out loud, hysterical sobs, and his mother hugged him to her, rocking him, and Hal looked out on the porch and saw two policemen standing there. The squad car in which they had conveyed Bill home was at the curb. Then he began to cry himself . . . but his tears were tears of relief.

It was Bill's turn to have nightmares now—dreams in which Charlie Silverman died over and over again, knocked out of his Red Ryder cowboy boots, and flipped onto the hood of the old Hudson Hornet the drunk driver had been driving. Charlie Silverman's head and the Hudson's windshield had met with an explosive noise, and both had shattered. The drunk driver, who owned a candy store in Milford, suffered a heart attack shortly after being taken into custody (perhaps it was the sight of Charlie Silverman's brains drying on his pants), and his lawyer was quite successful at the trial with his "this man has been punished enough" theme. The drunk was given sixty days (suspended) and lost his privilege to operate a motor vehicle in the state of Connecticut for five years . . . which was about as long as Bill Shelburn's nightmares lasted. The monkey was hidden away again in the back closet. Bill never noticed it was gone from his shelf . . . or if he did, he never said.

Hal felt safe for a while. He even began to forget about the monkey again, or to believe it had only been a bad dream. But when he came home from school on the afternoon his mother died, it was back on his shelf, cymbals poised, grinning down at him.

He approached it slowly as if from outside himself—as if his own body had been turned into a wind-up toy at the sight of the monkey. He saw his hand reach out and take it down. He felt the nappy fur crinkle under his hand, but the feeling was muffled, mere pressure, as if someone had shot him full of Novocaine. He could hear his breathing, quick and dry, like the rattle of wind through straw.

He turned it over and grasped the key and years later he would think that his drugged fascination was like that of a man who puts a six-shooter with one loaded chamber against a closed and jittering eyelid and pulls the trigger.

No don't—let it alone throw it away don't touch it——

He turned the key and in the silence he heard a perfect tiny series of winding-up clicks. When he let the key go, the monkey began to clap its cymbals together and he could feel its body jerking, bend-and-*jerk*, bend-and-*jerk*, as if it were live, it *was* alive, writhing in his hand like some loathsome pygmy, and the vibration he felt through its balding brown fur was not that of turning cogs but the beating of its black and cindered heart.

With a groan, Hal dropped the monkey and backed away, fingernails digging into the flesh under his eyes, palms pressed to his mouth. He stumbled over something and nearly lost his balance (then he would have been right down on the floor with it, his bulging blue eyes looking into its glassy hazel ones). He scrambled toward the door, backed through it, slammed it, and leaned against it. Suddenly he bolted for the bathroom and vomited.

It was Mrs. Stukey from the helicopter plant who brought the news and stayed with them those first two endless nights, until Aunt Ida got down from Maine. Their mother had died of a brain embolism in the middle of the afternoon. She had been standing at the water cooler with a cup of water in one hand and had crumpled as if shot, still holding the paper cup in one hand. With the other she had clawed at the water cooler and had pulled the great glass bottle of Poland water down with her. It had shattered . . . but the plant doctor, who came on the run, said later that he believed Mrs. Shelburn was dead before the water had soaked through her dress and her underclothes to wet her skin. The boys were never told any of this, but Hal knew anyway. He dreamed it again and again on the long nights following his mother's death. *You still have trouble gettin to sleep, little brother?* Bill had asked him, and Hal supposed Bill thought all the thrashing and bad dreams had to do with their mother dying so suddenly, and that was right . . . but only partly right. There was the guilt: the certain, deadly knowledge that he had killed his mother by winding the monkey up on that sunny afterschool afternoon.

When Hal finally fell asleep, his sleep must have been deep. When he awoke, it was nearly noon. Petey was sitting cross-legged in a chair across the room, methodically eating an orange section by section and watching a game show on TV.

Hal swung his legs out of bed, feeling as if someone had punched him down into sleep . . . and then punched him back out of it. His head throbbed. "Where's your mom, Petey?"

Petey glanced around. "She and Dennis went shopping. I said I'd stay here with you. Do you always talk in your sleep, Dad?"

Hal looked at his son cautiously. "No, I don't think so. What did I say?"

"It was all muttering. I couldn't make it out. It scared me, a little."

"Well, here I am in my right mind again," Hal said, and managed a small grin. Petey grinned back, and Hal felt simple love for the boy again, an emotion that was bright and strong and uncomplicated. He wondered why he had always been able to feel so good about Petey, to feel he understood Petey and could help him, and why Dennis seemed a window too dark to look through, a mystery in his ways and habits, the sort of boy he could not understand because he had never been that sort of boy. It was too easy to say that the move from California had changed Dennis, or that——

His thoughts froze. The monkey. The monkey was sitting on the windowsill, cymbals poised. Hal felt his heart stop dead in his chest and then suddenly begin to gallop. His vision wavered, and his throbbing head began to ache ferociously.

It had escaped from the suitcase and now stood on the windowsill, grinning at him. *Thought you got rid of me, didn't you? But you've thought that before, haven't you?*

Yes, he thought sickly. Yes, I have.

"Pete, did you take that monkey out of my suitcase?" he asked, knowing the answer already. He had locked the suitcase and put the key in his overcoat pocket.

Petey glanced at the monkey, and something—Hal thought it was unease—passed over his face. "No," he said. "Mom put it there."

"Mom did?"

"Yeah. She took it from you. She laughed."

"Took it from me? What are you talking about?"

"You had it in bed with you. I was brushing my teeth, but Dennis saw. He laughed, too. He said you looked like a baby with a teddy bear."

Hal looked at the monkey. His mouth was too dry to swallow. He'd had it in *bed* with him? In *bed*? That loathsome fur against his cheek, maybe against his *mouth*, those glass eyes staring into his sleeping face, those grinning teeth near his neck? Dear *God*.

He turned abruptly and went to the closet. The Samsonite was there, still locked. The key was still in his overcoat pocket.

Behind him, the TV snapped off. He came out of the closet slowly. Petey was looking at him soberly. "Daddy, I don't like that monkey," he said, his voice almost too low to hear.

"Nor do I," Hal said.

Petey looked at him closely, to see if he was joking, and saw that he was not. He came to his father and hugged him tight. Hal could feel him trembling.

Petey spoke into his ear, then, very rapidly, as if afraid he might not have courage enough to say it again . . . or that the monkey might overhear.

"It's like it looks at you. Like it looks at you no matter where you are in the room. And if you go into the other room, it's like it's looking through the wall at you. I kept feeling like it . . . like it wanted me for something."

Petey shuddered. Hal held him tight.

"Like it wanted you to wind it up," Hal said.

Pete nodded violently. "It isn't really broken, is it, Dad?"

"Sometimes it is," Hal said, looking over his son's shoulder at the monkey. "But sometimes it still works."

"I kept wanting to go over there and wind it up. It was so quiet, and I thought, I can't, it'll wake up Daddy, but I still wanted to, and I went over and I . . . I *touched* it and I hate the way it feels . . . but I liked it, too . . . and it was like it was saying, Wind me up, Petey, we'll play, your father isn't going to wake up, he's never going to wake up at all, wind me up, wind me up . . ."

The boy suddenly burst into tears.

"It's bad, I know it is. There's something wrong with it. Can't we throw it out, Daddy? Please?"

The monkey grinned its endless grin at Hal. He could feel Petey's tears between them. Late morning sun glinted off the monkey's brass cymbals—the light reflected upward and put sunstreaks on the motel's plain white stucco ceiling.

"What time did your mother think she and Dennis would be back, Petey?"

"Around one." He swiped at his red eyes with his shirt-sleeve, looking embarrassed at his tears. But he wouldn't look at the monkey. "I turned on the TV," he whispered. "And I turned it up loud."

"That was all right, Petey."

"I had a crazy idea," Petey said. "I had this idea that if I wound that monkey up, you . . . you would have just died there in bed. In your sleep. Wasn't that a crazy idea, Daddy?" His voice had dropped again, and it trembled helplessly.

How would it have happened? Hal wondered. *Heart attack? An embolism, like my mother? What? It doesn't really matter, does it?*

And on the heels of that, another, colder thought: *Get rid of it, he says. Throw it out. But can it be gotten rid of? Ever?*

The monkey grinned mockingly at him, its cymbals held a foot apart. Did it suddenly come to life on the night Aunt Ida died? he wondered suddenly. Was that the last sound she heard, the muffled *jang-jang-jang* of the monkey beating its cymbals together up in the black attic while the wind whistled along the drainpipe?

"Maybe not so crazy," Hal said slowly to his son. "Go get your flight bag, Petey."

Petey looked at him uncertainly. "What are we going to do?"

Maybe it can be got rid of. Maybe permanently, maybe just for a while . . . a long while or a short while. Maybe it's just going to come back and come back and that's what all this is about . . . but maybe I—we—can say good-bye to it for a long time. It took twenty years to come back this time. It took twenty years to get out of the well . . .

"We're going to go for a ride," Hal said. He felt fairly calm, but somehow too heavy inside his skin. Even his eyeballs seemed to have gained weight. "But first I want you to take your flight bag out there by the edge of the parking lot and find three or four good-sized rocks. Put them inside the bag and bring it back to me. Got it?"

Understanding flickered in Petey's eyes. "All right, Daddy."

Hal glanced at his watch. It was nearly 12:15. "Hurry. I want to be gone before your mother gets back."

"Where are we going?"

"To Uncle Will's and Aunt Ida's," Hal said. 'To the home place."

Hal went into the bathroom, looked behind the toilet, and got the bowl brush leaning there. He took it back to the window and stood there with it in his hand like a cut-rate magic wand. He looked out at Petey in his melton shirt-jacket, crossing the parking lot with his flight bag, DELTA showing clearly in white letters against a blue field. A fly bumbled in an upper corner of the window, slow and stupid with the end of the warm season. Hal knew how it felt.

He watched Petey hunt up three good-sized rocks and then start back across the parking lot. A car came around the corner of the motel, a car that was moving too fast, much too fast, and without thinking, reaching with the kind of reflex a good short-stop shows going to his right, his hand flashed down, as if in a karate chop . . . and stopped.

The cymbals closed soundlessly on his intervening hand, and he felt something in the air. Something like rage.

The car's brakes screamed. Petey flinched back. The driver motioned to him impatiently, as if what had almost happened was Petey's fault, and Petey ran across the parking lot with his collar flapping and into the motel's rear entrance.

Sweat was running down Hal's chest; he felt it on his forehead like a drizzle of oily rain. The cymbals pressed coldly against his hand, numbing it.

Go on, he thought grimly. *Go on, I can wait all day. Until hell freezes over, if that's what it takes.*

The cymbals drew apart and came to rest. Hal heard one faint *click!* from inside the monkey. He withdrew his hand and looked at it. On both the back and the palm there were grayish semicircles printed into the skin, as if he had been frostbitten.

The fly bumbled and buzzed, trying to find the cold October sunshine that seemed so close.

Petey came bursting in, breathing quickly, cheeks rosy. "I got three good ones, Dad, I—" He broke off. "Are you all right, Daddy?"

"Fine," Hal said. "Bring the bag over."

Hal hooked the table by the sofa over to the window with his foot, so it stood below the sill, and put the flight bag on it. He spread its mouth open like lips. He could see the stones Petey had collected glimmering inside. He used the toilet-bowl brush to hook the monkey forward. It teetered for a moment and then fell into the bag. There was a faint *jing!* as one of its cymbals struck one of the rocks.

"Dad? Daddy?" Petey sounded frightened. Hal looked around at him. Something was different; something had changed. What was it?

Then he saw the direction of Petey's gaze and he knew.

The buzzing of the fly had stopped. It lay dead on the win-dowsill.

"Did the monkey do that?" Petey whispered.

"Come on," Hal said, zipping the bag shut. "I'll tell you while we ride out to the home place."

"How can we go? Mom and Dennis took the car."

"I'll get us there," Hal said, and ruffled Petey's hair.

He showed the desk clerk his driver's license and a twenty-dollar bill. After taking Hal's Texas Instruments digital watch as further collateral, the clerk handed Hal the keys to his own car—a battered AMC Gremlin. As they drove east on Route 302 toward Casco, Hal began to talk, haltingly at first, then a little faster. He began by telling Petey that his father had probably brought the monkey home with him from overseas, as a gift for his sons. It wasn't a particularly unique toy; there was nothing strange or valuable about it. There must have been hundreds of thousands of wind-up monkeys in the world, some made in Hong Kong, some in Taiwan, some in Korea. But somewhere along the line—perhaps even in the dark back closet of the house in Connecticut where the two boys had begun their growing up—something had happened to the monkey. Something bad, evil. It might be, Hal told Petey as he tried to coax the clerk's Gremlin up past forty (he was very aware of the zipped-up flight bag on the back seat, and Petey kept glancing around at it), that some evil—maybe even most evil—isn't even sentient and aware of what it is. It might be that most evil is very much like a monkey full of clock-work that you wind up; the clockwork turns, the cymbals begin to beat, the teeth grin, the stupid glass eyes laugh . . . or appear to laugh. . . .

He told Petey about finding the monkey, but he found him-self skipping over large chunks of the story, not wanting to terrify his already scared boy any more than he was already. The story thus became disjointed, not really clear, but Petey asked no questions; perhaps he was filling in the blanks for himself, Hal thought, in much the same way that he had dreamed his mother's death over and over, although he had not been there.

Uncle Will and Aunt Ida had both been there for the funeral. Afterward, Uncle Will had gone back to Maine—it was harvest-time—and Aunt Ida had stayed on for two weeks with the boys to neaten up her sister's affairs. But more than that, she spent the time making herself known to the boys, who were so stunned by their mother's sudden death that they were nearly sleepwalking. When they couldn't sleep, she was there with warm milk; when Hal woke at three in the morning with nightmares (nightmares in which his mother approached the water cooler without seeing the monkey that floated and bobbed in its cool sapphire depths, grinning and clapping its cymbals, each converging pair of sweeps leaving trails of bubbles behind); she was there when Bill came down with first a fever and then a rash of painful mouth sores and then hives three days after the funeral; she was there. She made herself known to the boys, and before they rode the New England Flyer from Hartford to Portland with her, both Bill and Hal had come to her separately and wept on her lap while she held them and rocked them, and the bonding began.

The day before they left Connecticut for good to go "down Maine" (as it was called in those days), the rag-man came in his great old rattly truck and picked up the huge pile of useless stuff that Bill and Hal had carried out to the sidewalk from the back closet. When all the junk had been set out by the curb for pick-up, Aunt Ida had asked them to go through the back closet again and pick out any souvenirs or remembrances they wanted specially to keep. We just don't have room for it all, boys, she told them, and Hal supposed Bill had taken her at her word and had gone through all those fascinating boxes their father had left behind one final time. Hal did not join his older brother. Hal had lost his taste for the back closet. A terrible idea had come to him during those first two weeks of mourning; perhaps his father hadn't just disappeared, or run away because he had an itchy foot and had discovered marriage wasn't for him.

Maybe the monkey had gotten him.

When he heard the rag-man's truck roaring and farting and backfiring its way down the block, Hal nerved himself, snatched the scruffy wind-up monkey from his shelf where it had been since the day his mother died (he had not dared to touch it until then, not even to throw it back into the closet), and ran downstairs with it. Neither Bill nor Aunt Ida saw him. Sitting on top of a barrel filled with broken souvenirs and mouldy books was the Ralston-Purina carton, filled with similar junk. Hal had slammed the monkey back into the box it had originally come out of, hysterically daring it to begin clapping its cymbals (*go on, go on, I dare you, dare you, DARE YOU*), but the monkey only waited there, leaning back nonchalantly, as if expecting a bus, grinning its awful knowing grin.

Hal stood by, a small boy in old corduroy pants and scuffed Buster Browns, as the rag-man, an Italian gent who wore a crucifix and whistled through the space in his teeth, began loading boxes and barrels into his ancient truck with the high wooden sides. Hal watched as he lifted both the barrel and the Ralston-Purina box balanced atop it; he watched the monkey disappear into the maw of the truck; he watched as the rag-man climbed back into the cab, blew his nose mightily into the palm of his hand, wiped his hand with a huge red handkerchief, and started the truck's engine with a mighty roar and a stinking blast of oily blue smoke; he watched the truck draw away. And a great weight had dropped away from his heart—he actually felt it go. He had jumped up and down twice, as high as he could jump, his arms spread, palms held out, and if any of the neighbors had seen him, they would have thought it odd almost to the point of blasphemy, perhaps—*why is that boy jumping for joy* (for that was surely what it was; a jump for joy can hardly be disguised) *with his mother not even a month in her grave?*

He was jumping for joy because the monkey was gone, gone forever. Gone forever, but not three months later Aunt Ida had sent him up into the attic to get the boxes of Christmas decorations, and as he crawled around looking for them, getting the knees of his pants dusty, he had suddenly come face to face with it again, and his wonder and terror had been so great that he had to bite sharply into the side of his hand to keep from screaming . . . or fainting dead away. There it was, grinning its toothy grin, cymbals poised a foot apart and ready to clap, leaning nonchalantly back against one corner of the Ralston-Purina carton as if waiting for a bus, seeming to say: *Thought you got rid of me, didn't you? But I'm not that easy to get rid of, Hal. I like you, Hal. We were made for each other, just a boy and his pet monkey, a couple of good old buddies. And somewhere south of here there's a stupid old Italian rag-man lying in a claw-foot tub with his eyeballs bulging and his dentures half-popped out of his mouth, his screaming mouth, a rag-man who smells like a burned-out Exide battery. He was saving me for his grandson, Hal, he put me on the shelf with his soap and his razor and his Burma-Shave and the Philco radio he listened to the Brooklyn Dodgers on, and I started to clap, and one of my cymbals hit that old radio and into the tub it went, and then I came to you, Hal, I worked my way along country roads at night and the moonlight shone off my teeth at three in the morning and I left death in my wake, Hal, I came to you, I'm your Christmas present, Hal, wind me up, who's dead? Is it Bill? Is it Uncle Will? Is it you, Hal? Is it you?*

Hal had backed away, grimacing madly, eyes rolling, and nearly fell going downstairs. He told Aunt Ida he hadn't been able to find the Christmas decorations—it was the first lie he had ever told her, and she had seen the lie on his face but had not asked him why he had told it, thank God—and later when Bill came in she asked him to look and he brought the Christmas decorations down. Later, when they were alone, Bill hissed at him that he was a dummy who couldn't find his own ass with both hands and a flashlight. Hal said nothing. Hal was pale and silent, only picking at his supper. And that night he dreamed of the monkey again, one of its cymbals striking the Philco radio as it babbled out Dean Martin singing Whenna da moon hitta you eye like a big pizza pie *ats-a moray*, the radio tumbling into the bathtub as the monkey grinned and beat its cymbals together with a *JANG* and a *JANG* and a *JANG*; only it wasn't the Italian rag-man who was in the tub when the water turned electric.

It was him.

Hal and his son scrambled down the embankment behind the home place to the boathouse that jutted out over the water on its old pilings. Hal had the flight bag in his right hand. His throat was dry, his ears were attuned to an unnaturally keen pitch. The bag seemed very heavy.

"What's down here, Daddy?" Petey asked.

Hal didn't answer. He set down the flight bag. "Don't touch that," he said, and Petey backed away from it. Hal felt in his pocket for the ring of keys Bill had given him and found one neatly labeled B'HOUSE on a scrap of adhesive tape.

The day was clear and cold, windy, the sky a brilliant blue. The leaves of the trees that crowded up to the verge of the lake had gone every bright fall shade from blood red to sneering yellow. They rattled and talked in the wind. Leaves swirled round Petey's sneakers as he stood anxiously by, and Hal could smell November on the wind, with winter crowding close behind it.

The key turned in the padlock and he pulled the swing doors open. Memory was strong; he didn't even have to look to kick down the wooden block that held the door open. The smell in here was all summer; canvas and bright wood, a lingering, musty warmth.

Uncle Will's rowboat was still here, the oars neatly shipped as if he had last loaded it with his fishing tackle and two six-packs of Black Label on ice yesterday afternoon. Bill and Hal had both gone out fishing with Uncle Will many times, but never together; Uncle Will maintained the boat was too small for three. The red trim, which Uncle Will had touched up each spring, was now faded and peeling, though, and spiders had spun their silk in the boat's bow.

Hal laid hold of it and pulled it down the ramp to the little shingle of beach. The fishing trips had been one of the best parts of his childhood with Uncle Will and Aunt Ida. He had a feeling that Bill felt much the same. Uncle Will was ordinarily the most taciturn of men; but once he had the boat positioned to his liking, some sixty or seventy yards offshore, lines set and bobbers floating on the water, he would crack a beer for himself and one for Hal (who rarely drank more than half of the one can Uncle Will would allow, always with the ritual admonition from Uncle Will that Aunt Ida must never be told because "she'd shoot me for a stranger if she knew I was givin you boys beer, don't you know"), and wax expansive. He would tell stories, answer questions, rebait Hal's hook when it needed rebaiting; and the boat would drift where the wind and the mild current wanted it to be.

"How come you never go right out to the middle, Uncle Will?" Hal had asked once.

"Look over the side there, Hal," Uncle Will had answered.

Hal did. He saw blue water and his fish line going down into black.

"You're looking into the deepest part of Crystal Lake," Uncle Will said, crunching his empty beer can in one hand and selecting a fresh one with the other. "A hundred feet if she's an inch. Amos Culligan's old Studebaker is down there somewhere. Damn fool took it out on the lake one early December, before the ice was made. Lucky to get out of it alive, he was. They'll never get that Studebaker out, nor see it until Judgment Trump blows. Lake's one deep son of a whore right here, it is. Big ones are right here, Hal. No need to go out no further. Let's see how your worm looks. Reel that son of a whore right in."

Hal did, and while Uncle Will put a fresh crawler from the old Crisco tin that served as his bait box on his hook, he stared into the water, fascinated, trying to see Amos Culligan's old Studebaker all rust and waterweed drifting out of the open driver's side window through which Amos had escaped at the absolute last moment, waterweed festooning the steering wheel like a rotting necklace, waterweed dangling from the rearview mirror and drifting back and forth in the currents like some strange rosary. But he could see only blue shading to black, and there was the shape of Uncle Will's night-crawler, the hook hidden inside its knots, hung up there in the middle of things, its own sun-shafted version of reality. Hal had a brief, dizzying vision of being suspended over a mighty gulf, and he had closed his eyes for a moment until the vertigo passed. That day, he seemed to recollect, he had drunk his entire can of beer.

. . . *the deepest part of Crystal Lake* . . . *a hundred feet if she's an inch*.

He paused a moment, panting, and looked up at Petey, still watching anxiously. "You want some help, Daddy?"

"In a minute."

He had his breath again, and now he pulled the rowboat

across the narrow strip of sand to the water, leaving a groove. The paint had peeled, but the boat had been kept under cover and it looked sound.

When he and Uncle Will went out, Uncle Will would pull the boat down the ramp, and when the bow was afloat, he would clamber in, grab an oar to push with, and say: "Push me off, Hal . . . this is where you earn your truss!"

"Hand that bag in, Petey, and then give me a push," he said. And smiling, a little, he added: "This is where you earn your truss."

Petey didn't smile back. "Am I coming, Daddy?"

"Not this time. Another time I'll take you out fishing, but . . . not this time."

Petey hesitated. The wind tumbled his brown hair and a few yellow leaves, crisp and dry, wheeled past his shoulders and landed at the edge of the water, bobbing like boats themselves.

"You should have muffled them," he said, low.

"What?" But he thought he understood what Petey had meant.

"Put cotton over the cymbals. Taped it on. So it couldn't . . . make that noise."

Hal suddenly remembered Daisy coming toward him—not walking but lurching—and how, quite suddenly, blood had burst from both of Daisy's eyes in a flood that soaked her ruff and pattered down on the floor of the barn, how she had collapsed on her forepaws . . . and on that still, rainy spring air of that day he had heard the sound, not muffled but curiously clear, coming from the attic of the house fifty feet away: *Jang-jang-jang-jang!*

He began to scream hysterically, dropping the armload of wood he had been getting for the fire. He ran for the kitchen to get Uncle Will, who was eating scrambled eggs and toast, his suspenders not even up over his shoulders yet.

She was an old dog, Hal, Uncle Will had said, his face haggard and unhappy—he looked old himself. *She was twelve, and that's old for a dog. You mustn't take on, now— old Daisy wouldn't like that.*

Old, the vet had echoed, but he had looked troubled all the same, because dogs don't die of explosive brain hemorrhages, even at twelve ("like as if someone had stuck a fire-cracker in his head," Hal overheard the vet saying to Uncle

Will as Uncle Will dug a hole in back of the barn not far from the place where he had buried Daisy's mother in 1950; "I never seen the beat of it, Will").

And later, terrified almost out of his mind but unable to help himself, Hal had crept up to the attic.

Hello, Hal, how you doing? the monkey grinned from its shadowy corner. Its cymbals were poised, a foot or so apart. The sofa cushion Hal had stood on end between them was now all the way across the attic. Something—some force—had thrown it hard enough to split its cover, and stuffing foamed out of it. *Don't worry about Daisy,* the monkey whispered inside his head, its glassy hazel eyes fixed on Hal Shelburn's wide blue ones. *Don't worry about Daisy, she was old, old, Hal, even the vet said so, and by the way, did you see the blood coming out of her eyes, Hal? Wind me up, Hal. Wind me up, let's play, and who's dead, Hal? Is it you?*

And when he came back to himself he had been crawling toward the monkey as if hypnotized. One hand had been outstretched to grasp the key. He scrambled backward then, and almost fell down the attic stairs in his haste—probably would have if the stairwell had not been so narrow. A little whining noise had been coming from his throat.

Now he sat in the boat, looking at Petey. "Muffling the cymbals doesn't work," he said. "I tried it once."

Petey cast a nervous glance at the flight bag. "What happened, Daddy?"

"Nothing I want to talk about now," Hal said, "and nothing you want to hear about. Come on and give me a push."

Petey bent to it, and the stern of the boat grated along the sand. Hal dug in with an oar, and suddenly that feeling of being tied to the earth was gone and the boat was moving lightly, its own thing again after years in the dark boathouse, rocking on the light waves. Hal unshipped the oars one at a time and clicked the oarlocks shut.

"Be careful, Daddy," Petey said. His face was pale.

"This won't take long," Hal promised, but he looked at the flight bag and wondered.

He began to row, bending to the work. The old, familiar ache in the small of his back and between his shoulder blades began. The shore receded. Petey was magically eight again, six, a four-year-old standing at the edge of the water. He shaded his eyes with one infant hand.

Hal glanced casually at the shore but would not allow himself to actually study it. It had been nearly fifteen years, and if he studied the shoreline carefully, he would see the changes rather than the similarities and become lost. The sun beat on his neck, and he began to sweat. He looked at the flight bag, and for a moment he lost the bend-and-pull rhythm. The flight bag seemed . . . seemed to be bulging. He began to row faster.

The wind gusted, drying the sweat and cooling his skin. The boat rose and the bow slapped water to either side when it came down. Hadn't the wind freshened, just in the last minute or so? And was Petey calling something? Yes. Hal couldn't make out what it was over the wind. It didn't matter. Getting rid of the monkey for another twenty years—or maybe forever (please God, forever)—that was what mattered.

The boat reared and came down. He glanced left and saw baby whitecaps. He looked shoreward again and saw Hunter's Point and a collapsed wreck that must have been the Burdon's boathouse when he and Bill were kids. Almost there, then. Almost over the spot where Amos Culligan's Studebaker had plunged through the ice one long-ago December. Almost over the deepest part of the lake.

Petey was screaming something; screaming and pointing. Hal still couldn't hear. The rowboat rocked and bucked, flatting off clouds of thin spray to either side of its peeling bow. A tiny rainbow glowed in one, was pulled apart. Sunlight and shadow raced across the lake in shutters and the waves were not mild now; the whitecaps had grown up. His sweat had dried to gooseflesh, and spray had soaked the back of his jacket. He rowed grimly, eyes alternating between the shore-line and the flight bag. The boat rose again, this time so high that for a moment the left oar pawed at air instead of water.

Petey was pointing at the sky, his screams now only a faint, bright runner of sound.

Hal looked over his shoulder.

The lake was a frenzy of waves. It had gone a deadly dark shade of blue sewn with white seams. A shadow raced across the water toward the boat and something in its shape was familiar, so terribly familiar, that Hal looked up and then the scream was there, struggling in his tight throat.

The sun was behind the cloud, turning it into a hunched working shape with two gold-edged crescents held apart. Two holes were torn in one end of the cloud, and sunshine poured through in two shafts.

As the cloud crossed over the boat, the monkey's cymbals, barely muffled by the flight bag, began to beat. *Jang-jang-jang-jang, it's you. Hal, it's finally you, you're over the deepest part of the lake now and it's your turn, your turn, your turn—*

All the necessary shoreline elements had clicked into their places. The rotting bones of Amos Culligan's Studebaker lay somewhere below, this was where the big ones were, this was the place.

Hal shipped the oars to the locks in one quick jerk, leaned forward unmindful of the wildly rocking boat, and snatched the flight bag. The cymbals made their wild, pagan music; the bag's sides bellowed as if with tenebrous respiration.

"*Right here, you sonofabitch!*" Hal screamed. "*RIGHT HERE!*"

He threw the bag over the side.

It sank fast. For a moment he could see it going down, sides moving, and for that endless moment *he could still hear the cymbals beating*. And for a moment the black waters seemed to clear and he could see down into that terrible gulf of waters to where the big ones lay; there was Amos Culligan's Studebaker, and Hal's mother was behind its slimy wheel, a grinning skeleton with a lake bass staring coldly from the skull's nasal cavity. Uncle Will and Aunt Ida lolled beside her, and Aunt Ida's gray hair trailed upward as the bag fell, turning over and over, a few silver bubbles trailing up: *jang-jang-jang-jang . . .*

Hal slammed the oars back into the water, scraping blood from his knuckles (*and ah God the back of Amos Culligan's Studebaker had been full of dead children! Charlie Silverman . . . Johnny McCabe . . .*), and began to bring the boat about.

There was a dry pistol-shot crack between his feet, and suddenly clear water was welling up between two boards. The boat was old; the wood had shrunk a bit, no doubt; it was just a small leak. But it hadn't been there when he rowed out. He would have sworn to it.

The shore and lake changed places in his view. Petey was at his back now. Overhead, that awful, simian cloud was breaking up. Hal began to row. Twenty seconds was enough to convince him he was rowing for his life. He was only a so-so swimmer, and even a great one would have been put to the test in this suddenly angry water.

Two more boards suddenly shrank apart with that pistol-shot sound. More water poured into the boat, dousing his shoes. There were tiny metallic snapping sounds that he realized were nails breaking. One of the oarlocks snapped and flew off into the water—would the swivel itself go next?

The wind now came from his back, as if trying to slow him down or even to drive him into the middle of the lake. He was terrified, but he felt a crazy kind of exhilaration through the terror. The monkey was gone for good this time. He knew it somehow. Whatever happened to him, the monkey would not be back to draw a shadow over Dennis's life, or Petey's. The monkey was gone, perhaps resting on the roof or the hood of Amos Culligan's Studebaker at the bottom of Crystal Lake. Gone for good.

He rowed, bending forward and rocking back. That cracking, crimping sound came again, and now the rusty old bait can that had been lying in the bow of the boat was floating in three inches of water. Spray blew in Hal's face. There was a louder snapping sound, and the bow seat fell in two pieces and floated next to the bait box. A board tore off the left side of the boat, and then another, this one at the waterline, tore off at the right. Hal rowed. Breath rasped in his mouth, hot and dry, and his throat swelled with the coppery taste of exhaustion. His sweaty hair flew.

Now a crack ran directly up the bottom of the rowboat, zigzagged between his feet, and ran up to the bow. Water gushed in; he was in water up to his ankles, then to the swell of calf. He rowed, but the boat's shoreward movement was sludgy now. He didn't dare look behind him to see how close he was getting.

Another board tore loose. The crack running up the center of the boat grew branches, like a tree. Water flooded in.

Hal began to make the oars sprint, breathing in great, failing gasps. He pulled once . . . twice . . . and on the third pull both oar swivels snapped off. He lost one oar, held onto the other. He rose to his feet and began to flail at the water with it. The boat rocked, almost capsized, and spilled him back onto his seat with a thump.

Moments later more boards tore loose, the seat collapsed, and he was lying in the water which filled the bottom of the boat, astounded at its coldness. He tried to get on his knees, desperately thinking: *Petey must not see this, must not see his father drown right in front of his eyes, you're going to swim, dog-paddle if you have to, but do, do something—*

There was another splintering crack—almost a crash—and he was in the water, swimming for the shore as he never had swum in his life . . . and the shore was amazingly close. A minute later he was standing waist-deep in water, not five yards from the beach.

Petey splashed toward him, arms out, screaming and crying and laughing. Hal started toward him and floundered. Petey, chest-deep, floundered.

They caught each other.

Hal, breathing in great, winded gasps, nevertheless hoisted the boy into his arms and carried him up to the beach where both of them sprawled, panting.

"Daddy? Is it really gone? That monkey?"

"Yes. I think it's really gone."

"The boat fell apart. It just . . . fell apart all around you."

Disintegrated, Hal thought, and looked at the boards floating loose on the water forty feet out. They bore no resemblance to the tight, handmade rowboat he had pulled out of the boathouse.

"It's all right now," Hal said, leaning back on his elbows. He shut his eyes and let the sun warm his face.

"Did you see the cloud?" Petey whispered.

"Yes. But I don't see it now . . . do you?"

They looked at the sky. There were scattered white puffs here and there, but no large dark cloud. It was gone, as he had said.

Hal pulled Petey to his feet. "There'll be towels up at the

house. Come on.'' But he paused, looking at his son. ''You were crazy, running out there like that.''

Petey looked at him solemnly. ''You were brave, Daddy.''

''Was I?'' The thought of bravery had never crossed his mind. Only his fear. The fear had been too big to see anything else. If anything else had indeed been there. ''Come on, Pete.''

''What are we going to tell Mom?''

Hal smiled. ''I dunno, big guy. We'll think of something.''

He paused a moment longer, looking at the boards floating on the water. The lake was calm again, sparkling with small wavelets. Suddenly Hal thought of summer people he didn't even know—a man and his son, perhaps, fishing for the big one. *I've got something Dad!* the boy screams. *Well reel it up and let's see,* the father says, and coming up from the depths, weeds draggling from its cymbals, grinning its terrible, welcoming grin . . . the monkey.

He shuddered—but those were only things that might be.

''Come on,'' he said to Petey again, and they walked up the path through the flaming October woods toward the home place.

From the *Bridgton News*
October 24, 1980:

MYSTERY
OF THE DEAD FISH

BY BETSY MORIARTY

HUNDREDS of dead fish were found floating belly-up on Crystal Lake in the neighboring township of Casco late last week. The largest numbers appeared to have died in the vicinity of Hunter's Point, although the lake's currents make this a bit difficult to determine. The dead fish included all types commonly found in these waters—bluegills, pickerel, sunnies, carp, brown and rainbow trout, even one land-locked salmon. Fish and Game authorities say they are mystified, and caution fishermen and women not to eat any sort of fish from Crystal Lake until tests have determined . . .

Michael Bishop

WITHIN THE WALLS OF TYRE

Michael Bishop is one of the most distinguished SF
writers of contemporary times. On occasion he ventures into horror, with such success that Arkham
House released a collection of his dark fantasy, *One
Winter in Eden* (1983). "Within the Walls of Tyre" is
among his strongest and most effective pieces, with
echoes of William Faulkner and Flannery O'Connor
underpinning an ironic Christmas ghost story without
a ghost . . . perhaps. The Southern Gothic tradition
underlies this disturbing contemporary cityscape
wherein Marilyn Odau maintains the illusion of psychological control. Bishop's ability to examine character and his exquisite control of imagery and detail
make his small body of work in horror a significant
contribution to the field.

As she eased her Nova into the lane permitting access to
the perimeter highway, Marilyn Odau reflected that the
hardest time of year for her was the Christmas season. From
late November to well into January her nerves were invariably as taut as harp strings. The traffic on the expressway—
lane-jumping vans and pickups, sleek sports cars, tailgating
semis, and all the blurred, indistinguishable others—was no
help, either. Even though she could see her hands on the
wheel, trembling inside beige, leather-tooled gloves, her Nova
seemed hardly to be under her control; instead, it was a piece
of machinery given all its impetus and direction by an invisible slot in the concrete beneath it. Her illusion of control
was exactly that—an illusion.

Looking quickly over her left shoulder, Marilyn Odau had to laugh at herself as she yanked the automobile around a bearded young man on a motorcycle. If your car's in someone else's control, why is it so damn hard to steer?

Nerves; balky Yuletide nerves.

Marilyn Odau was fifty-five; she had lived in this city—*her* city—ever since leaving Greenville during the first days of World War II to begin her own life and to take a job clerking at Satterwhite's. Ten minutes ago, before reaching the perimeter highway, she had passed through the heart of the city and driven beneath the great, grey, cracking backside of Satterwhite's (which was now a temporary warehouse for an electronics firm located in a suburban industrial complex). Like the heart of the city itself, Satterwhite's was dead—its great silver escalators, its pneumatic message tubes, its elevator bell tones, and its perfume-scented mezzanines as surely things of the past as . . . well, as Tojo, Tarawa Atoll, and a young marine named Jordan Burk. That was why, particularly at this time of year, Marilyn never glanced at the old department store as she drove beneath it on her way to Summerstone.

For the past two years she had been the manager of the Creighton's Corner Boutique at Summerstone Mall, the largest self-contained shopping facility in the five-county metropolitan area. Business had been shifting steadily, for well over a decade, from downtown to suburban and even quasi-rural commercial centers. And when a position had opened up for her at the new tri-level mecca bewilderingly dubbed Summerstone, Marilyn had shifted too, moving from Creighton's original franchise near Capitol Square to a second-level shop in an acre-square monolith sixteen miles to the city's northwest—a building more like a starship hangar than a shopping center.

Soon, she supposed, she ought also to shift residences. There were town houses closer to Summerstone, after all, with names just as ersatz-elegant as that of the Brookmist complex in which she now lived: Chateau Royale, Springhaven, Tivoli, Smoke Glade, Eden Manor, Sussex Wood . . . *There,* she told herself, glancing sidelong at the Matterhorn Heights complex nestled below the highway to her left, its cheesebox-and-cardboard-shingle chalets distorted by a teepee of glaring window panes on a glass truck cruising abreast of her.

Living at Matterhorn Heights would have put Marilyn fifteen minutes closer to her job, but it would have meant enduring a gaudier lapse of taste than she had opted for at Brookmist. There were degrees of artificiality, she knew, and each person found his own level. . . . Above her, a green and white highway sign indicated the Willowglen and Summerstone exits. Surprised as always by its sudden appearance, she wrestled the Nova into an off-ramp lane and heard behind her the inevitable blaring of horns.

Pack it in, she told the driver on her bumper—an expression she had learned from Jane Sidney, one of her employees at the boutique. Pack it in, laddie.

Intent on the traffic light at the end of the off-ramp, conscious too of the wetness under the arms of her pantsuit jacket, Marilyn managed to giggle at the incongruous *feel* of these words. In her rearview mirror she could see the angry features of a modishly long-haired young man squinting at her over the hood of a Le Mans—and it was impossible to imagine herself confronting him, outside their automobiles, with the imperative, "Pack it in, laddie!" Absolutely impossible. All she could do was giggle at the thought and jab nervously at her clutch and brake pedals. Morning traffic—Christmas traffic—was bearable only if you remembered that impatience was a self-punishing sin.

At 8:50 she reached Summerstone and found a parking place near a battery of army-green trash bins. A security guard was passing in mall employees through a second-tier entrance near Montgomery-Ward's: and when Marilyn showed him her ID card, he said almost by way of ritual shibboleth, "Have a good day, Miss Odau." Then, with a host of people to whom she never spoke, she was on the enclosed promenade of machined wooden beams and open carpeted shops. As always, the hour could have been high noon or twelve midnight—there was no way to tell. The season was identifiable only because of the winter merchandise on display and the Christmas decorations suspended overhead or twining like tinfoil helixes through the central shaft of the mall. The smells of ammonia, confectionery goods, and perfumes commingled piquantly, even at this early hour, but Marilyn scarcely noticed.

Managing Creighton's Corner had become her life, the enterprise for which she lived; and because Summerstone contained Creighton's Corner, she went into it daily with less philosophical scrutiny than a coal miner gives his mine. Such speculation, Marilyn knew from thirty-five years on her own, was worse than useless—it imprisoned you in doubts and misapprehensions largely of your own devising. She was glad to be but a few short steps from Creighton's, glad to feel her funk disintegrating beneath the prospect of an efficient day at work. . . .

"Good morning, Ms. Odau," Jane Sidney said as she entered Creighton's.

"Good morning. You look nice today."

The girl was wearing a green and gold jersey, a kind of gaucho skirt of imitation leather, and suede boots. Her hair was not much longer than a military cadet's. She always pronounced "Ms." as a muted buzz—either out of feminist conviction or, more likely, her fear that "Miss" would betray her more-than-middle-aged superior as unmarried . . . as if that were a shameful thing in one of Marilyn's generation. Only Cissy Campbell of the three girls who worked in the boutique could address her as "Miss Odau" without looking flustered. Or maybe Marilyn imagined this. She didn't try to plumb the personal feelings of her employees, and they in turn didn't try to cast her in the role of a mother confessor. They liked her well enough, though. Everyone got along.

"I'm working for Cissy until three, Ms. Odau. We've traded shifts. Is that all right?" Jane followed her toward her office.

"Of course it is. What about Terri?"

The walls were mercury-colored mirrors; there were mirrors overhead. Racks of swirl-patterned jerseys, erotically tailored jumpsuits, and flamboyant scarves were reiterated around them like the refrain of a toothpaste or cola jingle. Macramé baskets with plastic flowers and exotic bath soaps hung from the ceiling. Black-light and pop-art posters went in and out of the walls, even though they never moved—and looking up at one of them, Marilyn had a vision of Satterwhite's during the austere days of 1942–43, when the war had begun to put money in people's pockets for the first time since the twenties but it was unpatriotic to spend it. She remembered the Office of Price Administration and ration-stamp booklets. Because of leather shortages, you couldn't have more than two pairs of shoes a year. . . .

Jane was looking at her fixedly.

"I'm sorry, Jane. I didn't hear you."

"I said Terri'll be here at twelve, but she wants to work all day tomorrow too, if that's okay. There aren't any Tuesday classes at City College, and she wants to get in as many hours as she can before final exams come up." Terri was still relatively new to the boutique.

"Of course, that's fine. Won't you be here too?"

"Yes, ma'am. In the afternoon."

"Okay, good. . . . I've got some order forms to look over and a letter or two to write." She excused herself and went behind a tie-dyed curtain into an office as plain and practical as Creighton's decor was peacockish and orgiastic. She sat down to a small metal filing cabinet with an audible moan—a moan at odds with the satisfaction she felt in getting down to work. What was wrong with her? She knew, she knew, dear God wasn't she perfectly aware. . . . Marilyn pulled her gloves off. As her fingers went to the onion-skin order forms and bills of lading in her files, she was surprised by the deep oxblood color of her nails. Why? She had worn this polish for a week, since well before Thanksgiving. . . .

The answer of course was Maggie Hood. During the war Marilyn and Maggie had roomed together in a clapboard house not far from Satterwhite's, a house with two poplars in the small front yard but not a single blade of grass. Maggie had worked for the telephone company (an irony, since they had no phone in their house) and she always wore oxblood nail polish. Several months before the Axis surrender, Maggie married a 4-F telephone-company official and moved to Mobile. The little house on Greenbriar Street was torn down during the mid-fifties to make way for an office building. Maggie Hood and oxblood nail polish—

Recollections that skirted the heart of the matter, Marilyn knew. She shook them off and got down to business.

Tasteful rock was playing in the boutique, something from Stevie Wonder's *Songs in the Key of Life*—Jane had flipped the music on. Through it, Marilyn could hear the morning herds passing along the concourses and interior bridges of Summerstone. Sometimes it seemed that half the population of the state was out there. Twice the previous Christmas season the structural vibrations had become so worrisome that security guards were ordered to keep new shoppers out until enough people had left to avert the danger of collapse. That was the rumor, anyway, and Marilyn almost believed it. Summerstone's several owners, on the other hand, claimed that the doors had been locked simply to minimize crowding. But how many times did sane business people turn away customers solely to "minimize crowding?"

Marilyn helped Jane wait on shoppers until noon. Then Terri Bready arrived, and she went back to her office. Instead of eating she checked outstanding accounts and sought to square away records. She kept her mind wholly occupied with the minutiae of running her business for its semiretired owners, Charlie and Agnes Creighton. It didn't bother her at all that they were ten years younger than she, absentee landlords with a condominium apartment on the gulf coast. She did a good job for them, working evenings as well as lunch hours, and the Creightons were smart enough to realize her worth. They trusted her completely and paid her well.

At one o'clock Terri Bready stepped through Marilyn's curtain and made an apologetic noise in her throat.

"Hey, Terri. What is it?"

"There's a salesman out here who'd like to see you." Bending a business card between her thumb and forefinger, the girl gave an odd baritone chuckle. Tawny-haired and lean, she was a freshman drama major who made the most fashionable clothes look like off-the-racks from a Salvation Army outlet. But she was sweet—so sweet that Marilyn had been embarrassed to hear her discussing with Cissy Campbell the boy with whom she was living.

"Is he someone we regularly buy from, Terri?"

"I don't know. I don't know who we buy from."

"Is that his card?"

"Yeah, it is."

"Why don't you let me see it, then?"

"Oh. Okay. Sorry, Ms. Odau. Here." Trying to hand it over, the girl popped the card out of her fingers; it struck Marilyn's chest and fluttered into her lap. "Sorry again. Sheesh, I really am." Terri chuckled her baritone chuckle, and Marilyn, smiling briefly, retrieved the card.

It said: *Nicholas Anson/Products Consultant & Sales Representative/Latter-Day Novelties/Los Angeles, California.* Also on the card were two telephone numbers and a zip code.

Terri Bready wet her lips and her tongue. "He's a hunk, Ms. Odau, I'm not kidding you—he's as pretty as a naked Swede."

"Is that right? How old?"

"Oh, he's too old for me. He's got to be in his thirties at least."

"Decrepit, dear."

"Oh, he's not decrepit, any. But I'm out of the market. You know."

"Off the auction block?"

"Yes, ma'am. Yeah."

"What's he selling? We don't often work through independent dealers—the Creightons don't, that is—and I've never heard of this firm."

"Jane says she thinks he's been hitting the stores up and down the mall for the last couple of days. Don't know what he's pushing. He's got a samples case, though—and really the most incredible kiss-me eyes."

"If he's been here two days, I'm surprised he hasn't already sold those."

"Do you want me to send him back? He's too polite to burst in. He's been calling Jane and me 'Ms. Sidney' and 'Ms. Bready,' like that."

"Don't send him back yet." Marilyn had a premonition, almost a fear. "Let me take a look at him first."

Terri Bready barked a laugh and had to cover her mouth. "Hey, Ms. Odau, I wouldn't talk him up like Robert Redford and then send you a bald frog. I mean, why would I?"

"Go on, Terri. I'll talk to him in a couple of minutes."

"Yeah. Okay." The girl was quickly gone, and at the curtain's edge Marilyn looked out. Jane was waiting on a heavy-set woman in a fire-engine-red pantsuit, and just inside the boutique's open threshold the man named Nicholas Anson was watching the crowds and countercrowds work through each other like grim armies.

Anson's hair was modishly long, and he reminded Marilyn a bit of the man who had grimaced at her on the off-ramp. Then, however, the sun had been ricocheting off windshields, grilles, and hood ornaments, and any real identification of the man in the Le Mans with this composed sales representative was impossible, if not downright pointless. A person in an automobile was not the same person you met on common ground. . . . Now Terri was approaching this Anson fellow, and he was turning toward the girl.

Marilyn Odau felt her fingers tighten on the curtain. Already she had taken in the man's navy blue leisure jacket and, beneath it, his silky shirt the color and pattern of a cumulus-filled sky. Already she had noted the length and the sun-flecked blondness of his hair, the etched-out quality of his profile. . . . But when he turned, the only thing apparent to her was Anson's resemblance to a dead marine named Jordan Burk, even though he was older than Jordan had lived to be. Ten or twelve years older, at the very least. Jordan Burk had died at twenty-four taking an amphibious tractor ashore at Betio, a tiny island near Tarawa Atoll in the Gilbert Islands. Nicholas Anson, however, had crow's-feet at the corners of his eyes and glints of silver in his sideburns. These things didn't matter much—the resemblance was still a heartbreaking one, and Marilyn found that she was staring at Anson like a starstruck teenager. She let the curtain fall.

This has happened before, she told herself. In a world of four billion people, over a period of thirty-five years, it isn't surprising that you should encounter two or more young men who look like each other. For God's sake, Odau, don't go to pieces over the sight of still another man who reminds you of Jordan—a stranger from Los Angeles who in just a couple of years is going to be old enough to be the *father* of your forever-twenty-four Jordan darling.

It's the season, Marilyn protested, answering her relentlessly rational self. It's especially cruel that this should happen now.

It happens all the time. You're just more susceptible at this time of year. Odau, you haven't outgrown what amounts to a basically childish syndrome, and it's beginning to look as if you never will.

Old enough in just a couple of years to be Jordan's father? He's old enough right now to be Jordan's and my child. *Our* child.

Marilyn could feel tears welling up from some ancient spring; susceptible, she had an unexpected mental glimpse of the upstairs bedroom in her Brookmist town house, the bedroom next to hers, the bedroom she had made a sort of shrine. In its corner, a white wicker bassinet—

That's enough, Odau!

"That's enough!" she said aloud, clenching a fist at her throat.

The curtain drew back, and she was again face to face with Terri Bready. "I'm sorry, Ms. Odau. You talkin' to me?"

"No, Terri. To myself."

"He's a neat fella, really. Says he played drums for a rock band in Haight-Ashbury once upon a time. Says he was one of the original hippies. He's been straight since Nixon resigned, he says—his faith was restored. . . . Whyn't you talk to him, Ms. Odau? Even if you don't place an order with him, he's an interesting person to talk to. Really. He says he's heard good things about you from the other managers on the mall. He thinks our place is just the sort of place to handle one of his products."

"I bet he does. You certainly got a lot out of him in the short time he's been here."

"Yeah. All my doing, too. I thought maybe, being from Los Angeles, he knew somebody in Hollywood. I sorta told him I was a drama major. You know. . . . Let me send him back, okay?"

"All right. Send him back."

Marilyn sat down at her desk. Almost immediately Nicholas Anson came through the curtain with his samples case. They exchanged polite greetings, and she was struck again by his resemblance to Jordan. Seeing him at close range didn't dispel the illusion of an older Jordan Burk, but intensified it. This was the reverse of the way it usually happened, and when he put his case on her desk, she had to resist a real urge to reach out and touch his hand.

No wonder Terri had been snowed. Anson's presence was a mature and amiable one, faintly sexual in its undertones. Haight-Ashbury? No, that was wrong. Marilyn couldn't imagine this man among Jesus freaks and flower children, begging small change, the ankles of his grubby blue jeans frayed above a pair of falling-to-pieces sandals. Altogether wrong. Thank God, he had found his calling. He seemed born to move gracefully among boutiques and front-line department stores, making recommendations, giving of his smile. Was it possible that he had once turned his gaunt young face upward to the beacon of a strobe and howled his heart out to the rhythms of his own acid drumming? Probably. A great many things had changed since the sixties. . . .

"You're quite far afield," Marilyn said, to be saying something. "I've never heard of Latter-Day Novelties."

"It's a consortium of independent business people and manufacturers," Anson responded. "We're trying to expand our markets, go nation-wide. I'm not really used to acting as—what does it say on my card?—a sales representative. My first job—my real love—is being a products consultant. If your company is a novelties company, it has to have novelties, products that are new and appealing and unusual. Prior to coming East on this trip, my principal responsibility was making product suggestions. That seems to be my forte, and that's what I really like to do."

"Well, I think you'll be an able enough sales representative too."

"Thank you, Miss Odau. Still, I always feel a little hesitation opening this case and going to bat for what it contains. There's an element of egotism in going out and pushing your own brainchildren on the world."

"There's an element of egotism in almost every human enterprise. I don't think you need to worry."

"I suppose not."

"Why don't you show me what you have?"

Nicholas Anson undid the catches on his case. "I've only brought you a single product. It was my judgment you wouldn't be interested in celebrity T-shirts, cartoon-character paperweights—products of that nature. Have I judged fairly, Miss Odau?''

''We've sold novelty T-shirts and jerseys, Mr. Anson, but the others sound like gift-shop gim-cracks and we don't ordinarily stock that sort of thing. Clothing, cosmetics, toiletries, a few handicraft or decorator items if they correlate well with the Creightons' image of their franchise.''

''Okay.'' Anson removed a glossy cardboard package from his case and handed it across the desk to Marilyn. The kit was blue and white, with two triangular windows in the cardboard. Elegant longhand lettering on the package spelled out the words *Liquid Sheers*. Through one of the triangular windows she could see a bottle of mahogany-colored liquid, a small foil tray, and a short bristled brush with a grip on its back; through the other window was visible an array of colored pencils.

''Liquid Sheers?''

''Yes, ma'am. The idea struck me only about a month ago, I drew up a marketing prospectus, and the Latter-Day consortium rushed the concept into production so quickly that the product's already selling quite well in a number of West Coast boutiques. Speed is one of the keynotes of our company's early success. By cutting down the elapsed time between concept-visualization and actual manufacture of the product, we've been able to stay ahead of most of our California competitors. . . . If you like Liquid Sheers, we have the means to keep you in a good supply.''

Marilyn was reading the instructions on the kit. Her attention refused to stay fixed on the words and they kept slipping away from her. Anson's matter-of-fact monologue about his company's business practices didn't help her concentration. She gave up and set the package down.

''But what are . . . these Liquid Sheers?''

''They're a novel substitute—a decorator substitute—for pantyhose or nylons, Miss Odau. A woman mixes a small amount of the Liquid Sheer solution with water and rubs or paints it on her legs. The pencils can be used to draw on seams or color in some of the applicator designs we've included in the kit—butterflies, flowers, that sort of thing. Placement's up to the individual. . . . We have kits for dark-as well as light-complexioned women, and the application process takes much less time than you might expect. It's fun too, some of our products-testers have told us. Several boutiques have even reported increased sales of shorts, abbreviated skirts, and short culotte outfits once they began stocking Liquid Sheers. This, I ought to add, right here at the beginning of winter.'' Anson stopped, his spiel dutifully completed and his smile expectant.

"They're bottled stockings," Marilyn said.

"Yes, ma'am. I suppose you could phrase it that way."

"We sold something very like this at Satterwhite's during the war," Marilyn went on, careful not to look at Anson. "Without the design doodads and the different colored pencils, at any rate. Women painted on their stockings and set the seams with mascara pencils."

Anson laughed. "To tell you the truth, Miss Odau, that's where I got part of my original idea. I rummage old mail-order catalogues and the ads in old magazines. Of course, Liquid Sheers also derive a little from the bodypainting fad of the sixties—but in our advertising we plan to lay heavy stress on their affinity to the World War era."

"Why?"

"Nostalgia sells. Girls who don't know World War II from the Peloponnesian War—girls who've worn seamless stockings all their lives, if they've worn stockings at all—are painting on Liquid Sheers and setting grease-pencil seams because they've seen Lauren Bacall and Ann Sheridan in Bogart film revivals and it makes them feel vaguely heroic. It's amazing, Miss Odau. In the last few years we've had sales and entertainment booms featuring nostalgia for the twenties, the thirties, the fifties, and the sixties. The forties—if you except Bogart—have been pretty much bypassed, and Liquid Sheers purposely play to that era while recalling some of the art-deco creations of the Beatles period too."

Marilyn met Anson's gaze and refused to fall back from it. "Maybe the forties have been 'pretty much bypassed' because it's hard to recall World War II with unfettered joy."

"I don't really buy that," Anson replied, earnest and undismayed. "The twenties gave us Harding and Coolidge, the thirties the Great Depression, the fifties the Cold War, and the sixties Vietnam. There's no accounting what people are going to remember with fondness—but I can assure you that Liquid Sheers are doing well in California.''

Marilyn pushed her chair back on its coasters and stood up. "I sold bottled stockings, Mr. Anson. I painted them on my legs. You couldn't *pay* me to use a product like that again—even with colored pencils and butterflies thrown in gratis.''

Seemingly out of deference to her Anson also stood. "Oh, no, Miss Odau—I wouldn't expect you to. This is a product aimed at adolescent girls and post-adolescent young women. We fully realize it's a fad product. We expect booming sales for a year and then a rapid tapering off. But it won't matter— our overhead on Liquid Sheers is low and when sales have bottomed out we'll drop 'em and move on to something else. You understand the transience of items like this.''

"Mr. Anson, do you know why bottled stockings existed at all during the Second World War?''

"Yes, ma'am. There was a nylon shortage.''

"The nylon went into the war effort—parachutes, I don't know what else." She shook her head, trying to remember. "All I know is that you didn't see them as often as you'd been used to. They were an important commodity on the domestic black market, just like alcohol and gasoline and shoes.''

Anson's smile was sympathetic, but he seemed to know he was defeated. "I guess you're not interested in Liquid Sheers?''

"I don't see how I could have them on my shelves, Mr. Anson.''

He reached across her desk, picked up the kit he had given her, and dropped it in his samples case. When he snapped its lid down, the reports of the catches were like distant gunshot. "Maybe you'll let me try you with something else, another time.''

"You don't have anything else with you?''

"To tell you the truth, I was so certain you'd like these I didn't bring another product along. I've placed Liquid Sheers with another boutique on the first level, though, and sold a few things to gift and novelty stores. Not a complete loss, this trip.'' He paused at the curtain. ''Nice doing business with you, Miss Odau.''

''I'll walk you to the front.''

Together they strolled through an aisleway of clothes racks and toiletry shelves over a mulberry carpet. Jane and Terri were busy with customers. . . . *Why am I being so solicitous?* Marilyn asked herself. Anson didn't look a bit broken by her refusal, and Liquid Sheers were definitely offensive to her—she wanted nothing to do with them. Still, any rejection was an intimation of failure, and Marilyn knew how this young man must feel. It was a shame her visitor would have to plunge himself back into the mall's motivelessly surging bodies on a note, however small, of defeat. He would be lost to her, borne to oblivion on the tide. . . .

''I'm sorry, Jordan,'' she said. ''Please do try us again with something else.''

The man beside her flinched and cocked his head. ''You called me Jordan, Miss Odau.''

Marilyn covered the lower portion of her face with her hand. She spread her fingers and spoke through them. ''Forgive me.'' She dropped her hand. ''Actually, I'm surprised it didn't happen before now. You look very much like someone I once knew. The resemblance is uncanny.''

''You did say Jordan, didn't you?''

''Yes, I guess I did—that was his name.''

''Ah.'' Anson seemed on the verge of some further comment but all he came out with was, ''Goodbye, Miss Odau. Hope you have a good Christmas season,'' after which he set himself adrift and disappeared in the crowd.

The tinfoil decorations in the mall's central shaft were like columns of a strange scarlet coral, and Marilyn studied them intently until Terri Bready spoke her name and returned her to the present. She didn't leave the boutique until ten that evening.

Tuesday, ten minutes before noon.

He wore the same navy blue leisure jacket, with an open collar shirt of gentle beige and bold indigo. He carried no samples case, and speaking with Cissy Campbell and then Terri, he seemed from the vantage of Marilyn's office, her curtain partially drawn back, less certain of his ground. Marilyn knew a similar uncertainty—Anson's presence seemed ominous, a challenge. She put a hand to her hair, then rose and went through the shop to meet him.

"You didn't bring me something else to look at, did you?"

"No; no, I didn't." He revealed his empty hand. "I didn't come on business at all . . . unless . . ." He let his voice trail away. "You haven't changed your mind about Liquid Sheers, have you?"

This surprised her. Marilyn could hear the stiffness in her voice. "I'm afraid I haven't."

Anson waved a hand. "Please forget that. I shouldn't have brought it up—because I *didn't* come on business." He raised his palm, like a Boy Scout pledging his honor. "I was hoping you'd have lunch with me."

"Why?"

"Because you seem *simpático*—that's the Spanish word for the quality you have. And it would be nice to sit down and talk with someone congenial about something other than Latter-Day Novelties. I've been on the road a week."

Out of the corner of her eye she could see Terri Bready straining to interpret her response to this proposal. Cissy Campbell, Marilyn's black clerk, had stopped racking a new supply of puff-sleeved blouses, and Marilyn had a glimpse of orange eyeliner and iridescent lipstick—the girl's face was that of an alert and self-confident panther.

"I don't usually eat lunch, Mr. Anson."

"Make an exception today. Not a word about business, I promise you."

"Go with him," Terri urged from the cash computer. "Cissy and I can take care of things here, Ms. Odau." Then she chuckled.

"Excellent advice," Anson said. "If I were you, I'd take it."

"Okay," Marilyn agreed. "So long as we don't leave Summerstone and don't stay gone too long. Let me get my bag."

Inevitably, they ended up at the McDonald's downstairs—yellow and orange wall paneling, trash bins covered with wood-grained contact paper, rows of people six and seven deep at the shiny metal counters. Marilyn found a table for two and eased herself into one of the attached, scoop-shaped plastic chairs. It took Anson almost fifteen minutes to return with two cheeseburgers and a couple of soft-drinks, which he nearly spilled squeezing his way out of the crowd to their tiny table.

"Thank God for plastic tops. Is it always like this?"

"Worse at Christmas. Aren't there any McDonald's in Los Angeles?"

"Nothing but. But it's three whole weeks till Christmas. Have these people no piety?"

"None."

"It's the same in Los Angeles."

They ate. While they were eating, Anson asked that she use his first name and she in turn felt obligated to tell him hers. Now they were Marilyn and Nicholas, mother and son on an outing to McDonalds's. Except that his attention to her wasn't filial—it was warm and direct, with a wooer's deliberately restrained urgency. His manner reminded her again of Jordan Burk, and at one point she realized that she had heard nothing at all he'd said for the last several minutes. Listen to this man, she cautioned herself. Come back to the here and now. After that, she managed better.

He told her that he'd been born in the East, raised single-handedly by his mother until her remarriage in the late forties, and after his new family's removal to Encino, educated entirely on the West Coast. He told her of his abortive career as a rock drummer, his early resistance to the war in Southeast Asia, and his difficulties with the United States military.

"I had no direction at all until my thirty-second birthday, Marilyn. Then I discovered where my talent lay and I haven't looked back since. I tell you, if I had the sixties to do over again—well, I'd gladly do them. I'd finagle myself a place in an Army reserve unit, be a weekend soldier, and get right down to products-consulting on a full-time basis. If I'd done that in '65, I'd probably be retired by now."

"You have plenty of time. You're still young."

"I've just turned thirty-six."

"You look less."

"But not much. Thanks anyway, though—it's nice to hear."

"Did you fight in Vietnam?" Marilyn asked on impulse.

"I *went* there in '68. I don't think you could say I fought. I was one of the oldest enlisted men in my unit, with a history of anti-war activity and draft-card burning. I'm going to tell you something, though—once I got home and turned myself around, I wept when Saigon fell. That's the truth—I wept. Saigon was some city, if you looked at it right."

Mentally counting back, Marilyn realized that Nicholas was the right age to be her and Jordan's child. Exactly. In early December, 1942, she and Jordan had made their last farewells in the little house on Greenbriar Street. . . . She attached no shame to his memory, had no regrets about it. The shame had come twenty-six years later—the same year, strangely enough, that Nicholas Anson was reluctantly pulling a tour of duty in Vietnam. The white wicker bassinet in her upstairs shrine was a perpetual reminder of this shame, of her secret monstrousness, and yet she could not dispose of the evidence branding her a freak, if only to herself, for the simple reason that she loved it. She loved it because she had once loved Jordan Burk. . . . Marilyn put her cheeseburger down. There was no way—no way at all—that she was going to be able to finish eating.

"Are you all right?"

"I need to get back to the boutique."

"Let me take you out to dinner this evening. You can hardly call this a relaxed and unhurried get-together. I'd like to take you somewhere nice. I'd like to buy you a snifter of brandy and a nice rare cut of prime rib."

"Why?"

"You use that word like a stiletto, Marilyn. Why not?"

"Because I don't go out. My work keeps me busy. And there's a discrepancy in our ages that embarrasses me. I don't know whether your motives are commercial, innocently social, or . . . Go ahead, then—laugh." She was wadding up the wrapper from her cheeseburger, squeezing the paper tighter and tighter, and she could tell that her face was crimsoning.

"I'm not laughing," Nicholas said. "I don't either—know

what my motives are, I mean. Except that they're not blame-worthy or unnatural.''

"I'd better go." She eased herself out of the underslung plastic chair and draped her bag over her shoulder.

"When can I see you?" His eyes were full of remonstrance and appeal. "The company wants me here another week or so—problems with a delivery. I don't know anyone in this city. I'm living out of a suitcase. And I've never in my life been married, if that's worrying you."

"Maybe I should worry because you haven't."

Nicholas smiled at her, a self-effacing charmer's smile. "When?"

"Wednesdays and Sundays are the only nights I don't work. And tomorrow's Wednesday."

"What time?"

"I don't know," she said distractedly. "Call me. Or come by the boutique. Or don't. Whatever you want."

She stepped into the aisle beside their table and quickly worked her way through the crowd to the capsule-lift outside McDonald's. Her thoughts were jumbled, and she hoped fee-bly—willing the hope—that Nicholas Anson would simply disappear from her life.

The next morning, before any customers had been admit-ted to the mall, Marilyn Odau went down to Summerstone's first level and walked past the boutique whose owner had elected to sell Nicholas' Liquid Sheers. The kits were on display in two colorful pyramids just inside the shop's en-trance.

That afternoon a leggy, dark-haired girl came into Creigh-ton's Corner to browse, and when she let her fur-trimmed coat fall open Marilyn saw a small magenta rose above her right knee. The girl's winter tan had been rubbed or brushed on, and there were magenta seams going up the backs of her legs. Marilyn didn't like the effect, but she understood that others might not find it unattractive.

At six o'clock Nicholas Anson showed up in sports clothes and an expensive deerskin coat. Jane Sidney and Cissy Campbell left, and Marilyn had a mall attendant draw the shop's movable grating across its entrance. Despite the early

Wednesday closing time, people were still milling about as shopkeepers transacted last-minute business or sought to shoo away their last heel-dragging customers. This was the last Wednesday evening before Christmas that Summerstone would be closed.

Marilyn began walking, and Nicholas fell in beside her like an assigned escort at a military ball. "Did you think I wasn't coming?"

"I didn't know. What now?"

"Dinner."

"I'd like to go home first. To freshen up."

"I'll drive you."

"I have a car."

"Lock it and let it sit. This place is about as well guarded as Fort Knox. I've rented a car from the service at the airport."

Marilyn didn't want to see Nicholas Anson's rental car. "Let *yours* sit. You can drive me home in mine." He started to protest. "It's either that or an early goodbye. I worry about my car."

So he drove her to Brookmist in her '68 Nova. The perimeter highway was yellow-grey under its ghostly lamps and the traffic was bewilderingly swift. Twilight had already edged over into evening—a dreary winter evening. The Nova's gears rattled even when Nicholas wasn't touching the stick on the steering column.

"I'm surprised you don't have a newer car. Surely you can afford one."

"I could, I suppose, but I like this one. It's easy on gas, and during the oil embargo I felt quite smart. . . . What's the matter with it?"

"Nothing. It's just that I'd imagined you in a bigger or a sportier one. I shouldn't have said anything." He banged his temple with the heel of his right hand. "I'm sorry, Marilyn."

"Don't apologize. Jane Sidney asked me the same thing one day. I told her that my parents were dirt-poor during the Depression and that as soon as I was able to sock any money away for them, that's what I did. It's a habit I haven't been able to break—even today, with my family dead and no real financial worries."

They rode in silence beneath the haloed lamps on the overpass and the looming grey shadow of Satterwhite's.

"A girl came into the boutique this afternoon wearing Liquid Sheers," Marilyn said. "It does seem your product's selling."

"Hooo," Nicholas replied, laughing mirthlessly. "Just remember that *I* didn't bring that up, okay?"

They left the expressway and drove down several elm-lined residential streets. The Brookmist complex of town houses came into the Nova's headlights like a photographic image emerging from a wash of chemicals, everything gauzy and indistinct at first. Marilyn directed Nicholas to the community carport against a brick wall behind one of the rows of houses, and he parked the car. They walked hunch-shouldered in the cold to a tall redwood fence enclosing a concrete patio not much bigger than a phone booth. Marilyn pushed the gate aside, let the latch fall behind them, and put her key into the lock on the kitchen door. Two or three flower pots with drooping, unrecognizable plants in them sat on a peeling windowsill beside the door.

"I suppose you think I could afford a nicer place to live, too."

"No, but you do give yourself a long drive to work."

"This place is paid for, Nicholas. It's mine."

She left him sitting under a table lamp with several old copies of *McCall's* and *Cosmopolitan* in front of him on her stonework coffee table and went upstairs to change clothes. She came back down wearing a long-sleeved black jumpsuit with a peach-colored sweater and a single polished-stone pendant at her throat. The heat had kicked on, and the downstairs was cozily warm.

Nicholas stood up. "You've set things up so that I'm going to have to drive your car and you're going to have to navigate. I hope you'll let me buy the gas."

"Why couldn't I drive and you just sit back and enjoy the ride?" Her voice was tight again, with uneasiness and mild disdain. For a products consultant Nicholas didn't seem quite as imaginative as he ought. Liquid Sheers were a rip-off of an idea born out of necessity during World War II, and the "novelties" he'd mentioned in his spiel on Monday were for the most part variations on the standard fare of gift shops and bookstores. He wasn't even able to envision her doing the driving while he relaxed and played the role of a passenger. And *he* was the one who'd come to maturity during the sixties, that fabled decade of egalitarian upheaval and heightened social awareness. . . .

"The real point, Marilyn, is that I wanted to do something for *you*. But you've taken the evening out of my hands."

All right, she could see that. She relented. "Nicholas, I'm not trying to stage-manage this—this *date*, if that's what it is. I was surprised that you came by the shop. I wasn't ready. And I'm not ready to go out this evening, either—I'm cold and I'm tired. I have a pair of steaks and a bottle of cold duck in the refrigerator, and enough fixings for a salad. Let me make dinner."

"A *pair* of steaks?"

"There's a grocery store off the perimeter highway that stays open night and day. I stopped there last night after work."

"But you didn't think I'd come by today?"

"No. Not really. And despite buying the steaks, I'm not sure I really wanted you to. I know that sounds backwards somehow but it's the truth."

Nicholas ignored this. "But you'll have to cook. I wanted to spare you that. I wanted to do something *for* you."

"Spare me another trip down the highway in my car and the agony of waiting for service in one of this city's snooty night spots."

He gave in, and she felt kindlier toward him. They ate at the coffee table in the living room, sitting on the floor in their stocking feet and listening to an FM radio station. They talked cursorily about sports and politics and movies, which neither of them was particularly interested in anymore; and then, because they had both staked their lives to it, Marilyn lifted the taboo that Nicholas had promised to observe and they talked business. They didn't talk about Liquid Sheers or profit margins or tax shelters, they talked about the involvement of their feelings with what they were doing and the sense of satisfaction that they derived from their work. That was common ground, and the evening passed—as Jane Sidney might have put it—"like sixty."

They were finishing the bottle of cold duck. Nicholas shifted positions, catching his knees with his right arm and rocking back a little.

"Marilyn?"

"Mmm?"

"You would never have let me drive you over here if I hadn't reminded you of this fellow you once knew, would you? This fellow named Jordan? Tell me the truth. No bet-hedging."

Her uneasiness returned. "I don't know."

"Yes, you do. Your answer won't hurt my feelings. I'd like to think that now that you know me a little better my resemblance to this person doesn't matter anymore—that you like me for myself." He waited.

"Okay, then. You're right."

"I'm right," he echoed her dubiously.

"I wouldn't have let you bring me home if you hadn't looked like Jordan. But now that I know you a little better it doesn't make any difference."

Not much, Marilyn told herself. At least I've stopped putting you in a marine uniform and trimming back the hair over your ears. . . . She felt a quiet tenderness for both men, the dead Jordan and the boyish Nicholas Anson who in many ways seemed younger than Jordan ever had. . . . That's because Jordan was almost three years older than you, Odau, and Nicholas is almost twenty years younger. Think a little.

The young man who resembled Jordan Burk drained his glass and hoisted himself nimbly off the floor.

"I'm staying at the Holiday Inn near the airport," he said. "Let me call a cab so you won't have to get out again."

"Cabs aren't very good about answering night calls anymore. The drivers are afraid to come."

"I hate for you to have to drive me, Marilyn." His look was expectant, and she hated to disappoint him.

"Why don't you just spend the night here?" she said.

They went upstairs together, and she was careful to close the door to the bedroom containing the wicker bassinet before following him into her own. They undressed in the greenish light sifting through the curtains from the arc lamp in the elm trees. Her heart raced. Then his body covered its beating, and afterwards she lay staring wide-eyed and be-mused at her acoustic ceiling panels as he slept beside her with a hand on her hip. Then she fell asleep too, and woke when her sleeping mind noted that his hand was gone, and sat up to discover that Nicholas was no longer there. The wind in the leafless elms was making a noise like angry surf.

"Nick!" she called.

He didn't answer.

She swung her feet to the carpet, put on her gown, and found him standing in a pair of plaid boxer shorts beside the wicker bassinet. He had put on a desk lamp, and its glow made a pool of light that contained and illuminated every-thing in that corner of the room. There was no doubt that he had discovered the proof of her monstrousness there, even if he didn't know what it meant.

Instead of screaming or flying at him like a drunken doxy, she sank to the floor in the billow of her dressing gown, shamefully conscious of her restraint and too well satisfied by Nicholas' snooping to be shocked by it. If she hadn't wanted this to happen, she would never have let him come. Or she would have murdered Nicholas in the numb sleep of his fulfillment. Any number of things. But this was what she had wanted.

Confession and surcease.

"I was looking for the bathroom," Nicholas said. "I didn't know where the upstairs bathroom was. But when I saw the baby bed. . . . well, I didn't know why you'd have a baby bed and—" He broke off.

"Don't explain, Nicholas." She gave him an up-from-under look and wondered what her own appearance must sug-gest. Age, promiscuousness, dissolution? You grew old, that you couldn't stop. But the others . . . those were lies. She wanted confession and surcease, that was all, and he was too intent on the bassinet to escape giving them to her, too intent to see how downright *old* she could look at two in the morn-ing. Consumed by years. Consumed by that which life itself is nourished by. Just one of a world of consumer goods.

Nicholas lifted something from the bassinet. He held it

in the palm of one hand. "What is this?" he asked. "Marilyn . . . ?"

"Lithopedion," she said numbly. "The medical term is lithopedion. And lithopedion is the word I use when I want to put myself at a distance from it. With you here, that's what I think I want to do—put myself at a distance from it. I don't know. Do you understand?"

He stared at her blankly.

"It means stone child, Nicholas. I was delivered of it during the first week of December, 1968. A petrified fetus."

"Delivered of it?"

"That's wrong. I don't know why I say that. It was removed surgically, cut from my abdominal cavity. Lithopedion." Finally she began to cry. "Bring him to me."

The unfamiliar man across from her didn't move. He held the stone child questioningly on his naked palm.

"Damn it, Nicholas, I asked you to bring him to me! He's mine! Bring him here!"

She put a fist to one of her eyes and drew it away to find black makeup on the back of her hand. Anson brought her the lithopedion, and she cradled it against the flimsy bodice of her dressing gown. A male child, calcified, with a tiny hand to the side of its face and its eyes forever shut; a fossil before it had ever really begun to live.

"This is Jordan's son," Marilyn told Anson, who was still standing over her. "Jordan's and mine."

"But how could that be? He died during the Pacific campaign."

Marilyn took no notice of either the disbelief in Anson's voice or his unaccountable knowledge of the circumstances of Jordan's death. "We had a honeymoon in the house on Greenbriar while Maggie was off for Christmas," she said, cradling her son. "Then Jordan had to return to his Division. In late March of '43 I collapsed while I was clerking at Satterwhite's. I was stricken with terrible cramps and I collapsed. Maggie drove me home to Greenville, and I was treated for intestinal flu. That was the diagnosis of a local doctor. I was in a coma for a while. I had to be forcibly fed. But after a while I got well again, and the manager of the notions department at Satterwhite's let me have my job back. I came back to the city.''

"And twenty-five years later you had your baby?"

Even the nastiness that Anson imparted to this question failed to dismay her. "Yes. It was an ectopic pregnancy. The fetus grew not in my womb, you see, but in the right Fallopian tube—where there isn't much room for it to grow. I didn't know, I didn't suspect anything. There were no signs.''

"Until you collapsed at Satterwhite's?"

"Dr. Rule says that was the fetus bursting the Fallopian tube and escaping into the abdominal cavity. I didn't know. I was twenty years old. It was diagnosed as flu, and they put me to bed. I had a terrible time. I almost died. Later in the year, just before Thanksgiving, Jordan was killed at Tarawa, and I wished that I had died before him.''

"He never lived to see his son," Anson said bitterly.

"No. I was frightened of doctors. I'm still frightened by them. But in 1965 I went to work for the Creightons at Capitol Square, and when I began having severe pains in my side a couple of years later, they *made* me go to Dr. Rule. They told me I'd have to give up my job if I didn't go.'' Marilyn brought a fold of her nightgown around the calcified infant in her arms. "He discovered what was wrong. He delivered my baby. A lithopedion, he said. . . . Do you know that there've been only a few hundred of them in all recorded history? That makes me a freak, all my love at the beck and call of a father and son who'll never be able to hear me.'' Marilyn's shoulders began to heave and her mouth fell slack to let the sounds of her grief work clear. "A freak," she repeated, sobbing.

"No more a freak than that thing's father."

She caught Anson's tone and turned her eyes up to see his face through a blur of tears.

"Its father was Jordan Burk," Anson told her. "My father was Jordan Burk. He even went so far as to *marry* my mother, Miss Odau. But when he discovered she was pregnant, he deserted her to enlist in a Division bound for combat. And he came here first and found another pretty piece to slip it to before he left. You.''

"No," Marilyn said, her sobs suddenly stilled.

"Yes. My mother found Burk in this city and asked him to come back to her. He pleaded his overmastering love for another woman and refused. *I* was no enticement at all—I was an argument for remaining with you. Once during her futile visit here Burk took my mother into Satterwhite's by a side-street entrance and pointed you out to her from one of the mezzanines. The 'other woman' was prettier than she was, my mother said. She gave up and returned home. She permitted Burk to divorce her without alimony while he was in the Pacific. Don't ask me why. I don't know. Later my mother married a man named Samuel Anson and we moved with him to California. . . . That thing in your arms, Miss Odau, is my half-brother."

It was impossible to cry now. Marilyn could hear her voice growing shrill and accusative. "That's why you asked me to lunch yesterday, isn't it? And why you asked me to dinner this evening. A chance for revenge. A chance to defile a memory you could have easily left untouched." She slapped Anson across the thigh, harmlessly. "I didn't know anything about your mother or you! I never suspected and I wasn't responsible! I'm not that kind of freak! Why have you set out to destroy both me and one of the few things in my life I've truly been able to cherish? Why do you turn on me with a nasty 'truth' that doesn't have any significance for me and never can? What kind of vindictive jackal are you?"

Anson looked bewildered. He dropped onto his knees in front of her and tried to grip her shoulders. She shook his hands away.

"Marilyn, I'm sorry. I asked you to lunch because you called me Jordan, just like you let me drive you home because I resembled him."

" 'Marilyn?' What happened to 'Miss Odau?' "

"Never mind that." He tried to grip her shoulders again, and she shook him off. "Is my crime greater than yours? If I've spoiled your memory of the man who fathered me, it's because of the bitterness I've carried against him for as long as I can remember. My intention wasn't to hurt you. The 'other woman' that my mother always used to talk about, even after she married Anson, has always been an abstract to me. Revenge wasn't my motive. Curiosity, maybe. But not revenge. Please believe me.''

''You have no imagination, Nicholas.''

He looked at her searchingly. ''What does that mean?''

''It means that if you'd only . . . Why should I explain this to you? I want you to get dressed and take my car and drive back to your motel. You can drop it off at Summerstone tomorrow when you come to get your rental car. Give the keys to one of the girls, I don't want to see you.''

''Out into the cold, huh?''

''Please go, Nicholas. I might resort to screaming if you don't.''

He rose, went into the other room, and a few minutes later descended the carpeted stairs without saying a word. Marilyn heard the flaring of her Nova's engine and a faint grinding of gears. After that, she heard nothing but the wind in the skeletal elm trees.

Without rising from the floor in her second upstairs bedroom, she sang a lullaby to the fossil child in her arms. ''Dapples and greys,'' she crooned. ''Pintos and bays,/All the pretty little horses. . . .''

It was almost seven o'clock of the following evening before Anson returned her key case to Cissy Campbell at the cash computer up front. Marilyn didn't hear him or see him, and she was happy that she had been in her office when he at last came by. The episode was over. She hoped that she never saw Anson again, even if he was truly Jordan's son—and she believed that Anson understood her wishes.

Four hours later she pulled into the carport at Brookmist and crossed the parking lot to her small patio. The redwood gate was standing open. She pulled it shut behind her and set its latch. Then, inside, she felt briefly on the verge of swooning because there was an odor in the air like that of a man's cologne, a fragrance Anson had worn. For a moment she considered running back onto the patio and shouting for assistance. If Anson was upstairs waiting for her, she'd be a fool to go up there alone. She'd be a fool to go up there at all. Who could read the mind of an enigma like Anson?

He's not up there waiting for you, Marilyn told herself. He's been here and gone.

But why?

Your baby, Marilyn—see to your baby. Who knows what Anson might have done for spite? Who knows what sick destruction he might have—

"Oh, God!" Marilyn cried aloud. She ran up the stairs unmindful of the intensifying smell of cologne and threw the door to her second bedroom open. The wicker bassinet was not in its corner but in the very center of the room. She ran to it and clutched its side, very nearly tipping it over.

Unharmed, her and Jordan's tiny child lay on the satin bolster she had made for him.

Marilyn stood over the baby trying to catch her breath. Then she moved his bed back into the corner where it belonged. Not until the following morning was the smell of that musky cologne dissipated enough for her to forget that Anson—or someone—had been in her house. Because she had no evidence of theft, she rationalized that the odor had drifted into her apartment through the ventilation system from the town house next to hers.

The fact that the bassinet had been moved she conveniently put out of her mind.

Two weeks passed. Business at Creighton's Corner Boutique was brisk, and if Marilyn thought of Nicholas Anson at all, it was to console herself with the thought that by now he was back in Los Angeles. A continent away. But on the last weekend before Christmas, Jane Sidney told Marilyn that she thought she had seen Anson going through the center of one of Summerstone's largest department stores carrying his samples case. He looked tan and happy, Jane said.

"Good. But if he shows up here, I'm not in. If I'm waiting on a customer and he comes by, you or Terri will have to take over for me. Do you understand?"

"Yes, ma'am."

But later that afternoon the telephone in her office rang, and when she answered it, the voice coming through the receiver was Anson's.

"Don't hang up, Miss Odau. I knew you wouldn't see me in person, so I've been reduced to telephoning."

"What do you want?"

"Take a walk down the mall toward Davner's. Take a walk down the mall and meet me there."

"Why should I do that? I thought that's why you phoned."

Anson hung up.

You can wait forever, then, she told him. The phone didn't ring again, and she busied herself with the onionskin order forms and bills of lading. It was hard to pay attention to them, though.

At last she got up and told Jane she was going to stroll down the mall to stretch her legs. The crowd was shoulder to shoulder. She saw old people being pushed along in wheelchairs and, as if they were dogs or monkeys, small children in leather harnesses. There were girls whose legs had been painted with Liquid Sheers, and young men in Russian hats and low-heeled shoes who made no secret of their appreciation of these girls' legs. The benches lining the shaft at the center of the promenade were all occupied, and the people sitting on them looked fatigued and irritable.

A hundred or so yards ahead of her, in front of the jewelry store called Davner's, there was a Santa Claus and a live reindeer.

She kept walking.

An odd display caught Marilyn's eye. She did a double-take and halted amid the traffic surging in both directions around her.

"Hey," a man said. He shoved past.

The shop window to her right was lined with eight or ten chalk-white effigies not much longer than her hand. They were eyeless. A small light played on them like the revolving blue strobe on a police vehicle. A sign in the window said: *Stone Children for Christmas, from Latter-Day Novelties.* Marilyn put a hand to her mouth and made a gagging sound that no one else on the mall paid any mind. She spun around. It seemed that Summerstone itself was swaying under her. Across from the gift shop, on one of the display cases of the bookstore located there, were a dozen more of these minute statuettes. Tiny figures, tiny feet, tiny eyeless faces. She looked down the collapsing mall and saw still another window displaying replicas of her and Jordan's baby. And in the windows that they weren't displayed, they were endlessly reflected.

Tiny fingers, tiny feet, tiny eyeless faces.

"Anson!" Marilyn shouted hoarsely, trying to find something to hang on to. "Anson, God damn you! God *damn* you!" She rushed on the gift-shop window and broke it with her fists. Then, not knowing what else to do, she withdrew her hands—with their worn oxblood nail polish—and held them bleeding above her head. A woman screamed, and the crowd fell back from her aghast.

In front of Davner's, only three or four stores away now, Nicholas Anson was stroking the head of the live reindeer. When he saw Marilyn, he gave her a friendly boyish smile.

H. P. Lovecraft

THE RATS IN THE WALLS

As Barton L. St. Armand pointed out in his extraordinary study of Lovecraft (*The Roots of Horror*), although Lovecraft overtly rejected contemporary psychoanalytic theory, "The Rats in the Walls" is a masterpiece of psychological structure, precisely paralleling a famous dream of C. G. Jung. This is a compelling story of psychological devolution and, at the same time, one of the most unusual of haunted house stories. Only traces, herein, can one find of the cosmic Lovecraftian strain—and "The Rats in the Walls" is in structure, it seems to me, more comparable to M. R. James' "The Ash-Tree" than has been heretofore noted. In Lovecraft's own work this story is an interesting contrast to "The Shunned House," his other, and very different, house story in the antiquarian vein.

On July 16, 1923, I moved into Exham Priory after the last workman had finished his labours. The restoration had been a stupendous task, for little had remained of the deserted pile but a shell-like ruin; yet because it had been the seat of my ancestors I let no expense deter me. The place had not been inhabited since the reign of James the First, when a tragedy of intensely hideous, though largely unexplained, nature had struck down the master, five of his children, and several servants; and driven forth under a cloud of suspicion and terror the third son, my lineal progenitor and the only survivor of the abhorred line. With this sole heir denounced as a murderer, the estate had reverted to the crown, nor had the accused man made any attempt to exculpate himself or regain his property. Shaken by some horror greater than that of conscience or the law, and expressing only a frantic wish to exclude the ancient edifice from his sight and memory, Walter de la Poer, eleventh Baron Exham, fled to Virginia and there founded the family which by the next century had become known as Delapore.

Exham Priory had remained untenanted, though later allotted to the estates of the Norrys family and much studied because of its peculiarly composite architecture; an architecture involving Gothic towers resting on a Saxon or Romanesque substructure, whose foundation in turn was of a still earlier order or blend of orders—Roman, and even Druidic or native Cymric, if legends speak truly. This foundation was a very singular thing, being merged on one side with the solid limestone of the precipice from whose brink the priory overlooked a desolate valley three miles west of the village of Anchester. Architects and antiquarians loved to examine this strange relic of forgotten centuries, but the country folk hated it. They had hated it hundreds of years before, when my ancestors lived there, and they hated it now, with the moss and mould of abandonment on it. I had not been a day in Anchester before I knew I came of an accursed house. And this week workmen have blown up Exham Priory, and are busy obliterating the traces of its foundations.

The bare statistics of my ancestry I had always known, together with the fact that my first American forbear had come to the colonies under a strange cloud. Of details, however, I had been kept wholly ignorant through the policy of reticence always maintained by the Delapores. Unlike our planter neighbours, we seldom boasted of crusading ancestors or other mediaeval and Renaissance heroes; nor was any kind of tradition handed down except what may have been recorded in the sealed envelope left before the Civil War by every squire to his eldest son for posthumous opening. The glories we cherished were those achieved since the migration; the glories of a proud and honourable, if somewhat reserved and unsocial Virginia line.

During the war our fortunes were extinguished and our

whole existence changed by the burning of Carfax, our home on the banks of the James. My grandfather, advanced in years, had perished in that incendiary outrage, and with him the envelope that bound us all to the past. I can recall that fire today as I saw it then at the age of seven, with the Federal soldiers shouting, the women screaming, and the negroes howling and praying. My father was in the army, defending Richmond, and after many formalities my mother and I were passed through the lines to join him. When the war ended we all moved north, whence my mother had come; and I grew to manhood, middle age, and ultimate wealth as a stolid Yankee. Neither my father nor I ever knew what our hereditary envelope had contained, and as I merged into the greyness of Massachusetts business life I lost all interest in the mysteries which evidently lurked far back in my family tree. Had I suspected their nature, how gladly I would have left Exham Priory to its moss, bats, and cobwebs!

My father died in 1904, but without any message to leave to me, or to my only child, Alfred, a motherless boy of ten. It was this boy who reversed the order of family information; for although I could give him only jesting conjectures about the past, he wrote me of some very interesting ancestral legends when the late war took him to England in 1917 as an aviation officer. Apparently the Delapores had a colourful and perhaps sinister history, for a friend of my son's, Capt. Edward Norrys of the Royal Flying Corps, dwelt near the family seat at Anchester and related some peasant superstitions which few novelists could equal for wildness and incredibility. Norrys himself, of course, did not take them seriously; but they amused my son and made good material for his letters to me. It was this legendry which definitely turned my attention to my transatlantic heritage, and made me resolve to purchase and restore the family seat which Norrys shewed to Alfred in its picturesque desertion, and offered to get for him at a surprisingly reasonable figure, since his own uncle was the present owner.

I bought Exham Priory in 1918, but was almost immediately distracted from my plans of restoration by the return of my son as a maimed invalid. During the two years that he lived I thought of nothing but his care, having even placed my business under the direction of partners. In 1921, as I found myself bereaved and aimless, a retired manufacturer no longer young, I resolved to divert my remaining years with my new possession. Visiting Anchester in December, I was entertained by Capt. Norrys, a plump, amiable young man who had thought much of my son, and secured his assistance in gathering plans and anecdotes to guide in the coming restoration. Exham Priory itself I saw without emotion, a jumble of tottering mediaeval ruins covered with lichens and honeycombed with rooks' nests, perched perilously upon a precipice, and denuded of floors or other interior features save the stone walls of the separate towers.

As I gradually recovered the image of the edifice as it had been when my ancestors left it over three centuries before, I began to hire workmen for the reconstruction. In every case I was forced to go outside the immediate locality, for the Anchester villagers had an almost unbelievable fear and hatred of the place. This sentiment was so great that it was sometimes communicated to the outside labourers, causing numerous desertions; whilst its scope appeared to include both the priory and its ancient family.

My son had told me that he was somewhat avoided during his visits because he was a de la Poer, and I now found myself subtly ostracised for a like reason until I convinced the peasants how little I knew of my heritage. Even then they sullenly disliked me, so that I had to collect most of the village traditions through the mediation of Norrys. What the people could not forgive, perhaps, was that I had come to restore a symbol so abhorrent to them; for, rationally or not, they viewed Exham Priory as nothing less than a haunt of fiends and werewolves.

Piecing together the tales which Norrys collected for me, and supplementing them with the accounts of several savants who had studied the ruins, I deduced that Exham Priory stood on the site of a prehistoric temple; a Druidical or ante-Druidical thing which must have been contemporary with Stonehenge. That indescribable rites had been celebrated there, few doubted; and there were unpleasant tales of the transference of these rites into the Cybele-worship which the Romans had introduced. Inscriptions still visible in the sub-cellar bore such unmistakable letters as "DIV . . . OPS . . . MAGNA.MAT . . ." sign of the Magna Mater whose dark worship was once vainly forbidden to Roman citizens. Anchester had been the camp of the third Augustan legion, as many remains attest, and it was said that the temple of Cybele was splendid and thronged with worshippers who performed nameless ceremonies at the bidding of a Phrygian priest. Tales added that the fall of the old religion did not end the orgies at the temple, but that the priests lived on in the new faith without real change. Likewise was it said that the rites did not vanish with the Roman power, and that certain among the Saxons added to what remained of the temple, and gave it the essential outline it subsequently preserved, making it the centre of a cult feared through half the heptarchy. About 1000 A.D. the place is mentioned in a chronicle as being a substantial stone priory housing a strange and powerful monastic order and surrounded by extensive gardens which needed no walls to exclude a frightened populace. It was never destroyed by the Danes, though after the Norman Conquest it must have declined tremendously; since there was no impediment when Henry the Third granted the site to my ancestor, Gilbert de la Poer, First Baron Exham, in 1261.

Of my family before this date there is no evil report, but something strange must have happened then. In one chronicle there is a reference to a de la Poer as "cursed of God" in 1307, whilst village legendry had nothing but evil and frantic fear to tell of the castle that went up on the foundations of the old temple and priory. The fireside tales were of the most grisly description, all the ghastlier because of their frightened reticence and cloudy evasiveness. They represented my ancestors as a race of hereditary daemons beside whom Gilles de Retz and the Marquis de Sade would seem the veriest tyros, and hinted whisperingly at their responsibility for the occasional disappearances of villagers through several generations.

The worst characters, apparently, were the barons and their direct heirs; at least, most was whispered about these. If of healthier inclinations, it was said, an heir would early and mysteriously die to make way for another more typical scion. There seemed to be an inner cult in the family, presided over by the head of the house, and sometimes closed except to a few members. Temperament rather than ancestry was evidently the basis of this cult, for it was entered by several who married into the family. Lady Margaret Trevor from Cornwall, wife of Godfrey, the second son of the fifth baron, became a favourite bane of children all over the countryside, and the daemon heroine of a particularly horrible old ballad not yet extinct near the Welsh border. Preserved in balladry, too, though not illustrating the same point, is the hideous tale of Lady Mary de la Poer, who shortly after her marriage to the Earl of Shrewsfield was killed by him and his mother, both of the slayers being absolved and blessed by the priest to whom they confessed what they dared not repeat to the world.

These myths and ballads, typical as they were of crude superstition, repelled me greatly. Their persistence, and their application to so long a line of my ancestors, were especially annoying; whilst the imputations of monstrous habits proved unpleasantly reminiscent of the one known scandal of my immediate forbears—the case of my cousin, young Randolph Delapore of Carfax, who went among the negroes and became a voodoo priest after he returned from the Mexican War.

I was much less disturbed by the vaguer tales of wails and howlings in the barren, windswept valley beneath the limestone cliff; of the graveyard stenches after the spring rains; of the floundering, squealing white thing on which Sir John Clave's horse had trod one night in a lonely field; and of the servant who had gone mad at what he saw in the priory in the full light of day. These things were hackneyed spectral lore, and I was at that time a pronounced sceptic. The accounts of vanished peasants were less to be dismissed, though not especially significant in view of mediaeval custom. Prying curiosity meant death, and more than one severed head had been publicly shewn on the bastions—now effaced—around Exham Priory.

A few of the tales were exceedingly picturesque, and made me wish I had learnt more of comparative mythology in my youth. There was, for instance, the belief that a legion of bat-winged devils kept Witches' Sabbath each night at the pri-

ory—a legion whose sustenance might explain the dispropor-
tionate abundance of coarse vegetables harvested in the vast
gardens. And, most vivid of all, there was the dramatic epic
of the rats—the scampering army of obscene vermin which
had burst forth from the castle three months after the tragedy
that doomed it to desertion—the lean, filthy, ravenous army
which had swept all before it and devoured fowl, cats, dogs,
hogs, sheep, and even two hapless human beings before its
fury was spent. Around that unforgettable rodent army a
whole separate cycle of myths revolves, for it scattered among
the village homes and brought curses and horrors in its train.

Such was the lore that assailed me as I pushed to completion, with an elderly obstinacy, the work of restoring my ancestral home. It must not be imagined for a moment that
these tales formed my principal psychological environment.
On the other hand, I was constantly praised and encouraged
by Capt. Norrys and the antiquarians who surrounded and
aided me. When the task was done, over two years after its
commencement, I viewed the great rooms, wainscotted walls,
vaulted ceilings, mullioned windows, and broad staircases
with a pride which fully compensated for the prodigious expense of the restoration. Every attribute of the Middle Ages
was cunningly reproduced, and the new parts blended perfectly with the original walls and foundations. The seat of
my fathers was complete, and I looked forward to redeeming
at last the local fame of the line which ended in me. I would
reside here permanently, and prove that a de la Poer (for I
had adopted again the original spelling of the name) need not
be a fiend. My comfort was perhaps augmented by the fact
that, although Exham Priory was mediaevally fitted, its interior was in truth wholly new and free from old vermin and
old ghosts alike.

As I have said, I moved in on July 16, 1923. My household
consisted of seven servants and nine cats, of which latter
species I am particularly fond. My eldest cat, "Nigger-Man",
was seven years old and had come with me from my home
in Bolton, Massachusetts; the others I had accumulated whilst
living with Capt. Norrys' family during the restoration of the
priory. For five days our routine proceeded with the utmost
placidity, my time being spent mostly in the codification of

old family data. I had now obtained some very circumstantial accounts of the final tragedy and flight of Walter de la Poer, which I conceived to be the probable contents of the hereditary paper lost in the fire at Carfax. It appeared that my ancestor was accused with much reason of having killed all the other members of his household, except four servant confederates, in their sleep, about two weeks after a shocking discovery which changed his whole demeanour, but which, except by implication, he disclosed to no one save perhaps the servants who assisted him and afterward fled beyond reach.

This deliberate slaughter, which included a father, three brothers, and two sisters, was largely condoned by the villagers, and so slackly treated by the law that its perpetrator escaped honoured, unharmed, and undisguised to Virginia; the general whispered sentiment being that he had purged the land of an immemorial curse. What discovery had prompted an act so terrible, I could scarcely even conjecture. Walter de la Poer must have known for years the sinister tales about his family, so that this material could have given him no fresh impulse. Had he, then, witnessed some appalling ancient rite, or stumbled upon some frightful and revealing symbol in the priory or its vicinity? He was reputed to have been a shy, gentle youth in England. In Virginia he seemed not so much hard or bitter as harassed and apprehensive. He was spoken of in the diary of another gentleman-adventurer, Francis Harley of Bellview, as a man of unexampled justice, honour, and delicacy.

On July 22 occurred the first incident which, though lightly dismissed at the time, takes on a preternatural significance in relation to later events. It was so simple as to be almost negligible, and could not possibly have been noticed under the circumstances; for it must be recalled that since I was in a building practically fresh and new except for the walls, and surrounded by a well-balanced staff of servitors, apprehension would have been absurd despite the locality. What I afterward remembered is merely this—that my old black cat, whose moods I know so well, was undoubtedly alert and anxious to an extent wholly out of keeping with his natural character. He roved from room to room, restless and disturbed, and sniffed constantly about the walls which formed part of the old Gothic structure. I realize how trite this sounds—like the inevitable dog in the ghost story, which always growls before his master sees the sheeted figure—yet I cannot consistently suppress it.

The following day a servant complained of restlessness among all the cats in the house. He came to me in my study, a lofty west room on the second story, with groined arches, black oak panelling, and a triple Gothic window overlooking the limestone cliff and desolate valley; and even as he spoke I saw the jetty form of Nigger-Man creeping along the west wall and scratching at the new panels which overlaid the ancient stone. I told the man that there must be some singular odour or emanation from the old stonework, imperceptible to human senses, but affecting the delicate organs of cats even through the new woodwork. This I truly believed, and when the fellow suggested the presence of mice or rats, I mentioned that there had been no rats there for three hundred years, and that even the field mice of the surrounding country could hardly be found in these high walls, where they had never been known to stray. That afternoon I called on Capt. Norrys, and he assured me that it would be quite incredible for field mice to infest the priory in such a sudden and unprecedented fashion.

That night, dispensing as usual with a valet, I retired in the west tower chamber which I had chosen as my own, reached from the study by a stone staircase and short gallery —the former partly ancient, the latter entirely restored. This room was circular, very high, and without wainscotting, being hung with arras which I had myself chosen in London. Seeing that Nigger-Man was with me, I shut the heavy Gothic door and retired by the light of the electric bulbs which so cleverly counterfeited candles, finally switching off the light and sinking on the carved and canopied four-poster, with the venerable cat in his accustomed place across my feet. I did not draw the curtains, but gazed out at the narrow north window which I faced. There was a suspicion of aurora in the sky, and the delicate traceries of the window were pleasantly silhouetted.

At some time I must have fallen quietly asleep, for I recall a distinct sense of leaving strange dreams, when the cat started violently from his placid position. I saw him in the faint auroral glow, head strained forward, fore feet on my ankles, and hind feet stretched behind. He was looking intensely at a point on the wall somewhat west of the window, a point which to my eye had nothing to mark it, but toward which all my attention was now directed. And as I watched, I knew that Nigger-Man was not vainly excited. Whether the arras actually moved I cannot say. I think it did, very slightly. But what I can swear to is that behind it I heard a low, distinct scurrying as of rats or mice. In a moment the cat had jumped bodily on the screening tapestry, bringing the affected section to the floor with his weight, and exposing a damp, ancient wall of stone; patched here and there by the restorers, and devoid of any trace of rodent prowlers. Nigger-Man raced up and down the floor by this part of the wall, clawing the fallen arras and seemingly trying at times to insert a paw between the wall and the oaken floor. He found nothing, and after a time returned wearily to his place across my feet. I had not moved, but I did not sleep again that night.

In the morning I questioned all the servants, and found that none of them had noticed anything unusual, save that the cook remembered the actions of a cat which had rested on her windowsill. This cat had howled at some unknown hour of the night, awaking the cook in time for her to see him dart purposefully out of the open door down the stairs. I drowsed away the noontime, and in the afternoon called again on Capt. Norrys, who became exceedingly interested in what I told him. The odd incidents—so slight yet so curious—appealed to his sense of the picturesque, and elicited from him a number of reminiscences of local ghostly lore. We were genuinely perplexed at the presence of rats, and Norrys lent me some traps and Paris green, which I had the servants place in strategic localities when I returned.

I retired early, being very sleepy, but was harassed by dreams of the most horrible sort. I seemed to be looking down from an immense height upon a twilit grotto, knee-deep with filth, where a white-bearded daemon swineherd drove about with his staff a flock of fungous, flabby beasts whose appearance filled me with unutterable loathing. Then, as the swineherd paused and nodded over his task, a mighty swarm of rats rained down on the stinking abyss and fell to devouring beasts and man alike.

From this terrific vision I was abruptly awaked by the motions of Nigger-Man, who had been sleeping as usual across my feet. This time I did not have to question the source of his snarls and hisses, and of the fear which made him sink his claws into my ankle, unconscious of their effect; for on every side of the chamber the walls were alive with nauseous sound—the verminous slithering of ravenous, gigantic rats. There was now no aurora to shew the state of the arras—the fallen section of which had been replaced—but I was not too frightened to switch on the light.

As the bulbs leapt into radiance I saw a hideous shaking all over the tapestry, causing the somewhat peculiar designs to execute a singular dance of death. This motion disappeared almost at once, and the sound with it. Springing out of bed, I poked at the arras with the long handle of a warming-pan that rested near, and lifted one section to see what lay beneath. There was nothing but the patched stone wall, and even the cat had lost his tense realization of abnormal presences. When I examined the circular trap that had been placed in the room, I found all of the openings sprung, though no trace remained of what had been caught and had escaped.

Further sleep was out of the question, so, lighting a candle, I opened the door and went out in the gallery toward the stairs to my study, Nigger-Man following at my heels. Before we had reached the stone steps, however, the cat darted ahead of me and vanished down the ancient flight. As I descended the stairs myself, I became suddenly aware of sounds in the great room below; sounds of a nature which could not be mistaken. The oak-panelled walls were alive with rats, scampering and milling, whilst Nigger-Man was racing about with the fury of a baffled hunter. Reaching the bottom, I switched on the light, which did not this time cause the noise to subside. The rats continued their riot, stampeding with such force and distinctness that I could finally assign to their motions a definite direction. These creatures, in numbers apparently inexhaustible, were engaged in one stupendous migration from inconceivable heights to some depth conceivably, or inconceivably, below.

I now heard steps in the corridor, and in another moment two servants pushed open the massive door. They were searching the house for some unknown source of disturbance which had thrown all the cats into a snarling panic and caused them to plunge precipitately down several flights of stairs and squat, yowling, before the closed door to the sub-cellar. I asked them if they had heard the rats, but they replied in the negative. And when I turned to call their attention to the sounds in the panels, I realized that the noise had ceased. With the two men, I went down to the door of the sub-cellar, but found the cats already dispersed. Later I resolved to explore the crypt below, but for the present I merely made a round of the traps. All were sprung, yet all were tenantless. Satisfying myself that no one had heard the rats save the felines and me, I sat in my study till morning; thinking profoundly, and recalling every scrap of legend I had unearthed concerning the building I inhabited.

I slept some in the forenoon, leaning back in the one comfortable library chair which my mediaeval plan of furnishing could not banish. Later I telephoned to Capt. Norrys, who came over and helped me explore the sub-cellar. Absolutely nothing untoward was found, although we could not repress a thrill at the knowledge that this vault was built by Roman hands. Every low arch and massive pillar was Roman—not the debased Romanesque of the bungling Saxons, but the severe and harmonious classicism of the age of the Caesars; indeed, the walls bounded with inscriptions familiar to the antiquarians who had repeatedly explored the place—things like "P.GETAE.PROP . . . TEMP . . . DONA . . ." and "L.PRAEC . . . VS . . . PONTIFI . . . ATYS. . . ."

The reference to Atys made me shiver, for I had read Catullus and knew something of the hideous rites of the Eastern god, whose worship was so mixed with that of Cybele. Norrys and I, by the light of lanterns, tried to interpret the odd and nearly effaced designs on certain irregularly rectangular blocks of stone generally held to be altars, but could make nothing of them. We remembered that one pattern, a sort of rayed sun, was held by students to imply a non-Roman origin, suggesting that these altars had merely been adopted by the Roman priests from some older and perhaps aboriginal temple on the same site. On one of these blocks were some brown stains which made me wonder. The largest, in the center of the room, had certain features on the upper surface which indicated its connexion with fire—probably burnt offerings.

Such were the sights in that crypt before whose door the cats had howled, and where Norrys and I now determined to pass the night. Couches were brought down by the servants, who were told not to mind any nocturnal actions of the cats, and Nigger-Man was admitted as much for help as for companionship. We decided to keep the great oak door—a modern replica with slits for ventilation—tightly closed; and, with this attended to, we retired with lanterns still burning to await whatever might occur.

The vault was very deep in the foundations of the priory, and undoubtedly far down on the face of the beetling limestone cliff overlooking the waste valley. That it had been the goal of the scuffling and unexplainable rats I could not doubt, though why, I could not tell. As we lay there expectantly, I found my vigil occasionally mixed with half-formed dreams from which the uneasy motions of the cat across my feet would rouse me. These dreams were not wholesome, but horribly like the one I had had the night before. I saw again the twilit grotto, and the swineherd with his unmentionable fungous beasts wallowing in filth, and as I looked at these things they seemed nearer and more distinct—so distinct that I could almost observe their features. Then I did observe the flabby features of one of them—and awaked with such a scream that Nigger-Man started up, whilst Capt. Norrys, who had not slept, laughed considerably. Norrys might have laughed more—or perhaps less—had he known what it was that made me scream. But I did not remember myself till later. Ultimate horror often paralyses memory in a merciful way.

Norrys waked me when the phenomena began. Out of the same frightful dream I was called by his gentle shaking and his urging to listen to the cats. Indeed, there was much to listen to, for beyond the closed door at the head of the stone steps was a veritable nightmare of feline yelling and clawing, whilst Nigger-Man, unmindful of his kindred outside, was running excitedly around the bare stone walls, in which I heard the same babel of scurrying rats that had troubled me the night before.

An acute terror now rose within me, for here were anomalies which nothing normal could well explain. These rats, if not the creatures of a madness which I shared with the cats alone, must be burrowing and sliding in Roman walls I had thought to be of solid limestone blocks . . . unless perhaps the action of water through more than seventeen centuries had eaten winding tunnels which rodent bodies had worn clear and ample. . . . But even so, the spectral horror was no less; for if these were living vermin why did not Norrys hear their disgusting commotion? Why did he urge me to watch Nigger-Man and listen to the cats outside, and why did he guess wildly and vaguely at what could have aroused them?

By the time I had managed to tell him, as rationally as I could, what I thought I was hearing, my ears gave me the last fading impression of the scurrying; which had retreated *still downward*, far underneath this deepest of sub-cellars till it seemed as if the whole cliff below were riddled with questing rats. Norrys was not as skeptical as I had anticipated, but instead seemed profoundly moved. He motioned to me to notice that the cats at the door had ceased their clamour, as if giving up the rats for lost; whilst Nigger-Man had a burst of renewed restlessness, and was clawing frantically around the bottom of the large stone altar in the centre of the room, which was nearer Norrys' couch than mine.

My fear of the unknown was at this point very great. Something astounding had occurred, and I saw that Capt. Norrys, a younger, stouter, and presumably more naturally materialistic man, was affected fully as much as myself— perhaps because of his lifelong and intimate familiarity with local legend. We could for the moment do nothing but watch the old black cat as he pawed with decreasing fervour at the base of the altar, occasionally looking up and mewing to me in that persuasive manner which he used when he wished me to perform some favour for him.

Norrys now took a lantern close to the altar and examined the place where Nigger-Man was pawing; silently kneeling and scraping away the lichens of centuries which joined the massive pre-Roman block to the tessellated floor. He did not find anything, and was about to abandon his efforts when I noticed a trivial circumstance which made me shudder, even though it implied nothing more than I had already imagined. I told him of it, and we both looked at its almost imperceptible manifestation with the fixedness of fascinated discovery and acknowledgment. It was only this—that the flame of the lantern set down near the altar was slightly but certainly flickering from a draught of air which it had not before received, and which came indubitably from the crevice between floor and altar where Norrys was scraping away the lichens.

We spent the rest of the night in the brilliantly lighted study, nervously discussing what we should do next. The discovery that some vault deeper than the deepest known masonry of the Romans underlay this accursed pile—some vault unsuspected by the curious antiquarians of three centuries—would have been sufficient to excite us without any background of the sinister. As it was, the fascination became twofold; and we paused in doubt whether to abandon our search and quit the priory forever in superstitious caution, or to gratify our sense of adventure and brave whatever horrors might await us in the unknown depths. By morning we had compromised, and decided to go to London to gather a group of archaeologists and scientific men fit to cope with the mystery. It should be mentioned that before leaving the sub-cellar we had vainly tried to move the central altar which we now recognized as the gate to a new pit of nameless fear. What secret would open the gate, wiser men than we would have to find.

During many days in London Capt. Norrys and I presented our facts, conjectures, and legendary anecdotes to five eminent authorities, all men who could be trusted to respect any family disclosures which future explorations might develop. We found most of them little disposed to scoff, but instead intensely interested and sincerely sympathetic. It is hardly necessary to name them all, but I may say that they included Sir William Brinton, whose excavations in the Troad excited most of the world in their day. As we all took the train for Anchester I felt myself poised on the brink of frightful revelations, a sensation symbolized by the air of mourning among the many Americans at the unexpected death of the President on the other side of the world.

On the evening of August 7th we reached Exham Priory, where the servants assured me that nothing unusual had occurred. The cats, even old Nigger-Man, had been perfectly placid; and not a trap in the house had been sprung. We were to begin exploring on the following day, awaiting which I assigned well-appointed rooms to all my guests. I myself retired in my own tower chamber, with Nigger-Man across my feet. Sleep came quickly, but hideous dreams assailed me. There was a vision of a Roman feast like that of Trimalchio, with a horror in a covered platter. Then came that damnable, recurrent thing about the swineherd and his filthy drove in the twilit grotto. Yet when I awoke it was full daylight, with normal sounds in the house below. The rats, living or spectral, had not troubled me; and Nigger-Man was still quietly asleep. On going down, I found that the same tranquility had prevailed elsewhere; a condition which one of the assembled savants—a fellow named Thornton, devoted to the psychic—rather absurdly laid to the fact that I had now been shewn the thing which certain forces had wished to shew me.

All was now ready, and at 11 a.m. our entire group of seven men, bearing powerful electric searchlights and implements of excavation, went down to the sub-cellar and bolted the door behind us. Nigger-Man was with us, for the investigators found no occasion to despise his excitability, and were indeed anxious that he be present in case of obscure rodent manifestations. We noted the Roman inscriptions and unknown altar designs only briefly, for three of the savants had already seen them, and all knew their characteristics. Prime attention was paid to the momentous central altar, and within an hour Sir William Brinton had caused it to tilt backward, balanced by some unknown species of counterweight.

There now lay revealed such a horror as would have overwhelmed us had we not been prepared. Through a nearly square opening in the tiled floor, sprawling on a flight of stone steps so prodigiously worn that it was little more than an inclined plane at the centre, was a ghastly array of human or semi-human bones. Those which retained their collocation as skeletons shewed attitudes of panic fear, and over all were the marks of rodent gnawing. The skulls denoted nothing short of utter idiocy, cretinism, or primitive semi-apedom. Above the hellishly littered steps arched a descending passage seemingly chiselled from the solid rock, and conducting a current of air. This current was not a sudden and noxious rush as from a closed vault, but a cool breeze with something of freshness in it. We did not pause long, but shiveringly began to clear a passage down the steps. It was then that Sir William, examining the hewn walls, made the odd observation that the passage, according to the direction of the strokes, must have been chiselled *from beneath*.

I must be very deliberate now, and choose my words.

After ploughing down a few steps amidst the gnawed bones we saw that there was light ahead; not any mystic phosphorescence, but a filtered daylight which could not come except from unknown fissures in the cliff that overlooked the waste valley. That such fissures had escaped notice from outside was hardly remarkable, for not only is the valley wholly uninhabited, but the cliff is so high and beetling that only an aëronaut could study its face in detail. A few steps more, and our breaths were literally snatched from us by what we saw; so literally that Thornton, the psychic investigator, actually fainted in the arms of the dazed man who stood behind him. Norrys, his plump face utterly white and flabby, simply cried out inarticulately; whilst I think that what I did was to gasp or hiss, and cover my eyes. The man behind me—the only one of the party older than I—croaked the hackneyed "My God!" in the most cracked voice I ever heard. Of seven cultivated men, only Sir William Brinton retained his composure; a thing the more to his credit because he led the party and must have seen the sight first.

It was a twilit grotto of enormous height, stretching away farther than any eye could see; a subterraneous world of limitless mystery and horrible suggestion. There were buildings and other architectural remains—in one terrified glance I saw a weird pattern of tumuli, a savage circle of monoliths, a low-domed Roman ruin, a sprawling Saxon pile, and an early English edifice of wood—but all these were dwarfed by the ghoulish spectacle presented by the general surface of the ground. For yards about the steps extended an insane tangle of human bones, or bones at least as human as those on the steps. Like a foamy sea they stretched, some fallen apart, but others wholly or partly articulated as skeletons; these latter invariably in postures of daemoniac frenzy, either fighting off some menace or clutching other forms with cannibal intent.

When Dr. Trask, the anthropologist, stooped to classify the skulls, he found a degraded mixture which utterly baffled him. They were mostly lower than the Piltdown man in the scale of evolution, but in every case definitely human. Many were of higher grade, and a very few were the skulls of supremely and sensitively developed types. All the bones were gnawed, mostly by rats, but somewhat by others of the half-human drove. Mixed with them were many tiny bones of rats—fallen members of the lethal army which closed the ancient epic.

I wonder that any man among us lived and kept his sanity through that hideous day of discovery. Not Hoffmann or Huysmans could conceive a scene more wildly incredible, more frenetically repellent, or more Gothically grotesque than the twilit grotto through which we seven staggered; each stumbling on revelation after revelation, and trying to keep for the nonce from thinking of the events which must have taken place there three hundred, or a thousand, or two thousand, or ten thousand years ago. It was the antechamber of hell, and poor Thornton fainted again when Trask told him that some of the skeleton things must have descended as quadrupeds through the last twenty or more generations.

Horror piled on horror as we began to interpret the architectural remains. The quadruped things—with their occasional recruits from the biped class—had been kept in stone pens, out of which they must have broken in their last delirium of hunger or rat-fear. There had been great herds of them, evidently fattened on the coarse vegetables whose remains could be found as a sort of poisonous ensilage at the bottom of huge stone bins older than Rome. I knew now why my ancestors had had such excessive gardens—would to heaven I could forget! The purpose of the herds I did not have to ask.

Sir William, standing with his searchlight in the Roman ruin, translated aloud the most shocking ritual I have ever known; and told of the diet of the antediluvian cult which the priests of Cybele found and mingled with their own. Norrys, used as he was to the trenches, could not walk straight when he came out of the English building. It was a butcher shop and kitchen—he had expected that—but it was too much to see familiar English implements in such a place, and to read familiar English *graffiti* there, some as recent as 1610. I could not go in that building—that building whose daemon activities were stopped only by the dagger of my ancestor Walter de la Poer.

What I did venture to enter was the low Saxon building, whose oaken door had fallen, and there I found a terrible row of ten stone cells with rusty bars. Three had tenants, all skeletons of high grade, and on the bony forefinger of one I found a seal ring with my own coat-of-arms. Sir William found a vault with far older cells below the Roman chapel, but these cells were empty. Below them was a low crypt with cases of formally arranged bones, some of them bearing terrible parallel inscriptions carved in Latin, Greek, and the tongue of Phrygia. Meanwhile, Dr. Trask had opened one of the prehistoric tumuli, and brought to light skulls which were slightly more human than a gorilla's, and which bore indescribable ideographic carvings. Through all this horror my cat stalked unperturbed. Once I saw him monstrously perched atop a mountain of bones, and wondered at the secrets that might lie behind his yellow eyes.

Having grasped to some slight degree the frightful revelations of this twilit area—an area so hideously foreshadowed by my recurrent dream—we turned to that apparently boundless depth of midnight cavern where no ray of light from the cliff could penetrate. We shall never know what sightless Stygian worlds yawn beyond the little distance we went, for it was decided that such secrets are not good for mankind. But there was plenty to engross us close at hand, for we had not gone far before the searchlights shewed that accursed infinity of pits in which the rats had feasted, and whose sudden lack of replenishment had driven the ravenous rodent army first to turn on the living herds of starving things, and then to burst forth from the priory in that historic orgy of devastation which the peasants will never forget.

God! those carrion black pits of sawed, picked bones and opened skulls! Those nightmare chasms choked with the pithecanthropoid, Celtic, Roman, and English bones of countless unhallowed centuries! Some of them were full, and none can say how deep they had once been. Others were still bottomless to our searchlights, and peopled by unnamable fancies. What, I thought, of the hapless rats that stumbled into such traps amidst the blackness of their quests in this grisly Tartarus?

Once my foot slipped near a horribly yawning brink, and I had a moment of ecstatic fear. I must have been musing a long time, for I could not see any of the party but the plump Capt. Norrys. Then there came a sound from that inky, boundless, farther distance that I thought I knew; and I saw my old black cat dart past me like a winged Egyptian god, straight into the illimitable gulf of the unknown. But I was not far behind, for there was no doubt after another second. It was the eldritch scurrying of those fiend-born rats, always questing for new horrors, and determined to lead me on even unto those grinning caverns of earth's centre where Nyarlathotep, the mad faceless god, howls blindly in the darkness to the piping of two amorphous idiot flute-players.

My searchlight expired, but still I ran. I heard voices, and yowls, and echoes, but above all there gently rose that impious, insidious scurrying; gently rising, rising, as a stiff bloated corpse gently rises above an oily river that flows under endless onyx bridges to a black, putrid sea. Something bumped into me—something soft and plump. It must have been the rats; the viscous, gelatinous, ravenous army that feast on the dead and the living. . . . Why shouldn't rats eat a de la Poer as a de la Poer eats forbidden things? . . . The war ate my boy, damn them all . . . and the Yanks ate Carfax with flames and burnt Grandsire Delapore and the secret . . . No, no, I tell you, I am *not* that daemon swineherd in the twilit grotto! It was *not* Edward Norrys' fat face on that flabby, fungous thing! Who says I am a de la Poer? He lived, but my boy died! . . . Shall a Norrys hold the lands of a de la Poer? . . . It's voodoo, I tell you . . . that spotted snake . . . Curse you, Thornton, I'll teach you to faint at what my family do! . . . 'Sblood, thou stinkard, I'll learn ye how to gust . . . wolde ye swynke me thilke wys? . . . *Magna Mater! Magna Mater!* . . . *Atys* . . . *Dia ad aghaidh's ad aodann . . . agus bas dunach ort! Dhonas's dholas ort, agus leat-sa!* . . . *Ungl . . . ungl . . . rrrlh . . . chchch . . .*

That is what they say I said when they found me in the blackness after three hours; found me crouching in the blackness over the plump, half-eaten body of Capt. Norrys, with my own cat leaping and tearing at my throat. Now they have blown up Exham Priory, taken my Nigger-Man away from me, and shut me into this barred room at Hanwell with fearful whispers about my heredity and experiences. Thornton is in the next room, but they prevent me from talking to him. They are trying, too, to suppress most of the facts concerning the priory. When I speak of poor Norrys they accuse me of a hideous thing, but they must know that I did not do it. They must know it was the rats; the slithering, scurrying rats whose scampering will never let me sleep; the daemon rats that race behind the padding in this room and beckon me down to greater horrors than I have ever known; the rats they can never hear; the rats, the rats in the walls.

J. Sheridan Le Fanu

SCHALKEN THE PAINTER

At the historical moment when the short story and the horror story were being invented, Poe and Le Fanu introduced psychological metaphor into the center of concern in many of their major fictions, de-emphasizing the moral didacticism of, say, Dickens, and influencing the later development of all short fiction in English in the direction of psychological investigation. "Schalken the Painter" (1839) is an historical tale with quite modern concerns: an innocent woman is married to a supernatural monster and no one can do anything about it. This tale is a direct ancestor of Charlotte Perkins Gilman's masterpiece, "The Yellow Wallpaper," and the horror derives in part from the impotence of the good man and the irrelevance of virtue in the face of quotidian but extraordinary evil. Allegorical interpretation is not to the point. Le Fanu's fantastic world in "Schalken the Painter" has more in common with Kafka and Joseph Conrad than with his contemporaries.

"For he is not a man as I am that we should come together; neither is there any that might lay his hand upon us both. Let him, therefore, take his rod away from me, and let not his fear terrify me."

There exists, at this moment, in good preservation a re-markable work of Schalken's. The curious management of its lights constitutes, as usual in his pieces, the chief apparent merit of the picture. I say *apparent*, for in its subject, and not in its handling, however exquisite, consists its real value. The picture represents the interior of what might be a chamber in some antique religious building; and its foreground is occupied by a female figure, in a species of white robe, part of which is arranged so as to form a veil. The dress, however, is not that of any religious order. In her hand the figure bears a lamp, by which alone her figure and face are illuminated; and her features wear such an arch smile, as well becomes a pretty woman when practising some prankish roguery; in the background, and, excepting where the dim red light of an expiring fire serves to define the form, in total shadow, stands the figure of a man dressed in the old Flemish fashion, in an attitude of alarm, his hand being placed upon the hilt of his sword, which he appears to be in the act of drawing.

There are some pictures, which impress one, I know not how, with a conviction that they represent not the mere ideal shapes and combinations which have floated through the imagination of the artist, but scenes, faces, and situations which have actually existed. There is in that strange picture, something that stamps it as the representation of a reality.

And such in truth it is, for it faithfully records a remarkable and mysterious occurrence, and perpetuates, in the face of the female figure, which occupies the most prominent place in the design, an accurate portrait of Rose Velderkaust, the niece of Gerard Douw, the first, and I believe, the only love of Godfrey Schalken. My great grandfather knew the painter well; and from Schalken himself he learned the fearful story of the painting, and from him too he ultimately received the picture itself as a bequest. The story and the picture have become heirlooms in my family, and having described the latter, I shall, if you please, attempt to relate the tradition which has descended with the canvas.

There are few forms on which the mantle of romance hangs more ungracefully than upon that of the uncouth Schalken—the boorish but most cunning worker in oils, whose pieces delight the critics of our day almost as much as his manners disgusted the refined of his own; and yet this man, so rude, so dogged, so slovenly, in the midst of his celebrity, had in his obscure, but happier days, played the hero in a wild romance of mystery and passion.

When Schalken studied under the immortal Gerard Douw, he was a very young man; and in spite of his phlegmatic temperament, he at once fell over head and ears in love with the beautiful niece of his wealthy master. Rose Velderkaust was still younger than he, having not yet attained her seventeenth year, and, if tradition speaks truth, possessed all the soft and dimpling charms of the fair, light-haired Flemish maidens. The young painter loved honestly and fervently. His frank adoration was rewarded. He declared his love, and extracted a faltering confession in return. He was the happiest and proudest painter in all Christendom. But there was somewhat to dash his elation; he was poor and undistinguished. He dared not ask old Gerard for the hand of his sweet ward. He must first win a reputation and a competence.

There were, therefore, many dread uncertainties and cold days before him; he had to fight his way against sore odds. But he had won the heart of dear Rose Velderkaust, and that was half the battle. It is needless to say his exertions were redoubled, and his lasting celebrity proves that his industry was not unrewarded by success.

These ardent labours, and worse still, the hopes that elevated and beguiled them, were however, destined to experience a sudden interruption—of a character so strange and mysterious as to baffle all inquiry and to throw over the events themselves a shadow of preternatural horror.

Schalken had one evening outstayed all his fellow-pupils, and still pursued his work in the deserted room. As the daylight was fast falling, he laid aside his colours, and applied himself to the completion of a sketch on which he had expressed extraordinary pains. It was a religious composition, and represented the temptations of a pot-bellied Saint Anthony. The young artist, however destitute of elevation, had, nevertheless, discernment enough to be dissatisfied with his own work, and many were the patient erasures and improvements which saint and devil underwent, yet all in vain. The large, old-fashioned room was silent, and, with the exception of himself, quite emptied of its usual inmates. An hour had thus passed away, nearly two, without any improved result.

Daylight had already declined, and twilight was deepening into the darkness of night. The patience of the young painter was exhausted, and he stood before his unfinished production, angry and mortified, one hand buried in the folds of his long hair, and the other holding the piece of charcoal which had so ill-performed its office, and which he now rubbed, without much regard to the sable streaks it produced, with irritable pressure upon his ample Flemish inexpressibles. "Curse the subject!" said the young man aloud; "curse the picture, the devils, the saint—"

At this moment a short, sudden sniff uttered close behind him made the artist turn sharply round, and he now, for the first time, became aware that his labours had been overlooked by a stranger. Within about a yard and half, and rather behind him, there stood the figure of an elderly man in a cloak and broad-brimmed, conical hat; in his hand, which was protected with a heavy gauntlet-shaped glove, he carried a long ebony walking-stick, surmounted with what appeared, as it glittered dimly in the twilight, to be a massive head of gold, and upon his breast, through the folds of the cloak, there shone the links of a rich chain of the same metal. The room was so obscure that nothing further of the appearance of the figure could be ascertained, and his hat threw his features into profound shadow. It would not have been easy to conjecture the age of the intruder; but a quantity of dark hair escaping from beneath his sombre hat, as well as his firm and upright carriage served to indicate that his years could not yet exceed threescore, or thereabouts. There was an air of gravity and importance about the garb of the person, and something indescribably odd, I might say awful, in the perfect, stone-like stillness of the figure, that effectually checked the testy comment which had at once risen to the lips of the irritated artist. He, therefore, as soon as he had sufficiently recovered his surprise, asked the stranger, civilly, to be seated, and desired to know if he had any message to leave for his master.

"Tell Gerard Douw," said the unknown, without altering his attitude in the smallest degree, "that Minheer Vanderhausen, of Rotterdam, desires to speak with him on tomorrow evening at this hour, and if he please, in this room, upon matters of weight; that is all.''

The stranger, having finished this message, turned abruptly, and, with a quick, but silent step quitted the room, before Schalken had time to say a word in reply. The young man felt a curiosity to see in what direction the burgher of Rotterdam would turn, on quitting the *studio*, and for that purpose he went directly to the window which commanded the door. A lobby of considerable extent intervened between the inner door of the painter's room and the street entrance, so that Schalken occupied the post of observation before the old man could possibly have reached the street. He watched in vain, however. There was no other mode of exit. Had the queer old man vanished, or was he lurking about the recesses of the lobby for some sinister purpose? This last suggestion filled the mind of Schalken with a vague uneasiness, which was so unaccountably intense as to make him alike afraid to remain in the room alone, and reluctant to pass through the lobby. However, with an effort which appeared very disproportioned to the occasion, he summoned resolution to leave the room, and, having locked the door and thrust the key in his pocket, without looking to the right or left, he traversed the passage which so recently, perhaps still, contained the person of his mysterious visitant, scarcely venturing to breathe till he had arrived in the open street.

''Minheer Vanderhausen!'' said Gerard Douw within himself, as the appointed hour approached, ''Minheer Vanderhausen, of Rotterdam! I never heard of the man till yesterday. What can he want of me? A portrait, perhaps, to be painted; or a poor relation to be apprenticed; or a collection to be valued; or—pshaw! there's no one in Rotterdam to leave me a legacy. Well, whatever the business may be, we shall soon know it all.''

It was now the close of day, and again every easel, except that of Schalken, was deserted. Gerard Douw was pacing the apartment with the restless step of impatient expectation, sometimes pausing to glance over the work of one of his absent pupils, but more frequently placing himself at the window, from whence he might observe the passengers who threaded the obscure by-street in which his studio was placed.

"Said you not, Godfrey," exclaimed Douw, after a long and fruitful gaze from his post of observation, and turning to Schalken, "that the hour he appointed was about seven by the clock of the Stadhouse?"

"It had just told seven when I first saw him, sir," answered the student.

"The hour is close at hand, then," said the master, consulting a horologe as large and as round as an orange. "Minheer Vanderhausen from Rotterdam—is it not so?"

"Such was the name."

"And an elderly man, richly clad?" pursued Douw, musingly.

"As well as I might see," replied his pupil; "he could not be young, nor yet very old, neither; and his dress was rich and grave, as might become a citizen of wealth and consideration."

At this moment the sonorous boom of the Stadhouse clock told, stroke after stroke, the hour of seven; the eyes of both master and student were directed to the door; and it was not until the last peal of the bell had ceased to vibrate, that Douw exclaimed—

"So, so; we shall have his worship presently, that is, if he means to keep his hour; if not, you may wait for him, Godfrey, if you court his acquaintance. But what, after all, if it should prove but a mummery got up by Vankarp, or some such wag? I wish you had run all risks, and cudgelled the old burgomaster soundly. I'd wager a dozen of Rhenish, his worship would have unmasked, and pleaded old acquaintance in a trice."

"Here he comes, sir," said Schalken, in a low monitory tone; and instantly, upon turning towards the door, Gerard Douw observed the same figure which had, on the day before, so unexpectedly greeted his pupil Schalken.

There was something in the air of the figure which at once satisfied the painter that there was no masquerading in the case, and that he really stood in the presence of a man of worship; and so, without hesitation, he doffed his cap, and courteously saluting the stranger, requested him to be seated. The visitor waved his hand slightly, as if in acknowledgment of the courtesy, but remained standing.

"I have the honour to see Minheer Vanderhausen of Rotterdam?" said Gerard Douw.

"The same," was the laconic reply of his visitor.

"I understand your worship desires to speak with me," continued Douw, "and I am here by appointment to wait your commands."

"Is that a man of trust?" said Vanderhausen, turning towards Schalken, who stood at a little distance behind his master.

"Certainly," replied Gerard.

"Then let him take this box, and get the nearest jeweller or goldsmith to value its contents, and let him return hither with a certificate of the valuation."

At the same time, he placed a small case about nine inches square in the hands of Gerard Douw, who was as much amazed at its weight as at the strange abruptness with which it was handed to him. In accordance with the wishes of the stranger, he delivered it into the hands of Schalken, and repeating his direction, despatched him upon the mission.

Schalken disposed his precious charge securely beneath the folds of his cloak, and rapidly traversing two or three narrow streets, he stopped at a corner house, the lower part of which was then occupied by the shop of a Jewish goldsmith. He entered the shop, and calling the little Hebrew into the obscurity of its back recesses, he proceeded to lay before him Vanderhausen's casket. On being examined by the light of a lamp, it appeared entirely cased with lead, the outer surface of which was much scraped and soiled, and nearly white with age. This having been partially removed, there appeared beneath a box of some hard wood; which also they forced open and after the removal of two or three folds of linen, they discovered its contents to be a mass of golden ingots, closely packed, and, as the Jew declared, of the most perfect quality. Every ingot underwent the scrutiny of the little Jew, who seemed to feel an epicurean delight in touching and testing these morsels of the glorious metal; and each one of them was replaced in its berth with the exclamation: "*Mein Gott*, how very perfect! not one grain of alloy—beautiful, beautiful!" The task was at length finished, and the Jew certified under his hand the value of the ingots submitted to his examination, to amount to many thousand rix-dollars. With the desired document in his pocket, and the rich box of gold carefully pressed under his arm, and concealed by his cloak, he retraced his way, and entering the studio, found his master and the stranger in close conference. Schalken had no sooner left the room, in order to execute the commission he had taken in charge, than Vanderhausen addressed Gerard Douw in the following terms:—

"I cannot tarry with you tonight more than a few minutes, and so I shall shortly tell you the matter upon which I come. You visited the town of Rotterdam some four months ago, and then I saw in the church of St. Lawrence your niece, Rose Velderkaust. I desire to marry her; and if I satisfy you that I am wealthier than any husband you can dream of for her, I expect that you will forward my suit with your authority. If you approve my proposal, you must close with it here and now, for I cannot wait for calculations and delays."

Gerard Douw was hugely astonished by the nature of Minheer Vanderhausen's communication, but he did not venture to express surprise; for besides the motives supplied by prudence and politeness, the painter experienced a kind of chill and oppression like that which is said to intervene when one is placed in unconscious proximity with the object of a natural antipathy—an undefined but overpowering sensation, while standing in the presence of the eccentric stranger, which made him very unwilling to say anything which might reasonably offend him.

"I have no doubt," said Gerard, after two or three prefatory hems, "that the alliance which you propose would prove alike advantageous and honourable to my niece; but you must be aware that she has a will of her own, and may not acquiesce in what *we* may design for her advantage."

"Do not seek to deceive me, sir painter," said Vanderhausen; "you are her guardian—she is your ward—she is mine if *you* like to make her so."

The man of Rotterdam moved forward a little as he spoke, and Gerard Douw, he scarce knew why, inwardly prayed for the speedy return of Schalken.

"I desire," said the mysterious gentleman, "to place in your hands at once an evidence of my wealth, and a security for my liberal dealing with your niece. The lad will return in a minute or two with a sum in value five times the fortune which she has a right to expect from her husband. This shall lie in your hands, together with her dowry, and you may apply the united sum as suits her interest best; it shall be all exclusively hers while she lives: is that liberal?''

Douw assented, and inwardly acknowledged that fortune had been extraordinarily kind to his niece; the stranger, he thought, must be both wealthy and generous, and such an offer was not to be despised, though made by a humourist, and one of no very prepossessing presence. Rose had no very high pretensions for she had but a modest dowry, which she owed entirely to the generosity of her uncle; neither had she any right to raise exceptions on the score of birth, for her own origin was far from splendid, and as the other objections, Gerard resolved, and indeed, by the usages of the time, was warranted in resolving, not to listen to them for a moment.

"Sir," said he, addressing the stranger, "your offer is liberal, and whatever hesitation I may feel in closing with it immediately, arises solely from my not having the honour of knowing anything of your family or station. Upon these points you can, of course, satisfy me without difficulty?"

"As to my respectability," said the stranger, drily, "you must take that for granted at present; pester me with no inquiries; you can discover nothing more about me than I choose to make known. You shall have sufficient security for my respectability—my word, if you are honourable: if you are sordid, my gold."

"A testy old gentleman," thought Douw, "he must have his own way; but, all things considered, I am not justified to declining his offer. I will not pledge myself unnecessarily, however."

"You will not pledge yourself unnecessarily," said Vanderhausen, strangely uttering the very words which had just floated through the mind of his companion; "but you will do so if it *is* necessary, I presume; and I will show you that I consider it indispensable. If the gold I mean to leave in your hands satisfy you, and if you don't wish my proposal to be at once withdrawn, you must, before I leave this room, write your name to this engagement.''

Having thus spoken, he placed a paper in the hands of the master, the contents of which expressed an engagement entered into by Gerard Douw, to give to Wilken Vanderhausen of Rotterdam, in marriage, Rose Velderkaust, and so forth, within one week of the date thereof. While the painter was employed in reading this covenant, by the light of a twinkling oil lamp in the far wall of the room, Schalken, as we have stated, entered the studio, and having delivered the box and the valuation of the Jew, into the hands of the stranger, he was about to retire, when Vanderhausen called to him to wait; and, presenting the case and the certificate to Gerard Douw, he paused in silence until he had satisfied himself, by an inspection of both, respecting the value of the pledge left in his hands. At length he said—

"Are you content?''

The painter said he would fain have another day to consider.

"Not an hour,'' said the suitor, apathetically.

"Well then,'' said Douw, with a sore effort, "I *am* content, it is a bargain.''

"Then sign at once,'' said Vanderhausen, "for I am weary.''

At the same time he produced a small case of writing materials, and Gerard signed the important document.

"Let this youth witness the covenant,'' said the old man; and Godfrey Schalken unconsciously attested the instrument which for ever bereft him of his dear Rose Velderkaust.

The compact being thus completed, the strange visitor folded up the paper, and stowed it safely in an inner pocket.

"I will visit you tomorrow night at nine o'clock, at your own house, Gerard Douw, and will see the object of our contract;'' and so saying Wilken Vanderhausen moved stiffly, but rapidly, out of the room.

Schalken, eager to resolve his doubts, had placed himself by the window, in order to watch the street entrance; but the experiment served only to support his suspicions, for the old man did not issue from the door. This was *very* strange, odd, nay fearful. He and his master returned together, and talked but little on the way, for each had his own subjects of reflection, of anxiety, and of hope. Schalken, however, did not know the ruin which menaced his dearest projects.

Gerard Douw knew nothing of the attachment which had sprung up between his pupil and his niece; and even if he had, it is doubtful whether he would have regarded its existence as any serious obstruction to the wishes of Minheer Vanderhausen. Marriages were then and there matters of traffic and calculation; and it would have appeared as absurd in the eyes of the guardian to make a mutual attachment an essential element in a contract of the sort, as it would have been to draw up his bonds and receipts in the language of romance.

The painter, however, did not communicate to his niece the important step which he had taken in her behalf, a forebearance caused not by any anticipated opposition on her part, but solely by a ludicrous consciousness that if she were to ask him for a description of her destined bridegroom, he would be forced to confess that he had not once seen his face, and if called upon, would find it absolutely impossible to identify him. Upon the next day, Gerard Douw, after dinner, called his niece to him and having scanned her person with an air of satisfaction, he took her hand, and looking upon her pretty innocent face with a smile of kindness, he said:—

"Rose, my girl, that face of yours will make your fortune." Rose blushed and smiled. "Such faces and such tempers seldom go together, and when they do, the compound is a love charm, few heads or hearts can resist; trust me, you will soon be a bride, girl. But this is trifling, and I am pressed for time, so make ready the large room by eight o'clock tonight, and give directions for supper at nine. I expect a friend; and observe me, child, do you trick yourself out handsomely. I will not have him think us poor or sluttish."

With these words he left her, and took his way to the room in which his pupils worked.

When the evening closed in, Gerard called Schalken, who was about to take his departure to his own obscure and comfortless lodgings, and asked him to come home and sup with Rose and Vanderhausen. The invitation was, of course, ac-

cepted and Gerard Douw and his pupil soon found themselves
in the handsome and, even then, antique chamber, which had
been prepared for the reception of the stranger. A cheerful
wood fire blazed in the hearth, a little at one side of which
an old-fashioned table, which shone in the fire-light like bur-
nished gold, was awaiting the supper, for which preparations
were going forward; and ranged with exact regularity, stood
the tall-backed chairs, whose ungracefulness was more than
compensated by their comfort. The little party, consisting of
Rose, her uncle, and the artist, awaited the arrival of the
expected visitor with considerable impatience. Nine o'clock
at length came, and with it a summons at the street door,
which being speedily answered, was followed by a slow and
emphatic tread upon the staircase; the steps moved heavily
across the lobby, the door of the room in which the party we
have described were assembled slowly opened, and there entered a figure which startled, almost appalled, the phlegmatic
Dutchmen, and nearly made Rose scream with terror. It was
the form, and arrayed in the garb of Minheer Vanderhausen;
the air, the gait, the height were the same, but the features
had never been seen by any of the party before. The stranger
stopped at the door of the room, and displayed his form and
face completely. He wore a dark-coloured cloth cloak, which
was short and full, not falling quite to his knees; his legs
were cased in dark purple silk stockings, and his shoes were
adorned with roses of the same colour. The opening of the
cloak in front showed the under-suit to consist of some very
dark, perhaps sable material, and his hands were enclosed in
a pair of heavy leather gloves, which ran up considerably
above the wrist, in the manner of a gauntlet. In one hand he
carried his walking-stick and his hat, which he had removed,
and the other hung heavily by his side. A quantity of grizzled
hair descended in long tresses from his head, and rested upon
the plaits of a stiff ruff, which effectually concealed his neck.
So far all was well; but the face!—all the flesh of the face
was coloured with the bluish leaden hue, which is sometimes
produced by metallic medicines, administered in excessive
quantities; the eyes showed an undue proportion of muddy
white, and had a certain indefinable character of insanity; the
hue of the lips bearing the usual relation to that of the face,

was, consequently, nearly black; and the entire character of the face was sensual, malignant, and even satanic. It was remarkable that the worshipful stranger suffered as little as possible of his flesh to appear, and that during his visit he did not once remove his gloves. Having stood for some moments at the door, Gerard Douw at length found breath and collectedness to bid him welcome, and with a mute inclination of the head, the stranger stepped forward into the room. There was something indescribably odd, even horrible, about all his motions, something undefinable, that was unnatural, unhuman; it was as if the limbs were guided and directed by a spirit unused to the management of bodily machinery. The stranger spoke hardly at all during his visit, which did not exceed half an hour; and the host himself could scarcely muster courage enough to utter the few necessary salutations and courtesies; and, indeed, such was the nervous terror which the presence of Vanderhausen inspired, that very little would have made all his entertainers fly in downright panic from the room. They had not so far lost all self-possession, however, as to fail to observe two strange peculiarities of their visitor. During his stay his eyelids did not once close, or, indeed, move in the slightest degree; and farther, there was a deathlike stillness in his whole person, owing to the absence of the heaving motion of the chest, caused by the process of respiration. These two peculiarities, though when told they may appear trifling, produced a very striking and unpleasant effect when seen and observed. Vanderhausen at length relieved the painter of Leyden of his inauspicious presence; and with no trifling sense of relief the little party heard the street door close after him.

"Dear uncle," said Rose, "what a frightful man! I would not see him again for the wealth of the States."

"Tush, foolish girl," said Douw, whose sensations were anything but comfortable. "A man may be as ugly as the devil, and yet, if his heart and actions are good, he is worth all the pretty-faced perfumed puppies that walk the Mall. Rose, my girl, it is very true he has not thy pretty face, but I know him to be wealthy and liberal; and were he ten times more ugly, these two virtues would be enough to counterbalance all his deformity, and if not sufficient actually to alter the shape and hue of his features, at least enough to prevent one thinking them so much amiss."

"Do you know, uncle," said Rose, "when I saw him standing at the door, I could not get it out of my head that I saw the old painted wooden figure that used to frighten me so much in the Church of St. Laurence at Rotterdam."

Gerard laughed, though he could not help inwardly acknowledging the justness of the comparison. He was resolved, however, as far as he could, to check his niece's disposition to dilate upon the ugliness of her intended bridegroom, although he was not a little pleased, as well as puzzled, to observe that she appeared totally exempt from that mysterious dread of the stranger which, he could not disguise it from himself, considerably affected him, as also his pupil Godfrey Schalken.

Early on the next day there arrived, from various quarters of the town, rich presents of silk, velvets, jewellery, and so forth, for Rose; and also a packet directed to Gerard Douw, which on being opened, was found to contain a contract of marriage, formally drawn up, between Wilken Vanderhausen of the *Boom-quay*, in Rotterdam, and Rose Velderkaust of Leyden, niece to Gerard Douw, master in the art of painting, also of the same city; and containing engagements on the part of Vanderhausen to make settlements upon his bride, far more splendid than he had before led her guardian to believe likely, and which were to be secured to her use in the most unexceptionable manner possible—the money being placed in the hand of Gerard Douw himself.

I have no sentimental scenes to describe, no cruelty of guardians, no magnanimity of wards, no agonies, or transport of lovers. The record I have to make is one of sordidness, levity, and heartlessness. In less than a week after the first interview which we have just described, the contract of marriage was fulfilled, and Schalken saw the prize which he would have risked existence to secure, carried off in solemn pomp by his repulsive rival. For two or three days he absented himself from the school; he then returned and worked, if with less cheerfulness, with far more dogged resolution than before; the stimulus of love had given place to that of ambition. Months passed away, and, contrary to his expectation, and, indeed, to the direct promise of the parties, Gerard Douw heard nothing of his niece or her worshipful spouse. The interest of the money, which was to have been demanded in quarterly sums, lay unclaimed in his hands.

He began to grow extremely uneasy. Minheer Vanderhausen's direction in Rotterdam he was fully possessed of; after some irresolution he finally determined to journey thither—a trifling undertaking, and easily accomplished—and thus to satisfy himself of the safety and comfort of his ward, for whom he entertained an honest and strong affection. His search was in vain, however; no one in Rotterdam had ever heard of Minheer Vanderhausen. Gerard Douw left not a house in the Boom-quay untried, but all in vain. No one could give him any information whatever touching the object of his inquiry, and he was obliged to return to Leyden nothing wiser and far more anxious, than when he had left it.

On his arrival he hastened to the establishment from which Vanderhausen had hired the lumbering, though, considering the times, most luxurious vehicle, which the bridal party had employed to convey them to Rotterdam. From the driver of this machine he learned, that having proceeded by slow stages, they had late in the evening approached Rotterdam; but that before they entered the city, and while yet nearly a mile from it, a small party of men, soberly clad, and after the old fashion, with peaked beards and moustaches, standing in the centre of the road, obstructed the further progress of the carriage. The driver reined in his horses, much fearing, from the obscurity of the hour, and the loneliness, of the road, that some mischief was intended. His fears were, however, somewhat allayed by his observing that these strange men carried a large litter, of an antique shape, and which they immediately set down upon the pavement, whereupon the bridegroom, having opened the coach-door from within, descended, and having assisted his bride to do likewise, led her, weeping bitterly, and wringing her hands, to the litter, which they both entered. It was then raised by the men who surrounded it, and speedily carried towards the city, and before it had proceeded very far, the darkness concealed it from the view of the Dutch coachman. In the inside of the vehicle he found a purse, whose contents more than thrice paid the hire of the carriage and man. He saw and could tell nothing more of Minheer Vanderhausen and his beautiful lady.

This mystery was a source of profound anxiety and even grief to Gerard Douw. There was evidently fraud in the dealing of Vanderhausen with him, though for what purpose committed he could not imagine. He greatly doubted how far it was possible for a man possessing such a countenance to be anything but a villain, and every day that passed without his hearing from or of his niece, instead of inducing him to forget his fears, on the contrary tended more and more to aggravate them. The loss of her cheerful society tended also to depress his spirits; and in order to dispel the gloom, which often crept upon his mind after his daily occupations were over, he was wont frequently to ask Schalken to accompany him home, and share his otherwise solitary supper.

One evening, the painter and his pupil were sitting by the fire, having accomplished a comfortable meal, and had yielded to the silent and delicious melancholy of digestion, when their ruminations were disturbed by a loud sound at the street door, as if occasioned by some person rushing and scrambling vehemently against it. A domestic had run without delay to ascertain the cause of the disturbance, and they heard him twice or thrice interrogate the applicant for admission, but without eliciting any other answer but a sustained reiteration of sounds. They heard him then open the hall-door, and immediately there followed a light and rapid tread on the staircase. Schalken advanced towards the door. It opened before he reached it, and Rose rushed into the room. She looked wild, fierce and haggard with terror and exhaustion, but her dress surprised them as much as even her unexpected appearance. It consisted of a kind of white woollen wrapper, made close about the neck, and descending to the very ground. It was much deranged and travel-soiled. The poor creature had hardly entered the chamber when she fell senseless on the floor. With some difficulty they succeeded in reviving her, and on recovering her senses, she instantly exclaimed, in a tone of terror rather than mere impatience:—

"Wine! wine! quickly, or I'm lost!"

Astonished and almost scared at the strange agitation in which the call was made, they at once administered to her wishes, and she drank some wine with a haste and eagerness which surprised them. She had hardly swallowed it, when she exclaimed, with the same urgency:

"Food, for God's sake, food, at once, or I perish."

A considerable fragment of a roast joint was upon the table, and Schalken immediately began to cut some, but he was anticipated, for no sooner did she see it than she caught it, a more than mortal image of famine, and with her hands, and even with her teeth, she tore off the flesh, and swallowed it. When the paroxysm of hunger had been a little appeased, she appeared on a sudden overcome with shame, or it may have been that other more agitating thoughts overpowered and scared her, for she began to weep bitterly and to wring her hands.

"Oh, send for a minister of God," said she; "I am not safe till he comes; send for him speedily."

Gerard Douw despatched a messenger instantly, and prevailed on his niece to allow him to surrender his bed chamber to her use. He also persuaded her to retire to it at once to rest; her consent was extorted upon the condition that they would not leave her for a moment.

"Oh that the holy man were here," she said; "he can deliver me: the dead and the living can never be one: God has forbidden it."

With these mysterious words she surrendered herself to their guidance, and they proceeded to the chamber which Gerard Douw had assigned to her use.

"Do not, do not leave me for a moment," said she; "I am lost forever if you do."

Gerard Douw's chamber was approached through a spacious apartment, which they were now about to enter. He and Schalken each carried a candle, so that a sufficiency of light was cast upon all surrounding objects. They were now entering the large chamber, which as I have said, communicated with Douw's apartment, when Rose suddenly stopped, and, in a whisper which thrilled them both with horror, she said:—

"Oh, God! he is here! he is here! See, see! there he goes!"

She pointed towards the door of the inner room, and Schalken thought he saw a shadowy and ill-defined form gliding into that apartment. He drew his sword, and, raising the candle so as to throw its light with increased distinctness upon the objects in the room, he entered the chamber into which the shadow had glided. No figure was there—nothing but the furniture which belonged to the room, and yet he could not be deceived as to the fact that something had moved before them into the chamber. A sickening dread came upon him, and the cold perspiration broke out in heavy drops upon his forehead; nor was he more composed, when he heard the increased urgency and agony of entreaty, with which Rose implored them not to leave her for a moment.

"I saw him," said she; "he's here. I cannot be deceived; I know him; he's by me; he is with me; he's in the room. Then, for God's sake, as you would save me, do not stir from beside me."

They at length prevailed upon her to lie down upon the bed, where she continued to urge them to stay by her. She frequently uttered incoherent sentences, repeating, again and again, "the dead and the living cannot be one: God has forbidden it." And then again, "Rest to the wakeful—sleep to the sleep-walkers." These and such mysterious and broken sentences, she continued to utter until the clergyman arrived. Gerard Douw began to fear, naturally enough, that terror or ill-treatment, had unsettled the poor girl's intellect, and he half suspected, by the suddenness of her appearance, the unseasonableness of the hour, and above all, from the wildness and terror of her manner, that she had made her escape from some place of confinement for lunatics, and was in imminent fear of pursuit. He resolved to summon medical advice as soon as the mind of his niece had been in some measure set at rest by the offices of the clergyman whose attendance she had so earnestly desired; and until this object had been attained, he did not venture to put any questions to her, which might possibly, by reviving painful or horrible recollections, increase her agitation. The clergyman soon arrived—a man of ascetic countenance and venerable age—one whom Gerard Douw respected very much, forasmuch as he was a veteran polemic, though one perhaps more dreaded as a combatant than beloved as a Christian—of pure morality, subtle brain, and frozen heart. He entered the chamber which communicated with that in which Rose reclined and immediately on his arrival, she requested him to pray for her, as for one who lay in the hands of Satan, and who could hope for deliverance only from heaven.

That you may distinctly understand all the circumstances of the event which I am going to describe, it is necessary to state the relative position of the parties who were engaged in it. The old clergyman and Schalken were in the anteroom of which I have already spoken; Rose lay in the inner chamber, the door of which was open; and by the side of the bed, at her urgent desire, stood her guardian; a candle burned in the bedchamber, and three were lighted in the outer apartment. The old man now cleared his voice as if about to commence, but before he had time to begin, a sudden gust of air blew out the candle which served to illuminate the room in which the poor girl lay, and she, with hurried alarm, exclaimed:—

"Godfrey, bring in another candle; the darkness is unsafe."

Gerard Douw forgetting for the moment her repeated injunctions, in the immediate impulse, stepped from the bedchamber into the other, in order to supply what she desired.

"Oh God! do not go, dear uncle," shrieked the unhappy girl—and at the same time she sprung from the bed, and darted after him, in order, by her grasp, to detain him. But the warning came too late, for scarcely had he passed the threshold, and hardly had his niece had time to utter the startling exclamation, when the door which divided the two rooms closed violently after him, as if swung by a strong blast of wind. Schalken and he both rushed to the door, but their united and desperate efforts could not avail so much as to shake it. Shriek after shriek burst from the inner chamber, with all the piercing loudness of despairing terror. Schalken and Douw applied every nerve to force open the door; but all in vain. There was no sound of struggling from within, but the screams seemed to increase in loudness, and at the same time they heard the bolts of the latticed window withdrawn, and the window itself grated upon the sill as if thrown open. One *last* shriek, so long and piercing and agonized as to be scarcely human, swelled from the room, and suddenly there followed a death-like silence. A light step was heard crossing the floor, as if from the bed to the window; and almost at the same instant the door gave way, and, yielding to the pressure of the external applicants, nearly precipitated them into the room. It was empty. The window was open, and Schalken sprung to a chair and gazed out upon the street and canal below. He saw no form, but he saw, or thought he saw, the waters of the broad canal beneath settling ring after ring in heavy circles, as if a moment before disturbed by the submission of some ponderous body.

No trace of Rose was ever after found, nor was anything certain respecting her mysterious wooer discovered or even suspected—no clue whereby to trace the intricacies of the labyrinth and to arrive at its solution, presented itself. But an incident occurred, which, though it will not be received by our rational readers in lieu of evidence, produced nevertheless a strong and a lasting impression upon the mind of Schalken. Many years after the events which we have detailed, Schalken, then residing far away received an intimation of his father's death, and of his intended burial upon a fixed day in the church of Rotterdam. It was necessary that a very considerable journey should be performed by the funeral procession, which as it will be readily believed, was not very numerously attended. Schalken with difficulty arrived in Rotterdam late in the day upon which the funeral was appointed to take place. It had not then arrived. Evening closed in, and still it did not appear.

Schalken strolled down to the church; he found it open; notice of the arrival of the funeral had been given, and the vault in which the body was to be laid had been opened. The sexton, on seeing a well-dressed gentleman, whose object was to attend the expected obsequies, pacing the aisle of the church, hospitably invited him to share with him the comforts of a blazing fire, which, as was his custom in winter time upon such occasions, he had kindled in the hearth of a chamber in which he was accustomed to await the arrival of such grisly guests and which communicated, by a flight of steps, with the vault below. In this chamber, Schalken and his entertainer seated themselves; and the sexton, after some fruitless attempts to engage his guest in conversation, was obliged to apply himself to his tobacco-pipe and can, to solace his solitude. In spite of his grief and cares, the fatigues of a rapid journey of nearly forty hours gradually overcame the mind and body of Godfrey Schalken, and he sank into a deep sleep, from which he awakened by someone's shaking him gently by the shoulder. He first thought that the old sexton had called him, but *he* was no longer in the room. He roused himself, and as soon as he could clearly see what was around him, he perceived a female form, clothed in a kind of light robe of white, part of which was so disposed as to form a veil, and in her hand she carried a lamp. She was moving rather away from him, in the direction of the flight of steps which conducted towards the vaults. Schalken felt a vague alarm at the sight of this figure and at the same time an irresistible impulse to follow its guidance. He followed it towards the vaults, but when it reached the head of the stairs, he paused; the figure paused also, and, turning gently round, displayed, by the light of the lamp it carried, the face and features of his first love, Rose Velderkaust. There was nothing horrible, or even sad, in the countenance. On the contrary, it wore the same arch smile which used to enchant the artist long before in his happy days. A feeling of awe and interest, too intense to be resisted, prompted him to follow the spectre, if spectre it were. She descended the stairs—he followed—and turning to the left, through a narrow passage, she led him, to his infinite surprise, into what appeared to be an old-fashioned Dutch apartment, such as the pictures of Gerard Douw have served to immortalize. Abundance of costly antique furniture was disposed about the room, and in one corner stood a four-post bed, with heavy black cloth curtains around it; the figure frequently turned towards him with the same arch smile; and when she came to the side of the bed, she drew the curtains, and, by the light of the lamp, which she held towards its contents, she disclosed to the horror-stricken painter, sitting bolt upright in the bed, the livid and demoniac form of Vanderhausen. Schalken had hardly seen him, when he fell senseless upon the floor, where he lay until discovered, on the next morning, by persons employed in closing the passages into the vaults. He was lying in a cell of considerable size, which had not been disturbed for a long time, and he had fallen beside a large coffin, which was supported upon small pillars, a security against the attacks of vermin.

To his dying day Schalken was satisfied of the reality of the vision which he had witnessed, and he has left behind him a curious evidence of the impression which it wrought upon his fancy, in a painting executed shortly after the event I have narrated, and which is valuable as exhibiting not only the peculiarities which have made Schalken's pictures sought after, but even more so as presenting a portrait of his early love, Rose Velderkaust, whose mysterious fate must always remain matter of speculation.

Charlotte Perkins Gilman

THE YELLOW WALLPAPER

Charlotte Perkins Gilman, feminist and reformer, wrote only one horror story and that one such an outstanding masterpiece that it has seldom been equalled in this century, only, perhaps, in the work of Shirley Jackson and Joanna Russ. "The Yellow Wallpaper" is either a haunted house story or a story of insanity, but in either case it is a monument of feminist horror, pointing out subtly and effectively all the restrictions which bring the central character to the moment of the story. This is the classic response to the story of male guilt and horror at how badly a woman has been treated, making the case for all time that the horror story need not be conservative.

It is very seldom that mere ordinary people like John and myself secure ancestral halls for the summer.

A colonial mansion, a hereditary estate, I would say a haunted house, and reach the height of romantic felicity—but that would be asking too much of fate!

Still I will proudly declare that there is something queer about it.

Else, why should it be let so cheaply? And why have stood so long untenanted?

John laughs at me, of course, but one expects that in marriage.

John is practical in the extreme. He has no patience with faith, an intense horror of superstition, and he scoffs openly at any talk of things not to be felt and seen and put down in figures.

John is a physician, and *perhaps*—(I would not say it to a living soul, of course, but this is dead paper and a great relief to my mind)—*perhaps* that is one reason I do not get well faster.

You see he does not believe I am sick!

And what can one do?

If a physician of high standing, and one's own husband, assures friends and relatives that there is really nothing the matter with one but temporary nervous depression—a slight hysterical tendency—what is one to do?

My brother is also a physician, and also of high standing, and he says the same thing.

So I take phosphates or phospites—whichever it is, and tonics, and journeys, and air, and exercise, and am absolutely forbidden to "work" until I am well again.

Personally, I disagree with their ideas.

Personally, I believe that congenial work, with excitement and change, would do me good.

But what is one to do?

I did write for a while in spite of them; but it *does* exhaust me a good deal—having to be so sly about it, or else meet with heavy opposition.

I sometimes fancy that in my condition if I had less opposition and more society and stimulus—but John says the very worst thing I can do is to think about my condition, and I confess it always makes me feel bad.

So I will let it alone and talk about the house.

The most beautiful place! It is quite alone, standing well back from the road, quite three miles from the village. It makes me think of English places that you read about, for there are hedges and walls and gates that lock, and lots of separate little houses for the gardeners and people.

There is a *delicious* garden! I never saw such a garden—large and shady, full of box-bordered paths, and lined with long grape-covered arbors with seats under them.

There were greenhouses, too, but they are all broken now.

There was some legal trouble, I believe, something about the heirs and coheirs; anyhow, the place has been empty for years.

That spoils my ghostliness, I am afraid, but I don't care—there is something strange about the house—I can feel it.

I even said so to John one moonlight evening, but he said what I felt was a *draught*, and shut the window.

I get unreasonably angry with John sometimes. I'm sure I never used to be so sensitive. I think it is due to this nervous condition.

But John says if I feel so, I shall neglect proper self-control; so I take pains to control myself—before him, at least, and that makes me very tired.

I don't like our room a bit. I wanted one downstairs that opened on the piazza and had roses all over the window, and such pretty old-fashioned chintz hangings! but John would not hear of it.

He said there was only one window and not room for two beds, and no near room for him if he took another.

He is very careful and loving, and hardly lets me stir without special direction.

I have a schedule prescription for each hour in the day; he takes all care from me, and so I feel basely ungrateful not to value it more.

He said we came here solely on my account, that I was to have perfect rest and all the air I could get. "Your exercise depends on your strength, my dear," said he, "and your food somewhat on your appetite; but air you can absorb all the time." So we took the nursery at the top of the house.

It is a big, airy room, the whole floor nearly, with windows that look all ways, and air and sunshine galore. It was nursery first and then playroom and gymnasium, I should judge; for the windows are barred for little children, and there are rings and things in the walls.

The paint and paper look as if a boys' school had used it. It is stripped off—the paper—in great patches all around the head of my bed, about as far as I can reach, and in a great place on the other side of the room low down. I never saw a worse paper in my life.

One of those sprawling flamboyant patterns committing every artistic sin.

It is dull enough to confuse the eye in following, pronounced enough to constantly irritate and provoke study, and when you follow the lame uncertain curves for a little distance they suddenly commit suicide—plunge off at outrageous angles, destroy themselves in unheard of contradictions.

The color is repellent, almost revolting; a smouldering unclean yellow, strangely faded by the slow-turning sunlight.

It is a dull yet lurid orange in some places, a sickly sulphur tint in others.

No wonder the children hated it! I should hate it myself if I had to live in this room long.

There comes John, and I must put this away,—he hates to have me write a word.

We have been here two weeks, and I haven't felt like writing before, since that first day.

I am sitting by the window now, up in this atrocious nursery, and there is nothing to hinder my writing as much as I please, save lack of strength.

John is away all day, and even some nights when his cases are serious.

I am glad my case is not serious!

But these nervous troubles are dreadfully depressing.

John does not know how much I really suffer. He knows there is no *reason* to suffer, and that satisfies him.

Of course it is only nervousness. It does weigh on me so not to do my duty in any way!

I meant to be such a help to John, such a real rest and comfort, and here I am a comparative burden already!

Nobody would believe what an effort it is to do what little I am able,—to dress and entertain, and order things.

It is fortunate Mary is so good with the baby. Such a dear baby!

And yet I *cannot* be with him, it makes me so nervous.

I suppose John never was nervous in his life. He laughs at me so about this wall-paper!

At first he meant to repaper the room, but afterwards he said that I was letting it get the better of me, and that nothing was worse for a nervous patient than to give way to such fancies.

He said that after the wall-paper was changed it would be

the heavy bedstead, and then the barred windows, and then that gate at the head of the stairs, and so on.

"You know the place is doing you good," he said, "and really, dear, I don't care to renovate the house just for a three months' rental."

"Then do let us go downstairs," I said, "there are such pretty rooms there."

Then he took me in his arms and called me a blessed little goose, and said he would go down to the cellar, if I wished, and have it whitewashed into the bargain.

But he is right enough about the beds and windows and things.

It is an airy and comfortable room as any one need wish, and, of course, I would not be so silly as to make him uncomfortable just for a whim.

I'm really getting quite fond of the big room, all but that horrid paper.

Out of one window I can see the garden, those mysterious deepshaded arbors, the riotous old-fashioned flowers, and bushes and gnarly trees.

Out of another I get a lovely view of the bay and a little private wharf belonging to the estate. There is a beautiful shaded lane that runs down there from the house. I always fancy I see people walking in these numerous paths and arbors, but John has cautioned me not to give way to fancy in the least. He says that with my imaginative power and habit of story-making, a nervous weakness like mine is sure to lead to all manner of excited fancies, and that I ought to use my will and good sense to check the tendency. So I try.

I think sometimes that if I were only well enough to write a little it would relieve the press of ideas and rest me.

But I find I get pretty tired when I try.

It is so discouraging not to have any advice and companionship about my work. When I get really well, John says we will ask Cousin Henry and Julia down for a long visit; but he says he would as soon put fireworks in my pillow-case as to let me have those stimulating people about now.

I wish I could get well faster.

But I must not think about that. This paper looks to me as if it *knew* what a vicious influence it had!

There is a recurrent spot where the pattern lolls like a broken neck and two bulbous eyes stare at you upside down.

I get positively angry with the impertinence of it and the everlastingness. Up and down and sideways they crawl, and those absurd, unblinking eyes are everywhere. There is one place where two breaths didn't match, and the eyes go all up and down the line, one a little higher than the other.

I never saw so much expression in an inanimate thing before, and we all know how much expression they have! I used to lie awake as a child and get more entertainment and terror out of blank walls and plain furniture than most children could find in a toy-store.

I remember what a kindly wink the knobs of our big, old bureau used to have, and there was one chair that always seemed like a strong friend.

I used to feel that if any of the other things looked too fierce I could always hop into that chair and be safe.

The furniture in this room is no worse than inharmonious, however, for we had to bring it all from downstairs. I suppose when this was used as a playroom they had to take the nursery things out, and no wonder! I never saw such ravages as the children have made here.

The wall-paper, as I said before, is torn off in spots, and it sticketh closer than a brother—they must have had perseverance as well as hatred.

Then the floor is scratched and gouged and splintered, the plaster itself is dug out here and there, and this great heavy bed which is all we found in the room, looks as if it had been through the wars.

But I don't mind it a bit—only the paper.

There comes John's sister. Such a dear girl as she is, and so careful of me! I must not let her find me writing.

She is a perfect and enthusiastic housekeeper, and hopes for no better profession. I verily believe she thinks it is the writing which made me sick!

But I can write when she is out, and see her a long way off from these windows.

There is one that commands the road, a lovely shaded winding road, and one that just looks off over the country. A lovely country, too, full of great elms and velvet meadows.

This wall-paper has a kind of sub-pattern in a different shade, a particularly irritating one, for you can only see it in certain lights, and not clearly then.

But in the places where it isn't faded and where the sun is just so—I can see a strange, provoking, formless sort of figure, that seems to skulk about behind that silly and conspicuous front design.

There's sister on the stairs!

Well, the Fourth of July is over! The people are all gone and I am tired out. John thought it might do me good to see a little company, so we just had mother and Nellie and the children down for a week.

Of course I didn't do a thing. Jennie sees to everything now.

But it tired me all the same.

John says if I don't pick up faster he shall send me to Weir Mitchell in the fall.

But I don't want to go there at all. I had a friend who was in his hands once, and she says he is just like John and my brother, only more so!

Besides, it is such an undertaking to go so far.

I don't feel as if it was worth while to turn my hand over for anything, and I'm getting dreadfully fretful and querulous.

I cry at nothing, and cry most of the time.

Of course I don't when John is here, or anybody else, but when I am alone.

And I am alone a good deal just now. John is kept in town very often by serious cases, and Jennie is good and lets me alone when I want her to.

So I walk a little in the garden or down that lovely lane, sit on the porch under the roses, and lie down up here a good deal.

I'm getting really fond of the room in spite of the wall-paper. Perhaps *because* of the wall-paper.

It dwells in my mind so!

I lie here on this great immovable bed—it is nailed down, I believe—and follow that pattern about by the hour. It is as good as gymnastics, I assure you. I start, we'll say, at the bottom, down in the corner over there where it has not been touched, and I determine for the thousandth time that I *will* follow that pointless pattern to some sort of a conclusion.

I know a little of the principle of design, and I know this thing was not arranged on any laws of radiation, or alternation, or repetition, or symmetry, or anything else that I ever heard of.

It is repeated, of course, by the breadths, but not otherwise.

Looked at in one way each breadth stands alone, the bloated curves and flourishes—a kind of "debased Romanesque" with *delirium tremens*—go waddling up and down in isolated columns of fatuity.

But, on the other hand, they connect diagonally, and the sprawling outlines run off in great slanting waves of optic horror, like a lot of wallowing seaweeds in full chase.

The whole thing goes horizontally, too, at least it seems so, and I exhaust myself in trying to distinguish the order of its going in that direction.

They have used a horizontal breadth for a frieze, and that adds wonderfully to the confusion.

There is one end of the room where it is almost intact, and there, when the crosslights fade and the low sun shines directly upon it, I can almost fancy radiation after all,—the interminable grotesques seem to form around a common centre and rush off in headlong plunges of equal distraction.

It makes me tired to follow it. I will take a nap I guess.

I don't know why I should write this.

I don't want to.

I don't feel able.

And I know John would think it absurd. But I *must* say what I feel and think in some way—it is such a relief!

But the effort is getting to be greater than the relief.

Half the time now I am awfully lazy, and lie down ever so much.

John says I mustn't lose my strength, and has me take cod liver oil and lots of tonics and things, to say nothing of ale and wine and rare meat.

Dear John! He loves me very dearly, and hates to have me sick. I tried to have a real earnest reasonable talk with him the other day, and tell him how I wish he would let me go and make a visit to Cousin Henry and Julia.

But he said I wasn't able to go, nor able to stand it after I got there; and I did not make out a very good case for myself, for I was crying before I had finished.

It is getting to be a great effort for me to think straight. Just this nervous weakness I suppose.

And dear John gathered me up in his arms, and just carried me upstairs and laid me on the bed, and sat by me and read to me till it tired my head.

He said I was his darling and his comfort and all he had, and that I must take care of myself for his sake, and keep well.

He says no one but myself can help me out of it, that I must use my will and self-control and not let any silly fancies run away with me.

There's one comfort, the baby is well and happy, and does not have to occupy this nursery with the horrid wall-paper.

If we had not used it, that blessed child would have! What a fortunate escape! Why, I wouldn't have a child of mine, an impressionable little thing, live in such a room for worlds.

I never thought of it before, but it is lucky that John kept me here after all, I can stand it so much easier than a baby, you see.

Of course I never mention it to them any more—I am too wise,—but I keep watch of it all the same.

There are things in that paper that nobody knows but me, or ever will.

Behind that outside pattern the dim shapes get clearer every day.

It is always the same shape, only very numerous.

And it is like a woman stooping down and creeping about behind that pattern. I don't like it a bit. I wonder—I begin to think—I wish John would take me away from here!

It is so hard to talk with John about my case, because he is so wise, and because he loves me so.

But I tried it last night.

It was moonlight. The moon shines in all around just as the sun does.

I hate to see it sometimes, it creeps so slowly, and always comes in by one window or another.

John was asleep and I hated to waken him, so I kept still and watched the moonlight on that undulating wall-paper till I felt creepy.

The faint figure behind seemed to shake the pattern, just as if she wanted to get out.

I got up softly and went to feel and see if the paper *did* move, and when I came back John was awake.

"What is it, little girl?" he said. "Don't go walking about like that—you'll get cold."

I thought it was a good time to talk, so I told him that I really was not gaining here, and that I wished he would take me away.

"Why darling!" said he, "our lease will be up in three weeks, and I can't see how to leave before.

"The repairs are not done at home, and I cannot possibly leave town just now. Of course if you were in any danger, I could and would, but you really are better, dear, whether you can see it or not. I am a doctor, dear, and I know. You are gaining flesh and color, your appetite is better, I feel really much easier about you."

"I don't weigh a bit more," said I, "nor as much; and my appetite may be better in the evening when you are here, but it is worse in the morning when you are away!"

"Bless her little heart!" said he with a big hug, "she shall be as sick as she pleases! But now let's improve the shining hours by going to sleep, and talk about it in the morning!"

"And you won't go away?" I asked gloomily.

"Why, how can I, dear? It is only three weeks more and then we will take a nice little trip of a few days while Jennie is getting the house ready. Really dear you are better!"

"Better in body perhaps—" I began, and stopped short, for he sat up straight and looked at me with such a stern, reproachful look that I could not say another word.

"My darling," said he, "I beg of you, for my sake and for our child's sake, as well as for your own, that you will never for one instant let that idea enter your mind! There is nothing so dangerous, so fascinating, to a temperament like yours. It is a false and foolish fancy. Can you not trust me as a physician when I tell you so?"

So of course I said no more on that score, and we went to

sleep before long. He thought I was asleep first, but I wasn't, and lay there for hours trying to decide whether that front pattern and the back pattern really did move together or separately.

On a pattern like this, by daylight, there is a lack of sequence, a defiance of law, that is a constant irritant to a normal mind.

The color is hideous enough, and unreliable enough, and infuriating enough, but the pattern is torturing.

You think you have mastered it, but just as you get well underway in following, it turns a backsomersault and there you are. It slaps you in the face, knocks you down, and tramples upon you. It is like a bad dream.

The outside pattern is a florid arabesque, reminding one of a fungus. If you can imagine a toadstool in joints, an interminable string of toadstools, budding and sprouting in endless convolutions—why, that is something like it.

That is, sometimes!

There is one marked peculiarity about this paper, a thing nobody seems to notice but myself, and that is that it changes as the light changes.

When the sun shoots in through the east window—I always watch for that first long, straight ray—it changes so quickly that I never can quite believe it.

That is why I watch it always.

By moonlight—the moon shines in all night when there is a moon—I wouldn't know it was the same paper.

At night in any kind of light, in twilight, candle light, lamplight, and worst of all by moonlight, it becomes bars! The outside pattern I mean, and the woman behind it is as plain as can be.

I didn't realize for a long time what the thing was that showed behind, that dim sub-pattern, but now I am quite sure it is a woman.

By daylight she is subdued, quiet. I fancy it is the pattern that keeps her so still. It is so puzzling. It keeps me quiet by the hour.

I lie down ever so much now. John says it is good for me, and to sleep all I can.

Indeed he started the habit by making me lie down for an hour after each meal.

It is a very bad habit I am convinced, for you see I don't sleep.

And that cultivates deceit, for I don't tell them I'm awake— O no!

The fact is I am getting a little afraid of John.

He seems very queer sometimes, and even Jennie has an inexplicable look.

It strikes me occasionally, just as a scientific hypothesis,— that perhaps it is the paper!

I have watched John when he did not know I was looking, and come into the room suddenly on the most innocent excuses, and I've caught him several times *looking at the paper*! And Jennie too. I caught Jennie with her hand on it once.

She didn't know I was in the room, and when I asked her in a quiet, a very quiet voice, with the most restrained manner possible, what she was doing with the paper—she turned around as if she had been caught stealing, and looked quite angry—asked me why I should frighten her so!

Then she said that the paper stained everything it touched, that she had found yellow smooches on all my clothes and John's, and she wished we would be more careful!

Did not that sound innocent? But I know she was studying that pattern, and I am determined that nobody shall find it out but myself!

Life is very much more exciting now than it used to be. You see I have something more to expect, to look forward to, to watch. I really do eat better, and am more quiet than I was.

John is so pleased to see me improve! He laughed a little the other day, and said I seemed to be flourishing in spite of my wall-paper.

I turned it off with a laugh. I had no intention of telling him it was *because* of the wall-paper—he would make fun of me. He might even want to take me away.

I don't want to leave now until I have found it out. There is a week more, and I think that will be enough.

* * *

I'm feeling ever so much better! I don't sleep much at night, for it is so interesting to watch developments; but I sleep a good deal in the daytime.

In the daytime it is tiresome and perplexing.

There are always new shoots on the fungus, and new shades of yellow all over it. I cannot keep count of them, though I have tried conscientiously.

It is the strangest yellow, that wall-paper! It makes me think of all the yellow things I ever saw—not beautiful ones like buttercups, but old foul, bad yellow things.

But there is something else about that paper—the smell! I noticed it the moment we came into the room, but with so much air and sun it was not bad. Now we have had a week of fog and rain, and whether the windows are open or not, the smell is here.

It creeps all over the house.

I find it hovering in the dining-room, skulking in the parlor, hiding in the hall, lying in wait for me on the stairs.

It gets into my hair.

Even when I go to ride, if I turn my head suddenly and surprise it—there is that smell!

Such a peculiar odor, too! I have spent hours in trying to analyze it, to find what it smelled like.

It is not bad—at first, and very gentle, but quite the subtlest, most enduring odor I ever met.

In this damp weather it is awful, I wake up in the night and find it hanging over me.

It used to disturb me at first. I thought seriously of burning the house—to reach the smell.

But now I am used to it. The only thing I can think of that it is like is the *color* of the paper! A yellow smell.

There is a very funny mark on this wall, low down, near the mopboard. A streak that runs round the room. It goes behind every piece of furniture, except the bed, a long, straight, even *smooch*, as if it had been rubbed over and over.

I wonder how it was done and who did it, and what they did it for. Round and round and round—round and round and round—it makes me dizzy!

* * *

I really have discovered something at last.

Through watching so much at night, when it changes so, I have finally found out.

The front pattern *does* move—and no wonder! The woman behind shakes it!

Sometimes I think there are a great many women behind, and sometimes only one, and she crawls around fast, and her crawling shakes it all over.

Then in the very bright spots she keeps still, and in the very shady spots she just takes hold of the bars and shakes them hard.

And she is all the time trying to climb through. But nobody could climb through that pattern—it strangles so; I think that is why it has so many heads.

They get through, and then the pattern strangles them off and turns them upside down, and makes their eyes white!

If those heads were covered or taken off it would not be half so bad.

I think that woman gets out in the daytime!

And I'll tell you why—privately—I've seen her!

I can see her out of every one of my windows!

It is the same woman, I know, for she is always creeping, and most women do not creep by daylight.

I see her on that long road under the trees, creeping along, and when a carriage comes she hides under the blackberry vines.

I don't blame her a bit. It must be very humiliating to be caught creeping by daylight!

I always lock the door when I creep by daylight. I can't do it at night, for I know John would suspect something at once.

And John is so queer now, that I don't want to irritate him. I wish he would take another room! Besides, I don't want anybody to get that woman out at night but myself.

I often wonder if I could see her out of all the windows at once.

But, turn as fast as I can, I can only see out of one at one time.

And though I always see her, she *may* be able to creep faster than I can turn!

I have watched her sometimes away off in the open country, creeping as fast as a cloud shadow in a high wind.

If only that top pattern could be gotten off from the under one! I mean to try it, little by little.

I have found out another funny thing, but I shan't tell it this time! It does not do to trust people too much.

There are only two more days to get this paper off, and I believe John is beginning to notice. I don't like the look in his eyes.

And I heard him ask Jennie a lot of professional questions about me. She had a very good report to give.

She said I slept a good deal in the daytime.

John knows I don't sleep very well at night, for all I'm so quiet!

He asked me all sorts of questions, too, and pretended to be very loving and kind.

As if I couldn't see through him!

Still, I don't wonder he acts so, sleeping under this paper for three months.

It only interests me, but I feel sure John and Jennie are secretly affected by it.

Hurrah! This is the last day, but it is enough. John to stay in town over night, and won't be out until this evening.

Jennie wanted to sleep with me—the sly thing! but I told her I should undoubtedly rest better for a night all alone.

That was clever, for really I wasn't alone a bit! As soon as it was moonlight and that poor thing began to crawl and shake the pattern, I got up and ran to help her.

I pulled and she shook, I shook and she pulled, and before morning we had peeled off yards of that paper.

A strip about as high as my head and half around the room.

And then when the sun came and that awful pattern began to laugh at me, I declared I would finish it to-day!

We go away to-morrow, and they are moving all my furniture down again to leave things as they were before.

Jennie looked at the wall in amazement, but I told her merrily that I did it out of pure spite at the vicious thing.

She laughed and said she wouldn't mind doing it herself, but I must not get tired.

How she betrayed herself that time!

But I am here, and no person touches this paper but me, —not *alive*!

She tried to get me out of the room—it was too patent! But I said it was so quiet and empty and clean now that I believed I would lie down again and sleep all I could; and not to wake me even for dinner—I would call when I woke.

So now she is gone, and the servants are gone, and the things are gone, and there is nothing left but the great bedstead nailed down, with the canvas mattress we found on it.

We shall sleep downstairs to-night, and take the boat home to-morrow.

I quite enjoy the room, now it is bare again.

How those children did tear about here!

This bedstead is fairly gnawed!

But I must get to work.

I have locked the door and thrown the key down into the front path.

I don't want to go out, and I don't want to have anybody come in, till John comes.

I want to astonish him.

I've got a rope up here that even Jennie did not find. If that woman does get out, and tries to get away, I can tie her!

But I forgot I could not reach far without anything to stand on!

This bed will *not* move!

I tried to lift and push it until I was lame, and then I got so angry I bit off a little piece at one corner—but it hurt my teeth.

Then I peeled off all the paper I could reach standing on the floor. It sticks horribly and the pattern just enjoys it! All those strangled heads and bulbous eyes and waddling fungus growths just shriek with derision!

I am getting angry enough to do something desperate. To jump out of the window would be admirable exercise, but the bars are too strong even to try.

Besides I wouldn't do it. Of course not. I know well enough that a step like that is improper and might be misconstrued.

I don't like to *look* out of the windows even—there are so many of those creeping women, and they creep so fast.

I wonder if they all come out of that wall-paper as I did?

But I am securely fastened now by my well-hidden rope—you don't get *me* out in the road there!

I suppose I shall have to get back behind the pattern when it comes night, and that is hard!

It is so pleasant to be out in this great room and creep around as I please!

I don't want to go outside. I won't, even if Jennie asks me to.

For outside you have to creep on the ground, and everything is green instead of yellow.

But here I can creep smoothly on the floor, and my shoulder just fits in that long smooch around the wall, so I cannot lose my way.

Why there's John at the door!

It is no use, young man, you can't open it!

How he does call and pound!

Now he's crying for an axe.

It would be a shame to break down that beautiful door!

"John dear!" said I in the gentlest voice, "the key is down by the front steps, under a plantain leaf!"

That silenced him for a few moments.

Then he said—very quietly indeed, "Open the door, my darling!"

"I can't," said I. "The key is down by the front door under a plantain leaf!"

And then I said it again, several times, very gently and slowly, and said it so often that he had to go and see, and he got it of course, and came in. He stopped short by the door.

"What is the matter?" he cried. "For God's sake, what are you doing!"

I kept on creeping just the same, but I looked at him over my shoulder.

"I've got out at last," said I, "in spite of you and Jane. And I've pulled off most of the paper, so you can't put me back!"

Now why should that man have fainted? But he did, and right across my path by the wall, so that I had to creep over him every time!

William Faulkner

A ROSE FOR EMILY

Psychological investigation in the Gothic mode is a characteristic of Faulkner's major work. One thinks of the central chapter of *As I Lay Dying* (the interior monologue of a corpse) or the brutal horrors of *Sanctuary*. But the precision and clarity and quiet monstrosity of "A Rose for Emily" represents his central contribution to horror fiction, in the period of transition from supernatural to psychological horror as the major mode of the literature, when D. H. Lawrence and Conrad Aiken and many others were investigating the abnormal in some of the major short fiction of the period. Often reprinted, "A Rose for Emily" is one of the most perfect and enduring classics of the century.

I

When Miss Emily Grierson died, our whole town went to her funeral: the men through a sort of respectful affection for a fallen monument, the women mostly out of curiosity to see the inside of her house, which no one save an old man-servant—a combined gardener and cook—had seen in at least ten years.

It was a big, squarish frame house that had once been white, decorated with cupolas and spires and scrolled balconies in the heavily lightsome style of the Seventies, set on what had once been our most select street. But garages and cotton gins had encroached and obliterated even the august names of that neighborhood; only Miss Emily's house was left, lifting its stubborn and coquettish decay above the cotton wagons and the gasoline pumps—an eyesore among eyesores. And now Miss Emily had gone to join the representatives of those august names where they lay in the cedar-bemused cemetery among the ranked and anonymous graves of Union and Confederate soldiers who fell at the battle of Jefferson.

Alive, Miss Emily had been a tradition, a duty, and a care; a sort of hereditary obligation upon the town, dating from that day in 1891 when Colonel Sartoris, the mayor—he who fathered the edict that no Negro woman should appear on the streets without an apron—remitted her taxes, the dispensation dating from the death of her father on into perpetuity. Not that Miss Emily would have accepted charity. Colonel Sartoris invented an involved tale to the effect that Miss Emily's father had loaned money to the town, which the town, as a matter of business, preferred this way of repaying. Only a man of Colonel Sartoris' generation and thought could have invented it, and only a woman could have believed it.

When the next generation, with its more modern ideas, became mayors and aldermen, this arrangement created some little dissatisfaction. On the first of the year they mailed her a tax notice. February came, and there was no reply. They wrote her a formal letter, asking her to call at the sheriff's office at her convenience. A week later the mayor wrote her himself, offering to call or send his car for her, and received in reply a note on paper of an archaic shape, in a thin, flowing calligraphy in faded ink, to the effect that she no longer went out at all. The tax notice was also enclosed, without comment.

They called a special meeting of the Board of Aldermen. A deputation waited upon her, knocked at the door through which no visitor had passed since she ceased giving china-painting lessons eight or ten years earlier. They were admitted by the old Negro into a dim hall from which a stairway mounted into still more shadow. It smelled of dust and disuse—a close, dank smell. The Negro led them into the parlor. It was furnished in heavy, leather-covered furniture. When the Negro opened the blinds of one window, they could see that the leather was cracked; and when they sat down, a faint dust rose sluggishly about their thighs, spinning with slow motes in the single sun-ray. On a tarnished gilt easel before the fireplace stood a crayon portrait of Miss Emily's father.

They rose when she entered—a small, fat woman in black, with a thin gold chain descending to her waist and vanishing into her belt, leaning on an ebony cane with a tarnished gold head. Her skeleton was small and spare; perhaps that was why what would have been merely plumpness in another was obesity in her. She looked bloated, like a body long submerged in motionless water, and of that pallid hue. Her eyes, lost in the fatty ridges of her face, looked like two small pieces of coal pressed into a lump of dough as they moved from one face to another while the visitors stated their errand.

She did not ask them to sit. She just stood in the door and listened quietly until the spokesman came to a stumbling halt. Then they could hear the invisible watch ticking at the end of the gold chain.

Her voice was dry and cold. "I have no taxes in Jefferson. Colonel Sartoris explained it to me. Perhaps one of you can gain access to the city records and satisfy yourselves."

"But we have. We are the city authorities, Miss Emily. Didn't you get a notice from the sheriff, signed by him?"

"I received a paper, yes," Miss Emily said. "Perhaps he considers himself the sheriff . . . . I have no taxes in Jefferson."

"But there is nothing on the books to show that, you see. We must go by the—"

"See Colonel Sartoris. I have no taxes in Jefferson."

"But, Miss Emily—"

"See Colonel Sartoris." (Colonel Sartoris had been dead almost ten years.) "I have no taxes in Jefferson. Tobe!" The Negro appeared. "Show these gentlemen out."

II

So she vanquished them, horse and foot, just as she had vanquished their fathers thirty years before about the smell. That was two years after her father's death and a short time after her sweetheart—the one we believed would marry her—

had deserted her. After her father's death she went out very little; after her sweetheart went away, people hardly saw her at all. A few of the ladies had the temerity to call, but were not received, and the only sign of life about the place was the Negro man—a young man then—going in and out with a market basket.

"Just as if a man—any man—could keep a kitchen properly," the ladies said; so they were not surprised when the smell developed. It was another link between the gross, teeming world and the high and mighty Griersons.

A neighbor, a woman, complained to the mayor, Judge Stevens, eighty years old.

"But what will you have me do about it, madam?" he said.

"Why, send her word to stop it," the woman said. "Isn't there a law?"

"I'm sure that won't be necessary," Judge Stevens said. "It's probably just a snake or a rat that nigger of hers killed in the yard. I'll speak to him about it."

The next day he received two more complaints, one from a man who came in diffident deprecation. "We really must do something about it, Judge. I'd be the last one in the world to bother Miss Emily, but we've got to do something." That night the Board of Aldermen met—three graybeards and one younger man, a member of the rising generation.

"It's simple enough," he said. "Send her word to have her place cleaned up. Give her a certain time to do it in, and if she don't . . ."

"Dammit, sir," Judge Stevens said, "will you accuse a lady to her face of smelling bad?"

So the next night, after midnight, four men crossed Miss Emily's lawn and slunk about the house like burglars, sniffing along the base of the brickwork and at the cellar openings while one of them performed a regular sowing motion with his hand out of a sack slung from his shoulder. They broke open the cellar door and sprinkled lime there, and in all the outbuildings. As they recrossed the lawn, a window that had been dark was lighted and Miss Emily sat in it, the light behind her, and her upright torso motionless as that of an idol. They crept quietly across the lawn and into the shadow of the locusts that lined the street. After a week or two the smell went away.

That was when people had begun to feel really sorry for her. People in our town, remembering how Old Lady Wyatt, her great-aunt, had gone completely crazy at last, believed that the Griersons held themselves a little too high for what they really were. None of the young men was quite good enough to Miss Emily and such. We had long thought of them as a tableau: Miss Emily a slender figure in white in the background, her father a spraddled silhouette in the foreground, his back to her and clutching a horsewhip, the two of them framed by the back-flung front door. So when she got to be thirty and was still single, we were not pleased exactly, but vindicated; even with insanity in the family she wouldn't have turned down all of her chances if they had really materialized.

When her father died, it got about that the house was all that was left to her; and in a way, people were glad. At last they could pity Miss Emily. Being left alone, and a pauper, she had become humanized. Now she too would know the old thrill and the old despair of a penny more or less.

The day after his death all the ladies prepared to call at the house and offer condolence and aid, as is our custom. Miss Emily met them at the door, dressed as usual and with no trace of grief on her face. She told them that her father was not dead. She did that for three days, with the ministers calling on her, and the doctors, trying to persuade her to let them dispose of the body. Just as they were about to resort to law and force, she broke down, and they buried her father quickly.

We did not say she was crazy then. We believed she had to do that. We remembered all the young men her father had driven away, and we knew that with nothing left, she would have to cling to that which had robbed her, as people will.

III

She was sick for a long time. When we saw her again, her hair was cut short, making her look like a girl, with a vague resemblance to those angels in colored church windows—sort of tragic and serene.

The town had just let the contracts for paving the sidewalks, and in the summer after her father's death they began the work. The construction company came with niggers and mules and machinery, and a foreman named Homer Barron, a Yankee—a big, dark, ready man, with a big voice and eyes lighter than his face. The little boys would follow in groups to hear him cuss the niggers, and the niggers singing in time to the rise and fall of picks. Pretty soon he knew everybody in town. Whenever you heard a lot of laughing anywhere about the square, Homer Barron would be in the center of the group. Presently we began to see him and Miss Emily on Sunday afternoons driving in the yellow-wheeled buggy and the matched team of bays from the livery stable.

At first we were glad that Miss Emily would have an interest, because the ladies all said, "Of course a Grierson would not think seriously of a Northerner, a day laborer." But there were still others, older people, who said that even grief could not cause a real lady to forget *noblesse oblige*—without calling it *noblesse oblige*. They just said, "Poor Emily. Her kinsfolk should come to her." She had some kin in Alabama; but years ago her father had fallen out with them over the estate of Old Lady Wyatt, the crazy woman, and there was no communication between the two families. They had not even been represented at the funeral.

And as soon as the old people said, "Poor Emily," the whispering began. "Do you suppose it's really so?" they said to one another. "Of course it is. What else could . . ." This behind their hands; rustling of craned silk and satin behind jalousies closed upon the sun of Sunday afternoon as the thin, swift clop-clop-clop of the matched team passed: "Poor Emily."

She carried her head high enough—even when we believed that she was fallen. It was as if she demanded more than ever the recognition of her dignity as the last Grierson; as if it had wanted that touch of earthiness to reaffirm her imperviousness. Like when she bought the rat poison, the arsenic. That was over a year after they had begun to say "Poor Emily," and while the two female cousins were visiting her.

"I want some poison," she said to the druggist. She was over thirty then, still a slight woman, though thinner than usual, with cold, haughty black eyes in a face the flesh of which was strained across the temples and about the eye-sockets as you imagine a lighthouse-keeper's face ought to look. "I want some poison," she said.

"Yes, Miss Emily. What kind? For rats and such? I'd recom—"

"I want the best you have. I don't care what kind."

The druggist named several. "They'll kill anything up to an elephant. But what you want is—"

"Arsenic," Miss Emily said. "Is that a good one?"

"Is . . . arsenic? Yes, ma'am. But what you want—"

"I want arsenic."

The druggist looked down at her. She looked back at him, erect, her face like a strained flag. "Why, of course," the druggist said. "If that's what you want. But the law requires you to tell what you are going to use it for."

Miss Emily just stared at him, her head tilted back in order to look him eye for eye, until he looked away and went and got the arsenic and wrapped it up. The Negro delivery boy brought her the package; the druggist didn't come back. When she opened the package at home there was written on the box, under the skull and bones: "For rats."

IV

So the next day we all said, "She will kill herself"; and we said it would be the best thing. When she had first begun to be seen with Homer Barron, we had said, "She will marry him." Then we said, "She will persuade him yet," because Homer himself had remarked—he liked men, and it was known that he drank with the younger men in the Elks' Club—that he was not a marrying man. Later we said, "Poor Emily'' behind the jalousies as they passed on Sunday afternoon in the glittering buggy, Miss Emily with her head high and Homer Barron with his hat cocked and a cigar in his teeth, reins and whip in a yellow glove.

Then some of the ladies began to say it was a disgrace to the town and a bad example to the young people. The men did not want to interfere, but at last the ladies forced the Baptist minister—Miss Emily's people were Episcopal—to call upon her. He would never divulge what happened during that interview, but he refused to go back again. The next Sunday they again drove about the streets, and the following day the minister's wife wrote to Miss Emily's relations in Alabama.

So she had blood-kin under her roof again and we sat back to watch developments. At first nothing happened. Then we were sure that they were to be married. We learned that Miss Emily had been to the jeweler's and ordered a man's toilet set in silver, with the letters H.B. on each piece. Two days later we learned that she had bought a complete outfit of men's clothing, including a nightshirt, and we said, ''They are married.'' We were really glad. We were glad because the two female cousins were even more Grierson than Miss Emily had ever been.

So we were not surprised when Homer Barron—the streets had been finished some time since—was gone. We were a little disappointed that there was not a public blowing-off, but we believed that he had gone on to prepare for Miss Emily's coming, or to give her a chance to get rid of the cousins. (By that time it was a cabal, and we were all Miss Emily's allies to help circumvent the cousins.) Sure enough, after another week they departed. And, as we had expected all along, within three days Homer Barron was back in town. A neighbor saw the Negro man admit him at the kitchen door at dusk one evening.

And that was the last we saw of Homer Barron. And of Miss Emily for some time. The Negro man went in and out with the market basket, but the front door remained closed. Now and then we would see her at a window for a moment, as the men did that night when they sprinkled the lime, but for almost six months she did not appear on the streets. Then we knew that this was to be expected too; as if that quality of her father which had thwarted her woman's life so many times had been too virulent and too furious to die.

When we next saw Miss Emily, she had grown fat and her hair was turning gray. During the next few years it grew grayer and grayer until it attainted an even pepper-and-salt iron-gray, when it ceased turning. Up to the day of her death at seventy-four it was still that vigorous iron-gray, like the hair of an active man.

From that time on her front door remained closed, save for a period of six or seven years, when she was about forty, during which she gave lessons in china-painting. She fitted up a studio in one of the downstairs rooms, where the daughters and granddaughters of Colonel Sartoris' contemporaries were sent to her with the same regularity and in the same spirit that they were sent to church on Sundays with a twenty-five-cent piece for the collection plate. Meanwhile her taxes had been remitted.

Then the newer generation became the backbone and the spirit of the town, and the painting pupils grew up and fell away and did not send their children to her with boxes of color and tedious brushes and pictures cut from the ladies' magazines. The front door closed upon the last one and remained closed for good. When the town got free postal delivery, Miss Emily alone refused to let them fasten the metal numbers above her door and attach a mailbox to it. She would not listen to them.

Daily, monthly, yearly we watched the Negro grow grayer and more stooped, going in and out with the market basket. Each December we sent her a tax notice, which would be returned by the post office a week later, unclaimed. Now and then we would see her in one of the downstairs windows—she had evidently shut up the top floor of the house—like the carven torso of an idol in a niche, looking or not looking at us, we could never tell which. Thus she passed from generation to generation—dear, inescapable, impervious, tranquil, and perverse.

And so she died. Fell ill in the house filled with dust and shadows, with only a doddering Negro man to wait on her. We did not even know she was sick; we had long since given up trying to get any information from the Negro. He talked to no one, probably not even to her, for his voice had grown harsh and rusty, as if from disuse.

She died in one of the downstairs rooms, in a heavy walnut bed with a curtain, her gray head propped on a pillow yellow and moldy with age and lack of sunlight.

V

The Negro met the first of the ladies at the front door and let them in, with their hushed, sibilant voices and their quick, curious glances, and then he disappeared. He walked right through the house and out the back and was not seen again.

The two female cousins came at once. They held the funeral on the second day, with the town coming to look at Miss Emily beneath a mass of bought flowers, with the crayon face of her father musing profoundly above the bier and the ladies sibilant and macabre; and the very old men—some in their brushed Confederate uniforms—on the porch and the lawn, talking of Miss Emily as if she had been a contemporary of theirs, believing that they had danced with her and courted her perhaps, confusing time with its mathematical progression, as the old do, to whom all the past is not a diminishing road but, instead, a huge meadow which no winter ever quite touches, divided from them now by the narrow bottle-neck of the most recent decade of years.

Already we knew that there was one room in that region above stairs which no one had seen in forty years, and which would have to be forced. They waited until Miss Emily was decently in the ground before they opened it.

The violence of breaking down the door seemed to fill this room with pervading dust. A thin, acrid pall as of the tomb seemed to lie everywhere upon this room decked and furnished as for a bridal: upon the valence curtains of faded rose color, upon the rose-shaded lights, upon the dressing table, upon the delicate array of crystal and the man's toilet things backed with tarnished silver, silver so tarnished that the monogram was obscured. Among them lay a collar and tie, as if they had just been removed, which, lifted, left upon the surface a pale crescent in the dust. Upon a chair hung the suit, carefully folded; beneath it the two mute shoes and the discarded socks.

The man himself lay in the bed.

For a long while we just stood there, looking down at the profound and fleshless grin. The body had apparently once lain in the attitude of an embrace, but now the long sleep that outlasts love, that conquers even the grimace of love, had cuckolded him. What was left of him, rotted beneath what was left of the nightshirt, had become inextricable from the bed in which he lay; and upon him and upon the pillow beside him lay that even coating of the patient and biding dust.

Then we noticed that in the second pillow was the indentation of a head. One of us lifted something from it, and leaning forward, that faint and invisible dust dry and acrid in the nostrils, we saw a long strand of iron-gray hair.

Robert Hichens

How Love Came to Professor Guildea

Hichens' masterpiece is one of the greatest of all horror stories, successful both as a moral investigation and as psychological anatomy, but it is in the latter area that it excels, rising above its contemporaries to stand beside Oliver Onions' "The Beckoning Fair One" and Le Fanu's "Carmilla" and Henry James' "The Turn of the Screw" as one of the landmarks of the novella form. It is a deconstruction of Victorian Christian morality under the guise of a moral tale that provides provocative contrasts on the one hand to Lucy Clifford's "The New Mother" and on the other to Oliver Onions' "The Beckoning Fair One." Onions alters the structure further by replacing Father Murchison's narrative view with that of an independent woman reporter, showing a break in horror and supernatural fiction of the period from the overt moral center to progressive interest in psychological investigation. Onions leads us toward the nonsupernatural and feminist consciousness of Gilman, and later, Russ.

I

Dull people often wondered how it came about that Father Murchison and Professor Frederic Guildea were intimate friends. The one was all faith, the other all scepticism. The nature of the Father was based on love. He viewed the world with an almost childlike tenderness above his long, black cassock; and his mild, yet perfectly fearless, blue eyes seemed always to be watching the goodness that exists in humanity, and rejoicing at what they saw. The Professor, on the other hand, had a hard face like a hatchet, tipped with an aggressive black goatee beard. His eyes were quick, piercing and irreverent. The lines about his small, thin-lipped mouth were almost cruel. His voice was harsh and dry, sometimes, when he grew energetic, almost soprano. It fired off words with a sharp and clipping utterance. His habitual manner was one of distrust and investigation. It was impossible to suppose that, in his busy life, he found any time for love, either of humanity in general or of an individual.

Yet his days were spend in scientific investigations which conferred immense benefits upon the world.

Both men were celibates. Father Murchison was a member of an Anglican order which forbade him to marry. Professor Guildea had a poor opinion of most things, but especially of women. He had formerly held a post as lecturer at Birmingham. But when his fame as a discoverer grew, he removed to London. There, at a lecture he gave in the East End, he first met Father Murchison. They spoke a few words. Perhaps the bright intelligence of the priest appealed to the man of science, who was inclined, as a rule, to regard the clergy with some contempt. Perhaps the transparent sincerity of this devotee, full of common sense, attracted him. As he was leaving the hall he abruptly asked the Father to call on him at his house in Hyde Park Place. And the Father, who seldom went into the West End, except to preach, accepted the invitation.

"When will you come?" said Guildea.

He was folding up the blue paper on which his notes were written in a tiny, clear hand. The leaves rustled drily in accompaniment to his sharp, dry voice.

"On Sunday week I am preaching in the evening at St. Saviour's, not far off," said the Father.

"I don't go to church."

"No," said the Father, without any accent of surprise or condemnation.

"Come to supper afterwards?"

"Thank you, I will."

"What time will you come?"

The Father smiled.

"As soon as I have finished my sermon. The service is at six-thirty."

"About eight then, I suppose. Don't make the sermon too long. My number in Hyde Park Place is 100. Good-night to you."

He snapped an elastic band round his papers and strode off without shaking hands.

On the appointed Sunday, Father Murchison preached to a densely crowded congregation at St. Saviour's. The subject of his sermon was sympathy, and the comparative uselessness of man in the world unless he can learn to love his neighbour as himself. The sermon was rather long, and when the preacher, in his flowing, black cloak, and his hard, round hat, with a straight brim over which hung the ends of a black cord, made his way towards the Professor's house, the hands of the illuminated clock disc at the Marble Arch pointed to twenty minutes past eight.

The Father hurried on, pushing his way through the crowd of standing soldiers, chattering women and giggling street boys in their Sunday best. It was a warm April night, and, when he reached number 100, Hyde Park Place, he found the Professor bareheaded on his doorstep, gazing out towards the Park railings, and enjoying the soft, moist air, in front of his lighted passage.

"Ha, a long sermon!" he exclaimed. "Come in."

"I fear it was," said the Father, obeying the invitation. "I am that dangerous thing—an extempore preacher."

"More attractive to speak without notes, if you can do it. Hang your hat and coat—oh, cloak—here. We'll have supper at once. This is the dining room."

He opened a door on the right and they entered a long, narrow room, with a gold paper and a black ceiling, from which hung an electric lamp with a gold-coloured shade. In the room stood a small oval table with covers laid for two. The Professor rang the bell. Then he said:

"People seem to talk better at an oval table than at a square one."

"Really? Is that so?"

"Well, I've had precisely the same party twice, once at a square table, once at an oval table. The first dinner was a dull failure, the second a brilliant success. Sit down, won't you?''

''How d'you account for the difference?'' said the Father, sitting down, and pulling the tail of his cassock well under him.

''H'm. I know how you'd account for it.''

''Indeed. How then?''

''At an oval table, since there are no corners, the chain of human sympathy—the electric current, is much more complete. Eh! Let me give you some soup.''

''Thank you.''

The Father took it, and, as he did so, turned his beaming blue eyes on his host. Then he smiled.

''What!'' he said, in his pleasant, light tenor voice. ''You do go to church sometimes, then?''

''To-night is the first time for ages. And, mind you, I was tremendously bored.''

The Father still smiled, and his blue eyes gently twinkled.

''Dear, dear!'' he said, ''what a pity!''

''But not by the sermon,'' Guildea added. ''I don't pay a compliment. I state a fact. The sermon didn't bore me. If it had, I should have said so, or said nothing.''

''And which would you have done?''

The Professor smiled almost genially.

''Don't know,'' he said. ''What wine d'you drink''

''None, thank you. I'm a teetotaller. In my profession and *milieu* it is necessary to be one. Yes, I will have some soda water. I think you would have done the first.''

''Very likely, and very wrongly. You wouldn't have minded much.''

''I don't think I should.''

They were intimate already. The Father felt most pleasantly at home under the black ceiling. He drank some soda water and seemed to enjoy it more than the Professor enjoyed his claret.

''You smile at the theory of the chain of human sympathy, I see,'' said the Father. ''Then what is your explanation of the failure of your square party with corners, the success of your oval party without them?''

''Probably on the first occasion the wit of the assembly

had a chill on his liver, while on the second he was in perfect health. Yet, you see, I stick to the oval table.''

''And that means—''

''Very little. By the way, your omission of any allusion to the notorious part liver plays in love was a serious one to-night.''

''Your omission of any desire for close human sympathy in your life is a more serious one.''

''How can you be sure I have no such desire?''

''I divine it. Your look, your manner, tell me it is so. You were disagreeing with my sermon all the time I was preaching. Weren't you?''

''Part of the time.''

The servant changed the plates. He was a middle-aged, blond, thin man, with a stony white face, pale, prominent eyes, and an accomplished manner of service. When he had left the room the Professor continued.

''Your remarks interested me, but I thought them exaggerated.''

''For instance?''

''Let me play the egoist for a moment. I spend most of my time in hard work, very hard work. The results of this work, you will allow, benefit humanity.''

''Enormously,'' assented the Father, thinking of more than one of Guildea's discoveries.

''And the benefit conferred by this work, undertaken merely for its own sake, is just as great as if it were undertaken because I loved my fellow man, and sentimentally desired to see him more comfortable than he is at present. I'm as useful precisely in my present condition of—in my present nonaffectional condition—as I should be if I were as full of gush as the sentimentalists who want to get murderers out of prison, or to put a premium on tyranny—like Tolstoi—by preventing the punishment of tyrants.''

''One may do great harm with affection; great good without it. Yes, that is true. Even *le bon motif* is not everything, I know. Still I contend that, given your powers, you would be far more useful in the world with sympathy, affection for your kind, added to them than as you are. I believe even that you would do still more splendid work.''

The Professor poured himself another glass of claret.

"You noticed my butler?" he said.

"I did."

"He's a perfect servant. He makes me perfectly comfortable. Yet he has no feeling of liking for me. I treat him civilly. I pay him well. But I never think about him, or concern myself with him as a human being. I know nothing of his character except what I read of it in his last master's letter. There are, you may say, no truly human relations between us. You would affirm that his work would be better done if I had made him personally like me as a man—of any class— can like a man—of any other class?"

"I should, decidedly."

"I contend that he couldn't do his work better than he does it at present."

"But if any crisis occurred?"

"What?"

"Any crisis, change in your condition. If you needed his help, not only as a man and a butler, but as a man and a brother? He'd fail you then, probably. You would never get from your servant that finest service which can only be prompted by an honest affection."

"You have finished?"

"Quite."

"Let us go upstairs then. Yes, those are good prints. I picked them up in Birmingham when I was living there. This is my workroom."

They came to a double room lined entirely with books, and brilliantly, rather hardly, lit by electricity. The windows at one end looked on to the Park, at the other on to the garden of a neighbouring house. The door by which they entered was concealed from the inner and smaller room by the jutting wall of the outer room, in which stood a huge writing table loaded with letters, pamphlets and manuscripts. Between the two windows of the inner room was a cage in which a large, grey parrot was clambering, using both beak and claws to assist him in his slow and meditative peregrinations.

"You have a pet," said the Father, surprised.

"I possess a parrot," the Professor answered drily. "I got

him for a purpose when I was making a study of the imitative powers of birds, and I have never got rid of him. A cigar?''

''Thank you.''

They sat down. Father Murchison glanced at the parrot. It has paused in its journey, and, clinging to the bars of its cage, was regarding them with attentive round eyes that looked deliberately intelligent, but by no means sympathetic. He looked away from it to Guildea, who was smoking, with his head thrown back, his sharp, pointed chin, on which the small black beard bristled, upturned. He was moving his under lip up and down rapidly. This action caused the beard to stir and look peculiarly aggressive. The Father suddenly chuckled softly.

''Why's that?'' cried Guildea, letting his chin drop down on his breast and looking at his guest sharply.

''I was thinking it would have to be a crisis indeed that could make you cling to your butler's affection for assistance.''

Guildea smiled too.

''You're right. It would. Here he comes.''

The man entered with coffee. He offered it gently, and retired like a shadow retreating on a wall.

''Splendid, inhuman fellow,'' remarked Guildea.

''I prefer the East End lad who does my errands in Bird Street,'' said the Father. ''I know all his worries. He knows some of mine. We are friends. He's more noisy than your man. He even breathes hard when he is especially solicitous, but he would do more for me than put the coals on my fire, or black my square-toed boots.''

''Men are differently made. To me the watchful eye of affection would be abominable.''

''What about that bird?''

The Father pointed to the parrot. It had got up on its perch and, with one foot uplifted in an impressive, almost benedictory, manner, was gazing steadily at the Professor.

''That's the watchful eye of imitation, with a mind at the back of it, desirous of reproducing the peculiarities of others. No, I thought your sermon to-night very fresh, very clever. But I have no wish for affection. Reasonable liking, of course, one desires''—he tugged sharply at his beard, as if to warn himself against sentimentality—"but anything more would be most irksome, and would push me, I feel sure, towards cruelty. It would also hamper one's work."

"I don't think so."

"The sort of work I do. I shall continue to benefit the world without loving it, and it will continue to accept the benefits without loving me. That's all as it should be."

He drank his coffee. Then he added rather aggressively:

"I have neither time nor inclination for sentimentality."

When Guildea let Father Murchison out, he followed the Father on to the doorstep and stood there for a moment. The Father glanced across the damp road into the Park.

"I see you've got a gate just opposite you," he said idly.

"Yes. I often slip across for a stroll to clear my brain. Good-night to you. Come again some day."

"With pleasure. Good-night."

The Priest strode away, leaving Guildea standing on the step.

Father Murchison came many times again to number 100, Hyde Park Place. He had a feeling of liking for most men and women whom he knew, and of tenderness for all, whether he knew them or not, but he grew to have a special sentiment towards Guildea. Strangely enough, it was a sentiment of pity. He pitied this hard-working, eminently successful man of big brain and bold heart, who never seemed depressed, who never wanted assistance, who never complained of the twisted skein of life or faltered in his progress along its way. The Father pitied Guildea, in fact, because Guildea wanted so little. He had told him so, for the intercourse of the two men, from the beginning, had been singularly frank.

One evening, when they were talking together, the Father happened to speak of one of the oddities of life, the fact that those who do not want things often get them, while those who seek them vehemently are disappointed in their search.

"Then I ought to have affection poured upon me," said Guildea, smiling rather grimly. "For I hate it."

"Perhaps some day you will."

"I hope not, most sincerely."

Father Murchison said nothing for a moment. He was

drawing together the ends of the broad band round his cassock. When he spoke he seemed to be answering someone.

"Yes," he said slowly, "yes, that *is* my feeling—pity."

"For whom?" said the Professor.

Then, suddenly, he understood. He did not say that he understood, but Father Murchison felt, and saw, that it was quite unnecessary to answer his friend's question. So Guildea, strangely enough, found himself closely acquainted with a man—his opposite in all ways—who pitied him.

The fact that he did not mind this, and scarcely ever thought about it, shows perhaps as clearly as anything could, the peculiar indifference of his nature.

II

One Autumn evening, a year and a half after Father Murchison and the Professor had first met, the Father called in Hyde Park Place and enquired of the blond and stony butler—his name was Pitting—whether his master was at home.

"Yes, sir," replied Pitting. "Will you please come this way?"

He moved noiselessly up the rather narrow stairs, followed by Father, tenderly opened the library door, and in his soft, cold voice, announced:

"Father Murchison."

Guildea was sitting in an armchair, before a small fire. His thin, long-fingered hands lay outstretched upon his knees, his head was sunk down on his chest. He appeared to be pondering deeply. Pitting very slightly raised his voice.

"Father Murchison to see you, sir," he repeated.

The Professor jumped up rather suddenly and turned sharply round as the Father came in.

"Oh," he said. "It's you, is it? Glad to see you. Come to the fire."

The Father glanced at him and thought him looking unusually fatigued.

"You don't look well tonight," the Father said.

"No?"

"You must be working too hard. That lecture you are go-ing to give in Paris is bothering you?"

"Not a bit. It's all arranged. I could deliver it to you at this moment verbatim. Well, sit down."

The Father did so, and Guildea sank once more into his chair and stared hard into the fire without another word. He seemed to be thinking profoundly. His friend did not inter-rupt him, but quietly lit a pipe and began to smoke reflec-tively. The eyes of Guildea were fixed upon the fire. The Father glanced about the room, at the walls of soberly bound books, at the crowded writing-table, at the windows, before which hung heavy, dark-blue curtains of old brocade, at the cage, which stood between them. A green baize covering was thrown over it. The Father wondered why. He had never seen Napoleon—so the parrot was named—covered up at night before. While he was looking at the baize, Guildea suddenly jerked up his head, and, taking his hands from his knees and clasping them, said abruptly:

"D'you think I'm an attractive man?"

Father Murchison jumped. Such a question coming from such a man astounded him.

"Bless me!" he ejaculated. "What makes you ask? Do you mean attractive to the opposite sex?"

"That's what I don't know," said the Professor gloomily, and staring again into the fire. "That's what I don't know."

The Father grew more astonished.

"Don't know!" he exclaimed.

And he laid down his pipe.

"Let's say—d'you think I'm attractive, that there's any-thing about me which might draw a—a human being, or an animal irresistibly to me?"

"Whether you desired it or not?"

"Exactly—or—no, let us say definitely—if I did not desire it."

Father Murchison pursed up his rather full, cherubic lips, and little wrinkles appeared about the corners of his blue eyes.

"There might be, of course," he said, after a pause. "Hu-man nature is weak, engagingly weak, Guildea. And you're inclined to flout it. I could understand a certain class of lady—

the lion-hunting, the intellectual lady, seeking you. Your reputation, your great name—''

''Yes, yes,'' Guildea interrupted, rather irritably—''I know all that, I know.''

He twisted his long hands together, bending the palms outwards till his thin, pointed fingers cracked. His forehead was wrinkled in a frown.

''I imagine,'' he said—he stopped and coughed drily, almost shrilly—''I imagine it would be very disagreeable to be liked, to be run after—that is the usual expression, isn't it—by anything one objected to.''

And now he half turned in his chair, crossed his legs one over the other, and looked at his guest with an unusual, almost piercing interrogation.

''Anything?'' said the Father.

''Well—well, anyone. I imagine nothing could be more unpleasant.''

''To you—no,'' answered the Father. ''But—forgive me, Guildea, I cannot conceive your permitting such intrusion. You don't encourage adoration.''

Guildea nodded his head gloomily.

''I don't,'' he said, ''I don't. That's just it. That's the curious part of it, that I—''

He broke off deliberately, got up and stretched.

''I'll have a pipe, too,'' he said.

He went over to the mantelpiece, got his pipe, filled it and lighted it. As he held the match to the tobacco, bending forward with an enquiring expression, his eyes fell upon the green baize that covered Napoleon's cage. He threw the match into the grate, and pulled at the pipe as he walked forward to the cage. When he reached it he put out his hand, took hold of the baize and began to pull it away. Then suddenly he pushed it back over the cage.

''No,'' he said, as if to himself, ''no.''

He returned rather hastily to the fire and threw himself once more into his armchair.

''You're wondering,'' he said to Father Murchison. ''So am I. I don't know at all what to make of it. I'll just tell you the facts and you must tell me what you think of them. The night before last, after a day of hard work—but no harder than usual—I went to the front door to get a breath of air. You know I often do that.''

"Yes, I found you on the doorstep when I first came here.''

"Just so. I didn't put on hat or coat. I just stood on the step as I was. My mind, I remember, was still full of my work. It was rather a dark night, not very dark. The hour was about eleven, or a quarter past. I was staring at the Park, and presently I found that my eyes were directed towards somebody who was sitting, back to me, on one of the benches. I saw the person—if it was a person—through the railings.''

"If it was a person!'' said the Father. "What do you mean by that?''

"Wait a minute. I say that because it was too dark for me to know. I merely saw some blackish object on the bench, rising into view above the level of the back of the seat. I couldn't say it was man, woman or child. But something there was, and I found that I was looking at it.''

"I understand.''

"Gradually, I also found that my thoughts were becoming fixed upon this thing or person. I began to wonder, first, what it was doing there; next, what it was thinking; lastly, what it was like.''

"Some poor creature without a home, I suppose,'' said the Father.

"I said that to myself. Still, I was taken with an extraordinary interest about this object, so great an interest that I got my hat and crossed the road to go into the Park. As you know, there's an entrance almost opposite to my house. Well, Murchison, I crossed the road, passed through the gate in the railings, went up to the seat, and found that there was—nothing on it.''

"Were you looking at it as you walked?''

"Part of the time. But I removed my eyes from it just as I passed through the gate, because there was a row going on a little way off, and I turned for an instant in that direction. When I saw that the seat was vacant I was seized by a most absurd sensation of disappointment, almost of anger. I stopped and looked about me to see if anything was moving away, but I could see nothing. It was a cold night and misty, and there were few people about. Feeling, as I say, foolishly and unnaturally disappointed, I retraced my steps to this house. When I got here I discovered that during my short absence I had left the hall door open—half open.''

''Rather imprudent in London.''

''Yes. I had no idea, of course, that I had done so, till I got back. However, I was only away three minutes or so.''

''Yes.''

''It was not likely that anybody had gone in.''

''I suppose not.''

''Was it?''

''Why do you ask me that, Guildea?''

''Well, well!''

''Besides, if anybody had gone in, on your return you'd have caught him, surely.''

Guildea coughed again. The Father, surprised, could not fail to recognise that he was nervous and that his nervousness was affecting him physically.

''I must have caught cold that night,'' he said, as if he had read his friend's thought and hastened to contradict it. Then he went on:

''I entered the hall, or passage, rather.''

He paused again. His uneasiness was becoming very apparent.

''And you did catch somebody?'' said the Father.

Guildea cleared his throat.

''That's just it,'' he said, ''now we come to it. I'm not imaginative, as you know.''

''You certainly are not.''

''No, but hardly had I stepped into the passage before I felt certain that somebody had got into the house during my absence. I felt convinced of it, and not only that, I also felt convinced that the intruder was the very person I had dimly seen sitting upon the seat in the Park. What d'you say to that?''

''I begin to think you are imaginative.''

''H'm! It seemed to me that the person—the occupant of the seat—and I had simultaneously formed the project of interviewing each other, had simultaneously set out to put that project into execution. I became so certain of this that I

walked hastily upstairs into this room, expecting to find the
visitor awaiting me. But there was no one. I then came down
again and went into the dining-room. No one. I was actually
astonished. Isn't that odd?''

''Very,'' said the Father, quite gravely.

The Professor's chill and gloomy manner, and uncomfortable, constrained appearance kept away the humour that might
well have lurked round the steps of such a discourse.

''I went upstairs again,'' he continued, ''sat down and
thought the matter over. I resolved to forget it, and took up
a book. I might perhaps have been able to read, but suddenly
I thought I noticed—''

He stopped abruptly. Father Murchison observed that he
was staring towards the green baize that covered the parrot's
cage.

''But that's nothing,'' he said. ''Enough that I couldn't
read. I resolved to explore the house. You know how small
it is, how easily one can go all over it. I went all over it. I
went into every room without exception. To the servants, who
were having supper, I made some excuse. They were surprised at my advent, no doubt.''

''And Pitting?''

''Oh, he got up politely when I came in, stood while I was
there, but never said a word. I muttered 'don't disturb yourselves,' or something of the sort, and came out. Murchison,
I found nobody new in the house—yet I returned to this room
entirely convinced that somebody had entered while I was in
the Park.''

''And gone out again before you came back?''

''No, had stayed, and was still in the house.''

''But, my dear Guildea,'' began the Father, now in great
astonishment. ''Surely—''

''I know what you want to say—what I should want to say
in your place. Now, do wait. I am also convinced that this
visitor has not left the house and is at this moment in it.''

He spoke with evident sincerity, with extreme gravity. Father Murchison looked him full in the face, and met his quick,
keen eyes.

''No,'' he said, as if in reply to an uttered question: ''I'm
perfectly sane, I assure you. The whole matter seems almost

as incredible to me as it must to you. But, as you know, I never quarrel with facts, however strange. I merely try to examine into them thoroughly. I have already consulted a doctor and been pronounced in perfect bodily health."

He paused, as if expecting the Father to say something.

"Go on, Guildea," he said, "you haven't finished."

"No. I felt that night positive that somebody had entered the house, and remained in it, and my conviction grew. I went to bed as usual, and, contrary to my expectation, slept as well as I generally do. Yet directly I woke up yesterday morning, I knew that my household had been increased by one."

"May I interrupt you for one moment? How did you know it?"

"By my mental sensation. I can only say that I was perfectly conscious of a new presence within my house, close to me."

"How very strange," said the Father. "And you feel absolutely certain that you are not overworked? Your brain does not feel tired? Your head is quite clear?"

"Quite. I was never better. When I came down to breakfast that morning I looked sharply into Pitting's face. He was as coldly placid and inexpressive as usual. It was evident to me that his mind was in no way distressed. After breakfast I sat down to work, all the time ceaselessly conscious of the fact of this intruder upon my privacy. Nevertheless, I laboured for several hours, waiting for any development that might occur to clear away the mysterious obscurity of this event. I lunched. About half-past two I was obliged to go out to attend a lecture. I therefore took my coat and hat, opened my door, and stepped on to the pavement. I was instantly aware that I was no longer intruded upon, and this although I was now in the street, surrounded by people. Consequently, I felt certain that the thing in my house must be thinking of me, perhaps even spying upon me."

"Wait a moment," interrupted the Father. "What was your sensation? Was it one of fear?"

"Oh, dear no. I was entirely puzzled—as I am now—and keenly interested, but not in any way alarmed. I delivered my lecture with my usual ease and returned home in the evening. On entering the house again I was perfectly conscious that the intruder was still there. Last night I dined alone and spent the hours after dinner in reading a scientific work in which I was deeply interested. While I read, however, I never for one moment lost the knowledge that some mind—very attentive to me—was within hail of mine. I will say more than this—the sensation constantly increased, and, by the time I got up to go to bed, I had come to a very strange conclusion.''

''What? What was it?''

''That whoever—or whatever—had entered my house during my short absence in the Park was more than interested in me.''

''More than interested in you?''

''Was fond, or was becoming fond, of me.''

''Oh!'' exclaimed the Father. ''Now I understand why you asked me just now whether I thought there was anything about you that might draw a human being or an animal irresistibly to you.''

''Precisely. Since I came to this conclusion, Murchison, I will confess that my feeling of strong curiosity has become tinged with another feeling.''

''Of fear?''

''No, of dislike, or irritation. No—not fear, not fear.''

As Guildea repeated unnecessarily this asseveration he looked again towards the parrot's cage.

''What is there to be afraid of in such a matter?'' he added. ''I am not a child to tremble before bogies.''

In saying the last words he raised his voice sharply; then he walked quickly to the cage, and, with an abrupt movement, pulled the baize covering from it. Napoleon was disclosed, apparently dozing upon his perch with his head held slightly on one side. As the light reached him, he moved, ruffled the feathers about his neck, blinked his eyes, and began slowly to sidle to and fro, thrusting his head forward and drawing it back with an air of complacent, though rather unmeaning, energy. Guildea stood by the cage, looking at him closely, and indeed with an attention that was so intense as to be remarkable, almost unnatural.

"How absurd these birds are!" he said at length, coming back to the fire.

"You have no more to tell me?" asked the Father.

"No. I am still aware of the presence of something in my house. I am still conscious of its close attention to me. I am still irritated, seriously annoyed—I confess it—by that attention."

"You say you are aware of the presence of something at this moment?"

"At this moment—yes."

"Do you mean in this room, with us, now?"

"I should say so—at any rate, quite near us."

Again he glanced quickly, almost suspiciously, towards the cage of the parrot. The bird was sitting still on its perch now. Its head was bent down and cocked sideways, and it appeared to be listening attentively to something.

"That bird will have the intonations of my voice more correctly than ever by to-morrow morning," said the Father, watching Guildea closely with his mild blue eyes. "And it has always imitated me very cleverly."

The Professor started slightly.

"Yes," he said. "Yes, no doubt. Well, what do you make of this affair?"

"Nothing at all. It is absolutely inexplicable. I can speak quite frankly to you, I feel sure."

"Of course. That's why I have told you the whole thing."

"I think you must be over-worked, over-strained, without knowing it."

"And that the doctor was mistaken when he said I was all right?"

"Yes."

Guildea knocked his pipe out against the chimney piece.

"It may be so," he said. "I will not be so unreasonable as to deny the possibility, although I feel as well as I ever did in my life. What do you advise then?"

"A week of complete rest away from London, in good air."

"The usual prescription. I'll take it. I'll go to-morrow to Westgate and leave Napoleon to keep house in my absence."

For some reason, which he could not explain to himself,

the pleasure which Father Murchison felt in hearing the first part of his friend's final remark was lessened, was almost destroyed, by the last sentence.

He walked towards the City that night, deep in thought, remembering and carefully considering the first interview he had with Guildea in the latter's house a year and a half before.

On the following morning Guildea left London.

III

Father Murchison was so busy a man that he had little time for brooding over the affairs of others. During Guildea's week at the sea, however, the Father thought about him a great deal, with much wonder and some dismay. This dismay was soon banished, for the mild-eyed priest was quick to discern weakness in himself, quicker still to drive it forth as a most undesirable inmate of the soul. But the wonder remained. It was destined to a crescendo. Guildea had left London on a Thursday. On a Thursday he returned, having previously sent a note to Father Murchison to mention that he was leaving Westgate at a certain time. When his train ran into Victoria Station, at five o'clock in the evening, he was surprised to see the cloaked figure of his friend standing upon the grey platform behind a line of porters.

"What, Murchison!" he said. "You here! Have you seceded from your order that you are taking this holiday?"

They shook hands.

"No," said the Father. "It happened that I had to be in this neighbourhood to-day, visiting a sick person. So I thought I would meet you."

"And see if I were still a sick person, eh?"

The Professor glanced at him kindly, but with a dry little laugh.

"Are you?" replied the Father gently, looking at him with interest. "No, I think not. You appear very well."

The sea air had, in fact, put some brownish red into Guildea's always thin cheeks. His keen eyes were shining with life and energy, and he walked forward in his loose grey suit and fluttering overcoat with a vigour that was noticeable, carrying easily in his left hand his well-filled Gladstone bag.

The Father felt completely reassured.

"I never saw you look better," he said.

"I never was better. Have you an hour to spare?"

"Two."

"Good. I'll send my bag up by cab, and we'll walk across the Park to my house and have a cup of tea there. What d'you say?"

"I shall enjoy it."

They walked out of the station yard, past the flower girls and newspaper sellers towards Grosvenor Place.

"And you have had a pleasant time?" the Father said.

"Pleasant enough, and lonely. I left my companion behind me in the passage at number 100, you know."

"And you'll not find him there now, I feel sure."

"H'm!" ejaculated Guildea. "What a precious weakling you think of me, Murchison."

As he spoke he strode forward more quickly, as if moved to emphasise his sensation of bodily vigour.

"A weakling—no. But anyone who uses his brain as persistently as you do yours must require an occasional holiday."

"And I required one very badly, eh?"

"You required one, I believe."

"Well, I've had it. And now we'll see."

The evening was closing in rapidly. They crossed the road at Hyde Park Corner, and entered the Park, in which were a number of people going home from work; men in corduroy trousers, caked with dried mud, and carrying tin cans slung over their shoulders, and flat panniers, in which lay their tools. Some of the younger ones talked loudly or whistled shrilly as they walked.

"Until the evening," murmured Father Murchison to himself.

"What?" asked Guildea.

"I was only quoting the last words of the text which seems written upon life, especially upon the life of pleasure: 'Man goeth forth to his work, and to his labour.' "

"Ah, those fellows are not half bad fellows to have in an

audience. There were a lot of them at the lecture I gave when I first met you, I remember. One of them tried to heckle me. He had a red beard. Chaps with red beards are always hecklers. I laid him low on that occasion. Well, Murchison, and now we're going to see.''

''What?''

''Whether my companion has departed.''

''Tell me—do you feel any expectation of—well—of again thinking something is there?''

''How carefully you choose language. No, I merely wonder.''

''You have no apprehension?''

''Not a scrap. But I confess to feeling curious.''

''Then the sea air hasn't taught you to recognise that the whole thing came from overstrain?''

''No,'' said Guildea, very drily.

He walked on in silence for a minute. Then he added:

''You thought it would?''

''I certainly thought it might.''

''Make me realise that I had a sickly, morbid, rotten imagination—eh? Come now, Murchison, why not say frankly that you packed me off to Westgate to get rid of what you considered an acute form of hysteria?''

The Father was quite unmoved by this attack.

''Come now, Guildea,'' he retorted, ''what did you expect me to think? I saw no indication of hysteria in you. I never have. One would suppose you the last man likely to have such a malady. But which is more natural—for me to believe in your hysteria or in the truth of such a story as you told me?''

''You have me there. No, I mustn't complain. Well, there's no hysteria about me now, at any rate.''

''And no stranger in your house, I hope.''

Father Murchison spoke the last words with earnest gravity, dropping the half-bantering tone—which they had both assumed.

''You take the matter very seriously, I believe,'' said Guildea, also speaking more gravely.

''How else can I take it? You wouldn't have me laugh at it when you tell it to me seriously?''

"No. If we find my visitor still in the house, I may even call upon you to exorcise it. But first I must do one thing."

"And that is?"

"Prove to you, as well as to myself, that it is still there."

"That might be difficult," said the Father, considerably surprised by Guildea's matter-of-fact tone.

"I don't know. If it has remained in my house I think I can find a means. And I shall not be at all surprised if it is still there—despite the Westgate air."

In saying the last words the Professor relapsed into his former tone of dry chaff. The Father could not quite make up his mind whether Guildea was feeling unusually grave or unusually gay. As the two men drew near to Hyde Park Place their conversation died away and they walked forward silently in the gathering darkness.

"Here we are!" said Guildea at last.

He thrust his key into the door, opened it and let Father Murchison into the passage, following him closely, and banging the door.

"Here we are!" he repeated in a louder voice.

The electric light was turned on in anticipation of his arrival. He stood still and looked round. "We'll have some tea at once," he said. "Ah, Pitting!"

The pale butler, who had heard the door bang, moved gently forward from the top of the stairs that led to the kitchen, greeted his master respectfully, took his coat and Father Murchison's cloak, and hung them on two pegs against the wall.

"All's right, Pitting? All's as usual?" said Guildea.

"Quite so, sir."

"Bring us up some tea to the library."

"Yes, sir."

Pitting retreated. Guildea waited till he had disappeared, then opened the dining-room door, put his head into the room and kept it there for a moment, standing perfectly still. Presently he drew back into the passage, shut the door, and said:

"Let's go upstairs."

Father Murchison looked at him enquiringly, but made no remark. They ascended the stairs and came into the library. Guildea glanced rather sharply round. A fire was burning on

the hearth. The blue curtains were drawn. The bright gleam
of the strong electric light fell on the long rows of books, on
the writing table—very orderly in consequence of Guildea's
holiday—and on the uncovered cage of the parrot. Guildea
went up to the cage. Napoleon was sitting humped up on his
perch with his feathers ruffled. His long toes, which looked
as if they were covered with crocodile skin, clung to the bar.
His round and blinking eyes were filmy, like old eyes. Guildea stared at the bird very hard, and then clucked with his
tongue against his teeth. Napoleon shook himself, lifted one
foot, extended his toes, sidled along the perch to the bars
nearest to the Professor and thrust his head against them.
Guildea scratched it with his forefinger two or three times,
still gazing attentively at the parrot; then he returned to the
fire just as Pitting entered with the tea-tray.

Father Murchison was already sitting in an armchair on
one side of the fire. Guildea took another chair and began to
pour out tea, as Pitting left the room, closing the door gently
behind him. The Father sipped his tea, found it hot, and set
the cup down on a little table at his side.

"You're fond of that parrot, aren't you?" he asked his
friend.

"Not particularly. It's interesting to study sometimes. The
parrot mind and nature are peculiar."

"How long have you had him?"

"About four years. I nearly got rid of him just before I
made your acquaintance. I'm very glad now I kept him."

"Are you? Why is that?"

"I shall probably tell you in a day or two."

The Father took his cup again. He did not press Guildea
for an immediate explanation, but when they had both finished their tea he said:

"Well, has the sea-air had the desired effect?"

"No," said Guildea.

The Father brushed some crumbs from the front of his
cassock and sat up higher in his chair.

"Your visitor is still here?" he asked, and his blue eyes
became almost ungentle and piercing as he gazed at his
friend.

"Yes," answered Guildea, calmly.

"How.do you know it, when did you know it—when you looked into the dining room just now?"

"No. Not until I came into this room. It welcomed me here."

"Welcomed you! In what way?"

"Simply by being here, by making me feel that it is here, as I might feel that a man was if I came into the room when it was dark."

He spoke quietly, with perfect composure in his usual dry manner.

"Very well," the Father said, "I shall not try to contend against your sensation, or to explain it away. Naturally, I am in amazement."

"So am I. Never has anything in my life surprised me so much. Murchison, of course I cannot expect you to believe more than that I honestly—imagine, if you like—that there is some intruder here, of what kind I am totally unaware. I cannot expect you to believe that there really is anything. If you were in my place, I in yours, I should certainly consider you the victim of some nervous delusion. I could not do otherwise. But—wait. Don't condemn me as a hysteria patient, or as a madman, for two or three days. I feel convinced that—unless I am indeed unwell, a mental invalid, which I don't think is possible—I shall be able very shortly to give you some proof that there is a newcomer in my house."

"You don't tell me what kind of proof?"

"Not yet. Things must go a little farther first. But, perhaps even to-morrow I may be able to explain myself more fully. In the meanwhile, I'll say this, that if, eventually, I can't bring any kind of proof that I'm not dreaming, I'll let you take me to any doctor you like, and I'll resolutely try to adopt your present view—that I'm suffering from an absurd delusion. That is your view, of course?"

Father Murchison was silent for a moment. Then he said, rather doubtfully:

"It ought to be."

"But isn't it?" asked Guildea, surprised.

"Well, you know, your manner is enormously convincing. Still, of course, I doubt. How can I do otherwise? The whole thing must be fancy."

The Father spoke as if he were trying to recoil from a mental position he was being forced to take up.

"It must be fancy," he repeated.

"I'll convince you by more than my manner, or I'll not try to convince you at all," said Guildea.

When they parted that evening, he said:

"I'll write to you in a day or two probably. I think the proof I am going to give you has been accumulating during my absence. But I shall soon know."

Father Murchison was extremely puzzled as he sat on the top of the omnibus going homeward.

IV

In two days' time he received a note from Guildea asking him to call, if possible, the same evening. This he was unable to do as he had an engagement to fulfil at some East End gathering. The following day was Sunday. He wrote saying he would come on the Monday, and got a wire shortly afterwards: "Yes Monday come to dinner seven-thirty Guildea." At half-past seven he stood on the doorstep of number 100.

Pitting let him in.

"Is the Professor quite well, Pitting?" the Father enquired as he took off his cloak.

"I believe so, sir. He has not made any complaint," the butler formally replied. "Will you come upstairs, sir?"

Guildea met them at the door of the library. He was very pale and sombre, and shook hands carelessly with his friend.

"Give us dinner," he said to Pitting.

As the butler retired, Guildea shut the door rather cautiously. Father Murchison had never before seen him look so disturbed.

"You're worried, Guildea," the Father said. "Seriously worried."

"Yes, I am. This business is beginning to tell on me a good deal."

"Your belief in the presence of something here continues then?"

"Oh, dear, yes. There's no sort of doubt about the matter.

The night I went across the road into the Park something got into the house, though what the devil it is I can't yet find out. But now, before we go down to dinner, I'll just tell you something about that proof I promised you. You remember?''

''Naturally.''

''Can't you imagine what it might be?''

Father Murchison moved his head to express a negative reply.

''Look about the room,'' said Guildea. ''What do you see?''

The Father glanced around the room, slowly and carefully.

''Nothing unusual. You do not mean to tell me there is any appearance of—''

''Oh, no, no, there's no conventional, white-robed, cloud-like figure. Bless my soul, no! I haven't fallen so low as that.''

He spoke with considerable irritation.

''Look again.''

Father Murchison looked at him, turned in the direction of his fixed eyes and saw the grey parrot clambering in its cage, slowly and persistently.

''What?'' he said, quickly. ''Will the proof come from there?''

The Professor nodded.

''I believe so,'' he said. ''Now let's go down to dinner. I want some food badly.''

They descended to the dining room. While they ate and Pitting waited upon them, the Professor talked about birds, their habits, their curiosities, their fears and their powers of imitation. He had evidently studied this subject with the thoroughness that was characteristic of him in all that he did.

''Parrots,'' he said presently, ''are extraordinarily observant. It is a pity that their means of reproducing what they see are so limited. If it were not so, I have little doubt that their echo of gesture would be as remarkable as their echo of voice often is.''

''But hands are missing.''

''Yes. They do many things with their heads, however. I once knew an old woman near Goring on the Thames. She was afflicted with the palsy. She held her head perpetually sideways and it trembled, moving from right to left. Her sailor son brought her home a parrot from one of his voyages. It used to reproduce the old woman's palsied movement of the head exactly. Those grey parrots are always on the watch.''

Guildea said the last sentence slowly and deliberately, glancing sharply over his wine at Father Murchison, and, when he had spoken it, a sudden light of comprehension dawned in the priest's mind. He opened his lips to make a swift remark. Guildea turned his bright eyes towards Pitting, who at the moment was tenderly bearing a cheese meringue from the lift that connected the dining room with the lower regions. The Father closed his lips again. But presently, when the butler had placed some apples on the table, had meticulously arranged the decanters, brushed away the crumbs and evaporated, he said, quickly:

"I begin to understand. You think Napoleon is aware of the intruder?''

"I know it. He has been watching my visitant ever since the night of that visitant's arrival.''

Another flash of light came to the priest.

"That was why you covered him with green baize one evening?''

"Exactly. An act of cowardice. His behaviour was beginning to grate upon my nerves.''

Guildea pursed up his thin lips and drew his brows down, giving to his face a look of sudden pain.

"But now I intend to follow his investigations,'' he added, straightening his features. "The week I wasted at Westgate was not wasted by him in London, I can assure you. Have an apple.''

"No, thank you; no, thank you.''

The Father repeated the words without knowing that he did so. Guildea pushed away his glass.

"Let us come upstairs, then.''

"No, thank you,'' reiterated the Father.

"Eh?''

"What am I saying?'' exclaimed the Father, getting up. "I was thinking over this extraordinary affair.''

"Ah, you're beginning to forget the hysteria theory?''

They walked out into the passage.

"Well, you are so very practical about the whole matter."

"Why not? Here's something very strange and abnormal come into my life. What should I do but investigate it closely and calmly?"

"What, indeed?"

The Father began to feel rather bewildered, under a sort of compulsion which seemed laid upon him to give earnest attention to a matter that ought to strike him—so he felt—as entirely absurd. When they came into the library his eyes immediately turned, with profound curiosity, towards the parrot's cage. A slight smile curled the Professor's lips. He recognised the effect he was producing upon his friend. The Father saw the smile.

"Oh, I'm not won over yet," he said in answer to it.

"I know. Perhaps you may be before the evening is over. Here comes the coffee. After we have drunk it we'll proceed to our experiment. Leave the coffee, Pitting, and don't disturb us again."

"No, sir."

"I won't have it black to-night," said the Father; "plenty of milk, please. I don't want my nerves played upon."

"Suppose we don't take coffee at all?" said Guildea. "If we do, you may trot out the theory that we are not in a perfectly normal condition. I know you, Murchison, devout priest and devout sceptic."

The Father laughed and pushed away his cup.

"Very well, then. No coffee."

"One cigarette, and then to business."

The grey-blue smoke curled up.

"What are we going to do?" said the Father.

He was sitting bolt upright as if ready for action. Indeed there was no suggestion of repose in the attitudes of either of the men.

"Hide ourselves, and watch Napoleon. By the way—that reminds me."

He got up, went to a corner of the room, picked up a piece of green baize and threw it over the cage.

"I'll pull that off when we are hidden."

"And tell me first if you have had any manifestation of this supposed presence during the last few days?"

"Merely an increasingly intense sensation of something here, perpetually watching me, perpetually attending to all my doings."

"Do you feel that it follows you about?"

"Not always. It was in this room when you arrived. It is here now—I feel. But, in going down to dinner, we seemed to get away from it. The conclusion is that it remained here. Don't let us talk about it just now."

They spoke of other things till their cigarettes were finished. Then, as they threw away the smouldering ends, Guildea said:

"Now, Murchison, for the sake of this experiment, I suggest that we should conceal ourselves behind the curtains on either side of the cage, so that the bird's attention may not be drawn towards us and so distracted from that which we want to know more about. I will pull away the green baize when we are hidden. Keep perfectly still, watch the bird's proceedings, and tell me afterwards how you feel about them, how you explain them. Tread softly."

The Father obeyed, and they stole towards the curtains that fell before the two windows. The Father concealed himself behind those on the left of the cage, the Professor behind those on the right. The latter, as soon as they were hidden, stretched out his arm, drew the baize down from the cage, and let it fall on the floor.

The parrot, which had evidently fallen asleep in the warm darkness, moved on its perch as the light shone upon it, ruffled the feathers round its throat, and lifted first one foot and then the other. It turned its head round on its supple, and apparently elastic, neck, and, diving its beak into the down upon its back, made some searching investigations with, as it seemed, a satisfactory result, for it soon lifted its head again, glanced around its cage, and began to address itself to a nut which had been fixed between the bars for its refreshment. With its curved beak it felt and tapped the nut, at first gently, then with severity. Finally it plucked the nut from the bars, seized it with its rough, grey toes, and, holding it down firmly on the perch, cracked it and pecked out its contents, scattering some on the floor of the cage and letting the fractured shell fall into the china bath that was fixed against the bars. This accomplished, the bird paused meditatively, extended one leg backwards, and went through an elaborate process of wing-stretching that made it look as if it were lopsided and deformed. With its head reversed, it again applied itself to a subtle and exhaustive search among the feathers of its wing. This time its investigation seemed interminable, and Father Murchison had time to realise the absurdity of the whole position, and to wonder why he had lent himself to it. Yet he did not find his sense of humour laughing at it. On the contrary, he was smitten by a sudden gust of horror. When he was talking to his friend and watching him, the Professor's manner, generally so calm, even so prosaic, vouched for the truth of his story and the well-adjusted balance of his mind. But when he was hidden this was not so. And Father Murchison, standing behind his curtain, with his eyes upon the unconcerned Napoleon, began to whisper to himself the word—madness, with a quickening sensation of pity and of dread.

The parrot sharply contracted one wing, ruffled the feathers around its throat again, then extended its other leg backwards, and proceeded to the cleaning of its other wing. In the still room the dry sound of the feathers being spread was distinctly audible. Father Murchison saw the blue curtains behind which Guildea stood tremble slightly, as if a breath of wind had come through the window they shrouded. The clock in the far room chimed, and a coal dropped into the grate, making a noise like dead leaves stirring abruptly on hard ground. And again a gust of pity and of dread swept over the Father. It seemed to him that he had behaved very foolishly, if not wrongly, in encouraging what must surely be the strange dementia of his friend. He ought to have declined to lend himself to a proceeding that, ludicrous, even childish in itself, might well be dangerous in the encouragement it gave to a diseased expectation. Napoleon's protruding leg, extended wing and twisted neck, his busy and unconscious devotion to the arrangement of his person, his evident sensation of complete loneliness and most comfortable solitude, brought home with vehemence to the Father the undignified buffoonery of his conduct, the more piteous buffoonery of his friend. He seized the curtains with his hand and was about to thrust them aside and issue forth, when an abrupt movement of the parrot stopped him. The bird, as if sharply attracted by something, paused in its pecking, and, with its head still bent backward and twisted sideways on its neck, seemed to listen intently. Its round eye looked glistening and strained, like the eye of a disturbed pigeon. Contracting its wing, it lifted its head and sat for a moment erect on its perch, shifting its feet mechanically up and down, as if a dawning excitement produced in it an uncontrollable desire of movement. Then it thrust its head forward in the direction of the further room and remained perfectly still. Its attitude so strongly suggested the concentration of its attention on something immediately before it, that Father Murchison instinctively stared about the room, half expecting to see Pitting advance softly, having entered through the hidden door. He did not come, and there was no sound in the chamber. Nevertheless, the parrot was obviously getting excited and increasingly attentive. It bent its head lower and lower, stretching out its neck until, almost falling from the perch, it half extended its wings, raising them slightly from its back, as if about to take flight, and fluttering them rapidly up and down. It continued this fluttering movement for what seemed to the Father an immense time. At length, raising its wings as far as possible, it dropped them slowly and deliberately down to its back, caught hold of the edge of its bath with its beak, hoisted itself on to the floor of the cage, waddled to the bars, thrust its head against them, and stood quite still in the exact attitude it always assumed when its head was being scratched by the Professor. So complete was the suggestion of this delight conveyed by the bird, that Father Murchison felt as if he saw a white finger gently pushed among the soft feathers of its head, and he was seized by a most strong conviction that something, unseen by him but seen and welcomed by Napoleon, stood immediately before the cage.

The parrot presently withdrew its head, as if the coaxing finger had been lifted from it, and its pronounced air of acute physical enjoyment faded into one of marked attention and alert curiosity. Pulling itself up by the bars it climbed again upon its perch, sidled to the left side of the cage, and began apparently to watch something with profound interest. It bowed its head oddly, paused for a moment, then bowed its head again. Father Murchison found himself conceiving—from this elaborate movement of the head—a distinct idea of a personality. The bird's proceedings suggested extreme sentimentality combined with that sort of weak determination which is often the most persistent. Such weak determination is a very common attribute of persons who are partially idiotic. Father Murchison was moved to think of these poor creatures who will often, so strangely and unreasonably, attach themselves with persistence to those who love them least. Like many priests, he had had some experience of them, for the amorous idiot is peculiarly sensitive to the attraction of preachers. This bowing movement of the parrot recalled to his memory a terrible, pale woman who for a time haunted all churches in which he ministered, who was perpetually endeavouring to catch his eye, and who always bent her head with an obsequious and cunningly conscious smile when she did so. The parrot went on bowing, making a short pause between each genuflection, as if it waited for a signal to be given that called into play its imitative faculty.

"Yes, yes, it's imitating an idiot," Father Murchison caught himself saying as he watched.

And he looked again about the room, but saw nothing; except the furniture, the dancing fire, and the serried ranks of the books. Presently the parrot ceased from bowing, and assumed the concentrated and stretched attitude of one listening very keenly. He opened his beak, showing his black tongue, shut it, then opened it again. The Father thought he was going to speak, but he remained silent, although it was obvious that he was trying to bring out something. He bowed again two or three times, paused, and then, again opening his beak, made some remark. The Father could not distinguish any words, but the voice was sickly and disagreeable, a cooing and, at the same time, querulous voice, like a woman's, he thought. And he put his ear nearer to the curtain, listening with almost feverish attention. The bowing was resumed, but this time Napoleon added to it a sidling movement, affectionate and affected, like the movement of a silly and eager thing, nestling up to someone, or giving someone a gentle and furtive nudge. Again the Father thought of that terrible, pale woman who had haunted churches. Several times he had come upon her waiting for him after evening services. Once she had hung her head smiling, and lolled out her tongue and pushed against him sideways in the dark. He remembered how his flesh had shrunk from the poor thing, the sick loathing of her that he could not banish by remembering that her mind was all astray. The parrot paused, listened, opened his beak, and again said something in the same dove-like, amorous voice, full of sickly suggestion and yet hard, even dangerous, in its intonation. A loathsome voice, the Father thought it. But this time, although he heard the voice more distinctly than before, he could not make up his mind whether it was like a woman's voice or a man's—or perhaps a child's. It seemed to be a human voice, and yet oddly sexless. In order to resolve his doubt he withdrew into the darkness of the curtains, ceased to watch Napoleon and simply listened with keen attention, striving to forget that he was listening to a bird, and to imagine that he was overhearing a human being in conversation. After two or three minutes' silence the voice spoke again, and at some length, apparently repeating several times an affectionate series of ejaculations with a cooing emphasis that was unutterably mawkish and offensive. The sickliness of the voice, its falling intonations and its strange indelicacy, combined with a die-away softness and meretricious refinement, made the Father's flesh creep. Yet he could not distinguish any words, nor could he decide on the voice's sex or age. One thing alone he was certain of as he stood still in the darkness—that such a sound could only proceed from something peculiarly loathsome, could only express a personality unendurably abominable to him, if not to everybody. The voice presently failed, in a sort of husky gasp, and there was a prolonged silence. It was broken by the Professor, who suddenly pulled away the curtains that hid the Father and said to him:

"Come out now, and look."

The Father came into the light, blinking, glanced towards the cage, and saw Napoleon poised motionless on one foot with his head under his wing. He appeared to be asleep. The Professor was pale, and his mobile lips were drawn into an expression of supreme disgust.

"Faugh!" he said.

He walked to the windows of the further room, pulled aside the curtains and pushed the glass up, letting in the air. The bare trees were visible in the grey gloom outside. Guildea leaned out for a minute drawing the night air into his lungs. Presently he turned round to the Father, and exclaimed abruptly:

"Pestilent! Isn't it?"

"Yes—most pestilent."

"Ever hear anything like it?"

"Not exactly."

"Nor I. It gives me nausea, Murchison, absolute physical nausea."

He closed the window and walked uneasily about the room.

"What d'you make of it?" he asked, over his shoulder.

"How d'you mean exactly?"

"Is it man's, woman's, or child's voice?"

"I can't tell, I can't make up my mind."

"Nor I."

"Have you heard it often?"

"Yes, since I returned from Westgate. There are never any words that I can distinguish. What a voice!"

He spat into the fire.

"Forgive me," he said, throwing himself down in a chair. "It turns my stomach—literally."

"And mine," said the Father truly.

"The worst of it is," continued Guildea, with a high, nervous accent, "that there's no brain with it, none at all—only the cunning of idiocy."

The Father started at this exact expression of his own conviction by another.

"Why d'you start like that?" said Guildea, with a quick suspicion which showed the unnatural condition of his nerves.

"Well, the very same idea had occurred to me."

"What?"

"That I was listening to the voice of something idiotic."

"Ah! That's the devil of it, you know, to a man like me. I could fight against brain—but this!"

He sprang up again, poked the fire violently, then stood

on the hearth-rug with his back to it, and his hands thrust
into the high pockets of his trousers.

"That's the voice of the thing that's got into my house,"
he said. "Pleasant, isn't it?"

And now there was really horror in his eyes and his voice.

"I must get it out," he exclaimed. "I must get it out. But
how?"

He tugged at his short black beard with a quivering hand.

"How?" he continued. "For what is it? Where is it?"

"You feel it's here—now?"

"Undoubtedly. But I couldn't tell you in what part of the
room."

He stared about, glancing rapidly at everything.

"Then you consider yourself haunted?" said Father Murchison. He, too, was much moved and disturbed, although
he was not conscious of the presence of anything near them
in the room.

"I have never believed in any nonsense of that kind, as
you know," Guildea answered. "I simply state a fact, which
I cannot understand, and which is beginning to be very painful to me. There is something here. But whereas most so-
called hauntings have been described to me as inimical, what
I am conscious of is that I am admired, loved, desired. This
is distinctly horrible to me, Murchison, distinctly horrible."

Father Murchison suddenly remembered the first evening
he had spent with Guildea, and the latter's expression almost
of disgust at the idea of receiving warm affection from anyone. In the light of that long-ago conversation, the present
event seemed supremely strange, and almost like a punishment for an offence committed by the Professor against humanity. But, looking up at his friend's twitching face, the
Father resolved not to be caught in the net of his hideous
belief.

"There can be nothing here," he said. "It's impossible."

"What does that bird imitate, then?"

"The voice of someone who has been here."

"Within the last week then. For it never spoke like that
before, and mind, I noticed that it was watching and striving
to imitate something before I went away, since the night that
I went into the Park, only since then."

"Somebody with a voice like that must have been here while you were away," Father Murchison repeated, with a gentle obstinacy.

"I'll soon find out."

Guildea pressed the bell. Pitting stole in almost immediately.

"Pitting," said the Professor, speaking in a high, sharp voice, "did anyone come into this room during my absence at the sea?"

"Certainly not, sir, except the maids—and me, sir."

"Not a soul? You are certain?"

"Perfectly certain, sir."

The cold voice of the butler sounded surprised, almost resentful. The Professor flung out his hands toward the cage.

"Has the bird been here the whole time?"

"Yes, sir."

"He was not moved, taken elsewhere, even for a moment?"

Pitting's pale face began to look almost expressive, and his lips were pursed.

"Certainly not, sir."

"Thank you. That will do."

The butler retired, moving with a sort of ostentatious rectitude. When he had reached the door, and was just going out, his master called:

"Wait a minute, Pitting."

The butler paused. Guildea bit his lips, tugged at his beard uneasily two or three times, and then said:

"Have you noticed—er—the parrot talking lately in a—a very peculiar, very disagreeable voice?"

"Yes, sir—a soft voice like, sir."

"Ha! Since when?"

"Since you went away, sir. He's always at it."

"Exactly. Well, and what did you think of it?"

"Beg pardon, sir?"

"What do you think about his talking in this voice?"

"Oh, that it's only his play, sir."

"I see. That's all, Pitting."

The butler disappeared and closed the door noiselessly behind him.

Guildea turned his eyes on his friend.

"There, you see!" he ejaculated.

"It's certainly very odd," said the Father. "Very odd indeed. You are certain you have no maid who talks at all like that?"

"My dear Murchison! Would you keep a servant with such a voice about you for two days?"

"No."

"My housemaid has been with me for five years, my cook for seven. You've heard Pitting speak. The three of them make up my entire household. A parrot never speaks in a voice it has not heard. Where has it heard that voice?"

"But we hear nothing?"

"No. Nor do we see anything. But it does. It feels something too. Didn't you observe it presenting its head to be scratched?"

"Certainly it seemed to be doing so."

"It was doing so."

Father Murchison said nothing. He was full of increasing discomfort that almost amounted to apprehension.

"Are you convinced?" said Guildea, rather irritably.

"No. The whole matter is very strange. But till I hear, see or feel—as you do—the presence of something, I cannot believe."

"You mean that you will not?"

"Perhaps. Well, it is time I went."

Guildea did not try to detain him, but said, as he let him out:

"Do me a favour, come again tomorrow night."

The Father had an engagement. He hesitated, looked into the Professor's face and said:

"I will. At nine I'll be with you. Good-night."

When he was on the pavement he felt relieved. He turned round, saw Guildea stepping into his passage, and shivered.

V

Father Murchison walked all the way home to Bird Street
that night. He required exercise after the strange and disagreeable evening he had spent, an evening upon which he
looked back already as a man looks back upon a nightmare.
In his ears, as he walked, sounded the gentle and intolerable
voice. Even the memory of it caused him physical discomfort. He tried to put it from him, and to consider the whole
matter calmly. The Professor had offered his proof that there
was some strange presence in his house. Could any reasonable man accept such proof? Father Murchison told himself
that no reasonable man could accept it. The parrot's proceedings were, no doubt, extraordinary. The bird had succeeded in producing an extraordinary illusion of an invisible
presence in the room. But that there really was such a presence the Father insisted on denying to himself. The devoutly
religious, those who believe implicitly in the miracles recorded in the Bible, and who regulate their lives by the messages they suppose themselves to receive directly from the
Great Ruler of a hidden World, are seldom inclined to accept
any notion of supernatural intrusion into the affairs of daily
life. They put it from them with anxious determination. They
regard it fixedly as hocus-pocus, childish if not wicked.

Father Murchison inclined to the normal view of the devoted churchman. He was determined to incline to it. He
could not—so he now told himself—accept the idea that his
friend was being supernaturally punished for his lack of humanity, his deficiency in affection, by being obliged to endure the love of some horrible thing, which could not be
seen, heard, or handled. Nevertheless, retribution did certainly seem to wait upon Guildea's condition. That which he
had unnaturally dreaded and shrunk from in his thought he
seemed to be now forced unnaturally to suffer. The Father
prayed for his friend that night before the little, humble altar
in the barely furnished, cell-like chamber where he slept.

On the following evening, when he called in Hyde Park
Place, the door was opened by the housemaid, and Father
Murchison mounted the stairs, wondering what had become

of Pitting. He was met at the library door by Guildea and was painfully struck by the alteration in his appearance. His face was ashen in hue, and there were lines beneath his eyes. The eyes themselves looked excited and horribly forlorn. His hair and dress were disordered and his lips twitched continually, as if he were shaken by some acute nervous apprehension.

"What has become of Pitting?" asked the Father, grasping Guildea's hot and feverish hand.

"He has left my service."

"Left your service!" exclaimed the Father in utter amazement.

"Yes, this afternoon."

"May one ask why?"

"I'm going to tell you. It's all part and parcel of this—this most odious business. You remember once discussing the relations men ought to have with their servants?"

"Ah!" cried the Father, with a flash of inspiration. "The crisis has occurred?"

"Exactly," said the Professor, with a bitter smile. "The crisis has occurred. I called upon Pitting to be a man and a brother. He responded by declining the invitation. I upbraided him. He gave me warning. I paid him his wages and told him he could go at once. And he has gone. What are you looking at me like that for?"

"I didn't know," said Father Murchison, hastily dropping his eyes, and looking away. "Why," he added, "Napoleon is gone too."

"I sold him today to one of those shops in Shaftesbury Avenue."

"Why?"

"He sickened me with his abominable imitation of—his intercourse with—well, you know what he was at last night. Besides, I have no further need of his proof to tell me I am not dreaming. And, being convinced as I now am, that all I have thought to have happened has actually happened, I care very little about convincing others. Forgive me for saying so, Murchison, but I am now certain that my anxiety to make you believe in the presence of something here really arose from some faint doubt on that subject—within myself. All doubt has now vanished.''

"Tell me why."

"I will."

Both men were standing by the fire. They continued to stand while Guildea went on:

"Last night I felt it.''

"What?'' cried the Father.

"I say that last night, as I was going upstairs to bed, I felt something accompanying me and nestling up against me.''

"How horrible!'' exclaimed the Father, involuntarily.

Guildea smiled drearily.

"I will not deny the horror of it. I cannot, since I was compelled to call on Pitting for assistance.''

"But—tell me—what was it, at least what did it seem to be?''

"It seemed to be a human being. It seemed, I say; and what I mean exactly is that the effect upon me was rather that of human contact than of anything else. But I could see nothing, hear nothing. Only, three times, I felt this gentle, but determined, push against me, as if to coax me and to attract my attention. The first time it happened I was on the landing outside this room, with my foot on the first stair. I will confess to you, Murchison, that I bounded upstairs like one pursued. That is the shameful truth. Just as I was about to enter my bedroom, however, I felt the thing entering with me, and, as I have said, squeezing, with loathsome, sickening tenderness, against my side. Then—''

He paused, turned towards the fire and leaned his head on his arm. The Father was greatly moved by the strange helplessness and despair of the attitude. He laid his hand affectionately on Guildea's shoulder.

"Then?''

Guildea lifted his head. He looked painfully abashed.

"Then, Murchison, I am ashamed to say, I broke down, suddenly, unaccountably, in a way I should have thought wholly impossible to me. I struck out with my hands to thrust the thing away. It pressed more closely to me. The pressure, the contact became unbearable to me. I shouted out for Pitting. I—I believe I must have cried—'Help.' ''

"He came, of course?"

"Yes, with his usual soft, unemotional quiet. His calm—its opposition to my excitement of disgust and horror—must, I suppose, have irritated me. I was not myself, no, no!"

He stopped abruptly. Then—

"But I need hardly tell you that," he added, with most piteous irony.

"But what did you say to Pitting?"

"I said that he should have been quicker. He begged my pardon. His cold voice really maddened me, and I burst out into some foolish, contemptible diatribe, called him a machine, taunted him, then—as I felt that loathsome thing nestling once more to me—begged him to assist me, to stay with me, not to leave me alone—I meant in the company of my tormentor. Whether he was frightened, or whether he was angry at my unjust and violent manner and speech a moment before, I don't know. In any case he answered that he was engaged as a butler, and not to sit up all night with people. I suspect he thought I had taken too much to drink. No doubt that was it. I believe I swore at him as a coward—I! This morning he said he wished to leave my service. I gave him a month's wages, a good character as a butler, and sent him off at once."

"But the night? How did you pass it?"

"I sat up all night."

"Where? In your bedroom?"

"Yes—with the door open—to let it go."

"You felt that it stayed?"

"It never left me for a moment, but it did not touch me again. When it was light I took a bath, lay down for a little while, but did not close my eyes. After breakfast I had the explanation with Pitting and paid him. Then I came up here. My nerves were in a very shattered condition. Well, I sat down, tried to write, to think. But the silence was broken in the most abominable manner."

"How?"

"By the murmur of that appalling voice, that voice of a lovesick idiot, sickly but determined. Ugh!"

He shuddered in every limb. Then he pulled himself to-

gether, assumed, with a self-conscious effort, his most determined, most aggressive, manner, and added:

"I couldn't stand that. I had come to the end of my tether;
so I sprang up, ordered a cab to be called, seized the cage
and drove with it to a bird shop in Shaftesbury Avenue. There
I sold the parrot for a trifle. I think, Murchison, that I must
have been nearly mad then, for, as I came out of the wretched
shop, and stood for an instant on the pavement among the
cages of rabbits, guinea-pigs, and puppy dogs, I laughed
aloud. I felt as if a load was lifted from my shoulders, as if
in selling that voice I had sold the cursed thing that torments
me. But when I got back to the house it was here. It's here
now. I suppose it will always be here."

He shuffled his feet on the rug in front of the fire.

"What on earth am I to do?" he said. "I'm ashamed of
myself, Murchison, but—but I suppose there are things in the
world that certain men simply can't endure. Well, I can't
endure this, and there's an end of the matter."

He ceased. The Father was silent. In presence of this extraordinary distress he did not know what to say. He recognised the uselessness of attempting to comfort Guildea, and
he sat with his eyes turned, almost moodily, to the ground.
And while he sat there he tried to give himself to the influences within the room, to feel all that was within it. He even,
half-unconsciously, tried to force his imagination to play
tricks with him. But he remained totally unaware of any third
person with them. At length he said:

"Guildea, I cannot pretend to doubt the reality of your
misery here. You must go away, and at once. When is your
Paris lecture?"

"Next week. In nine days from now."

"Go to Paris tomorrow then; you say you have never had
any consciousness that this—this thing pursued you beyond
your own front door?"

"Never—hitherto."

"Go tomorrow morning. Stay away till after your lecture.
And then let us see if the affair is at an end. Hope, my dear
friend, hope."

He had stood up. Now he clasped the Professor's hand.

"See all your friends in Paris. Seek distractions. I would ask you also to seek—other help."

He said the last words with a gentle, earnest gravity and simplicity that touched Guildea, who returned his handclasp almost warmly.

"I'll go," he said. "I'll catch the ten o'clock train, and tonight I'll sleep at an hotel, at the Grosvenor—that's close to the station. It will be more convenient for the train."

As Father Murchison went home that night he kept thinking of that sentence: "It will be more convenient for the train." The weakness in Guildea that had prompted its utterance appalled him.

VI   .

No letter came to Father Murchison from the Professor during the next few days, and this silence reassured him, for it seemed to betoken that all was well. The day of the lecture dawned, and passed. On the following morning, the Father eagerly opened the *Times*, and scanned its pages to see if there were any report of the great meeting of scientific men which Guildea had addressed. He glanced up and down the columns with anxious eyes, then suddenly his hands stiffened as they held the sheets. He had come upon the following paragraph:

"We regret to announce that Professor Frederic Guildea was suddenly seized with severe illness yesterday evening while addressing a scientific meeting in Paris. It was observed that he looked very pale and nervous when he rose to his feet. Nevertheless, he spoke in French fluently for about a quarter of an hour. Then he appeared to become uneasy. He faltered and glanced about like a man apprehensive, or in severe distress. He even stopped once or twice, and seemed unable to go on, to remember what he wished to say. But, pulling himself together with an obvious effort, he continued to address the audience. Suddenly, however, he paused again, edged furtively along the platform, as if pursued by something which he feared, struck out with his hands, uttered a loud, harsh cry and fainted. The sensation in the hall was indescribable. People rose from their seats. Women screamed, and, for a moment, there was a veritable panic. It is feared that the Professor's mind must have temporarily given way owing to overwork. We understand that he will return to England as soon as possible, and we sincerely hope that necessary rest and quiet will soon have the desired effect, and that he will be completely restored to health and enabled to prosecute further the investigations which have already so benefited the world.''

The Father dropped the paper, hurried out into Bird Street, sent a wire of inquiry to Paris, and received the same day the following reply: "Returning tomorrow. Please call evening. Guildea." On that evening the Father called in Hyde Park Place, was at once admitted, and found Guildea sitting by the fire in the library, ghastly pale, with a heavy rug over his knees. He looked like a man emaciated by a long and severe illness, and in his wide open eyes there was an expression of fixed horror. The Father started at the sight of him, and could scarcely refrain from crying out. He was beginning to express his sympathy when Guildea stopped him with a trembling gesture.

"I know all that," Guildea said, "I know. This Paris affair—" He faltered and stopped.

"You ought never to have gone," said the Father. "I was wrong. I ought not to have advised your going. You were not fit."

"I was perfectly fit," he answered, with the irritability of sickness. "But I was—I was accompanied by that abominable thing."

He glanced hastily round him, shifted his chair and pulled the rug higher over his knees. The Father wondered why he was thus wrapped up. For the fire was bright and red and the night was not very cold.

"I was accompanied to Paris," he continued, pressing his upper teeth upon his lower lip.

He paused again, obviously striving to control himself. But

the effort was vain. There was no resistance in the man. He writhed in his chair and suddenly burst forth in a tone of hopeless lamentation.

"Murchison, this being, thing—whatever it is—no longer leaves me even for a moment. It will not stay here unless I am here, for it loves me, persistently, idiotically. It accompanied me to Paris, stayed with me there, pursued me to the lecture hall, pressed against me, caressed me while I was speaking. It has returned with me here. It is here now"—he uttered a sharp cry—"now, as I sit here with you. It is nestling up to me, fawning upon me, touching my hands. Man, man, can't you feel that it is here?"

"No," the Father answered truly.

"I try to protect myself from its loathsome contact," Guildea continued, with fierce excitement, clutching the thick rug with both hands. "But nothing is of any avail against it. Nothing. What is it? What can it be? Why should it have come to me that night?"

"Perhaps as a punishment," said the Father, with a quick softness.

"For what?"

"You hated affection. You put human feeling aside with contempt. You had, you desired to have, no love for anyone. Nor did you desire to receive any love from anything. Perhaps this is a punishment."

Guildea stared into his face.

"D'you believe that?" he cried.

"I don't know," said the Father. "But it may be so. Try to endure it, even to welcome it. Possibly then the persecution will cease."

"I know it means me no harm," Guildea exclaimed, "It seeks me out of affection. It was led to me by some amazing attraction which I exercise over it ignorantly. I know that. But to a man of my nature that is the ghastly part of the matter. If it would hate me, I could bear it. If it would attack me, if it would try to do me some dreadful harm, I should become a man again. I should be braced to fight against it. But this gentleness, this abominable solicitude, this brainless worship of an idiot, persistent, sickly, horribly physical, I cannot endure. What does it want of me? What would it demand of me? It nestles to me. It leans against me. I feel its touch, like the touch of a feather, trembling about my heart, as if it sought to number my pulsations, to find out the inmost secrets of my impulses and desires. No privacy is left to me." He sprang up excitedly. "I cannot withdraw," he cried, "I cannot be alone, untouched, unworshipped, unwatched for even one-half second. Murchison, I am dying of this, I am dying."

He sank down again in his chair, staring apprehensively on all sides, with the passion of some blind man, deluded in the belief that by his furious and continued effort he will attain sight. The Father knew well that he sought to pierce the veil of the invisible, and have knowledge of the thing that loved him.

"Guildea," the Father said, with insistent earnestness, "try to endure this—do more—try to give this thing what it seeks."

"But it seeks my love."

"Learn to give it your love and it may go, having received what it came for."

"T'sh! You talk like a priest. Suffer your persecutors. Do good to them that despitefully use you. You talk as a priest."

"As a friend I spoke naturally, indeed, right out of my heart. The idea suddenly came to me that all this—truth or seeming, it doesn't matter which—may be some strange form of lesson. I have had lessons—painful ones. I shall have many more. If you could welcome—"

"I can't! I can't!" Guildea cried fiercely. "Hatred! I can give it that—always that, nothing but that—hatred, hatred."

He raised his voice, glared into the emptiness of the room, and repeated, "Hatred!"

As he spoke the waxen pallor his cheeks increased, until he looked like a corpse with living eyes. The Father feared that he was going to collapse and faint, but suddenly he raised himself upon his chair and said, in a high and keen voice, full of suppressed excitement:

"Murchison, Murchison!"

"Yes. What is it?"

An amazing ecstasy shone in Guildea's eyes.

"It wants to leave me," he cried. "It wants to go! Don't lose a moment! Let it out! The window—the window!"

The Father, wondering, went to the near window, drew aside the curtains and pushed it open. The branches of the trees in the garden creaked drily in the light wind. Guildea leaned forward on the arms of his chair. There was silence for a moment. Then Guildea, speaking in a rapid whisper, said:

"No, no. Open this door—open the hall door. I feel—I feel that it will return the way it came. Make haste—ah, go!"

The Father obeyed—to soothe him, hurried to the door and opened it wide. Then he glanced back to Guildea. He was standing up, bent forward. His eyes were glaring with eager expectation, and, as the Father turned, he made a furious gesture towards the passage with his thin hands.

The Father hastened out and down the stairs. As he descended in the twilight he fancied he heard a slight cry from the room behind him, but he did not pause. He flung the hall door open, standing back against the wall. After waiting a moment—to satisfy Guildea, he was about to close the door again, and had his hand on it, when he was attracted irresistibly to look forth towards the park. The night was lit by a young moon, and, gazing through the railings, his eyes fell upon a bench beyond them.

Upon the bench something was sitting, huddled together very strangely.

The Father remembered instantly Guildea's description of that former night, that night of Advent, and a sensation of horror-stricken curiosity stole through him.

Was there then really something that had indeed come to the Professor? And had it finished its work, fulfilled its desire and gone back to its former existence?

The Father hesitated a moment in the doorway. Then he stepped out resolutely and crossed the road, keeping his eyes fixed upon this black or dark object that leaned so strangely upon the bench. He could not tell yet what it was like, but he fancied it was unlike anything with which his eyes were acquainted. He reached the opposite path, and was about to pass through the gate in the railings, when his arm was brusquely grasped. He started, turned round, and saw a policeman eyeing him suspiciously.

"What are you up to?" said the policeman.

The Father was suddenly aware that he had no hat upon his head, and that his appearance, as he stole forward in his cassock, with his eyes intently fixed upon the bench in the park, was probably unusual enough to excite suspicion.

"It's all right, policeman," he answered quickly, thrusting some money into the constable's hand.

Then, breaking from him, the Father hurried towards the bench, bitterly vexed at the interruption. When he reached it, nothing was there. Guildea's experience had been almost exactly repeated and, filled with unreasonable disappointment, the Father returned to the house, entered it, shut the door and hastened up the narrow stairway into the library.

On the hearthrug, close to the fire, he found Guildea lying with his head lolled against the armchair from which he had recently risen. There was a shocking expression of terror on his convulsed face. On examining him the Father found that he was dead.

The doctor, who was called in, said that the cause of death was failure of the heart.

When Father Murchison was told this, he murmured:

"Failure of the heart! It was that then!"

He turned to the doctor and said:

"Could it have been prevented?"

The doctor drew on his gloves and answered:

"Possibly, if it had been taken in time. Weakness of the heart requires a great deal of care. The Professor was too much absorbed in his work. He should have lived very differently."

The Father nodded.

"Yes, yes," he said, sadly.

Richard Matheson

BORN OF MAN AND WOMAN

Richard Matheson, one of the great contemporary fantasists, burst upon the scene in 1950 with the publication of "Born of Man and Woman," which later became the title story for his first collection. He was one of the most prolific and important voices in horror in that decade, producing two of the most important horror novels of the contemporary period, *I Am Legend* (1954) and *The Shrinking Man*, (1956) both in the science fiction genre, before going to Hollywood to pursue a successful film-writing career. "Born of Man and Woman" is the contemporary monster story par excellence: concise, chilling, psychologically disturbing. The child is abused and is going to get even. And the world in which such a child exits is not our own, but the world of fantastic horror.

X—This day when it had light mother called me a retch. You retch she said. I saw in her eyes the anger. I wonder what it is a retch.

This day it had water falling from upstairs. It fell all around. I saw that. The ground of the back I watched from the little window. The ground it sucked up the water like thirsty lips. It drank too much and it got sick and runny brown. I didn't like it.

Mother is a pretty I know. In my bed place with cold walls around I have a paper thing that was behind the furnace. It says on it SCREEN-STARS. I see in the pictures faces like of mother and father. Father says they are pretty. Once he said it.

And also mother he said. Mother so pretty and me decent enough. Look at you he said and didn't have the nice face. I touched his arm and said it is alright father. He shook and pulled away where I couldn't reach.

Today mother let me off the chain a little so I could look out the little window. That's how I saw the water falling from upstairs.

XX—This day it had goldness in the upstairs. As I know, when I looked at it my eyes hurt. After I look at it the cellar is red.

I think this was church. They leave the upstairs. The big machine swallows them and rolls out past and is gone. In the back part is the *little* mother. She is much small than me. I am big. It is a secret but I have pulled the chain out of the wall. I can see out the little window all I like.

In this day when it got dark I had eat my food and some bugs. I hear laughs upstairs. I like to know why there are laughs for. I took the chain from the wall and wrapped it around me. I walked squish to the stairs. They creak when I walk on them. My legs slip on them because I don't walk on stairs. My feet stick to the wood.

I went up and opened a door. It was a white place. White as white jewels that come from upstairs sometime. I went in and stood quiet. I hear the laughing some more. I walk to the sound and look through to the people. More people than I thought was. I thought I should laugh with them.

Mother came out and pushed the door in. It hit me and hurt. I fell back on the smooth floor and the chain made noise. I cried. She made a hissing noise into her and put her hand on her mouth. Her eyes got big.

She looked at me. I heard father call. What fell he called. She said a iron board. Come help pick it up she said. He came and said now is *that* so heavy you need. He saw me and grew big. The anger came in his eyes. He hit me. I spilled some of the drip on the floor from one arm. It was not nice. It made ugly green on the floor.

Father told me to go to the cellar. I had to go. The light it hurt some now in my eyes. It is not so like that in the cellar.

Father tied my legs and arms up. He put me on my bed.

Upstairs I heard laughing while I was quiet there looking on a black spider that was swinging down to me. I thought what father said. Ohgod he said. And only eight.

XXX—This day father hit in the chain again before it had light. I have to try pull it out again. He said I was bad to come upstairs. He said never do that again or he would beat me hard. That hurts.

I hurt. I slept the day and rested my head against the cold wall. I thought of the white place upstairs.

XXXX—I got the chain from the wall out. Mother was upstairs. I heard little laughs very high. I looked out the window. I saw all little people like the little mother and little fathers too. They are pretty.

They were making nice noise and jumping around the ground. Their legs was moving hard. They are like mother and father. Mother says all right people look like they do.

One of the little fathers saw me. He pointed at the window. I let go and slid down the wall in the dark. I curled up as they would not see. I heard their talks by the window and foots running. Upstairs there was a door hitting. I heard the little mother call upstairs. I heard heavy steps and I rushed to my bed place. I hit the chain in the wall and lay down on my front.

I heard mother come down. Have you been at the window she said. I heard the anger. *Stay* away from the window. You have pulled the chain out again.

She took the stick and hit me with it. I didn't cry. I can't do that. But the drip ran all over the bed. She saw it and twisted away and made a noise. Oh mygod mygod she said why have you *done* this to me? I heard the stick go bounce on the stone floor. She ran upstairs. I slept the day.

XXXXX—This day it had water again. When mother was upstairs I heard the little one come slow down the steps. I hidded myself in the coal bin for mother would have anger if the little mother saw me.

She had a little live thing with her. It walked on the arms and had pointy ears. She said things to it.

It was all right except the live thing smelled me. It ran up the coal and looked down at me. The hairs stood up. In the throat it made an angry noise. I hissed but it jumped on me.

I didn't want to hurt it. I got fear because it bit me harder than the rat does. I hurt and the little mother screamed. I grabbed the live thing tight. It made sounds I never heard. I pushed it all together. It was all lumpy and red on the black coal.

I hid there when mother called. I was afraid of the stick. She left. I crept over the coal with the thing. I hid it under my pillow and rested on it. I put the chain in the wall again.

X—This is another times. Father chained me tight. I hurt because he beat me. This time I hit the stick out of his hands and made noise. He went away and his face was white. He ran out of my bed place and locked the door.

I am not so glad. All day it is cold in here. The chain comes slow out of the wall. And I have a bad anger with mother and father. I will show them. I will do what I did that once.

I will screech and laugh loud. I will run on the walls. Last I will hang head down by all my legs and laugh and drip green all over until they are sorry they didn't be nice to me.

If they try to beat me again I'll hurt them. I will.

Joanna Russ

MY DEAR EMILY

Joanna Russ is best known for her award-winning science fiction and her notable feminist criticism, but throughout her career she has been a persistent investigator of psychological horrors and has produced a small number of extraordinary tales of the highest quality in that mode. "My Dear Emily" is one of the finest vampire stories since Le Fanu's "Carmilla," monstrous and subversive in its conscious use of psychological metaphor. It is a love story that discovers transcendence through horror. Russ' short fiction is collected in the *The Zanzibar Cat* (Arkham House, 1983). Recently in the last decade the vampire story has staged a major comeback in the novels of Ann Rice, Chelsea Quinn Yarbro and Suzy McKee Charnas, Les Daniels and Stephen King. "My Dear Emily" is a nearly lone example from the previous decade and surpasses all but the best of them.

San Francisco, 188-

I am so looking forward to seeing my dear Emily at last, now she is grown, a woman, although I'm sure I will hardly recognize her. She must not be proud (as if she could be!) but will remember her friends, I know, and have patience with her dear Will who cannot help but remember the girl she was, and the sweet influence she had in her old home. I talk to your father about you every day, dear, and he longs to see you as I do. Think! a learned lady in our circle! But I know you have not changed . . .

Emily came home from school in April with her bosom friend Charlotte. They had loved each other in school, but they didn't speak much on the train. While Emily read Mr. Emerson's poems, Charlotte examined the scenery through opera-glasses. She expressed her wish to see "savages."

"That's foolish," says Emily promptly.

"If we were carried off," says Charlotte, "I don't think you would notice it in time to disapprove."

"That's very foolish," says Emily, touching her round lace collar with one hand. She looks up from Mr. Emerson to stare at Charlotte out of countenance, properly, morally, and matter-of-course young lady. It has always been her style.

"The New England look," Charlotte snaps resentfully. She makes her opera-glasses slap shut.

"I should like to be carried off," she proposes; "but then I don't have an engagement to look forward to. A delicate affair."

"You mustn't make fun," says Emily. Mr. Emerson drops into her lap. She stares unseeing at Charlotte's opera-glasses.

"Why do they close?" she asks helplessly.

"I beg your pardon?" blankly, from Charlotte.

"Nothing. You're much nicer than I am," says Emily.

"Look," urges Charlotte kindly, pressing the toy into her friend's hand.

"For savages?"

Charlotte nods, Emily pushes the spring that will open the little machine, and a moment later drops them into her lap where they fall on Mr. Emerson. There is a cut across one of her fingers and a blue pinch darkening the other.

"They hurt me," she says without expression, and as Charlotte takes the glasses up quickly, Emily looks with curious sad passivity at the blood from her little wound, which has bled an incongruous passionate drop on Mr. Emerson's clothbound poems. To her friend's surprise (and her own, too) she begins to cry, heavily, silently, and totally without reason.

He wakes up slowly, mistily, dizzily, with a vague memory of having fallen asleep on plush. He is intensely miserable, bound down to his bed with hoops of steel, and the memory adds nausea to his misery, solidifying ticklishly around his bare hands and the back of his neck as he drifts towards wakefulness. His stomach turns over with the dry brushy filthiness of it. With the caution of the chronically ill, he opens his eyelids, careful not to move, careful even to keep from focusing his gaze until—he thinks to himself—his bed stops holding him with the force of Hell and this intense miserable sickness goes down, settles . . . Darkness. No breath. A glimmer of light, a stone wall. He thinks: *I'm dead and buried, dead and buried, dead and*—With infinite care he attempts to breathe, sure that this time it will be easy; he'll be patient, discreet, sensible, he won't do it all at once—

He gags. Spasmodically, he gulps, cries out, and gags again, springing convulsively to his knees and throwing himself over the low wall by his bed, laboring as if he were breathing sand. He starts to sweat. His heartbeat comes back, then pulse, then seeing, hearing, swallowing . . . High in the wall a window glimmers, a star is out, the sky is pale evening blue. Trembling with nausea, he rises to his feet, sways a little in the gloom, then puts out one arm and steadies himself against the stone wall. He sees the window, sees the door ahead of him. In his tearing eyes the star suddenly blazes and lengthens like a knife; his head is whirling, his heart painful as a man's; he throws his hands over his face, longing for life and strength to come back, the overwhelming flow of force that will crest at sunrise, leaving him raging at the world and ready to kill anyone, utterly proud and contemptuous, driven to sleep as the last resort of a balked assassin. But it's difficult to stand, difficult to breathe: *I wish I were dead and buried, dead and buried, dead and buried*—But *there!* he whispers to himself like a charm. *There, it's going, it's going away.* He smiles slyly round at his companionable, merciful stone walls. With an involuntarily silent, gliding gait he moves towards the door, opens the iron gate, and goes outside. Life is coming back. The trees are black against the sky, which yet holds some light; far away in the West lie the radiant memories of a vanished sun. An always vanished sun.

"Alive!" he cries, in triumph. It is—as usual—his first word of the day.

* * *

Dear Emily, sweet Emily, met Martin Guevara three days after she arrived home. She had been shown the plants in the garden and the house plants in stands and had praised them; she had been shown the sun-pictures and had praised *them*; she had fingered antimacassars, promised to knit, exclaimed at gas-lights, and passed two evenings at home, doing nothing. Then in the hall that led to the pantry sweet Will had taken her hand and she had dropped her eyes because you were sup-posed to and that was her style. Charlotte (who slept in the same room as her friend) embraced her at bedtime, wept over the handtaking, and then Emily said to her dear, dear friend (without thinking):

"Sweet William."

Charlotte laughed.

"It's not a joke!"

"It's so funny."

"I love Will dearly." She wondered if God would strike her dead for a hypocrite. Charlotte was looking at her oddly, and smiling.

"You mustn't be full of levity," said Emily, peeved. It was then that sweet William came in and told them of to-morrow's garden-party, which was to be composed of her father's congregation. They were lucky, he said, to have ac-quaintances of such position and character. Charlotte slipped out on purpose and Will, seeing they were alone, attempted to take Emily's hand again.

"Leave me alone!" Emily said angrily. He stared.

"I said leave me alone!"

And she gave him such a look of angry pride that, in fact, he did.

Emily sees Guevara across the parlor by the abominable cherry-red sofa, talking animatedly and carelessly. In repose he is slight, undistinguished, and plain, but no one will ever see him in repose; Emily realizes this. His strategy is never to rest, to bewilder, he would (she thinks) slap you if only to confuse you, and when he can't he's always out of the way and attacking, making one look ridiculous. She knows no-body and is bored; she starts for the door to the garden.

At the door his hand closes over her wrist; he has somehow gotten there ahead of her.

"The lady of the house," he says.

"I'm back from school."

"And you've learned—?"

"Let me go, please."

"Never." He drops her hand and stands in the doorway. She says:

"I want to go outside."

"Never."

"I'll call my father."

"Do." She tries and can't talk; I wouldn't *bother*, she thinks to herself, loftily. She goes out into the garden with him. Under the trees his plainness vanishes like smoke.

"You want lemonade," he says.

"I'm not going to talk to you," she responds. "I'll talk to Will. Yes! I'll make him—"

"In trouble," says Mr. Guevara, returning silently with lemonade in a glass cup.

"No thank you."

"She wants to get away," says Martin Guevara. "I know."

"If I had your trick of walking like a cat," she says, "I could get out of anything."

"I *can* get out of anything," says the gentleman, handing Emily her punch, "Out of an engagement, a difficulty. I can even get *you* out of anything."

"I loathe you," whispers Emily suddenly. "You walk like a cat. You're ugly."

"Not out here," he remarks.

"Who has to be afraid of lights?" cries Emily energetically. He stands away from the paper lanterns strung between the trees, handsome, comfortable and collected, watching Emily's cut-glass cup shake in her hand.

"I can't move," she says miserably.

"Try." She takes a step towards him. "See; you can."

"But I wanted to go *away*!" With sudden hysteria she flings the lemonade (cup and all) into his face, but he is no longer there.

"What are you doing at a church supper, you hypocrite!" she shouts tearfully at the vacancy.

Sweet William has to lead her in to bed.

"You thought better of it," remarks Martin, head framed in an evening window, sounds of footsteps outside, ladies' heels clicking in the streets.

"I don't know you," she says miserably, "I just don't." He takes her light shawl, a pattern in India cashmere.

"That will come," he says, smiling. He sits again, takes her hand, and squeezes the skin on the wrist.

"Let me go, please?" she says like a child.

"I don't know."

"You talk like the smart young gentlemen at Andover; they were all fools."

"Perhaps you overawed them." He leans forward and puts his hand around the back of her neck for a moment. "Come on, dear."

"What are you talking about!" Emily cries.

"San Francisco is a lovely city. I had ancestors here three hundred years ago."

"Don't think that because I came here—"

"She doesn't," he whispers, grasping her shoulder, "She doesn't know a thing."

"God damn you!"

He blinks and sits back. Emily is weeping. The confusion of the room—an over-stuffed, over-draped hotel room—has gotten on her nerves. She snatches for her shawl, which is still in his grasp, but he holds it out of her reach, darting his handsome, unnaturally young face from side to side as she tries to reach round him. She falls across his lap and lies there, breathless with terror.

"You're cold," she whispers horrified, "you're cold as a corpse." The shawl descends lightly over her head and shoulders. His frozen hands help her to her feet. He is delighted; he bares his teeth in a smile.

"I think," he says, tasting it, "that I'm going to visit your family."

"But you don't—" she stumbles—"you don't want to . . . sleep with me. I know it."

"I can be a suitor like anyone else," he says.

* * *

That night Emily tells it all to Charlotte, who, afraid of the roué, stays up and reads a French novel as the light drains from the windows and the true black dark takes its place. It is towards dawn and Charlotte has been dozing, when Emily shakes her friend awake, kneeling by the bed with innocent blue eyes reflecting the dying night.

"I had a terrible dream," she complains.

"Hmmmm?"

"I dreamed," says Emily tiredly. "I had a nightmare. I dreamed I was walking by the beach and I decided to go swimming and then a . . . a thing, I don't know . . . it took me by the neck."

"Is that all?" says Charlotte peevishly.

"I'm sick," says Emily with childish satisfaction. She pushes Charlotte over in the bed and climbs in with her. "I won't have to see that man again if I'm sick."

"Pooh, why not?" mumbles Charlotte.

"Because I'll have to stay home."

"He'll visit you."

"William won't let him."

"Sick?" says Charlotte then, suddenly waking up. She moves away from her friend, for she has read more bad fiction than Emily and less moral poetry.

"Yes, I feel awful," says Emily simply, resting her head on her knees. She pulls away in tired irritation when her friend reaches for the collar of her nightdress. Charlotte looks and jumps out of bed.

"Oh," says Charlotte. "Oh—goodness—oh—" holding out her hands.

"What on earth's the matter with you?"

"He's—" whispers Charlotte in horror, "He's—"

In the dim light her hands are black with blood.

"You've come," he says. He is lying on his hotel sofa, reading a newspaper, his feet over one arm and a hand trailing on the rug.

"Yes," she answers, trembling with resolution.

"I never thought this place would have such a good use. But I never know when I'll manage to pick up money—"

With a blow of her hand, she makes a fountain of the newspaper; he lies on the sofa, mildly amused.

"Nobody knows I came," she says rapidly. "But I'm going to finish you off. I know how." She hunts feverishly in her bag.

"I wouldn't," he remarks quietly.

"Ah!" Hauling out her baby cross (silver), she confronts him with it like Joan of Arc. He is still amused, still mildly surprised.

"In your hands?" he says delicately. Her fingers are loosening, her face pitiful.

"My dear, the significance is in the feeling, the faith, not the symbol. You use that the way you would use a hypodermic needle. Now in your father's hands—"

"I dropped it," she says in a little voice. He picks it up and hands it to her.

"You can touch—" she says, her face screwing up for tears.

"I can."

"Oh my God!" she cries in despair.

"My dear." He puts one arm around her, holding her against him, a very strong man for she pushes frantically to free herself. "How many times have *I* said that! But you'll learn. Do I sound like the silly boys at Andover?" Emily's eyes are fixed and her throat contracts; he forces her head between her knees. "The way you go on, you'd think I was bad luck."

"I—I—"

"And you without the plentiful lack of brains that characterizes your friend. She'll be somebody's short work and I think I know whose."

Emily turns white again.

"I'll send her around to you afterwards. Good God! What do you think will happen to her?"

"She'll die," says Emily clearly. He grasps her by the shoulders.

"Ah!" he says with immense satisfaction. "And after that? Who lives forever after that? Did you know that?"

"Yes, people like you don't die," whispers Emily. "But you're not people—"

"No," he says intently, "No. We're not." He stands Emily on her feet. "We're a passion!" Smiling triumphantly, he puts his hands on each side of her head, flattening the pretty curls, digging his fingers into the hair, in a grip Emily can no more break than she could break a vise.

"We're passion," he whispers, amused. "Life is passion. Desire makes life."

"Ah, let me go," says Emily.

He smiles ecstatically at the sick girl.

"Desire," he says dreamily, "lives; *that* lives when nothing else does, and we're desire made purely, desire walking the Earth. Can a dead man walk? Ah! If you want, want, want . . ."

He throws his arms around her, pressing her head to his chest and nearly suffocating her, ruining her elaborate coiffure and crushing the lace at her throat. Emily breathes in the deadness about him, the queer absence of odor, or heat, or presence; her mouth is pressed against the cloth of his fashionable suit, expensive stuff, a good dollar a yard, gotten by—what? But his hands are strong enough to get anything.

"You see," he says gently, "I enjoy someone with intelligence, even with morals; it adds a certain—And besides—" here he releases her and holds her face up to his—"we like souls that come to us; these visits to the bedrooms of unconscious citizens are rather like frequenting a public brothel."

"I abhor you," manages Emily. He laughs. He's delighted.

"Yes, yes, dear," he says, "But don't imagine we're callous parasites. Followers of the Marquis de Sade, perhaps—you see Frisco has evening hours for its bookstores!—but sensitive souls, really, and apt to long for a little conscious partnership." Emily shuts her eyes. "I said," he goes on, with a touch of hardness, "that I am a genuine seducer. I flatter myself that I'm not an animal."

"You're a monster," says Emily, with utter conviction. Keeping one hand on her shoulder, he steps back a pace.

"Go." She stands, unable to believe her luck, then makes what seems to her a rush for the door; it carries her into his arms.

"You see?" He's pleased; he's proved a point.

"I can't," she says, with wide eyes and wrinkled forehead . . .

"You will." He reaches for her and she faints.

* * *

Down in the dark where love and some other things make their hiding-place, Emily drifts aimlessly, quite alone, quite cold, like a dead woman without a passion in her soul to make her come back to life.

She opens her eyes and finds herself looking at his face in the dark, as if the man carried his own light with him.

"I'll die," she says softly.

"Not for a while," he drawls, sleek and content.

"You've killed me."

"I've loved."

"Love!"

"Say 'taken' then, if you insist."

"I do! I do!" she cried bitterly.

"You decided to faint."

"Oh the hell with you!" she shouts.

"Good girl!" And as she collapses, weeping hysterically, "Now, now, come here, dear . . ." nuzzling her abused little neck. He kisses it in the tenderest fashion with an exaggerated, mocking sigh; she twists away, but is pulled closer and as his lips open over the teeth of an inhuman, dead desire, his victim finds—to her surprise—that there is no pain. She braces herself and then, unexpectedly, shivers from head to foot.

"Stop it!" she whispers, horrified. "Stop it! Stop it!"

But a vampire who has found a soul-mate (even a temporary one) will be immoderate. There's no stopping them.

Charlotte's books have not prepared her for *this*.

"You're to stay in the house, my dear, because you're ill."

"I'm not," Emily says, pulling the sheet up to her chin.

"Of course you are." The Reverend beams at her, under the portrait of Emily's dead mother which hangs in Emily's bedroom. "You've had a severe chill."

"But I have to get out!" says Emily, sitting up. "Because I have an appointment, you see."

"Not now," says the Reverend.

"But I *can't* have a severe chill in the *summer*!"

"You look so like your mother," says the Reverend, musing. After he has gone away, Charlotte comes in.

"I have to stay in the damned bed," says Emily forcefully, wiggling her toes under the sheet. Charlotte, who has been carrying a tray with tea and a posy on it, drops it on the washstand.

"Why, Emily!"

"I have to stay in the damned bed the whole damned day," Emily adds.

"Dear, why do you use those words?"

"Because the whole world's damned!"

After the duties of his employment were completed at six o'clock on a Wednesday, William came to the house with a doctor and introduced him to the Reverend and Emily's bosom friend. The street lamps would not be lit for an hour but the sun was just down and the little party congregated in the garden under remains of Japanese paper lanterns. No one ever worried that these might set themselves on fire. Lucy brought tea—they were one of the few civilized circles in Frisco—and over the tea, in the darkening garden, to the accompaniment of sugar-tongs and plopping cream (very musical) they talked.

"Do you think," says the Reverend, very worried, "that it might be consumption?"

"Perhaps the lungs are affected," says the doctor.

"She's always been such a robust girl." This is William, putting down the teapot which has a knitted tube about the handle, for insulation. Charlotte is stirring her tea with a spoon.

"It's very strange," says the doctor serenely, and he repeats "It's very strange" as shadows advance in the garden. "But young ladies, you know—especially at twenty—young ladies often take strange ideas into their heads; they do, they often do; they droop; they worry." His eyes are mild, his back sags, he hears the pleasant gurgle of more tea. A quiet consultation, good people, good solid people, a little illness, nothing serious—

"No," says Charlotte. Nobody hears her.

"I knew a young lady once—" ventures the doctor mildly.

"No," says Charlotte, more loudly. Everyone turns to her,

and Lucy, taking the opportunity, insinuates a plate of small-sized muffins in front of Charlotte.

"I can tell you all about it," mutters Charlotte, glancing up from under her eyebrows. "But you'll *laugh*."

"Now, dear—" says the Reverend.

"Now, miss—" says the doctor.

"As a friend—" says William.

Charlotte begins to sob.

"Oh," she says, "I'll—I'll tell you about it."

Emily meets Mr. Guevara at the Mansion House at seven, having recovered an appearance of health (through self-denial) and a good solid record of spending the evenings at home (through self-control). She stands at the hotel's wrought-iron gateway, her back rigid as a stick, drawing on white gloves. Martin materializes out of the blue evening shadows and takes her arm.

"I shall like living forever," says Emily, thoughtfully.

"God deliver me from Puritans," says Mr. Guevara.

"What?"

"You're a lady. You'll swallow me up."

"I'll do anything I please," remarks Emily severely, with a glint of teeth.

"Ah."

"I will." They walk through the gateway. "You don't care two pins for me."

"Unfortunately," says he, bowing.

"It's not unfortunate as long as *I* care for me," says Emily, smiling with great energy. "Damn them all."

"You proper girls would overturn the world." Along they walk in the evening, in a quiet, respectable rustle of clothes. Halfway to the restaurant she stops and says breathlessly:

"Let's go—somewhere else!"

"My dear, you'll ruin your health!"

"You know better. Three weeks ago I was sick as a dog and much you cared; I haven't slept for days and I'm fine."

"You look fine."

"Ah! You mean I'm beginning to look dead, like you." She tightens her hold on his arm, to bring him closer.

"Dead?" says he, slipping his arm around her.

"Fixed. Bright-eyed. Always at the same heat and not a moment's rest."

"It agrees with you."

"I adore you," she says.

When Emily gets home, there's a reckoning. The Reverend stands in the doorway and sad William, too, but not Charlotte, for she is on the parlor sofa, having had hysterics.

"Dear Emily," says the Reverend. "We don't know how to tell you this—"

"Why, Daddy, *what*?" exclaims Emily, making wide-eyes at him.

"Your little friend told us—"

"Has something happened to Charlotte?" cries Emily. "Oh tell me, tell me, what happened to Charlotte?" And before they can stop her she has flown into the parlor and is kneeling beside her friend, wondering if she dares pinch her under cover of her shawl. William, quick as a flash, kneels on one side of her and Daddy on the other.

"Dear Emily!" cries William with fervor.

"Oh sweetheart!" says Charlotte, reaching down and putting her arms around her friend.

"You're well!" shouts Emily, sobbing over Charlotte's hand and thinking perhaps to bite her. But the Reverend's arms lift her up.

"My dear," says he, "you came home unaccompanied. You were not at the Society."

"But," says Emily, smiling dazzlingly, "two of the girls took all my hospital sewing to their house because we must finish it right away and I have not—"

"You have been lying to us," the Reverend says. *Now*, thinks Emily, *sweet William will cover his face.* Charlotte sobs.

"She can't help it," says Charlotte brokenly. "It's the spell."

"Why, I think everyone's gone out of their minds," says Emily, frowning. Sweet William takes her from Daddy, leading her away from Charlotte.

"Weren't you with a gentleman tonight?" says Sweet Will firmly. Emily backs away.

"For shame!"

"She doesn't remember it," explains Charlotte; "it's part of his spell."

"I think you ought to get a doctor for *her*," observes Emily.

"You were with a gentleman named Guevara," says Will, showing less tenderness than Emily expects. "Weren't you? Well—weren't you?"

"Bad cess to you if I was!" snaps Emily, surprised at herself. The other three gasp. "I won't be questioned," she goes on, "and I won't be spied upon. And I think you'd better take some of Charlotte's books away from her; she's getting downright silly."

"You have too much color," says Will, catching her hands. "You're ill but you don't sleep. You stay awake all night. You don't eat. But look at you!"

"I don't understand you. Do you want me to be ugly?" says Emily, trying to be pitiful. Will softens; she sees him do it.

"My dear Emily," he says. "My dear girl—we're afraid for you."

"Me?" says Emily, enjoying herself.

"We'd better put you to bed," says the Reverend kindly.

"You're so kind," whispers Emily, blinking as if she held back tears.

"That's a good girl," says Will, approving. "We know you don't understand. But we'll take care of you, Em."

"*Will* you?"

"Yes, dear. You've been near very grave danger, but luckily we found out in time, and we found out what to do; we'll make you well, we'll keep you safe, we'll—"

"Not with *that* you won't," says Emily suddenly, rooting herself to the spot, for what William takes out of his vest pocket (where he usually keeps his watch) is a broad-leaved, prickle-faced dock called wolfsbane; it must distress any vampire of sense to be so enslaved to pure superstition. But enslaved they are, nonetheless.

"Oh, no!" says Emily swiftly. "That's silly, perfectly silly!"

"Common sense must give way in such a crisis," remarks the Reverend gravely.

"You bastard!" shouts Emily, turning red, attempting to tear the charm out of her fiance's hand and jump up and down on it. But the Reverend holds one arm and Charlotte the other and between them they pry her fingers apart and William puts his property gently in his vest-pocket again.

"She's far gone," says the Reverend fearfully, at his angry daughter. Emily is scowling, Charlotte stroking her hair.

"Ssssh," says Will with great seriousness. "We must get her to bed," and between them they half-carry Emily up the stairs and put her, dressed as she is, in the big double bed with the plush headboard that she has shared so far with Charlotte. Daddy and fiance confer in the room across the long, low rambling hall, and Charlotte sits by her rebellious friend's bed and attempts to hold her hand.

"I won't permit it; you're a damned fool!" says Emily.

"Oh, Emmy!"

"Bosh."

"It's true!"

"Is it?" With extraordinary swiftness, Emily turns round in the bed and rises to her knees. "Do you know anything about it?"

"I know it's horrid, I—"

"Silly!" Playfully Emily puts her hands on Charlotte's shoulders. Her eyes are narrowed, her nostrils widened to breathe; she parts her lips a little and looks archly at her friend. "You don't know anything about it," she says insinuatingly.

"I'll call your father," says Charlotte quickly.

Emily throws an arm around her friend's neck.

"Not yet! Dear Charlotte!"

"We'll save you," says Charlotte doubtfully.

"Sweet Charrie; you're my friend, aren't you?"

Charlotte begins to sob again.

"Give me those awful things, those leaves."

"Why, Emily, I *couldn't*!"

"But he'll come for me and I have to protect myself, don't I?"

"I'll call your father," says Charlotte firmly.

"No, I'm *afraid*." And Emily wrinkles her forehead sadly.

"Well—"

"Sometimes I—I—" falters Emily. "I can't move or run away and everything looks so—so strange and *horrible*—"

"Oh, here!" Covering her face with one hand, Charlotte holds out her precious dock leaves in the other.

"Dear, dear! Oh, sweet! Oh thank you! Don't be afraid. He isn't after you."

"I hope not," says the bosom friend.

"Oh no, he told me. It's me he's after."

"How awful," says Charlotte, sincerely.

"Yes," says Emily. "Look." And she pulls down the collar of her dress to show the ugly marks, white dots unnaturally healed up, like the pockmarks of a drug addict.

"Don't!" chokes Charlotte.

Emily smiles mournfully. "We really ought to put the lights out," she says.

"Out!"

"Yes, you can see him better that way. If the lights are on, he could sneak in without being seen; he doesn't mind lights, you know."

"I don't know, dear—"

"I do." (Emily is dropping the dock leaves into the washstand, under cover of her skirt.) "I'm afraid. Please."

"Well—"

"Oh, you must!" And leaping to her feet, she turns down the gas to a dim glow; Charlotte's face fades into the obscurity of the deepening shadows.

"So. The lights are out," says Emily quietly.

"I'll ask Will—" Charlotte begins . . .

"No, dear."

"But, Emily—"

"He's coming, dear."

"You mean Will is coming."

"No, not Will."

"Emily, you're a—"

"I'm a sneak," says Emily, chuckling. "Sssssh!" And, while her friend sits paralyzed, one of the windows swings open in the night breeze, a lead-paned window that opens on a hinge, for the Reverend is fond of culture and old architec-

ture. Charlotte lets out a little noise in her throat; and then—
with the smash of a pistol shot—the gaslight shatters and the
flame goes out. Gas hisses into the air, quietly, insinuatingly,
as if explaining the same thing over and over. Charlotte
screams with her whole heart. In the dark a hand clamps like
a vise on Emily's wrist. A moment passes.

"Charlotte?" she whispers.

"Dead," says Guevara.

Emily has spent most of the day asleep in the rubble, with
his coat rolled under her head where he threw it the moment
before sunrise, the moment before he staggered to his place
and plunged into sleep. She has watched the dawn come up
behind the rusty barred gate, and then drifted into sleep herself with his face before her closed eyes—his face burning
with a rigid, constricted, unwasting vitality. Now she wakes
aching and bruised, with the sun of late afternoon in her face.
Sitting against the stone wall, she sneezes twice and tries,
ineffectually, to shake the dust from her silk skirt.

Oh, how—she thinks vaguely—*how messy*. She gets to her
feet. *There's something I have to do.* The iron gate swings
open at a touch. *Trees and gravestones tilted every which
way. What did he say? Nothing would disturb it but a Historical Society.*

Having tidied herself as best she can, with his coat over
her arm and the address of his tailor in her pocket, she trudges
among the erupted stones, which tilt crazily to all sides as if
in an earthquake. Blood (Charlotte's, whom she does not
think about) has spread thinly on to her hair and the hem of
her dress, but her hair is done up with fine feeling, despite
the absence of a mirror, and her dress is dark gray; the spot
looks like a spot of dusk. She folds the coat into a neat package and uses it to wipe the dust off her shoes, then lightens
her step past the cemetery entrance, trying to look healthy
and respectable. She aches all over from sleeping on the
ground.

Once in town and having ascertained from a shop window
that she will pass muster in a crowd, Emily trudges up hills
and down hills to the tailor, the evidence over her arm. She
stops at other windows, to look or to admire herself; thinks

smugly of her improved coloring; shifts the parcel on her arm to show off her waist. In one window there is a display of religious objects—beads and crosses, books with fringed gilt bookmarks, a colored chromo of Madonna and Child. In this window Emily admires herself.

"It's Emily, dear!"

A Mrs. L——appears in the window beside her, with Constantia, Mrs. L——'s twelve-year-old offspring.

"Why, dear, whatever happened to you?" says Mrs. L——, noticing no hat, no gloves, and no veil.

"Nothing; whatever happened to you?" says Emily cockily. Constantia's eyes grow wide with astonishment at the fine, free audacity of it.

"Why, you look as if you'd been—"

"Picnicking," says Emily, promptly. "One of the gentlemen spilled beer on his coat." And she's in the shop now and hanging over the counter, flushed, counting the coral and amber beads strung around a crucifix.

Mrs. L——knocks doubtfully on the window-glass.

Emily waves and smiles.

Your father—form Mrs. L——'s lips in the glass.

Emily nods and waves cheerfully.

They do go away, finally.

"A fine gentleman," says the tailor earnestly, "a very fine man." He lisps a little.

"Oh very fine," agrees Emily, sitting on a stool and kicking the rungs with her feet. "Monstrous fine."

"But very careless," says the tailor fretfully, pulling Martin's coat nearer the window so he can see it, for the shop is a hole-in-the-wall and dark. "He shouldn't send a lady to this part of the town."

"I was a lady once," says Emily.

"Mmmmm."

"It's fruit stains—something awful, don't you think?"

"I cannot have this ready by tonight," looking up.

"Well, you must, that's all," says Emily calmly. "You always have and he has a lot of confidence in you, you know. He'd be awfully angry if he found out."

"Found out?" sharply.

"That you can't have it ready by tonight."

The tailor ponders.

"I'll positively stay in the shop while you work," says Emily flatteringly.

"Why, Reverend, I saw her on King Street as dirty as a gypsy, with her hair loose and the wildest eyes and I *tried* to talk to her, but she dashed into a shop—"

The sun goes down in a broad belt of gold, goes down over the ocean, over the hills and the beaches, makes shadows lengthen in the street near the quays where a lisping tailor smooths and alters, working against the sun (and very uncomfortable he is, too), watched by a pair of unwinking eyes that glitter a little in the dusk inside the stuffy shop. (*I think I've changed*, meditates Emily.)

He finishes, finally, with relief, and sits with an *ouf*! handing her the coat, the new and beautiful coat that will be worn as soon as the eccentric gentleman comes out to take the evening air. The eccentric gentleman, says Emily incautiously, will do so in an hour by the Mansion House when the last traces of light have faded from the sky.

"Then, my dear Miss," says the tailor unctuously, "I think a little matter of pay—"

"You don't think," says Emily softly, "or you wouldn't have gotten yourself into such a mess as to be this eccentric gentleman's tailor." And out she goes.

Now nobody can see the stains on Emily's skirt or in her hair; street lamps are being lit, there are no more carriages, and the number of people in the streets grows—San Francisco making the most of the short summer nights. It is perhaps fifteen minutes back to the fashionable part of town where Emily's hatless, shawlless state will be looked on with disdain; here nobody notices. Emily dawdles through the streets, fingering her throat, yawning, looking at the sky, thinking: I love, I love, I love—

She has fasted for the day but she feels fine; she feels busy, busy inside as if the life inside her is flowering and bestirring itself, populated as the streets. She remembers—

I love you. I hate you. You enchantment, you degrading

necessity, you foul and filthy life, you promise of endless love and endless time . . .

What words to say with Charlotte sleeping in the same room, no, the same bed, with her hands folded under her face! Innocent sweetheart, whose state must now be rather different.

Up the hills she goes, where the view becomes wider and wider, and the lights spread out like sparkles on a cake, out of the section which is too dangerous, too low, and too furtive to bother with a lady (or is it something in her eyes?), into the broader by-streets where shore-leave sailors try to make her acquaintance by falling into step and seizing her elbow; she snakes away with unbounded strength, darts into shadows, laughs in their faces: "I've got what I want!"

"Not like me!"

"Better!"

This is the Barbary Coast, only beginning to become a tourist attraction; there are barkers outside the restaurants advertising pretty waiter girls, dance halls, spangled posters twice the height of a man, crowds upon crowds of people, one or two guides with tickets in their hats, and Emily—who keeps to the shadows. She nearly chokes with laughter: *What a field of ripe wheat!* One of the barkers hoists her by the waist onto his platform.

"Do you see this little lady? Do you see this—"

"Let me go, God damn you!" she cries indignantly.

"This angry little lady—" pushing her chin with one sunburned hand to make her face the crowd. "This—" But here Emily hurts him, slashing his palm with her teeth, quite pleased with herself, but surprised, too, for the man was holding his hand cupped and the whole thing seemed to happen of itself. She escapes instantly into the crowd and continues up through the Coast, through the old Tenderloin, drunk with self-confidence, slipping like a shadow through the now genteel streets and arriving at the Mansion House gate having seen no family spies and convinced that none has seen her.

But nobody is there.

* * *

Ten by the clock, and no one is there, either; eleven by the clock and still no one. *Why didn't I leave this life when I had the chance!* Only one thing consoles Emily, that by some alchemy or nearness to the state she longs for, no one bothers or questions her and even the policemen pass her by as if in her little corner of the gate there is nothing but a shadow. Midnight and no one, half-past and she dozes; perhaps three hours later, perhaps four, she is startled awake by the sound of footsteps. She wakes: nothing. She sleeps again and in her dreams hears them for the second time, then she wakes to find herself looking into the face of a lady who wears a veil.

"What!" Emily's startled whisper.

The lady gestures vaguely, as if trying to speak.

"What is it?"

"Don't—" and the lady speaks with feeling but, it seems, with difficulty also—"don't go home."

"Home?" echoes Emily, stupefied, and the stranger nods, saying:

"In danger."

"Who?" Emily is horrified.

"He's in danger." Behind her veil her face seems almost to emit a faint light of its own.

"You're one of them," says Emily. "Aren't you?" and when the woman nods, adds desperately, "Then you must save him!"

The lady smiles pitifully; that much of her face can be seen as the light breeze plays with her net veil.

"But you must!" exclaims Emily, "You know how; I don't; you've got to!"

"I don't dare," very softly. Then the veiled woman turns to go, but Emily—quite hysterical now—seizes her hand, saying:

"Who are you? Who are you?"

The lady gestures vaguely and shakes her head.

"Who are you!" repeats Emily with more energy. "You tell me, do you hear?"

Somberly the lady raises her veil and stares at her friend with a tragic, dignified, pitiful gaze. In the darkness her face burns with unnatural and beautiful color.

It is Charlotte.

* * *

Dawn comes with a pellucid quickening, glassy and ghostly. Slowly, shapes emerge from darkness and the blue pours back into the world—twilight turned backwards and the natural order reversed. Destruction, which is simple, logical, and easy, finds a kind of mocking parody in the morning's creation. Light has no business coming back, but light does.

Emily reaches the cemetery just as the caldron in the east overflows, just as the birds (idiots! she thinks) begin a tentative cheeping and chirping. She sits at the gate for a minute to regain her strength, for the night's walking and worry have tried her severely. In front of her the stones lie on graves, almost completely hard and real, waiting for the rising of the sun to finish them off and make complete masterpieces of them. Emily rises and trudges up the hill, slower and slower as the ground rises to its topmost swell, where three hundred years of peaceful Guevaras fertilize the grass and do their best to discredit the one wild shoot that lives on, the only disrespectful member of the family. Weeping a little to herself, Emily lags up the hill, raising her skirts to keep them off the weeds, and murderously hating in her heart the increasing light and the happier celebrating of the birds. She rounds the last hillock of ground and raises her eyes to the Guevaras' eternal mansion, expecting to see nobody again. There is the corner of the building, the low iron gate—

In front of it stands Martin Guevara between her father and sweet sweet Will, captivated by both arms, his face pale and beautiful between two gold crosses that are just beginning to sparkle in the light of day.

"We are caught," says Guevara, seeing her, directing at her his fixed, white smile.

"You let him go," says Emily—very reasonably.

"You're safe, my Emily!" cries sweet Will.

"Let him go!" She runs to them, stops, looks at them, perplexed to the bottom of her soul.

"Let him go," she says. "Let him go, let him go!"

Between the two bits of jewelry, Emily's life and hope and only pleasure smiles painfully at her, the color drained out of his face, desperate eyes fixed on the east.

"You don't understand," says Emily, inventing. "He isn't dangerous now. If you let him go, he'll run inside and then you can come back any time during the day and finish him off. I'm sick. You—"

The words die in her throat. All around them, from every tree and hedge, from boughs that have sheltered the grave-yard for a hundred years, the birds begin their morning noise. A great hallelujah rises; after all, the birds have nothing to worry about. Numb, with legs like sticks, Emily sees sun-light touch the top of the stone mausoleum, sunlight slide down its face, sunlight reach the level of a standing man—

"I adore you," says Martin to her. With the slow bending over of a drowning man, he doubles up, like a man stuck with a knife in a dream; he doubles up, falls—

And Emily screams; What a scream! as if her soul were being haled out through her throat; and she is running down the other side of the little hill to regions as yet untouched by the sun, crying inwardly: I need help! help! help!—She knows where she can get it. Three hundred feet down the hill in a valley, a wooded protected valley sunk below the touch of the rising sun, there she runs through the trees, past the fence that separates the old graveyard from the new, expensive, polished granite—Charlotte is her friend, she loves her: Charlotte in her new home will make room for her.

Dennis Etchison

YOU CAN GO NOW

Dennis Etchison is an anthologist and writer whose occasional short stories have established a respectable following in the past fifteen years. The title story of his first collection, *The Dark Country*, won the World Fantasy Award for best short fiction (1982). He is an indefatigable supporter of horror fiction, especially in his anthology series, *The Cutting Edge* (1987), promoting new and different fiction. "You Can Go Now" is characteristic of his surreal psychological short fiction: intense, shifting, suggestive. What happens, happens offstage . . . the horror is internal, in the central character's mind at the moment of realization, which is the story. The maltreatment of women by men is a common theme in contemporary horror, nowhere more pointedly represented than in "You Can Go Now."

1

The receiver purred in his hand.

He glanced around the bedroom, feeling as if he had just awakened from a long, dreamless sleep.

A click, then recorded music. He had been placed on hold.

There was something he was trying to remember. Everything seemed to be ready, but—

"Thank-you-for-waiting-good-afternoon-Pacific-Southwest-Airlines-may-I-help-you?"

He told the voice about his reservation; he was sure he had one. Would she—

Yes. Confirmed.

He thanked her and hung up.

Wait. What was the flight number? He must have written it down—yes. It was probably in his wallet.

He bent over the coat on the bed, feeling for the slim leather billfold. There, in the breast pocket. He fumbled through business cards, odd papers, credit plates.

No.

But no matter. He would find out when he got there.

Still, there was *something*.

He pulled out the drawer in the nightstand, under the phone, and started poking around, not even sure of what he was looking for.

He found a long, unmarked envelope, near the bottom. He took it and held it tightly as he slipped the coat on, then put it into the inside pocket while he felt with his other hand for the keys. He patted his outer pockets, but they were not there.

Head down, he left the room.

His bags were stacked neatly by the wall of the foyer, but the keys were not there. He paced through the living room, the kitchen, checking the tables.

He went back to the bedroom, eyes down.

There.

By the door. The key ring was wedged by the bottom edge, between the door and the pile of the carpet, as though it had been flung or kicked there.

He picked it up, walked to the front door, lifted his bags, and went out to the car.

It was still early afternoon, so the freeway would be a clear shot most of the way.

He switched off the air conditioning—who had left it on?—and rolled down the window, stretching out. The seat was adjusted wrong again, damn it, so he had to grope for the lever and push with his feet, struggling to seat the runner back another notch.

He connected through to the San Diego Freeway, made the turn and tried to unwind the rest of the way. He sampled the radio, but it was only more of the same: back scratchings about love or the lack of it and the pleasure or the pain it brought or might bring; maybe, could be, possibly, for sure, always, never, too soon, not soon enough, in the wrong rain or the wrong style. *Wrong, wrong.* He flicked it off.

The airport turnoff would be coming up.

He flexed his arm, checking his watch. But it had stopped. The face was spattered with dry, flaking paint, so it would have been hard to read the numbers, anyway.

He toed the accelerator until he was moving five miles over the speed limit, then ten.

He was glad to have made such good time; a few extra minutes would mean a drink first, maybe two—

It was funny. The car ahead, at the foot of the ramp. The back-up lights were on, but not the brake lights. He did not slow, because it meant that the signal at the intersection would be—

Headlights. They were headlights.

Headed directly at him.

You can go now, said a voice.

He leaned on the horn, but then there was the heavy, bone-snapping impact and everything was driven into him with such force that the horn stayed on, bleating like a siren, whether or not he would have wanted it to or would even have thought of it or of anything, of anything else at all.

2

He was late getting to LAX, so he swung at once into the western parking lot, hoofed it over to the PSA building and sloughed his bags through the metal detector without stopping at the flight information desk. A couple of quick questions later, a hostess in a Halloween-colored uniform was pointing him toward the boarding tunnel, and then another was ushering him onto the plane and back to the smoking section.

He stashed his bags and found himself in a seat on the aisle, next to a pregnant woman and two drugged-looking hyperactive children. They continued to squirm, but slowly, as though underwater, as he tugged at the seat belt, trying to dislodge the oversized buckle from beneath his buttocks.

A double vodka and two cigarettes later, he was halfway to Oakland and swinging inland away from the silvery tilt of the sea. He drained the ice against his teeth and snared the elbow of a stewardess.

Another?

Well, the bottles were all put away, but—yes. Of course. Of course.

The smaller child was busy on the floor in front of the seat, trying to tear out the pages of a washable cloth picture book about animals who wore gloves and had one-syllable names. The child had already stripped the airline coloring book, the oxygen mask instruction card and the air sickness bag into piles of ragged chits. Now, however, he dropped his work and wobbled to his feet, straining to clamber up the seat and under his mother's smock.

But the mother was absorbed in the counting and recounting of empty punch cups—one, two, three, see? one, two three—over and over, for the older child, who was working with all his might to slide out from under his seat belt. He would flatten like a limbo dancer until his shoes touched the floor and his knees buckled; then the mother would reach down, hoist him back up and begin counting the cups for him again.

"One, two, three, see? Why don't you try, Joshua?"

Ignored, the smaller child twisted like a bendable rubber doll and, sucking the ink off two fingers, watched the man across from him.

Who looked away. He was, mercifully, beginning to feel something from the double: a familiar ease, faint but unmistakable. He folded his hands, cold against each other, and tried to unwind while there was still time. He caught a glimpse out the window of farmlands sectioned like the layers of a surgical operation, beyond the flashing tip of the wing.

The child followed his eyes. "Break-ing," the child announced.

Idly he watched the wing swaying slowly as it knifed through the air currents. He remembered seeing the wing moving up and down like that on his first flight, how he worried that it might break off until someone had explained to him about expansion and contraction and allowances for stress.

"What's breaking?" said the mother. "Nothing's breaking, Jeremiah. Look, look what Mommy's . . ."

The stewardess reappeared. She rattled the plastic serving tray, bending over his lap with the drink.

He reached into his back pocket for his wallet.

"Want more punch!" said the older child.

"More punch?" asked the stewardess.

The wallet wasn't there. He remembered. He reached inside his coat.

He felt a long envelope, and the billfold. He removed both, peeled off two bills and laid them on the tray.

"Break-ing!" said the smaller child.

At that moment a shadow passed over the tray and the stewardess's wet fingers. He glanced up.

Outside, heavy strands of mist had begun to drift above the wings, temporarily blocking the sun. Looking down, he saw the black outline of the plane passing over the manicured rectangles of land.

Suddenly, sharply, the plane dropped like an elevator falling between floors. Then just as suddenly it stopped.

"Looks like we might be hitting some turbulence," he said. "Sure you've got a pilot up there?"

His attention returned to the window. Now darker clouds clotted the view, turning the window opaque so that he saw a reflection of his own face within the thick glass.

He heard a voice say something he did not understand.

"What?" he said.

"I said, that's funny," said the stewardess, "like an open grave."

A flash of brilliant light struck outside, penetrating the cloud bank. She stopped pouring the drink. He looked up at her, then at the tray. He noticed that her hands were shaking.

Then a dull, muffled sound from the back of the plane. Then a series of jolts that rattled the bottle against the lip of the glass. He thought he heard a distant crackling, like ants crawling over aluminum foil. Then the quick, shocking smell of smoke wafted up the aisle.

"Oh my God," whispered the stewardess hoarsely, "we've been—"

"I know," he said, strangely calm, "I know," *with tears of blood I tell you I know.*

The tray, ice and drink went flying, and then they were falling, everything falling inward and children, pillows, oxygen masks, bottles, the envelope he still clutched stupidly in his hand, the whole thing, the plane and the entire world were falling, falling and would not, could not, be stopped.

3

It was dusk as he drove into the delta, and the river, washed over with the memory of the dying red eye of the sun, seemed to be reflecting a gradual darkening of the world.

He wound down the windows of the rented car, cranking back the wind wings so that he could feel the air. The smell of seed crops and of the rich, silted undergrowth of the banks blew around him, bathing him in the special dark parturience of the Sacramento Valley.

He had been away too long.

And soon he would be back, away for a time from the practices of the city, which he had come to think of more and more lately as the art of doing natural things in an unnatural way—something he was afraid he had learned all too well. But now, very soon, he would be back on the houseboat; for a while, at least.

He did not know how long.

He would anchor somewhere near The Meadows. He would tie up to that same tree in the deep, still water, near the striped bass hole, hearing the lowing of cattle from behind the clutch of wild blackberry bushes on shore . . .

And this time, he dared himself, he might not go back at all. Not, at least, for a long, long time.

He drove past the weathered, century-old mansions left from the gold days, past the dirt roads marked only by rural mailboxes, past the fanning rows of shadowy, pungent trees, past the collapsing wooden walkways of the abandoned settlement towns, past the broad landmark barn and the white-wash message fading on its doors, one he had never understood:

HIARA PERU RESH.

He geared down and took the last, unpaved mile in a growing rush of anticipation. Rocks and eucalyptus pods rained up under the car, the wheel jerking in his hands, the shocks and the leaf springs groaning and creaking.

Then he saw a curl of smoke beyond the next grove and caught the warm smell of catfish frying over open coals. And he knew, at last, that he was nearing the inlet, the diner and the dock.

He braked in the gravel and walked down the path to the riverbank. He heard the lapping of the tide and the low, heavy knocking of hulls against splintered pilings. Finally he saw the long pier, the planks glistening, the light and dark prows of cabin cruisers rocking in their berths, the dinghies tied up to battered cleats, their slack, frayed ropes swollen where they dipped into the water, the buoys bobbing slowly, the running lights of a smaller, rented houseboat chugging away around the bend, toward Wimpy's Landing.

The boards moved underfoot as he counted the steps, head down, and he smiled, reminding himself that it would take a few hours to regain his sea legs. He reached the spot, a few yards from the end of the docking area, where he knew the *Shelley Ann* would be waiting.

He tried to remember how long it had been. Since the spring. Yes, that was right, Memorial Day weekend. Sometimes friends rode him about paying for the year-round space—why, when he used her only a few times each year? Even Shelley had begun talking that way in the last few weeks. *Cut your losses on that albatross!* She had actually said that. But at times like this, coming to her after so many months, he forgot it all. It felt like coming home. It always did.

He looked up.

The space was empty.

His eyes darted around the landing, but she was nowhere that he could see.

Unless—of course. She had been moved. That was it. But why? His boat had never been assigned any other stall for as long as he had owned her. Something had happened, then. But there had been no long distance call, no word in the mail; Old John would not be one to hide anything as serious as an accident. Would he?

He took a few steps, his hands in his back pockets, scanning the river in both directions.

He could just make out the diner/office/tackle shop through the trees. A dim light was burning behind the peeling wooden panes.

Yes. Old John would know. Old John would be able to tell him the story, whatever it was.

Which was the trouble. Knowing him, it would take an hour, two. A beer, three beers, maybe even dinner. The lonely old man would not let him go with a simple explanation, of that he was sure.

And now he found he could think only of the *Shelley Ann*. He had waited and he had planned and he had come all this way, and at the moment nothing else seemed to matter. He needed to feel her swaying under him, rocking him. Now, right now.

Then. Everything. Would be. All right.

He stepped off the end to the bank, peering under the covered section of the landing, even though he knew that his boat would have been too large to clear the drooping canvas overhang.

He crouched at the edge, feeling suddenly very alone. The river smelled like dead stars. He watched the water purl gently around the floats and echo back and forth over the fine sand. A few small bubbles rode the surface, and a thin patina of oil shone with mirror-like luminescence under the dimming sky, reflecting a dark, swirling rainbow.

No stars were visible yet. In fact, the sky above the trees grew more steely as he watched.

He looked again at the water. He fingered a chip of gravel and tossed it. It made a plunking sound and settled quickly, and as it disappeared he found that he was straining to follow it with his eyes all the way down to the bottom.

He reached into his coat for a cigarette. His hands were still cold, and growing colder.

He felt the cigarette case and drew it out, along with something else.

He pushed a cigarette into his lips and stared at the envelope. It had no name and address on it. He couldn't remember—

He opened it, slipped out a neatly folded sheet of bond paper, unfolded it.

The leaves of the trees near him rustled, and then a light breeze strafed the water, tipping it with silver.

Still crouching, he fired up the lighter, lit the cigarette and squinted, trying to make out the words. It was written in careful longhand, a letter or—no. Something else.

He read the title.

The paper began to make a tapping sound. He held out his hand. Rain had started to fall, a light rain that danced on the river and left it glittering. As he blinked down at the paper, more drops hit the page. The ink began to run, blurring before his eyes.

The lighter became too hot to hold. He snapped it shut and stood. He heard the rain talking in the trees, on the canvas tarpaulin, on the struts of the rotting pier.

His legs were cramped. He made a staggering step forward. His shoes sloshed the water. He stepped still further, led by the swinging arc of his cigarette tip in the darkness, until the rain found the cigarette and extinguished it.

He dropped it and moved forward, ankle-deep in the river. Is she really there? he thought.

Then he waded out into the low tide, the rain striking around him with a sound like musical notes, the melting paper still gripped in his hand, trailing the water.

4 _____

Dazed, he glanced around the bedroom.

The receiver was in his hand. By now the plastic had become quite warm against his palm. He stared at it for a moment, then returned it to his ear.

He heard recorded music.

Click.

"Thank-you-for-waiting-good-afternoon-Pacific-Southwest-Airlines-may-I-help-you?"

There was something he wanted to tell her. He had been trying hard to remember, but—

His eyes continued to roam the lower half of the room. Then he spotted the keys, the car keys, wedged between the bottom edge of the door and the pile of the carpet, as though they had been flung or kicked there with great force.

It started to come back to him. Shelley had done it. She had thrown the key ring with all her strength, a while ago. Yes. That had happened.

He raised his head at last, rubbed his neck.

And saw her, there on the other side of the bed.

She lay with eyes closed, hands at her sides, fingers clutching the bedspread.

He didn't want to disturb her. He modulated his voice, cupping the mouthpiece with his hand.

He told the maddeningly cheerful voice on the phone—it reminded him of a Nichiren Shoshu recruiter who had buttonholed him on the street once—to cancel one reservation. His wife was not ready, would not be ready on time.

Yes. Only one. That's right. Thank you.

He hung up.

He lifted the phone and replaced it on the nightstand.

On the bed, where the phone had been, was an envelope.

He picked it up.

It was empty.

There was a sheet of paper on the floor, where Shelley had crumpled and thrown it. That was right, wasn't it?

He smoothed it out on his knee.

It was written in a very careful, painstaking longhand, much more legible than his own. He started to read it.

At the end of the first stanza he paused.

Yes, it was something Shelley had found—no, she had had it all along, saved (hidden?) in her drawer in the nightstand. She had taken it out earlier this morning, or perhaps it had been last night, and had shown it to him, and one of them had become angry and crumpled it onto the floor. That was how it had started.

He read it again, this time to the end.

> (1)
> brown hair
> curling smile
> shadowed eyes
> the line of your lips . . .
> hair tangled
> over me
>
> (2)
> warm skin
> tender breasts
> your mouth and
> sweet throat . . .
> hair moist
> under me
>
> (3)
> there will be more
> my eyes tell your eyes
> than love of touch
> *face lost in my face* . . .
> do you know what lives
> between our breathing palms?
>
> (4)
> twisted hair
> seashell ear
> soft sounds

stopped by my chest . . .
dark eyes sleep
while I speak to your heart

He turned to his wife.

It was true; she was beautiful. Whoever had written those words had loved her. He studied her intently until he began to feel an odd sense of dislocation, as if he were seeing her for the first time.

He looked again at the paper.

At the bottom of the page, following the last stanza, there was a name.

It was his own.

And in the corner, a date: almost fifteen years ago.

Quietly, almost imperceptibly, he began to cry.

For so much had changed over the years, much more than handwriting. He did not love her now, not in any traditional sense; instead, he thought, there was merely a sense of loving that seemed to exist somewhere between her and his mind.

As he sat there, he forced his eyes to trace the lines of her body, her face: the shrug of her shoulders, the sweep of her long, slender neck, the surprisingly full jaw and yet the almost weak point of the chin, the slight lips, the sad curve at the corners of her mouth, the smooth, even shade of her skin, the narrow nose, the nearly parallel lines that formed the sides of her small face, the close-set eyes, the thin and almond-shaped lids and delicately sketched lashes, the worried cast of her forehead and the baby-fine wisps at the hairline, the soft down that grew near her temples, the fuller curls that filled out a nimbus around her head, the hair bunched behind her neck, the ends hard and stiff now where the dried brown web had trickled out, just a spot at first but soon spreading onto the pillow after he had lain her down so gently. He had not meant it. He had not meant anything like it. He did not even remember what he had meant, and that was the truth. He had tried to tell her that, practically at the moment it had happened, but then it was too late. And it was too late now. It would always been too late.

He lowered his head.

When he opened his eyes again, he was looking at the paper.

At the top of the page, perfectly centered, was the title. It said:

YOU CAN GO NOW.

D. H. Lawrence

THE ROCKING-HORSE WINNER

D. H. Lawrence, the great critic, poet, novelist and short story writer, made only this one landmark contribution to the evolution of the horror story, a small masterpiece of Modern literature. During the era when the Modernists had for the most part assumed the death of the supernatural tale in the mainstream of literature, the investigation of abnormal human psychology remained nevertheless at the center of much fiction. So one of the mainstreams of horror, became prominent in such fiction as "The Rocking-horse Winner," a story of monstrosity using the form of the "possessed child" story but without supernatural paraphernalia. The child is haunted, possessed, but the most overt interpretation is Freudian, not moral, allegory.

There was a woman who was beautiful, who started with all the advantages, yet she had no luck. She married for love, and the love turned to dust. She had bonny children, yet she felt they had been thrust upon her, and she could not love them. They looked at her coldly, as if they were finding fault with her. And hurriedly she felt she must cover up some fault in herself. Yet what it was that she must cover up she never knew. Nevertheless, when her children were present, she always felt the centre of her heart go hard. This troubled her, and in her manner, she was all the more gentle and anxious for her children, as if she loved them very much. Only she herself knew that at the centre of her heart was a hard little place that could not feel love, no, not for anybody. Everybody else said of her, "She is such a good mother. She adores her children." Only she herself, and her children themselves, knew it was not so. They read it in each other's eyes.

There was a boy and two little girls. They lived in a pleasant house, with a garden, and they had discreet servants, and felt themselves superior to anyone in the neighbourhood.

Although they lived in style, they felt always an anxiety in the house. There was never enough money. The mother had a small income, and the father had a small income, but not nearly enough for the social position which they had to keep up. The father went into town to some office. But though he had good prospects, these prospects never materialized. There was always the grinding sense of the shortage of money, though the style was always kept up.

At last the mother said, "I will see if *I* can't make something." But she did not know where to begin. She racked her brains, and tried this thing and the other, but could not find anything successful. The failure made deep lines come into her face. Her children were growing up, they would have to go to school. There must be more money, there must be more money. The father, who was always very handsome and expensive in his tastes, seemed as if he never *would* be able to do anything worth doing. And the mother, who had a great belief in herself, did not succeed any better, and her tastes were just as expensive.

And so the house came to be haunted by the unspoken phrase: *There must be more money! There must be more money!* The children could hear it all the time, though nobody said it aloud. They heard it at Christmas, when the expensive and splendid toys filled the nursery. Behind the shining modern rocking-horse, behind the smart doll's-house, a voice would start whispering, "There *must* be more money! There *must* be more money!" And the children would stop playing, to listen for a moment. They would look into each other's eyes, to see if they had all heard. And each one saw in the eyes of the other two that they too had heard. "There *must* be more money! There *must* be more money!"

It came whispering from the springs of the still-swaying

rocking-horse, and even the horse, bending his wooden, champing head, heard it. The big doll, sitting so pink and smirking in her new pram, could hear it quite plainly, and seemed to be smirking all the more self-consciously because of it. The foolish puppy too, that took the place of the teddy-bear, he was looking so extraordinarily foolish for no other reason but that he heard the secret whisper all over the house. "There *must* be more money."

Yet nobody ever said it aloud. The whisper was everywhere, and therefore no one spoke it. Just as no one ever says: "We are breathing!" in spite of the fact that breath is coming and going all the time.

"Mother!" said the boy Paul one day. "Why don't we keep a car of our own? Why do we always use uncle's or else a taxi?"

"Because we're the poor members of the family," said the mother.

"But *why* are we, Mother?"

"Well—I suppose," she said slowly and bitterly, "it's because your father has no luck."

The boy was silent for some time.

"Is luck money, Mother?" he asked, rather timidly.

"No, Paul! Not quite. It's what causes you to have money."

"Oh!" said Paul vaguely. "I thought when Uncle Oscar said *filthy lucker*, it meant money."

"*Filthy lucre* does mean money," said the mother. "But it's lucre, not luck."

"Oh!" said the boy. "Then what *is* luck, Mother?"

"It's what causes you to have money. If you're lucky you have money. That's why it's better to be born lucky than rich. If you're rich, you may lose your money. But if you're lucky, you will always get more money."

"Oh! Will you! And is Father not lucky?"

"Very unlucky, I should say," she said, bitterly.

The boy watched her with unsure eyes.

"Why?" he asked.

"I don't know. Nobody ever knows why one person is lucky and another unlucky."

"Don't they? Nobody at all? Does *nobody* know?"

"Perhaps God! But He never tells."

"He ought to, then. And aren't you lucky either, Mother?"

"I can't be, if I married an unlucky husband."

"But by yourself, aren't you?"

"I used to think I was, before I married. Now I think I am very unlucky indeed."

"Why?"

"Well—never mind! Perhaps I'm not really," she said.

The child looked at her, to see if she meant it. But he saw, by the lines of her mouth, that she was only trying to hide something from him.

"Well, anyhow," he said stoutly. "I'm a lucky person."

"Why?" said his mother, with a sudden laugh.

He stared at her. He didn't even know why he had said it.

"God told me," he asserted, brazening it out.

"I hope He did, dear!" she said, again with a laugh, but rather bitter.

"He did, Mother!"

"Excellent!" said the mother, using one of her husband's exclamations.

The boy saw she did not believe him; or rather, that she paid no attention to his assertion. This angered him somewhere, and made him want to compel her attention.

He went off by himself, vaguely, in a childish way, seeking for the clue to "luck." Absorbed, taking no heed of other people, he went about with a sort of stealth, seeking inwardly for luck. He wanted luck, he wanted it, he wanted it. When the two girls were playing dolls, in the nursery, he would sit on his big rocking-horse, charging madly into space, with a frenzy that made the little girls peer at him uneasily. Wildly the horse careered, the waving dark hair of the boy tossed, his eyes had a strange glare in them. The little girls dared not speak to him.

When he had ridden to the end of his mad little journey, he climbed down and stood in front of his rocking-horse, staring fixedly into its lowered face. Its red mouth was slightly open, its big eye was wide and glassy bright.

"Now!" he would silently command the snorting steed. "Now take me where there is luck! Now take me!"

And he would slash the horse on the neck with the little whip he had asked Uncle Oscar for. He *knew* the horse could take him to where there was luck, if only he forced it. So he would mount again, and start on his furious ride, hoping at last to get there. He knew he could get there.

"You'll break your horse, Paul!" said the nurse.

"He's always riding like that! I wish he'd leave off!" said his elder sister Joan.

But he only glared down on them in silence. Nurse gave him up. She could make nothing of him. Anyhow he was growing beyond her.

One day his mother and his Uncle Oscar came in when he was on one of his furious rides. He did not speak to them.

"Hallo! you young jockey! Riding a winner?" said his uncle.

"Aren't you growing too big for a rocking-horse? You're not a very little boy any longer, you know," said his mother.

But Paul only gave a blue glare from his big, rather close-set eyes. He would speak to nobody when he was in full tilt. His mother watched him with an anxious expression on her face.

At last he suddenly stopped forcing his horse into the me-chanical gallop, and slid down.

"Well, I got there!" he announced fiercely, his blue eyes still flaring, and his sturdy long legs straddling apart.

"Where did you get to?" asked his mother.

"Where I wanted to go to," he flared back at her.

"That's right, son!" said Uncle Oscar. "Don't you stop till you get there. What's the horse's name?"

"He doesn't have a name," said the boy.

"Gets on without all right?" asked the uncle.

"Well, he has different names. He was called Sansovino last week."

"Sansovino, eh? Won the Ascot. How did you know his name?"

"He always talks about horse-races with Bassett," said Joan.

The uncle was delighted to find that his small nephew was posted with all the racing news. Bassett, the young gardener who had been wounded in the left foot in the war, and had got his present job through Oscar Cresswell, whose batman he had been, was a perfect blade of the "turf." He lived in the racing events, and the small boy lived with him.

Oscar Cresswell got it all from Bassett.

"Master Paul comes and asks me, so I can't do more than tell him, sir," said Bassett, his face terribly serious, as if he were speaking of religious matters

"And does he ever put anything on a horse he fancies?"

"Well—I don't want to give him away—he's a young sport, a fine sport, sir. Would you mind asking him himself? He sort of takes a pleasure in it, and perhaps he'd feel I was giving him away, sir, if you don't mind."

Bassett was serious as a church.

The uncle went back to his nephew, and took him off for a ride in the car.

"Say, Paul, old man, do you ever put anything on a horse?" the uncle asked.

The boy watched the handsome man closely.

"Why, do you think I oughtn't to?" he parried.

"Not a bit of it! I thought perhaps you might give me a tip for the Lincoln."

The car sped on into the country, going down to Uncle Oscar's place in Hampshire.

"Honour bright?" said the nephew.

"Honour bright, son!" said the uncle.

"Well, then, Daffodil."

"Daffodil! I doubt it, sonny. What about Mirza?"

"I only know the winner," said the boy. "That's Daffodil!"

"Daffodil, eh?"

There was a pause. Daffodil was an obscure horse, comparatively.

"Uncle!"

"Yes, son?"

"You won't let it go any further, will you? I promised Bassett."

"Bassett be damned, old man! What's he got to do with it?"

"We're partners! We've been partners from the first! Uncle, he lent me my first five shillings, which I lost. I promised him, honour bright, it was only between me and him: only you gave me that ten-shilling note I started winning with, so

I thought you were lucky. You won't let it go any further, will you?''

The boy gazed at his uncle from those big, hot, blue eyes, set rather close together. The uncle stirred and laughed uneasily.

''Right you are, son! I'll keep your tip private. Daffodil, eh! How much are you putting on him?''

''All except twenty pounds,'' said the boy. ''I keep that in reserve.''

The uncle thought it was a joke.

''You keep twenty pounds in reserve, do you, you young romancer? What are you betting, then?''

''I'm betting three hundred,'' said the boy gravely. ''But it's between you and me, Uncle Oscar! Honour bright?''

The uncle burst into a roar of laughter.

''It's between you and me all right, you young Nat Gould,'' he said, laughing. ''But where's your three hundred?''

''Bassett keeps it for me. We're partners.''

''You are, are you! And what is Bassett putting on Daffodil?''

''He won't go quite as high as I do, I expect. Perhaps he'll go a hundred and fifty.''

''What, pennies?'' laughed the uncle.

''Pounds,'' said the child, with a surprised look at his uncle. ''Bassett keeps a bigger reserve than I do.''

Between wonder and amusement, Uncle Oscar was silent. He pursued the matter no further, but he determined to take his nephew with him to the Lincoln races.

''Now, son,'' he said. ''I'm putting twenty on Mirza, and I'll put five for you on any horse you fancy. What's your pick?''

''Daffodil, uncle!''

''No, not the fiver on Daffodil!''

''I should if it was my own fiver,'' said the child.

''Good! Good! Right you are! A fiver for me and a fiver for you on Daffodil.''

The child had never been to a race-meeting before, and his eyes were blue fire. He pursed his mouth tight, and watched. A Frenchman just in front had put his money on Lancelot.

Wild with excitement, he flared his arms up and down, yelling *"Lancelot! Lancelot!"* in his French accent.

Daffodil came in first, Lancelot second, Mirza third. The child, flushed and with eyes blazing, was curiously serene. His uncle brought him five five-pound notes: four to one.

"What am I to do with these?" he cried, waving them before the boy's eyes.

"I suppose we'll talk to Bassett," said the boy. "I expect I have fifteen hundred now: and twenty in reserve: and this twenty."

His uncle studied him for some moments.

"Look here, son!" he said. "You're not serious about Bassett and that fifteen hundred, are you?"

"Yes, I am. But it's between you and me, uncle! Honour bright!"

"Honour bright, all right, son! But I must talk to Bassett."

"If you'd like to be a partner, uncle, with Bassett and me, we could all be partners. Only you'd have to promise, honour bright, uncle, not to let it go beyond us three. Bassett and I are lucky, and you must be lucky, because it was your ten shillings I started winning with . . ."

Uncle Oscar took both Bassett and Paul into Richmond Park for an afternoon, and there they talked.

"It's like this, you see, sir," Bassett said. "Master Paul would get me talking about racing events, spinning yarns, you know, sir. And he was always keen on knowing if I'd made or if I'd lost. It's about a year since, now, that I put five shillings on Blush of Dawn for him: and we lost. Then the luck turned, with that ten shillings he had from you: that we put on Singhalese. And since that time, it's been pretty steady, all things considering. What do you say, Master Paul?"

"We're all right when we're *sure*," said Paul. "It's when we're not quite sure that we go down."

"Oh, but we're careful then," said Bassett.

"But when are you *sure*?" smiled Uncle Oscar.

"It's Master Paul, sir," said Bassett, in a secret, religious voice. "It's as if he had it from heaven. Like Daffodil, now, for the Lincoln. That was as sure as eggs."

"Did you put anything on Daffodil?" asked Oscar Cresswell.

"Yes, sir. I made my bit."

"And my nephew?"

Bassett was obstinately silent, looking at Paul.

"I made twelve hundred, didn't I, Bassett? I told uncle I
was putting three hundred on Daffodil."

"That's right," said Bassett, nodding.

"But where's the money?" asked the uncle.

"I keep it safe locked up, sir. Master Paul, he can have it
any minute he likes to ask for it."

"What, fifteen hundred pounds?"

"And twenty! And *forty*, that is, with the twenty he made
on the course."

"It's amazing," said the uncle.

"If Master Paul offers you to be partners, sir, I would, if
I were you: if you'll excuse me," said Bassett.

Oscar Cresswell thought about it.

"I'll see the money," he said.

They drove home again, and sure enough, Bassett came
round to the garden-house with fifteen hundred pounds in
notes. The twenty pounds reserve was left with Joe Glee, in
the Turf Commission deposit.

"You see, it's all right, uncle, when I'm *sure*! Then we go
strong, for all we're worth. Don't we, Bassett?"

"We do that, Master Paul."

"And when are you sure?" said the uncle, laughing.

"Oh well, sometimes I'm absolutely sure, like about Daffodil," said the boy; "and sometimes I have an idea; and
sometimes I haven't an idea, have I, Bassett? Then we're
careful, because we mostly go down."

"You do, do you! And when you're sure, like about Daffodil, what makes you sure, sonny?"

"Oh, well, I don't know," said the boy uneasily. "I'm
sure, you know, uncle; that's all."

"It's as if he had it from heaven, sir," Bassett reiterated.

"I should say so!" said the uncle.

But he became a partner. And when the Leger was coming
on, Paul was "sure" about Lively Spark, which was a quite
inconsiderable horse. The boy insisted on putting a thousand

on the horse, Bassett went for five hundred, and Oscar Cresswell two hundred. Lively Spark came in first and the betting had been ten to one against him. Paul had made ten thousand.

"You see," he said, "I was absolutely sure of him."

Even Oscar Cresswell had cleared two thousand.

"Look here, son," he said, "this sort of thing makes me nervous."

"It needn't, uncle! Perhaps I shan't be sure again for a long time."

"But what are you going to do with your money?" asked the uncle.

"Of course," said the boy, "I started it for Mother. She said she had no luck, because Father is unlucky, so I thought if I was lucky, it might stop whispering."

"What might stop whispering?"

"Our house! I *hate* our house for whispering."

"What does it whisper?"

"Why—why"—the boy fidgeted—"why I don't know! But it's always short of money, you know, uncle."

"I know it, son, I know it."

"You know people send Mother writs, don't you uncle?"

"I'm afraid I do," said the uncle.

"And then the house whispers like people laughing at you behind your back. It's awful, that is! I thought if I was lucky—"

"You might stop it," added the uncle.

The boy watched him with big blue eyes, that had an uncanny cold fire in them, and he said never a word.

"Well, then!" said the uncle. "What are we doing?"

"I shouldn't like Mother to know I was lucky," said the boy.

"Why not, son?"

"She'd stop me."

"I don't think she would."

"Oh!"—and the boy writhed in an odd way—"I *don't* want her to know, uncle."

"All right, son! We'll manage it without her knowing."

They managed it very easily. Paul, at the other's suggestion, handed over five thousand pounds to his uncle, who deposited it with the family lawyer, who was then to inform

Paul's mother that a relative had put five thousand pounds into his hands, which sum was to be paid out a thousand pounds at a time, on the mother's birthday, for the next five years.

"So she'll have a birthday present of a thousand pounds for five successive years," said Uncle Oscar.

"I hope it won't make it all the harder for her later."

Paul's mother had her birthday in November. The house had been "whispering" worse than ever lately, and even in spire of his luck, Paul could not bear up against it. He was very anxious to see the effect of the birthday letter, telling his mother about the thousand pounds.

When there were no visitors, Paul now took his meals with his parents, as he was beyond the nursery control. His mother went into town nearly every day. She had discovered that she had an odd knack of sketching furs and dress materials, so she worked secretly in the studio of a friend who was the chief "artist" for the leading drapers. She drew the figures of ladies in furs and ladies in silk and sequins for the newspaper advertisements. This young woman artist earned several thousand pounds a year, but Paul's mother only made several hundreds, and she was again dissatisfied. She so wanted to be first in something, and she did not succeed, even in making sketches for drapery advertisements.

She was down to breakfast on the morning of her birthday. Paul watched her face as she read her letters. He knew the lawyer's letter. As his mother read it, her face hardened and became more expressionless. Then a cold, determined look came on her mouth. She hid the letter under the pile of others, and said not a word about it.

"Didn't you have anything nice in the post for your birthday, Mother?" said Paul.

"Quite moderately nice," she said, her voice cold and absent.

She went away to town without saying more.

But in the afternoon Uncle Oscar appeared. He said Paul's mother had had a long interview with the lawyer, asking if the whole five thousand could not be advanced at once, as she was in debt.

"What do you think, uncle?" said the boy.

"I leave it to you, son."

"Oh, let her have it, then! We can get some more with the other," said the boy.

"A bird in the hand is worth two in the bush, laddie!" said Uncle Oscar.

"But I'm sure to *know* for the Grand National; or the Lincolnshire; or else the Derby. I'm sure to know for *one* of them," said Paul.

So Uncle Oscar signed the agreement, and Paul's mother touched the whole five thousand. Then something very curious happened. The voices in the house suddenly went mad, like a chorus of frogs on a spring evening. There were certain new furnishings, and Paul had a tutor. He was *really* going to Eton, his father's school, in the following autumn. There were flowers in the winter, and a blossoming of the luxury Paul's mother had been used to. And yet the voices in the house, behind the sprays of mimosa and almond-blossom, and from under the piles of iridescent cushions, simply trilled and screamed in a sort of ecstasy: "There *must* be more money! Oh-h-h! There *must* be more money! Oh, now, now-w! now-w-w—there *must* be more money!—more than ever! More than ever!"

It frightened Paul terribly. He studied away at his Latin and Greek with his tutors. But his intense hours were spent with Bassett. The Grand National had gone by; he had not "known," and had lost a hundred pounds. Summer was at hand. He was in agony for the Lincoln. But even for the Lincoln he didn't "know," and he lost fifty pounds. He became wild-eyed and strange, as if something were going to explode in him.

"Let it alone, son! Don't you bother about it!" urged Uncle Oscar. But it was as if the boy couldn't really hear what his uncle was saying.

"I've got to know for the Derby! I've *got* to know for the Derby!" the child reiterated, his big blue eyes blazing with a sort of madness.

His mother noticed how overwrought he was.

"You'd better go to the seaside. Wouldn't you like to go now to the seaside, instead of waiting? I think you'd better," she said, looking down at him anxiously, her heart curiously heavy because of him.

But the child lifted his uncanny blue eyes.

"I couldn't possibly go before the Derby, Mother!" he said. "I couldn't possibly!"

"Why not?" she said, her voice becoming heavy when she was opposed. "Why not? You can still go from the seaside to see the Derby with your Uncle Oscar if that's what you wish. No need for you to wait here. Besides, I think you care too much about these races. It's a bad sign. My family has been a gambling family, and you won't know till you grow up how much damage it has done. But it has done damage. I shall have to send Bassett away and ask Uncle Oscar not to talk racing to you, unless you promise to be reasonable about it; go away to the seaside and forget it. You're all nerves!"

"I'll do what you like, Mother, so long as you don't send me away till after the Derby," the boy said.

"Send you away from where? Just from this house?"

"Yes," he said, gazing at her.

"Why, you curious child, what makes you care about this house so much, suddenly? I never knew you loved it!"

He gazed at her without speaking. He had a secret within a secret, something he had not divulged, even to Bassett or to his Uncle Oscar.

But his mother, after standing undecided and a little bit sullen for some moments, said:

"Very well, then! Don't go to the seaside till after the Derby, if you don't wish it. But promise me you won't let your nerves go to pieces! Promise you won't think so much about horse-racing and *events*, as you call them!"

"Oh no!" said the boy, casually. "I won't think much about them, Mother. You needn't worry. I wouldn't worry, Mother, if I were you."

"If you were me and I were you," said his mother, "I wonder what we *should* do!"

"But you know you needn't worry, Mother, don't you?" the boy repeated.

"I should be awfully glad to know it," she said wearily.

"Oh, well, you can, you know. I mean you ought to know you needn't worry!" he insisted.

"Ought I? Then I'll see about it," she said.

Paul's secret of secrets was his wooden horse, that which had no name. Since he was emancipated from a nurse and a nursery governess, he had had his rocking-horse removed to his own bedroom at the top of the house.

"Surely you're too big for a rocking-horse," his mother had remonstrated.

"Well, you see, Mother, till I can have a *real* horse, I like to have *some* sort of animal about," had been his quaint answer.

"Do you feel he keeps you company?" she laughed.

"Oh yes! He's very good, he always keeps me company, when I'm there," said Paul.

So the horse, rather shabby, stood in an arrested prance in the boy's bedroom.

The Derby was drawing near, and the boy grew more and more tense. He hardly heard what was spoken to him, he was very frail, and his eyes were really uncanny. His mother had sudden strange seizures of uneasiness about him. Sometimes, for half an hour, she would feel a sudden anxiety about him that was almost anguish. She wanted to rush to him at once, and know he was safe.

Two nights before the Derby, she was at a big party in town, when one of her rushes of anxiety about her boy, her first-born, gripped her heart till she could hardly speak. She fought with the feeling, might and main, for she believed in common-sense. But it was too strong. She had to leave the dance and go downstairs to telephone to the country. The children's nursery governess was terribly surprised and startled at being rung up in the night.

"Are the children all right, Miss Wilmot?"

"Oh yes, they are quite all right."

"Master Paul? Is he all right?"

"He went to bed as right as a trivet. Shall I run up and look at him?"

"No!" said Paul's mother reluctantly. "No! Don't trouble. It's all right. Don't sit up. We shall be home fairly soon." She did not want her son's privacy intruded upon.

"Very good," said the governess.

It was about one o'clock when Paul's mother and father drove up to their house. All was still. Paul's mother went to her room and slipped off her white fur cloak. She had told the maid not to wait up for her. She heard her husband downstairs, mixing a whisky-and-soda.

And then, because of the strange anxiety at her heart, she stole upstairs to her son's room. Noiselessly, she went along the upper corridor. Was there a faint noise? What was it?

She stood, with arrested muscles, outside his door, listening. There was a strange, heavy, and yet not loud noise. Her heart stood still. It was a soundless noise, yet rushing and powerful. Something huge, in violent, hushed motion. What was it? What in God's Name was it? She ought to know. She felt she *knew* the noise. She knew what it was.

Yet she could not place it. She couldn't say what it was. And on and on it went, like a madness.

Softly, frozen with anxiety and fear, she turned the doorhandle.

The room was dark. Yet in the space near the window, she heard and saw something plunging to and fro. She gazed in fear and amazement.

Then suddenly she switched on the light, and saw her son, in his green pyjamas, madly surging on his rocking-horse. The blaze of light suddenly lit him up, as he urged the wooden horse, and lit her up, as she stood, blonde, in her dress of pale green and crystal, in the doorway.

"Paul!" she cried. "Whatever are you doing?"

"It's Malabar!" he screamed, in a powerful, strange voice. "It's Malabar!"

His eyes blazed at her for one strange and senseless second, as he ceased urging his wooden horse. Then he fell with a crash to the ground, and she, all her tormented motherhood flooding upon her, rushed to gather him up.

But he was unconscious, and unconscious he remained, with some brain-fever. He talked and tossed, and his mother sat stonily by his side.

"Malabar! It's Malabar! Bassett, Bassett, I *know*: it's Malabar!"

So the child cried, trying to get up and urge the rocking-horse that gave him his inspiration.

"What does he mean by Malabar?" she asked her brother Oscar.

"It's one of the horses running for the Derby," was the answer.

And, in spite of himself Oscar Cresswell spoke to Bassett, and himself put a thousand on Malabar: at fourteen to one.

The third day of the illness was critical: they were watching for a change. The boy, with his rather long, curly hair, was tossing ceaselessly on the pillow. He neither slept nor regained consciousness, and his eyes were like blue stones. His mother sat, feeling her heart had gone, turned actually into a stone.

In the evening, Oscar Cresswell did not come, but Bassett sent a message, saying could he come up for one moment, just one moment? Paul's mother was very angry at the intrusion, but on second thoughts she agreed. The boy was the same. Perhaps Bassett might bring him to consciousness.

The gardener, a shortish fellow with a little brown moustache and sharp little brown eyes, tiptoed into the room, touched his imaginary cap to Paul's mother, and stole to the bedside, staring with glittering, smallish eyes at the tossing, dying child.

"Master Paul!" he whispered. "Master Paul! Malabar came in first all right, a clean win. I did as you told me. You've made over seventy thousand pounds, you have; you've got over eighty thousand. Malabar came in all right, Master Paul."

"Malabar! Malabar! Did I say Malabar, Mother? Did I say Malabar! Do you think I'm lucky, Mother? I knew Malabar, didn't I? Over eighty thousand pounds! I call that lucky, don't you, Mother? Over eighty thousand pounds! I knew, didn't I know I knew? Malabar came in all right. If I ride my horse till I'm sure, then I tell you, Bassett, you can go as high as you like. Did you go for all you were worth, Bassett?"

"I went a thousand on it, Master Paul."

"I never told you, Mother, that if I can ride my horse, and *get there*, then I'm absolutely sure—oh, absolutely! Mother, did I ever tell you? I *am* lucky!"

"No, you never did," said the mother.

But the boy died in the night.

And even as he lay dead, his mother heard her brother's voice saying to her: "My God, Hester, you're eighty-odd thousand to the good, and a poor devil of a son to the bad. But, poor devil, poor devil, he's best gone out of a life where he rides his rocking-horse to find a winner."

Tanith Lee

THREE DAYS

Tanith Lee, a popular and prolific author of fantastic novels and stories, often works in the horror mode in short fiction, although her principal reputation is as a genre fantasy writer. Her range is impressive, her effects dramatic, her imagery vivid. The principal focus in her fiction is often psycho-sexual, overtly or metaphorically. "Three Days" is one of her lesser known stories but one of her best. It is overtly a melodramatic romance in the historical genre, with overt reference to Poe, then a story of reincarnation, the occult rationalized, then undercut. Lee gives the essence of the horror story: "I went over the bridge with the strangest feeling imaginable. I find no name for it even now. It seemed for a moment I had glimpsed the rickety facade of all things and the boundless, restless, terrible truth beyond. But it faded, and I was glad of it." The self-consciously antiquated manner of the telling is an interesting comparison to Joyce Carol Oates' "Nightside."

The house was tall, impressive, peeling, and seemed old before its time. The only attractive thing about it, to my eyes, was the dark-lidded glance of an attic, looking out of the slope of the roof, which such houses sometimes have. The attic eye seemed to say: "There is something beautiful here, after all. Or, there *could* be something beautiful, if such a thing were allowed."

Below and before, a green haze of young chestnut trees

lined the street, which gave on the Bois Palais. Behind, rising above the walled gardens, were the stepped roads and blue slate caps of distant Montmoulin over the river, with, as their apparent apex, the white dome of the Sacré. All this was of course very pleasant. Yet I never come into the area now without a sense of misgiving. That is due to the house, and to what took place there.

One felt nothing extravagant could ever have issued from such a proper dwelling. And one would have been wrong. My friend (I use the term indiscriminately) Charles Laurent had issued from it. He was at that season making something of a star himself in the legal profession, and also by way of a series of books—fictionalized, witty, rather brilliant studies of past trials and case histories. It was in the latter capacity, the literary side, that our paths crossed. I took to him, it was difficult not to. Handsome and informed was Laurent, an easy companion, and a very entertaining one. I suppose too the best of us may agree it is no bad thing to be on good terms with a clever lawyer. I was at this time also attempting to become engaged, and the girl's father had suddenly begun to make my way stony. After a stormy, possibly hysterical scene, worthy of the opera, my love and I had agreed we should put some physical distance between us for a while, allowing Papa's temper to cool, and relying on letters and the connivance of the mother—who liked me, and was no less than an angel—to save our hopes and prevent our mutually going mad. It is a shabby thing for a young man to be in love with one he may not have. It puts an end to a number of solaces, without replacing them. In short, life was not at its nicest. To take up with a Charles Laurent was the ideal solution.

To say our relationship was superficial would be a perfect description; its superficiality was the shining crown of it. We knew just enough of each other as might be helpful. For the rest—food, drink, music, the arts—such as these were ably sufficient to carry us across whole continents of hours into the small ones before dawn. So it was with slight surprise that I found one day he had invited me to dine at his home.

"And well your face may fall," he said. "Believe me, it will be a hideous evening, I can promise you that. I'm asking

you selfishly, to relieve the tedium and horror. Not that anyone conceivably could.''

Not unnaturally, I inquired after details. He told me with
swift disdain that his father observed yearly the anniversary
of his mother's death.

''I'm a stranger,'' I said. ''At such a function I could hardly
be welcome.''

''We are *all* strangers. He hates everyone of us. My
brother, my sister. He hated my mother, too.'' He spoke
frivolously. That did not stop a slight frisson of interest from
going over me. ''Now I have you, I see,'' said Charles. ''The
writer has been woken up and is scenting the air.''

''Not at all. But you never mentioned a brother, or a sister.''

''Semery won't be there. He never comes near the house
on such occasions. Honorine lives there, as I do, and has no
choice.''

''Honorine, your sister?''

''My sister. Poor plain pitiful creation of an unjust God.''

I confess I did not like his way of referring to her. If it
were true, I felt he should have protected, not slandered her,
with that able tongue of his, to loose acquaintances such as
I. He saw me frowning and said, ''Don't be afraid, my friend.
We shan't try to marry her off to you. I recall too well la
bonne Anette.''

I frankly thought the entire dialogue would be forgotten,
but not so. The next morning an embossed invitation was
delivered. A couple of nights later I found myself under the
chestnut trees before that tall, unprepossessing house, and
presently inside, for good or ill.

I was uneasy—that was the least of it—but also, I confess,
extremely curious. Charles had hit home with that remark
about the writer in me waking up. What was I about to see
at this annual wake? Images of the American writer Mr. Poe
trooped across my mind: an embalmed corpse, black wreaths,
a vault, a creaking black-clad aristo with long tapering
hands. . . . Even the daughter had assumed some importance. I think I toyed with the picture of her playing an eastern harp.

Naturally, I was far out. The family, what there was of it, seemed familiarly normal. Monsieur Laurent was a wine-faced, portly *maître d'affaires*. He looked me up and down, found me wanting (of course), greeted me, and let me pass. He reminded me but too well of that other father I had to do with, Anette's, four miles to the west, and I felt an instant depression. There was also an uncle on the premises, who stammered and was not well dressed, two deaf and short-sighted old ladies whose connection I did not quite resolve, and a florid, limping servant. I began to feel I had come among a collection of the deaf, the dumb, the halt, and the lame. Charles, obviously, was not to be numbered among these. Like a firework, he had exploded from the dull genetic sink, as sometimes happens. The younger brother, Semery, who after all attended, was also an exception. Good-looking, he had a makeshift air; Charles and he hailed each other heartily, as rival bandits meeting unarmed in the hills. Semery was the ne'er-do-well with which so many families attempt to equip themselves. Some twist of fortune, some strain of energy, had denied the role to Charles who, I felt, might have handled it better.

The sister came down late. She did not have a harp about her, but alas, everything Charles had said seemed a fact.

The sons perhaps had taken their looks from the dead mother we were supposed to be celebrating. Poor Honorine did not even favor her father. She was that sad combination of small bones and heavy flesh that seems to indicate some mistake has been made in assembly. She ate very little, and one knew instinctively that her dumpy form and puffy features were not the results of gluttony, or even appetite. She was not ugly, but that is all that can be said. Indeed, had she been ugly, she would have possessed a greater advantage than she did. For she was unmemorable. Her small eyes, whose color I truly do, God forgive me, forget, were downcast. Her thin hair, drawn back into a false chignon that did not exactly match, made me actually miserable. We writers sometimes postulate future states of freedom for both sexes, regardless of physical advantage. Never had one seemed so necessary. Poor wretched girl.

That her father detested her was obvious, but—as Charles

had told me—Monsieur Laurent cared little for any of them. The dire lucklessness of it was that, while his sons escaped or absconded, the daughter was trapped. She had no option but to wait out, as how many do, the death of the tyrant. He was hale and hearty. It would be a long wait. How did she propose to spend it? How did she spend her days as it was?

No doubt my remarks on Monsieur Laurent sound unduly callous. Patently, they are colored by hindsight, but I took against him immediately, and he against me, I am sure. Yes, he resembled my own reluctant intended father-in-law, but there was more to it than that. Lest I do myself greater injustice than I must, I will hastily reproduce some of the conversation and the events of that first, really most unglittering, dinner party.

To begin with there was some sherry, or something rather like it, but very little talk. Monsieur Laurent maintained guard across the fireplace. Aside from snapping rudely a couple of times at the old ladies and the limping servant, he only stood eyeing us all, as if we were a squadron of raw troops foisted on him at the very eve of important hostilities. Annoyance, contempt, and actual exasperation were mingled in that glance, which generously included us all. I found it irritating. He knew nothing of me, as yet, to warrant such an opinion. In the case of Charles, most fathers would have been proud. We were meanwhile talking sotto voce and Charles said, as if reading my thoughts, "You can see what he thinks of me, go on, can't you?" "I assume," I said, "that his expression is misleading." "Not at all. When I won my first case, he looked at me just that way. When I foolishly spoke of it, the old wretch said to me, 'The stupidity of other men doesn't make *you* clever.' As for the first book—well, it was a success, and I recall we met on the stairs and he had a copy. I was stunned he'd even looked at it, and said so. At which he put the book in my hand as if I'd demanded it and replied, 'I suppose you'll sell this rubbish, since the majority of the populace is dustbin-brained.' "

Just then the food was ready and our host marched before us into the dining salon. No pretense was made of escort or invitation. Charles conducted the two elderly ladies. Semery idled through. I looked round to offer my arm to Mademoiselle Honorine, but she was making a great fuss over the discarded sherry goblets. I sensed too exactly the dreadful embarrassment of the unlovely, and left well alone.

Needless to say, I wondered how on earth, and why on earth, Charles had procured me a place at this specter's feast. I could only conclude that Monsieur Laurent's utter disgust with humanity en masse did not deign to distinguish between absence and arrival. Come or go as we would, we were a source of displeasure. Perhaps even, new specimens of the loathsome breed momentarily satisfied him, bringing him as they must the unassailable proof that nothing had altered, he was still quite right about us all.

"*Sit,*" rapped Monsieur Laurent, glaring around him.

Obedient as dogs, we sat.

Some kind of entrée was served and a vintage inspected. Monsieur Laurent then looked directly at me. "The wine isn't so good, but I expect you'll put up with it." This, as if I were some destitute who had scrounged a place at the board. A number of retorts bolted into my mind; but I curbed them, smiled politely, and had thereafter a schoolboy urge to kick Charles' shins under the table.

Whether the wine was good or not good, after a glass or two, the demon father began noticeably to brighten. I was struck by the flash of his eye, and realized that generalized contempt was about to flower into malice. I am afraid only two thoughts occurred to me at that moment. One was, I regret, that this was very intriguing. The other was concerned with wondering what *I* would do if he grossly insulted me. For I could sense, the way animals scent a coming storm, how the thunder was getting up. I reasoned though I was safe, being not such fun to attack as his own. He had not had time to learn my weaknesses and wants. While the rest of them—they had been his playground from birth.

Honorine—there was no attempt at fashionable order—sat three seats away from me, with Semery and an empty chair between. Behind Honorine, above the mahogany sideboard, a large framed photograph with black ribbon on it seemed to depict the dead wife and mother. My current angle prevented any perusal of this, but to it Monsieur Laurent now ordered our attention.

"That woman," he said, "was a very great nuisance while she lived. I drink, as you see, to her departure. Ah, what a nasty, wicked sentiment. Correction, an honest one. Besides, she had taken her revenge. Look what she saddled me with. All of you." There was a concerted dismal rustle round the table. One of the old ladies dabbed her face with a handkerchief, but one saw it was a sort of reflex. It was plainly not the only occasion all this had been voiced. I looked surreptitiously at Charles. He was a perfect blank, composed and cool. Small wonder he could keep his head in a courtroom after being raised to the tune of this!

Beside me, however, Semery either deliberately, or uncontrollably, acted out the role of foil by snarling: "Cher Papa. Can't you leave anything in decent peace?"

"Ah, my little Semery," said Cher Papa, smiling at him now. "You have toiled up from the slime of your slum to say this? And how is the painting going? Sell well, do you, my boy? You came to ask . . . now what was it for? Ah, yes. For money. And I told you I would think about it, but after all, what use is it to give you cash?" (Semery had gone white. I could hardly believe what I was hearing or that Semery could have given such a faultless cue for his own public castigation. It was as if he had *had* to do it.) "You squander everything. And have such slender talent. No, I really think after all you must do without. Tighten your belt. Or, you could return and live here. My doors are always open to you."

"I'd rather die in the gutter," shouted Semery.

"No you wouldn't. Or why are you here?"

"Not to ask anything from *you*, as you well know."

"Begging from your brother Charles then. This afternoon's most touching scene. Such a pity I disturbed you. But Charles isn't a fool with his money if he's a fool with everything else. You won't get it from him. And I promise you, you won't get it from me."

Semery rose. An amazing change reshaped the monster's face. It grew rock-hard, petrified. But the eyes were filled by potent electricity. "Down," rasped the father. The room seemed to shake at the command. Semery sank back into his chair and his trembling hands knocked over his wineglass. Seldom have I witnessed such a display of the casual, abso-

lute power one mortal thing may obtain over another. I felt
myself as if I had received a blow in the stomach, and yet
what had actually happened? To set it out here does not convey anything.

"Yes, Semery," Monsieur Laurent now said, "you should
return under my roof, and make your name painting portraits
of this beautiful sister of yours."

Having leveled one gun emplacement with his unerring
cannon, the warmonger had turned his fire from the rout of
the wounded to the demolition of the totally helpless. I could
not prevent myself glancing at her, in horrid fascination, to
see how she took it. Of course, she too was well used to such
treatment. She cowered, her eyes down, her terrible, un-
matched chignon shuddering. Yet the pose was native to her.
It seemed almost comfortable. Her body sagged in the lines
of abjection so readily, easily.

"Compliment your coiffeur, Honorine," said Monsieur
Laurent. "These enemies of yours have succeeded in making
of you, yet again, a fright. Heaven hurry the day," he added,
drinking his wine in greedy little sips, "when this pretense
at having hair is done. A daughter who is completely bald
will be a novelty. All this scraping and combing and messing.
Fate intended you as a catastrophe, my child. You should
accept the part. Look at you, my dear, graceless lump—" At
this point I put out my hand and picked up my own glass. I
believe I had every intention of throwing it at his head, anything to make him stop. But thank God Charles interrupted
with a (perhaps faked) gargantuan sneeze. The father turned
slowly, fire duly drawn. "And you," he said to the recovering Charles, "our own moneylender, the wealthy gigolo of
the bookstalls. What have you to say for yourself?"

Charles shrugged. "What I always say for myself. And
what you also have just said. I've a private income and you
don't frighten me. You could put me out on the street tomorrow—"

"I put none of my own tribe onto the street. They put
themselves there. As for your books—what are they? You
plagiarize and you steal, you botch and bungle—"

"And *livres* pour into my hands," said Charles.

My God, I thought, at last the razor of the father's tongue

was going into a block of cork. Naturally, the confounded devil knew it. This means of hurting pride no longer worked, it seemed, or at least without evidence. Talented, loved, an egoist, and lucky, Charles was not a happy target. Unerringly, the father retraced his aim.

"A pity," he said, "your sister has taken to reading your works. Filling her hairless skull with more predigested idiocy than is already in there. She puts her hat on her bald head and goes puttering off to the bookshop to discuss your successes. And so has fallen into the clutches of madwomen."

Strangely, Honorine was moved by this to murmur quickly, "No, Father, no, you mustn't say they are—"

"*Mustn't?* Mustn't I? You keep your mouth closed, my fat, balding daughter. I say what I know. Your great friends are lunatics, and I'm considering whether or not I shall approach the police—"

"Father!" The cry now was anguished.

"What? You think they're friends of yours, hah? You, with a friend? How should you have friends, you overweighted slug? Do you think they're captivated by your prettiness and charm? Eh? It's my money they like the idea of, and your insane acquaintances from the bookshop are a fine example of a certain animal known as a charlatan."

"I won't go there ever again," said Honorine.

This startled me. Her voice was altered when she spoke. It had grown deeper, it was definite. By agreeing with him she had, albeit temporarily, removed the bludgeon from his grasp.

At the time, the business of the "charlatan madwomen" and the bookshop were only a facet of an astonishing whole. I paid no particular attention. Nor do I think much more needs to be said of the dinner. Dishes came in and were taken away, and those with the heart to eat (they were few) did so. There were many and various further sallies from the indefatigable Monsieur Laurent. None were aimed at me, though I was now primed and eager for them and, I imagine, slightly drunk. In my confusion, even as I sat there, I was already mentally composing a letter to Anette, telling her everything, word for word, of this unspeakable affair. (It is from the same letter, penned fresh and with the vivid recall of insomniac indignation at two that morning, that I am able to quote fairly accurately what I have just set down.) I also wished him dead at least twenty times. I backed the big heavy body and the thick red face for an apoplexy, yet they looked more like ebullient good health.

As soon as I could, without augmenting the casualties of that war zone of a table by slamming out halfway through the meal, I left. I bade Charles a brisk adieu and walked by myself beside the river until well past midnight, powerlessly on the boil. As I told Anette, my entertaining friend was out of favor now completely. I reckoned never to see him again, for it was not simple, after the fact, to forgive him this exposure to alien filial strife. I even in a wild moment suspected some joke at my expense.

However, my having ignored two notes and a subsequent attempted visit, he finally caught me up in the gardens of the Palais. There was an argument, at least on my side, but Charles was not to be fought with if he had no mind for it.

"I can only apologize," he said, in broken accents. "What more can I say?"

"Why in God's name did you make me a party to the bloody affair?"

"Well, frankly, my friend, because—though you'll find it hard to credit—he is kinder to us when there is some stranger present."

I fell silent at that, moodily staring away between the green grove of trees. Now and then, Anette and I had contrived a meeting here, and the gardens filled me always with a piercing sweet sadness that tended to override other emotions. I looked at Charles, who seemed genuinely contrite, and acknowledged there might be some logic in his statement. Although the idea of Monsieur Laurent *un*kind, if such was a version of his restraint, filled one with laughing horror.

So, if you will, ends the first act.

The second act commences with a scene or two going on offstage. There had been an improvement in my own fortunes, to wit, Anette's father deeming it necessary, in the way of business, to travel to England. This brought an unexpected luster to the summer. It also meant that I saw very little of Charles Laurent.

Then one morning, strolling through the covered market near the cathedral, I literally bumped into Semery and, after the usual exchanges, was invited to an apartment above a chandler's, on the left bank of the river.

Here is the area of the Montmoulin, the medieval hill of the windmill, the namesake of which is long since gone. One hears the place referred to frequently as being of a "picturesque, quaint squalor." Certainly, the poor do live here, and the fallen angels of the bourgeoisie perch in the garrets and studios above the twisting cobbled lanes. The smell of cabbage soup and the good coffee even the poverty-stricken sometimes manage to get hold of, hang in the air, along with the marvelous inexpressible smell of the scarlet geraniums that explode over balconies and on walls above narrow stairways, and against a sky tangled with washing and pigeons.

We got up into a suitable attic studio and found a table already laid with cheese and bread and fruit and wine, and a fawn cat at play with an apple. A very pretty girl came from behind a curtain. She ran to kiss Semery and, her arms still around him, turned to beam at me in just the way women in love so often do when another man comes on the scene. Even in her loose blouse, I could tell she was carrying a child. Little doubt of the father, though her hand was ringless. I remembered, with a fleeting embarrassment, Semery's supposed request for money from his brother, or Monsieur Laurent. Here might be the excuse.

There were pictures, naturally, everywhere—on the walls, on easels, stacked up, or even horizontal on the floor for the cat to sit on.

"Courage," said Semery, seeing me glance around, "I won't try to sell anything to you. Not, at all." This in turn reflected Charles' avowal, on first inviting me to the gruesome dinner party, that they would not try to marry Honorine off to me. It was a little thing, but it made me conscious of some strange defensiveness inherent, and probably engendered in them by their disgusting father. "But," added Semery, "look, if you like." "Of course he will like," said the girl mischievously. "How nice the table is, Miou," said Semery. "Let's have some wine."

A very pleasant couple of hours ensued. Semery was acting at least as fine a companion as Charles; I was charmed by Miou, and by the cat, and the simple luncheon was appetizing. As for the art—I am no critic, but suppose I have some slight knowledge. While not being in that first startling rank of original genius, Semery's work seemed bright with talent. It had enormous energy, was attractive, sometimes lush, yet never too easy. Particularly, I liked two or three unusual night scenes of the city, one astonishingly lit by a flight of birds escaping from some baskets and streaming over a lamp-strung bridge.

"Yes," he said, coming to my side, "I call that one *Honorine*." I was at a loss to reply. "I don't mean to make you uncomfortable," he said. "But you've been blooded, after all. You were there just the last time I was."

"Hush, Semery," said Miou, who was rocking the cat in an armchair, practicing for her baby. "Talking of *him* makes you sick and gives you migraine."

"True," said Semery. He refilled our glasses with wine. "But I can talk of Honorine? Yes? No? But I must. That poor little sack of sadness. If there were any money, I'd take her in with me, though God knows she bores me to despair. Our dear father, you understand, has stamped and trampled all the life from her. She can no longer talk. She only answers questions. So you say to her, 'Would you care to do this?' And you get in return, 'Oh yes, if *you* wish.' And she drops things. And she stumbles when she walks even when there's nothing to stumble over. However," he said, with a boy's fierceness, "there was one service I think I did her. I first took her to the bookshop on the Rue Danton. And so introduced her to the three witches."

Miou began to sing a street song, quietly but firmly disowning us.

"That's the bookshop your father objected to? And the witches?"

"Well, three old ladies, in particular one, very gray and thin, read the tarot there in the backroom. And sometimes, when the moon is full, work the planchette of a Ouija board."

"And Honorine . . ."

"Honorine attended a session or two. She wouldn't reveal the results, but you could tell she enjoyed every moment. When you saw her after, her cheeks would be flushed, her eyes had a light in them. Unfortunately, that limping gargoyle who serves *mon père* found out about it all and duly informed. Now Honorine's one poor, pitiful pleasure is ended. Unless she can somehow evade the spies, and our confounded father—"

"Sur la chatte, le chat,/Et sur la reine le roi . . ." naughtily sang Miou to the cat-baby.

"On the other hand," Semery added, now with great nonchalance, "I did visit the shop today, and one of the eldritch sisters—good lord, I must paint them—no rush, they're each about three hundred years old and will outlive us all—well, Miou-who-has-stopped-singing-and-is-all-ears-and-eyes, well, one of them gave me a note to give to Honorine. Something the spirit guides had revealed that my sister apparently desired to know." And from his jacket Semery produced a piece of paper, unsealed, merely folded in the middle, which he held aloft quizzically. "I wonder what it can be?"

"You shouldn't have brought it here," said Miou. She crossed herself between fawn paws. "Magic. Ghosts."

"Where else then? Papa is out tomorrow afternoon and I can take it to the house. But I could hardly do so today, could I now? One foot on the threshold, and he'd have seized me in his jaws."

"Well," said Miou. "Put it away somewhere."

"Don't you think I should read it? Secret communications to my little sister . . ." He looked back at me. "Actually, I did. Here, what do you make of this?"

And he opened the paper and put it in my hand.

I admit I was curious. There seemed no harm in it, and I have always had a quiet disrespect for "supernatural" things.

On the paper from the mysterious bookshop were these words as follows:

As we have told you, she is to be found as a minor character in some of the history books, and there has also been at least one novel written about her. The name is correct, Lucie Belmains. She did indeed die as a result of hanging herself. The date of her death is the morning of the eighth April, 1760.

"Fascinating, isn't it," said Semery. "What does it mean? Who is Lucie Belmains?"

Miou and the cat were already peering between our shoulders at the paper.

"Lucie Belmains," said Miou, "was a minor aristocrat, very beautiful and very wicked. She would drink and ride a horse and swear better—or worse—than a man. She was the mistress of several princes and dukes. She once dressed as a bandit and waylaid the king on some road, and was his mistress too perhaps, till she became bored with all the riches he lavished on her. Then she fell in love with a man five years her junior. He loved her too, to distraction, and when he was killed in a duel over her, Lucie gave a great party, like a Roman empress, and in the morning she hanged herself like Antigone from a crimson cord."

Semery and I stood amazed until Miou stopped, breathless and in triumph.

"It seems," said Semery then, "there is indeed one novel, and you have read it."

"Yes. When I was a little girl," said Miou, all of seventeen now. "I remember my sister and I read the book aloud to each other when we were supposed to be asleep. And how we giggled. And we dressed up in lace curtains and our mother's hats and raised glasses of water pretending they were champagne and said, 'I am Lucie and you are my slave!' And fought like cats because neither of us would *be* the slave. And then one day Adèle hung her doll up by the neck from a red ribbon and we had a funeral party. Maman found us and we were both beaten."

"Quite right. These are most corrupting activities for a future wife of France's leading painter, and the mother of his heir." At which Miou smiled and laid her head on his shoulder. "But even so," said Semery, stroking her hair, "what has all this got to do with Honorine?"

I said, "She's making a study of this woman, or the period?"

"No. She has no interests anymore."

Later, toward evening, we strolled along the riverbank. The leveling rays of the sun flashed over the water. I had arranged to buy the picture of the escaping birds for Anette. I knew she would like it, as indeed she did—we have it still, and since Semery's name is now not unknown, it is worth rather a deal more than I paid for it. But there was some argument with Semery at the time, who thought I was patronizing him, or trying to pay for my luncheon. Thank God, all that had been settled, however, by the hour we emerged on the street, Miou in her light shawl and straw bonnet with cherries. When we reached the Pont Nouveau and I was about to cross over, Semery said to me, "You see, that business with the paper—belle Lucie Belmains. Something about it worries me. Perhaps I shouldn't let Honorine have it. Would that be dishonorable?"

"Yes."

"Or prudent?"

"Maybe that too. But as you don't know—"

"I think perhaps I do. The purpose of the witches' Ouija has often to do with reincarnation—the passage of the soul through many lives and many bodies."

We had all paused in mutual revelation.

"Do you mean your sister is being told she lived a previous life in which—"

"In which she was beautiful and notorious, kings slobbered at her feet, and duels were organized for her favors."

We looked at the river, the womb and fount of the city, glittering with sun, all sequins, which on the dark days of winter seems like lead.

"Well," Semery said at last, "why not? If it makes her happy for a moment. If it gives her something nice to think about. There's nothing now. What has she got? What can she hope to have? If she can say to herself, just one time in every day, *once* I was beautiful, *once* I was free, and crazy and lavish and adored, and loved."

I looked at him. His eyes were wet, and he was pale, as if at the onset of a headache. Impulsively, I clasped his hand.

"Why not?" I said. "Yes, Semery, why *not*?"

Miou let me kiss her blossomy cheek as a reward.

I went over the bridge with the strangest feeling imaginable. I find no name for it even now. It seemed for a moment
I had glimpsed the rickety facade of all things and the boundless, restless, terrible truth beyond. But it faded, and I was
glad of it.

As the glorious summer drew to its close, intimations of
winter and discontent appeared. The birds and golden leaves
began to be displaced by emptiness in the trees of the Bois;
Anette's father returned, foul-tempered, and shut his house
like a castle under siege against all comers, particularly one.

It was nearly three months since my chance meeting with
Semery. We had met deliberately a couple of times since; I
had even been invited to his wedding, the thought of which
now made me rather melancholy. As for Charles Laurent, I
was sitting at a café table one morning, curiously enough
reading a review of his latest book—as usual a success—when
I happened to look up and saw two women seating themselves
a few tables away. I was struck at once by a sense of confusion, such as comes when one is accosted by an old acquaintance whose name one forgets. But it was not that a name
had been forgotten, for frankly I was not familiar with either
of these women. It must be, then, that they put me in mind
of others with whom I was. Because of this I studied them
surreptitiously over my newspaper.

The nearer woman, with her back to me now, was apparently a maid or companion, and a withered specimen at that.
She seemed ill at ease, full of humble, insistent protestation.
No, I did not know her at all. The other, who sat facing
me, was not particularly remarkable. Not tall, quite slim, and
plainly dressed, her fine brown hair had been cut daringly
short and she was hatless. Two little silver earrings flickered
attractively in her earlobes. That was all. Her skin was sal-
low, her features ordinary. Then the waiter came and I was
struck again, this time by a quality of fearlessness, *boldness*,
out of all proportion to what she did, which was merely to
order a pot of chocolate. There was something gallant in this
minor action, such as you sometimes find in invalids taking
their first convalescent stroll, or the blind listening to music.

Quite suddenly, I realized who she was. It was the graceful

bravery, though I had never seen her exhibit it previously, that gave her away. Honorine, of course.

I resolved immediately I would not go over. I had no real wish to, heaven knows. Memories of her wounded social clumsiness did not inspire me. I could only be a ghastly reminder of a hideous event. Let her enjoy her chocolate in peace, while I stayed here, keeping stealthy watch from my covert of newspaper.

So I kept watch, true to my profession, taking rapid mental notes the while. Surely, she was not as I recalled. It was small wonder I had not recognized her at once. She had lost a great deal of weight, yet here she sat eating gateau, drinking chocolate, with the accustomed appetite of a famished child. And there truly was about her a gracefulness—of gesture, of attitude. And a strange air of laughter, mischievous and essentially womanly, that despite myself began to entice me to her vicinity. In the end I gave in, rose, walked across and stood before her.

"Mademoiselle Laurent. Can I hope you remember me?"

Her eyes came up. Those eyes not large nor bright—but they were altered. They shone, they were alive. The oddest thing happened now. The loud blush of shyness, which one might have expected, rushed over her face. It was the order of blush well known to the adolescent, which makes physically uncomfortable with its heat, the drumming in the ears, the feeling the brain may explode under its pressure. All is instant panic and surrender to panic. What is there to be said or done when such a mark of shame is branded on one's forehead? But the eyes of Honorine Laurent did not fall. She drew in a long breath and said, calmly, as if blood and body did not belong to each other, "Why, monsieur, of course I remember you. My brother's friend. Please, will you sit down? We have greedily eaten all the cake, but there's some chocolate left." And she smiled. As she did so, the red blush went out, defeated. Her smile was open, friendly, not afraid—nor false. And her eyes sparkled so they were pretty, just as the smile was pretty. One writes of auras. Honorine had just such an aura. I knew in that moment that I was in the presence of a woman who found her own lack of beauty no disadvantage, who therefore would not use pain or sullenness as a weapon, who believed that in the end she herself was all that she required, although others were quietly welcomed should they come close to warm themselves in the light. In short, the look of a confident woman, a woman who has known great love, and awaits, without impatience or aggression, some future, unhurried, certain joy.

As if I had been hypnotized, I drew out a chair and sat down. I had only just breakfasted, but I drank the chocolate that was poured for me in a daze. Presently, the withered lady companion, fretting like a horse for hay, was thankfully dispatched to collect some cotton, and arm in arm, Mademoiselle Honorine and I turned toward the graveled paths of the Bois Palais. I had offered to see her to her door, and she had said, "Yes, do. Charles is home in a filthy temper—one bad review, I think, of his excellent book. He'll be delighted to see you. And my father is . . . out." And there was that mischief again. She did not then hate Monsieur Laurent, this elfin woman with her slim hand so lightly through my arm. She did not hate me for being witness to his humiliation of her. And she was used to escorts, she was used to friends.

I recall she asked me about Anette, very graciously and tactfully, and abruptly all my cares came flooding out in a torrent of words that astonished me, so in the end we sat down by the fountain with the nymphs as I made my complaints to life and heaven. Sometimes Honorine patted my arm gently. "Oh, yes," she said, "ah, no?" with such unflurried kindness and sympathy—*she* with all her woes, so tender toward mine—and at the finish I remember too she said, "You have a sound literary reputation and I would say your prospects are fine. Besides, you and she love each other. Could you perhaps," and those eyes of hers flashed like her earrings, like the summer river, "run away together?" I realized, even at the time, that this last piece of advice came straight from the idiomatic guide book of Lucie Belmains.

For that, naturally, was who I had beside me, there on that bench: Lucie Belmains, who had died on the eight of April, 1760. Lucie Belmains, but at her softest, sweetest—who knew love, and love's fulfillment, and touched my hand from her greater knowledge, ready to listen, and to reassure me. Even to suggest a madcap means of how to win the age-old game. The means *she*, more daring than I, might have taken.

Why not? Semery had said. Why not let that poor little dumpy bundle of a sister, that sack of sadness, creation of an unjust God, think of some better chance she had been given, once, if it could make her glad? And, *Why not?* I had magnanimously echoed. My God, why not indeed, if this exquisite person was to be the result . . . No, I did not believe in her reincarnation. But her *alteration—this* I believed. How could I avoid belief? The living proof sat with limpid laughing eyes beside me. As tyrants are changed by faith to flawless saints, so faith of her own kind had changed this human failure to a glowing being. There was a loveliness about her—yes, loveliness. Some latent charm, extant in her brothers, formerly lost in her, had evolved and possessed her perfectly. And that smile, those eyes. And her walk. Her carriage. Years have gone by since that day, to dim the vista. I loved Anette then, I love her still, and no woman in the world, in my eyes, can equal Anette. And yet I look back to this Honorine I had the happiness to find that far-off morning, and I must set down the truth as it seemed to me then, and seems to me now, older, wiser, and less innocent as I am. I have never, save for my wife, met any woman who enchanted me so thoroughly. For she was beautiful. Her beauty lay all around us on the air. And even if I did not credit the transference of the soul, yet the soul I did credit. And it was the soul of Honorine that brought the loveliness and the beauty and the enchantment. For you see, she was then completely those things so few of us ever are, and if we are, so briefly: at peace, joyful, *sure.*

We reached the house, that dire house, and even this seemed less awful by her light. She was no longer afraid of it. She went up the steps and beckoned me in as if I might be comfortable there, and so I, too, felt no foreboding.

Charles was in the drawing room and jumped up when he saw me out of a snowfall of papers. Having brought us together, she was gone. I stared after her and then at the closed door. Presently, Charles left off talking of his book and said, "Well, what do you think of *her*?"

She had made me skittish too. I said, no doubt rudely, "This is not the same sister."

Charles nodded vigorously. "It can't be, can it? Isn't she a jewel?" He was proud of her. "If she keeps this up, we'll get her married to a rich potentate in half a year. You've seen Semery and know the cause, I understand?"

"Yes."

He gazed at me and said mock-seriously, "Of course, it's a form of madness. If she killed someone, I could get her off on a plea of this. My client reckons she is actually a lady who is dead."

"Surely she reckons she has *been*, not is, Lucie Belmains."

"Hairsplitting worthy of the bar. But it's a miracle. If she's gone a little mad, so nicely, why not?"

And thus the third culpable party added his careless *why not*? to Semery's and mine.

"But does she," I said, "know that you—"

"She know Semery and I—though not you, *cher ami*—are in on it. But she doesn't review the matter with us, nor we with her. Then again, considering the extravagance of the idea, not to mention results, she's very serene about it all. I don't think she's even read anything, no history of this woman. Save the smallest outline in some encyclopedia. On the other hand, I suspect her of writing about her feelings. I gather a diary has been started. But she only revealed that to me because I caught sight of the article on her vanité. She's said nothing else. After all, she knows we're a bunch of vile skeptics. As for father—well, no whisper must reach *his* ears. And you can guess, all this of hers has thrown him off balance. She eats more and grows more slight, she cuts off her hair and buys earrings. But you should see her with him. Stay and lunch with us and you will."

The prospect of encountering Monsieur Laurent again brought me to with a jolt.

"Unfortunately, I must be elsewhere."

"And anywhere but here? Well, you'll be missing a treat. And by the way, have you seen what this devil in the *Journal* has the wretched audacity to say about my book . . . ?"

Half an hour later, just as I got out into the hall, the limping servant hobbled by me and flung open the street door. And there stood Monsieur Laurent, his horrible puce face thrust forward, seeing me at once, before Charles and all things else. I felt like a seven-year-old boy caught stealing fruit in someone's orchard. I had been so determined to avoid the monster. Nor had I heard any summons to warn me of this collision; the sinister limper seemed to have known of his master's arrival by telepathic means alone.

"Good day," said the *maître* to me, advancing into his domain. "Hoping for lunch?"

I writhed to utter as I wanted, but did not.

"No, monsieur. I am lunching with friends."

"I thought my plagiarist son was your friend. Or have you grown wise to him, seen through him? I note," he added, directing his attention now to Charles, "one critic at least has had the wit to penetrate your sham nonsense. I must send him my congratulations."

Charles, touchy over the review (for which his father must truly have scoured the journals) was plainly for once caught on the raw spot. Without looking at him, I saw his anger reflected in the momentary pleasure of Monsieur Laurent's little eyes.

"And where's your beauteous sister? I've some news for her."

"Here I am," said a voice from the stairs.

Monsieur Laurent gave vent to that toneless, noisy amusement generally called a guffaw. "Yes, there you are. What plenteous abundance of hair! Where is it? Have I gone blind? Do you still go out on the street like that and make yourself a laughingstock?"

Turned to stone, my eyes only on the shut front door, I waited. And I heard her gentle voice say casually, light as down, "Yes, Papa, I'm afraid I do."

"You silly sheep. Look at you. Well, I suppose it's generous of you to give everyone, complete strangers, such a good laugh. But do I permit you to draw money to buy earrings and make yourself resemble a circus monkey?"

"No, Papa, the earrings were purchased from the small allowance Mother left me. But if they worry you, I'll take them off."

''Worry me? *You* worry me. You brainless thing, flapping about the house, scribbling, mooning. What's wrong with you?''

''I am very well, thank you, Papa.''

''That damnable fool, your female parent, what a curse she left me. A sniveling, profligate dunce and a literary jackal for sons. An idiot daughter.''

She was down the stairs now; I heard the rustle of her gown. She seemed to bring a coolness with her, a freshness, like open air, escape from the trap.

She said, ''Come and see the new sherry, Papa. I took your advice on the business of wines and have been trying to improve my knowledge. I'd like you to taste this latest bottle and see what you think.''

''If you chose the stuff, it must be worthless muck,'' said this charming father.

''Not necessarily,'' replied Honorine, for all the world as if she were talking to a sane and rational human being instead of to a thing from the Pit. ''I've tried, in my choice, to apply all you told me the other day. But if you think the sherry is poor and I'm mistaken again, of course I shall want you to correct me. How can I benefit from your superior understanding in these matters if you're lenient?''

What could he say, the beast? She had him, as seldom have I heard any so had. What had gone on? I can only conclude she had begun to take an interest in the ordering of the cellar, as la Belmains would certainly have done, and Monsieur, true to himself as always, had insulted her and attempted to belittle her over it, as over all else. Whereupon she must have assumed the attitude that she was being given an altruistic lesson for her own benefit, which notion she here continued. I have done just as you said, she informed him now. But if I am wrong—for naturally, I do not for a moment deny you are more clever than I am—you must let me know. And *do* be as harsh, as discourteous as you can be. I shall regard it as a mark of your concern and patronage. My God! I nearly laughed aloud. Whatever revolting abuse he threw at her now came with her awarded license. She would sit meekly before him, nodding as he ranted, presently thanking him for the tutorial. I was, despite everything, after all tempted to stay for lunch.

I compromised then, and indicated to Charles I would remain long enough to try the new sherry. And when the monster eyed me and made some remark about there being no luckier club for a minor writer than the free one of somebody else's house, I snatched a leaf from her book, grinned wildly at him, and cried, "And such an entertaining club, too."

It goes without saying he hated the sherry, which was a discerning one. But he said not much about it, save it was ditchwater. Honorine promised to bear this in mind. It was at this point that he recollected the news he wanted to tell her.

"Your hags of the tarot have gone," he said. "Did you know? An end to clandestine sorties to the bookshop and table tappings at my expense. Perhaps an end to the silliness you've been parading these last months, eh?"

"Ever since you showed such displeasure," said Honorine placidly, "I've not visited the shop."

"No. But things have come here from there. From your faker parasites. Bits of paper brought by your ugly maid. Or by dear Semery when I'm out—you thought I wasn't aware? There's not much I miss. I've read some of these secret notes, *billets doux*. Let me see. What did they say?"

We had all turned very silent. Honorine was pale and she put down her glass. From the erratic glitter of those delightful earrings of hers I could learn the quick, erratic motion of her pulse.

Monsieur Laurent made a great drama over recalling. He, like the soulless evil he was, had sound instincts for a victim's shrinking and fear. Yet, if he had got hold of any communications from Honorine's three witches, it seemed to me they would probably mean nothing to him. His was a sly mind, but not an intellectual slyness. He pulled the wings from insects to agonize them and prevent their flight, not to study the complexity of their pain and flightlessness. But the information of the Ouija board, ridiculous as it might be, was also intensely personal. He had, no doubt, always been in the habit of opening his children's private correspondence and taunting them with its closest passages.

Eventually, his head tilted back in a sort of cold, dry ecstasy, he announced: " 'Lucie Belmains. Born at Troy-la-Dianne in April 1729. Hanged dead on April 8, 1760.' Now do I quote that as it should be? Hah? And do I have *this* right—that you, my dollop of dough, unlovely, loveless, hopeless wreck that you are, are the reborn Lucie, so beautiful, kings paid ransoms for her company, and duels were fought to the death?''

There was a long terrible pause, with no noises in it save a patter of leafy rain on the road outside.

I did not look at her. I do not know how she seemed, but I can conjure it. Who needs to be told? This was her sacrament, holy, and hidden. And now he had it in his fangs, mauling and maiming it before us all. He had only been waiting, only *seeming* muzzled. But how could he be? All the servants were in his thrall. And her diary, maybe he had even got a grip on that, this savage, rabid dog. Yes, so he must have done, to come at the roots of her dream, the beautiful, abnormal structure that had made bearable her life. But it was not to be bearable. *He* could not bear that. She should not spring up from the crushing. He would pile on another weight.

I suppose seconds went by, no more, while I thought this, and suffered for her, and yearned again to kill him.

Then she spoke, and my head cleared of the black cloud, because her voice was steady, self-possessed. She had made a virtue of passivity. She gave no resistance now, since it would only lead the torturer on. She said, "Yes, Papa. Isn't it absurd? For me to imagine, even for an instant, I might have been such a person. But you seem to have discovered that I do imagine it. And I do. While, truly, thinking it every bit as unlikely and preposterous as you do yourself.''

The cold ecstasy left him at that. Temper came instead. For a moment I thought he would strike her, but physical blows were not what he enjoyed.

"And what gives you to think such errant twaddle? This salivatory drivel from what? A *Ouija board*? Fakers and schemers—they take your money—*my* money—and tell you anything you like to hear.''

"No, Father. They never asked a sou from me.''

"So you say. You *say*. But no doubt you make donations? Eh? And you've done their dubious reputation good, I expect, babbling to those you know of the *accomplishments* of this hocus-pocus. Lucie Belmains. *Lucie Belmains*. Does she even exist? Tell me that, you dunce. You'd swallow anything to make you out not the clod you are."

I could hold myself no longer, I regret it, but I think in the long term it made no difference. He was on the trail, this bloody dog. He would have found it all at length, whatever was done or said or omitted.

"Monsieur. Lucie Belmains most decidedly did exist. I'm surprised, sir, with your exceptional bent for knowing everything and missing nothing, that you've never heard of her."

"*Ah*," he said, turning his gaze on me. "So we're to be paid for our sherry with information. This is not," he said, "your concern. You may leave my house." And he smiled.

"I can think of nowhere, offhand, I could leave with greater pleasure."

"Brave words for a sponger," he said. "Or did you steal something while my back was turned?"

"In the sight of God!" shouted Charles.

But I, at the reckless, heedless spur of immaturity, answered, "Steal from you, monsieur? I'd be more fastidious."

"Would you?" he said. "From Anette Dupleys then, that fine, plump dowry of hers and her property in the south that goes with it. Indeed, a much juicier theft than anything the poor Laurents could offer you."

It seems he had done me the honor of finding out something about my circumstances also. And what he had found out, of course, was the thing set to cut me to the bone. I forget what I said or anything at all, until I got out, burning as if in flames and in an icy sweat, onto the street. Unfortunately, whatever I did in my passion, I did not seize a fire iron and murder him.

Charles came flying after me and grabbed my shoulder as I reached the Bois.

"In God's name—what can I say? Oh my God—forgive me."

I had chilled in the fire-following ice by then and said stiffly, "There's nothing to forgive you. I stayed when I was aware I should not. As for Anette's money, who doesn't know? That is all the argument between her father and myself. I am a fortunate hunter. Naturally.''

We quarreled about all this for a while, aimless and appalled. Finally, I accused him of leaving Honorine to face horror alone. "No, no," he said, "it was she sent me after you. She was quite calm still. He hasn't broken her. I thought he had. But she's talking to him so delicately, saying yes, she agrees with everything he says, but there it is.''

I thought of her grey face, I said, "Now he has the name of her hopes in front of him, he'll go on until he has destroyed them all.''

"How? She believes exactly what her witch ladies told her. He can't touch that.''

"He'll find some way," I said.

As I walked alone back along the leaf-lit paths I had traveled with Honorine, through the somber dusk of a coming storm, I knew my premonition was a true one.

The week before Semery's wedding to Miou, the two brothers and I dined in a good restaurant on the Boulevard du Pays. Charles seemed vaguely troubled at the outset, but he neither explained nor made a burden of it, the wine flowed, and soon enough there were no troubles in the world.

I judge it was about midnight when a written message was brought to Charles at the table. He read it and went very white.

"What?" said Semery. But a sense of dread and dismay had passed unsounded between them, not by any mystical means, but from old habit, a boyhood terror that came back whenever some dark shadow proceeded from their father.

I put down my glass and sat in silence.

Presently, Charles covered his eyes with his hand.

"We must go to the house," he said.

"Very well," said Semery, his bright tipsiness all gone. "But why?''

Charles took his hand from his eyes. He looked at me.

"This isn't your affair. There's no need for you to be caught up in it.''

"If you prefer," I said. It had had echoes of his father's words in showing me the door.

"No, no, I don't mean to offend you. Oh my God, my God." He stumbled to his feet and the chair chattered over. He did not even seem to see the obstacle as he avoided it.

In a few minutes we were out in the autumn night, still without an answer. Only a pall of black disaster hung about us, sure as the smell of death. It needed no name. In some degree, each of us knew.

I think he told us on the way to the house. I am not positive. It may have been on the very threshold. Or perhaps he did not tell us at all, was not required to. It seems to me now he never did say, in words. Yet I remember later, when we were in a room downstairs, lighted only by a lamp, and cold, he took up the open book left lying on a table and directed me to the place. I remember I read it and for a moment it made no sense, and then I fathomed the sense and my heart sank through me, leaden and afraid, for her sake.

To piece it together now will, perhaps, be better. What use is there, after all, to hesitate? As I had known, Monsieur Laurent must destroy her dream, and so he had, by the very simple expedient of doing what she had not. Honorine had taken her enlightenment almost solely from her ladies of the bookshop. What she had already read of Lucie Belmains had not been, presumably, specific in the matter of dates.

Honorine had trusted her mediums implicitly. She had believed what she had been told. Every fragment of it. But every fragment rested on every other. It was not a house of stone, not even of cards, but of glass, that whole, harmless, shining, starry edifice, and it shattered at a tiny mortal blow. How gratified he must have been, that demon, the weapon so easily come by, and so sharp.

They had told her—I had myself witnessed it—that Honorine's former self, her belle Lucie, had hanged herself, and died on the eighth of April, 1760. But if they were wrong in this, then the entire codex must be mistaken, a lie. And so it was proved. For this date was in error. Lucie Belmains, as history has recorded, as that very book Charles handed to me had recorded, had hanged herself on the morning of the fifth of April and, being cut down, was buried on the evening of the seventh, for the summer was forward that year. Of the eighth of April there was, and needed to be, no mention.

Three days out. Only that. Three days.

Monsieur Laurent had been at pains to tell her, and to show her, no doubt. I can envisage the scene that passed between them, father and daughter, there in that dank, fireless room, as *we* dined on the Boulevard du Pays. I have seen it often in my mind's eye, and listened to it over and over in those half dreams that come between sleep and waking when one is unhappy or very tired.

So she was rid of her fantasy and her madness. So he gave her back the single and only life she had, that dreary, pointless, loathing life, and her own former self, he gave her that, too. He widowed her of beauty and of love, love which had been, love which might yet come, if not as Honorine then in some future when she might be born once more another Lucie. And worse than all that, he throttled the sweet dignity and charm of what she was becoming, had become. God damn him. I do not ask for lives, but for a hell of fire and shrieking where he may burn and scream for all eternity.

After he had instructed her, Monsieur Laurent went out to his own gentleman's club. And Honorine, climbing up to that attic room whose window I had first admired, swallowed a dose of some poison kept for rats. She died in convulsions about an hour after we arrived.

She had written none of those parting notes so common in such cases. I do not think her wish was to instill in anyone feelings of guilt. In her father, the prime offender, it would have been impossible. I gather, though I never met him again, that his attitude remained consistent toward her, even after her death. She was a fool who had always displeased him, and displeased him only a fraction more by dying so violently under his roof. He used to say, I believe, that if she had desired an end so greatly, she should have drowned herself in the river and thereby saved them all the fuss and the expense her domestic suicide entailed. And of course, there was fuss and expense. The newspapers carried the story in a riot. This did Charles no good, but it was the shocking death itself, I am sure, which wore him down and eventually changed the pattern of his life, as is generally reckoned to its detriment. He left the bar less than a year after. His elegant and carefree wit, which had long deserted him, began to return in a strange little lay community attached to a monastery of the Languedoc. Occasionally, we correspond; I do not presume to understand his present existence, or to approve or disapprove of it, but he apparently does some good for himself and for those around him. Other than these messages to me or to Semery, he writes nothing now.

Semery himself, who in his way had already broken off the chains of a false life, was not fundamentally altered, but his grief and his remorse were awesome. Though the marriage went forward on the day assigned, he faltered through it all barely coherent and blind with tears. Later, I gather, he made some attempt to destroy his canvases, but fortunately, friends arrived and prevented it. Miou helped as only she could, by her persevering tenderness, until in the end some care of her and of their approaching child brought him to his senses.

But none of us was untouched.

Honorine, as I said, surely did not intend this torrent of guilt. That guilt should be experienced was unavoidable. Yet she, she was in that last hour so isolate, I would say she thought of no other, either to long for their comfort or to wish them ill. She must have climbed those stairs up through the house in an utter darkness of heart and mind, and soulless too, for her soul had been wrenched from her, as in the myths it is, by the devil. Her imaginings, or rather the black void within her—one shrinks from its contemplation.

However, though she left no concrete parting gift of bitterness in the form of a letter, there is that journal of hers, which Semery now possesses, and which he has allowed me to see. She wrote nothing in it of despair. It was all joy from start to finish. The finish being where she had left it off in the midst of a sentence, probably because she had been told her father required her downstairs. It is the joy, of course, which is unbearable. It is the unfinished sentence that fills one with terror, as if reading the order for an execution. What breaks the heart is the motto she has written just inside the cover: *Je suis parce que j'ai été.**

For none of us were untouched.

At six o'clock on the morning after her death, not having slept or shaved, nor completely in my right mind, I hurried westward across the city. The dawn was beginning to wash stealthily in along the dry riverbeds of the streets, and I remember I met a flock of sheep being ushered into the Faubourg St. Marie. When I reached the house of the Dupleys, I woke it, and its neighbors, by hammering on the door.

What was said and performed was madness, and I can recollect only fragments of it now, that to this day have the power to embarrass me, or sometimes to make me laugh. Suffice it to relate, I fought my way by means of shouted threats through several servants and eventually through Anette's father himself (who thought me dangerously insane), all the way to Anette's mother (who thought much as he did, but with more compassion). And so to Anette herself, who, whatever she thought, did not love me less. There in a corner of a room, her good, kind mother outside the door as our protector, the father in the hall roaring that the police should be called, I said nothing of what had happened, only perpetrated yet one more scene worthy of the opera, crying in Anette's arms and then seizing her hands and asking her to get dressed and come away with me at once. There was the briefest addendum to this plea. It concerned her trusting me, it concerned our being married by the quickest means the law allowed, it concerned my ability to support her, that she was of age but would lose all her money and inheritance. That maybe we should live without pecuniary margin forever. That she should bring warm clothing and whatever else she might need, and her pet kitten. And that I could not swear not to attack her father if he interfered any further. To all of which she listened gravely, then said that I must go away at once, and that she would then meet me, with her mother's help, complete with one small valise and the kitten, in an hour's time in the Bois Palais. At first I argued. Not because I thought she was putting me off—wretch that I was I had every

---

*I am because I was.

right to think that she might be—but simply because I was so shaken and wild I could not bear to leave her. Nevertheless, in the end she persuaded me. I went, while Monsieur Dupleys, standing on his steps in his dressing gown, with the manservant, waved a purportedly loaded pistol at my back. And in just over an hour mother, daughter, and kitten appeared in the Bois, and we and the fountains wept, and the little cat wailed in astonishment, and God alone knows what the early strollers made of it all.

As it turned out, there was a later reconciliation, and Anette lost nothing by her elopement. We were, though, a year married by then, and my own financial prospects had taken a soaring turn toward fortune. I like to suppose that even if they had not, we could still have possessed the great happiness we had from the commencement, and still share together. I am now received by Monsieur Dupleys, who pompously and placatingly, and also out of a need to make me uncomfortable, sometimes refers to that tempestuous morning, as if it were some game we all played. But it was nothing of the sort. Or, if so, it was Honorine's—Lucie's.

For it was because of Honorine that I risked, as I did, our chances. This I have since explained to my wife. Not only through the upheaval of that ghastly suicide. No, more because of those ephemeral moments of a woman's *life*, in which I had participated. I had been trying, desperately, to make at least one iota of the dream be true. *Could you perhaps run away together?* she had said to me. Lucie's scheme—brave, beautiful, reckless Lucie. Lucie gracious enough to assume Anette's money meant nothing to me, in which assumption she and Anette have been, probably, quite alone. And so I honored Lucie. I went to my love and asked her to run away with me, and she consented. I shall be grateful for that, to Honorine, until the day of my death.

The last act is now concluded, and yet there remains something in the way of an epilogue. I have said I have no leanings to superstition, or to esoteric occult ideas, and part of me clamors here to leave well alone. After all, if, as I believe, it proves nothing, then the circumstances I have outlined turn only darker, and they are surely dark enough. On the other hand, the inveterate storyteller finds it hard to reject such a gem. For gem it is, of a sort.

Some years had passed; the great-grandchildren of Anette's first cat were playing with two children of our own across the floors of our house. Researching in an area that had nothing whatever to do with Lucie Belmains, I suddenly came across a strange reference to her. It dealt, as did the rest of the rather obscure material I was examining, with the negligence, connivance, and ineptitude of some doctors when presented with various classic but misleading symptoms. There was, for instance, a case of hysteria amusingly and dreadfully diagnosed as *la rage*, and a nastier affair of the same rabid condition, genuine, thought to be lycanthropy. Then came an interim paragraph, and next a name (Lucie's) that caught me unawares and made me start. Some wounds, though they heal, retain a lifelong capacity for hurt.

"Lucie Belmains," my material went on after a token biography, "having slain herself on the morning of the fifth of April, was medically certified as mortal, and buried swiftly, due to the extreme and unusual heat of the season. Readers who have scanned the novel *La Prise En Geste* will be familiar with the following quotation from it." The quotation does indeed follow, but I will omit it here. It was from a flowery work, the very one I am sure Miou and her sister had giggled over under the covers, and as a result of which their poor doll was hanged on a ribbon. The substance of the quotation was this: That on the sixth of April, one of Lucie's living admirers, having entered the bedroom where the body was laid out, and kneeling by the bed in a transport of grief, was abruptly terrified to see the dead woman's left hand flutter as if beckoning to him. Hastening to uncover her face, however, he found only the discoloration and popping eyes such a corpse would exhibit and, running out of the room, he fainted.

"What is not widely known," the material went on, "is that this incident is a fact, and not merely a flight of fancy on the part of a romantic author. There are two other facts, even more slenderly recorded, and not utilized by the writer of *La Prise En Geste*. Firstly, that Belmains' maid, on the evening of the seventh, the actual night of burial, found disturbed the veil which covered the cadaver's face, it being partly pushed or drawn in between the lips. Secondly, that several comments were made on the suppleness of the limbs. This was put down to the hot weather. While the whole affair was meanwhile thought so scandalous, its sequels were largely rushed and overall camouflaged, to the point that for several years even the Duc de M——, who had been for so long the lady's intimate protector, thought she had died from accidental choking.''

The conclusion my material evolved from all this is a fairly obvious one. That though Lucie had sufficiently strangled herself as to induce a kind of catalepsy, she was not dead, and did not die until the injury of a mainly collapsed windpipe was augmented by the disadvantages of the grave. Not the material but I myself venture to suggest she could not, in this state, have lingered very much longer. No doubt only until the morning of the eighth of April.

Flannery O'Connor

GOOD COUNTRY PEOPLE

Flannery O'Connor is one of the finest American writers of the latter half of this century, an ironist in the Southern tradition of William Faulkner and Eudora Welty. She was not in any sense a category writer, but her contributions to horror literature place her beside Shirley Jackson and Joyce Carol Oates. A number of her stories of bleak, black humor show horrific insight into human psychology, of which "Good Country People" is a prime example. It forms an interesting couplet with Robert Aickman's "The Swords" as a story of sexual initiation dealing with body parts, and shows the strength of the nonsupernatural strain in American psychological horror fiction.

B esides the neutral expression that she wore when she was alone, Mrs. Freeman had two others, forward and reverse, that she used for all her human dealings. Her forward expression was steady and driving like the advance of a heavy truck. Her eyes never swerved to left or right but turned as the story turned as if they followed a yellow line down the center of it. She seldom used the other expression because it was not often necessary for her to retract a statement, but when she did, her face came to a complete stop, there was an almost imperceptible movement of her black eyes, during which they seemed to be receding, and then the observer would see that Mrs. Freeman, though she might stand there as real as several grain sacks thrown on top of each other, was no longer there in spirit. As for getting anything across to her when this was the case, Mrs. Hopewell had given it up. She might talk her head off. Mrs. Freeman could never be brought to admit herself wrong on any point. She would stand there and if she could be brought to say anything, it was something like, "Well, I wouldn't of said it was and I wouldn't of said it wasn't," or letting her gaze range over the top kitchen shelf where there was an assortment of dusty bottles, she might remark, "I see you ain't ate many of them figs you put up last summer."

They carried on their most important business in the kitchen at breakfast. Every morning Mrs. Hopewell got up at seven o'clock and lit her gas heater and Joy's. Joy was her daughter, a large blonde girl who had an artificial leg. Mrs. Hopewell thought of her as a child though she was thirty-two years old and highly educated. Joy would get up while her mother was eating and lumber into the bathroom and slam the door, and before long, Mrs. Freeman would arrive at the back door. Joy would hear her mother call, "Come on in," and then they would talk for a while in low voices that were indistinguishable in the bathroom. By the time Joy came in, they had usually finished the weather report and were on one or the other of Mrs. Freeman's daughters, Glynese, or Carramae. Joy called them Glycerin and Caramel. Glynese, a redhead, was eighteen and had many admirers; Carramae, a blonde, was only fifteen but already married and pregnant. She could not keep anything on her stomach. Every morning Mrs. Freeman told Mrs. Hopewell how many times she had vomited since the last report.

Mrs. Hopewell liked to tell people that Glynese and Carramae were two of the finest girls she knew and that Mrs. Freeman was a *lady* and that she was never ashamed to take her anywhere or introduce her to anybody they might meet. Then she would tell how she had happened to hire the Freemans in the first place and how they were a godsend to her and how she had had them four years. The reason for her keeping them so long was that they were not trash. They were good country people. She had telephoned the man whose name they had given as a reference and he had told her that Mr. Freeman was a good farmer but that his wife was the nosiest woman ever to walk the earth. "She's got to be into everything,'' the man said. ''If she don't get there before the dust settles, you can bet she's dead, that's all. She'll want to know all your business. I can stand him real good,'' he had said, ''but me nor my wife neither could have stood that woman one more minute on this place.'' That had put Mrs. Hopewell off for a few days.

She had hired them in the end because there were no other applicants but she had made up her mind beforehand exactly how she would handle the woman. Since she was the type who had to be into everything, then, Mrs. Hopewell had decided, she would not only let her be into everything, she would *see to it* that she was into everything—she would give her the responsibility of everything, she would put her in charge. Mrs. Hopewell had no bad qualities of her own but she was able to use other people's in such a constructive way that she never felt the lack. She had hired the Freemans and she had kept them four years.

Nothing is perfect. This was one of Mrs. Hopewell's favorite sayings. Another was: that is life! And still another, the most important, was: well, other people have their opinions too. She would make these statements, usually at the table, in a tone of gentle insistence as if no one held them but her, and the large hulking Joy, whose constant outrage had obliterated every expression from her face, would stare just a little to the side of her, her eyes icy blue, with the look of someone who has achieved blindness by an act of will and means to keep it.

When Mrs. Hopewell said to Mrs. Freeman that life was like that, Mrs. Freeman would say, ''I always said so myself.'' Nothing had been arrived at by anyone that had not first been arrived at by her. She was quicker than Mr. Freeman. When Mrs. Hopewell said to her after they had been on the place a while, ''You know, you're the wheel behind the wheel,'' and winked, Mrs. Freeman had said, ''I know it. I've always been quick. It's some that are quicker than others.''

''Everybody is different,'' Mrs. Hopewell said.

''Yes, most people is,'' Mrs. Freeman said.

''It takes all kinds to make the world.''

''I always said it did myself.''

The girl was used to this kind of dialogue for breakfast and more of it for dinner; sometimes they had it for supper too. When they had no guest they ate in the kitchen because that was easier. Mrs. Freeman always managed to arrive at some point during the meal and to watch them finish it. She would stand in the doorway if it were summer but in the winter she would stand with one elbow on top of the refrigerator and look down on them, or she would stand by the gas heater, lifting the back of her skirt slightly. Occasionally she would stand against the wall and roll her head from side to side. At no time was she in any hurry to leave. All this was very trying on Mrs. Hopewell but she was a woman of great patience. She realized that nothing is perfect and that in the Freemans she had good country people and that if, in this day and age, you get good country people, you had better hang onto them.

She had had plenty of experience with trash. Before the Freemans she had averaged one tenant family a year. The wives of these farmers were not the kind you would want to be around you for very long. Mrs. Hopewell, who had divorced her husband long ago, needed someone to walk over the fields with her; and when Joy had to be impressed for these services, her remarks were usually so ugly and her face so glum that Mrs. Hopewell would say, "If you can't come pleasantly, I don't want you at all," to which the girl, standing square and rigid-shouldered with her neck thrust slightly forward, would reply, "If you want me, here I am—LIKE I AM."

Mrs. Hopewell excused this attitude because of the leg (which had been shot off in a hunting accident when Joy was ten). It was hard for Mrs. Hopewell to realize that her child was thirty-two now and that for more than twenty years she had had only one leg. She thought of her still as a child because it tore her heart to think instead of the poor stout girl in her thirties who had never danced a step or had any *normal* good times. Her name was really Joy but as soon as she was twenty-one and away from home, she had had it legally changed. Mrs. Hopewell was certain that she had thought and thought until she had hit upon the ugliest name in any language. Then she had gone and had the beautiful name, Joy, changed without telling her mother until after she had done it. Her legal name was Hulga.

When Mrs. Hopewell thought the name, Hulga, she thought of the broad blank hull of a battleship. She would not use it. She continued to call her Joy to which the girl responded but in a purely mechanical way.

Hulga had learned to tolerate Mrs. Freeman who saved her from taking walks with her mother. Even Glynese and Carramae were useful when they occupied attention that might otherwise have been directed at her. At first she had thought she could not stand Mrs. Freeman for she had found that it was not possible to be rude to her. Mrs. Freeman would take on strange resentments and for days together she would be sullen but the source of her displeasure was always obscure; a direct attack, a positive leer, blatant ugliness to her face— these never touched her. And without warning one day, she began calling her Hulga.

She did not call her that in front of Mrs. Hopewell who would have been incensed but when she and the girl happened to be out of the house together, she would say something and add the name Hulga to the end of it, and the big spectacled Joy-Hulga would scowl and redden as if her privacy had been intruded upon. She considered the name her personal affair. She had arrived at it first purely on the basis of its ugly sound and then the full genius of its fitness had struck her. She had a vision of the name working like the ugly sweating Vulcan who stayed in the furnace and to whom, presumably, the goddess had to come when called. She saw it as the name of her highest creative act. One of her major triumphs was that her mother had not been able to turn her dust into Joy, but the greater one was that she had been able to turn it herself into Hulga. However, Mrs. Freeman's relish for using the name only irritated her. It was as if Mrs. Freeman's beady steelpointed eyes had penetrated far enough behind her face to reach some secret fact. Something about her seemed to fascinate Mrs. Freeman and then one day Hulga realized that it was the artificial leg. Mrs. Freeman had a special fondness for the details of secret infections, hidden deformities, assaults upon children. Of diseases, she preferred the lingering or incurable. Hulga had heard Mrs.

Hopewell give her the details of the hunting accident, how the leg had been literally blasted off, how she had never lost consciousness. Mrs. Freeman could listen to it any time as if it had happened an hour ago.

When Hulga stumped into the kitchen in the morning (she could walk without making the awful noise but she made it—Mrs. Hopewell was certain—because it was ugly-sounding), she glanced at them and did not speak. Mrs. Hopewell would be in her red kimono with her hair tied around her head in rags. She would be sitting at the table, finishing her breakfast and Mrs. Freeman would be hanging by her elbow outward from the refrigerator, looking down at the table. Hulga always put her eggs on the stove to boil and then stood over them with her arms folded, and Mrs. Hopewell would look at her—a kind of indirect gaze divided between her and Mrs. Freeman—and would think that if she would only keep herself up a little, she wouldn't be so bad looking. There was nothing wrong with her face that a pleasant expression wouldn't help. Mrs. Hopewell said that people who looked on the bright side of things would be beautiful even if they were not.

Whenever she looked at Joy this way, she could not help but feel that it would have been better if the child had not taken the Ph.D. It had certainly not brought her out any and now that she had it, there was no more excuse for her to go to school again. Mrs. Hopewell thought it was nice for girls to go to school to have a good time but Joy had "gone through." Anyhow, she would not have been strong enough to go again. The doctors had told Mrs. Hopewell that with the best of care, Joy might see forty-five. She had a weak heart. Joy had made it plain that if it had not been for this condition, she would be far from these red hills and good country people. She would be in a university lecturing to people who knew what she was talking about. And Mrs. Hopewell could very well picture her there, looking like a scarecrow and lecturing to more of the same. Here she went about all day in a six-year-old skirt and a yellow sweat shirt with a faded cowboy on a horse embossed on it. She thought this was funny; Mrs. Hopewell thought it was idiotic and showed simply that she was still a child. She was brilliant

but she didn't have a grain of sense. It seemed to Mrs. Hopewell that every year she grew less like other people and more
like herself—bloated, rude, and squint-eyed. And she said such
strange things! To her own mother she had said—without
warning, without excuse, standing up in the middle of a
meal with her face purple and her mouth half full—"Woman!
do you ever look inside? Do you ever look inside and see
what you are *not*? God!" she had cried sinking down again
and staring at her plate, "Malebranche was right: we are not
our own light. We are not our own light!" Mrs. Hopewell
had no idea to this day what brought that on. She had only
made the remark, hoping Joy would take it in, that a smile
never hurt anyone.

The girl had taken the Ph.D. in philosophy and this left
Mrs. Hopewell at a complete loss. You could say, "My
daughter is a nurse," or "My daughter is a school teacher,"
or even, "My daughter is a chemical engineer." You could
not say, "My daughter is a philosopher." That was something that had ended with the Greeks and Romans. All day
Joy sat on her neck in a deep chair, reading. Sometimes she
went for walks but she didn't like dogs or cats or birds or
flowers or nature or nice young men. She looked at nice
young men as if she could smell their stupidity.

One day Mrs. Hopewell had picked up one of the books
the girl had just put down and opening it at random, she read,
"Science, on the other hand, has to assert its soberness and
seriousness afresh and declare that it is concerned solely with
what-is. Nothing—how can it be for science anything but a
horror and a phantasm? If science is right, then one thing
stands firm: science wishes to know nothing of nothing. Such
is after all the strictly scientific approach to Nothing. We
know it by wishing to know nothing of Nothing." These
words had been underlined with a blue pencil and they worked
on Mrs. Hopewell like some evil incantation in gibberish.
She shut the book quickly and went out of the room as if she
were having a chill.

This morning when the girl came in, Mrs. Freeman was
on Carramae. "She thrown up four times after supper," she
said, "and was up twice in the night after three o'clock. Yesterday she didn't do nothing but ramble in the bureau drawer.

All she did. Stand up there and see what she could run up on.''

"She's got to eat," Mrs. Hopewell muttered, sipping her coffee, while she watched Joy's back at the stove. She was wondering what the child had said to the Bible salesman. She could not imagine what kind of a conversation she could possibly have had with him.

He was a tall gaunt hatless youth who had called yesterday to sell them a Bible. He had appeared at the door, carrying a large black suitcase that weighted him so heavily on one side that he had to brace himself against the door facing. He seemed on the point of collapse but he said in a cheerful voice, "Good morning, Mrs. Cedars!" and set the suitcase down on the mat. He was not a bad-looking young man though he had on a bright blue suit and yellow socks that were not pulled up far enough. He had prominent face bones and a streak of sticky-looking brown hair falling across his forehead.

"I'm Mrs. Hopewell," she said.

"Oh!" he said, pretending to look puzzled but with his eyes sparkling, "I saw it said 'The Cedars,' on the mailbox so I thought you was Mrs. Cedars!" and he burst out in a pleasant laugh. He picked up the satchel and under cover of a pant, he fell forward into her hall. It was rather as if the suitcase had moved first, jerking him after it. "Mrs. Hopewell!" he said and grabbed her hand. "I hope you are well!" and he laughed again and then all at once his face sobered completely. He paused and gave her a straight earnest look and said, "Lady, I've come to speak of serious things."

"Well, come in," she muttered, none too pleased because her dinner was almost ready. He came into the parlor and sat down on the edge of a straight chair and put the suitcase between his feet and glanced around the room as if he were sizing her up by it. Her silver gleamed on the two sideboards; she decided he had never been in a room as elegant as this.

"Mrs. Hopewell," he began, using her name in a way that sounded almost intimate, "I know you believe in Chrustian service."

"Well yes," she murmured.

"I know," he said and paused, looking very wise with his

head cocked on one side, "that you're a good woman. Friends have told me."

Mrs. Hopewell never liked to be taken for a fool. "What are you selling?" she asked.

"Bibles," the young man said and his eye raced around the room before he added, "I see you have no family Bible in your parlor, I see that is the one lack you got!"

Mrs. Hopewell could not say, "My daughter is an atheist and won't let me keep the Bible in the parlor." She said, stiffening slightly, "I keep my Bible by my bedside." This was not the truth. It was in the attic somewhere.

"Lady," he said, "The word of God ought to be in the parlor."

"Well, I think that's a matter of taste," she began. "I think . . ."

"Lady," he said, "for a Chrustian, the word of God ought to be in every room in the house besides in his heart. I know you're a Chrustian because I can see it in every line of your face."

She stood up and said, "Well, young man, I don't want to buy a Bible and I smell my dinner burning."

He didn't get up. He began to twist his hands and looking down at them, he said softly, "Well lady, I'll tell you the truth—not many people want to buy one nowadays and besides, I know I'm real simple. I don't know how to say a thing but to say it. I'm just a country boy." He glanced up into her unfriendly face. "People like you don't like to fool with country people like me!"

"Why!" she cried, "good country people are the salt of the earth! Besides, we all have different ways of doing, it takes all kinds to make the world go 'round. That's life!"

"You said a mouthful," he said.

"Why, I think there aren't enough good country people in the world!" she said, stirred. "I think that's what's wrong with it!"

His face had brightened. "I didn't inraduce myself," he said. "I'm Manley Pointer from out in the country around Willohobie, not even from a place, just from near a place."

"You wait a minute," she said. "I have to see about my

dinner." She went out to the kitchen and found Joy standing near the door where she had been listening.

"Get rid of the salt of the earth," she said, "and let's eat."

Mrs. Hopewell gave her a pained look and turned the heat down under the vegetables. "*I* can't be rude to anybody," she murmured and went back into the parlor.

He had opened the suitcase and was sitting with a Bible on each knee.

"You might as well put those up," she told him. "I don't want one."

"I appreciate your honesty," he said. "You don't see any more real honest people unless you go way out in the country."

"I know," she said, "real genuine folks!" Through the crack in the door she heard a groan.

"I guess a lot of boys come telling you they're working their way through college," he said, "but I'm not going to tell you that. Somehow," he said, "I don't want to go to college. I want to devote my life to Chrustian service. See," he said, lowering his voice, "I got this heart condition. I may not live long. When you know it's something wrong with you and you may not live long, well then, lady . . ." He paused, with his mouth open, and stared at her.

He and Joy had the same condition! She knew that her eyes were filling with tears but she collected herself quickly and murmured, "Won't you stay for dinner? We'd love to have you!" and was sorry the instant she heard herself say it.

"Yes mam," he said in an abashed voice, "I would sher love to do that!"

Joy had given him one look on being introduced to him and then throughout the meal had not glanced at him again. He had addressed several remarks to her, which she had pretended not to hear. Mrs. Hopewell could not understand deliberate rudeness, although she lived with it, and she felt she had always to overflow with hospitality to make up for Joy's lack of courtesy. She urged him to talk about himself and he did. He said he was the seventh child of twelve and that his father had been crushed under a tree when he himself was eight year old. He had been crushed very badly, in fact, almost cut in two and was practically not recognizable. His mother had got along the best she could by hard working and she had always seen that her children went to Sunday School and that they read the Bible every evening. He was now nineteen year old and he had been selling Bibles for four months. In that time he had sold seventy-seven Bibles and had the promise of two more sales. He wanted to become a missionary because he thought that was the way you could do most for people. "He who losest his life shall find it," he said simply and he was so sincere, so genuine and earnest that Mrs. Hopewell would not for the world have smiled. He prevented his peas from sliding onto the table by blocking them with a piece of bread which he later cleaned his plate with. She could see Joy observing sidewise how he handled his knife and fork and she saw too that every few minutes, the boy would dart a keen appraising glance at the girl as if he were trying to attract her attention.

After dinner Joy cleared the dishes off the table and disappeared and Mrs. Hopewell was left to talk with him. He told her again about his childhood and his father's accident and about various things that had happened to him. Every five minutes or so she would stifle a yawn. He sat for two hours until finally she told him she must go because she had an appointment in town. He packed his Bibles and thanked her and prepared to leave, but in the doorway he stopped and wrung her hand and said that not on any of his trips had he met a lady as nice as her and he asked if he could come again. She had said she would always be happy to see him.

Joy had been standing in the road, apparently looking at something in the distance, when he came down the steps toward her, bent to the side with his heavy valise. He stopped where she was standing and confronted her directly. Mrs. Hopewell could not hear what he said but she trembled to think what Joy would say to him. She could see that after a minute Joy said something and that then the boy began to speak again, making an excited gesture with his free hand. After a minute Joy said something else at which the boy began to speak once more. Then to her amazement, Mrs. Hopewell saw the two of them walk off together, toward the gate. Joy had walked all the way to the gate with him and Mrs.

Hopewell could not imagine what they had said to each other, and she had not yet dared to ask.

Mrs. Freeman was insisting upon her attention. She had moved from the refrigerator to the heater so that Mrs. Hopewell had to turn and face her in order to seem to be listening. "Glynese gone out with Harvey Hill again last night," she said. "She had this sty."

"Hill," Mrs. Hopewell said absently, "is that the one who works in the garage?"

"Nome, he's the one that goes to chiropracter school," Mrs. Freeman said. "She had this sty. Been had it two days. So she says when he brought her in the other night he says, 'Lemme get rid of that sty for you,' and she says, 'How?' and he says, 'You just lay yourself down acrost the seat of that car and I'll show you.' So she done it and he popped her neck. Kept on a-popping it several times until she made him quit. This morning," Mrs. Freeman said, "she ain't got no sty. She ain't got no traces of a sty."

"I never heard of that before," Mrs. Hopewell said.

"He ast her to marry him before the Ordinary," Mrs. Freeman went on, "and she told him she wasn't going to be married in no *office*."

"Well, Glynese is a fine girl," Mrs. Hopewell said. "Glynese and Carramae are both fine girls."

"Carramae said when her and Lyman was married Lyman said it sure felt sacred to him. She said he said he wouldn't take five hundred dollars for being married by a preacher."

"How much would he take?" the girl asked from the stove.

"He said he wouldn't take five hundred dollars," Mrs. Freeman repeated.

"Well we all have work to do," Mrs. Hopewell said.

"Lyman said it just felt more sacred to him," Mrs. Freeman said. "The doctor wants Carramae to eat prunes. Says instead of medicine. Says them cramps is coming from pressure. You know where I think it is?"

"She'll be better in a few weeks," Mrs. Hopewell said.

"In the tube," Mrs. Freeman said. "Else she wouldn't be as sick as she is."

Hulga had cracked her two eggs into a saucer and was bringing them to the table along with a cup of coffee that she had filled too full. She sat down carefully and began to eat, meaning to keep Mrs. Freeman there by questions if for any reason she showed an inclination to leave. She could perceive her mother's eye on her. The first round-about question would be about the Bible salesman and she did not wish to bring it on. "How did he pop her neck?" she asked.

Mrs. Freeman went into a description of how he had popped her neck. She said he owned a '55 Mercury but that Glynese said she would rather marry a man with only a '36 Plymouth who would be married by a preacher. The girl asked what if he had a '32 Plymouth and Mrs. Freeman said what Glynese had said was a '36 Plymouth.

Mrs. Hopewell said there were not many girls with Glynese's common sense. She said what she admired in those girls was their common sense. She said that reminded her that they had had a nice visitor yesterday, a young man selling Bibles. "Lord," she said, "he bored me to death but he was so sincere and genuine I couldn't be rude to him. He was just good country people, you know," she said, "—just the salt of the earth."

"I seen him walk up," Mrs. Freeman said, "and then later—I seen him walk off," and Hulga could feel the slight shift in her voice, the slight insinuation, that he had not walked off alone, had he? Her face remained expressionless but the color rose into her neck and she seemed to swallow it down with the next spoonful of egg. Mrs. Freeman was looking at her as if they had a secret together.

"Well, it takes all kinds of people to make the world go 'round," Mrs. Hopewell said. "It's very good we aren't all alike."

"Some people are more alike than others," Mrs. Freeman said.

Hulga got up and stumped, with about twice the noise that was necessary, into her room and locked the door. She was to meet the Bible salesman at ten o'clock at the gate. She had thought about it half the night. She had started thinking of it as a great joke and then she had begun to see profound implications in it. She had lain in bed imagining dialogues for them that were insane on the surface but that reached below to depths that no Bible salesman would be aware of. Their conversation yesterday had been of this kind.

He had stopped in front of her and had simply stood there. His face was bony and sweaty and bright, with a little pointed nose in the center of it, and his look was different from what it had been at the dinner table. He was gazing at her with open curiosity, with fascination, like a child watching a new fantastic animal at the zoo, and he was breathing as if he had run a great distance to reach her. His gaze seemed somehow familiar but she could not think where she had been regarded with it before. For almost a minute he didn't say anything. Then on what seemed an insuck of breath, he whispered, "You ever ate a chicken that was two days old?"

The girl looked at him stonily. He might have just put this question up for consideration at the meeting of a philosophical association. "Yes," she presently replied as if she had considered it from all angles.

"It must have been mighty small!" he said triumphantly and shook all over with little nervous giggles, getting very red in the face, and subsiding finally into his gaze of complete admiration, while the girl's expression remained exactly the same.

"How old are you?" he asked softly.

She waited some time before she answered. Then in a flat voice she said, "Seventeen."

His smiles came in succession like waves breaking on the surface of a little lake. "I see you got a wooden leg," he said. "I think you're real brave. I think you're real sweet."

The girl stood blank and solid and silent.

"Walk to the gate with me," he said. "You're a brave sweet little thing and I liked you the minute I seen you walk in the door."

Hulga began to move forward.

"What's your name?" he asked, smiling down on the top of her head.

"Hulga," she said.

"Hulga," he murmured, "Hulga. Hulga. I never heard of anybody name Hulga before. You're shy, aren't you, Hulga?" he asked.

She nodded, watching his large red hand on the handle of the giant valise.

"I like girls that wear glasses," he said. "I think a lot. I'm not like these people that a serious thought don't ever enter their heads. It's because I may die."

"I may die too," she said suddenly and looked up at him. His eyes were very small and brown, glittering feverishly.

"Listen," he said, "don't you think some people was meant to meet on account of what all they got in common and all? Like they both think serious thoughts and all?" He shifted the valise to his other hand so that the hand nearest her was free. He caught hold of her elbow and shook it a little. "I don't work on Saturday," he said. "I like to walk in the woods and see what Mother Nature is wearing. O'er the hills and far away. Pic-nics and things. Couldn't we go on a pic-nic tomorrow? Say yes, Hulga," he said and gave her a dying look as if he felt his insides about to drop out of him. He had even seemed to sway slightly toward her.

During the night she had imagined that she seduced him. She imagined that the two of them walked on the place until they came to the storage barn beyond the two back fields and there, she imagined, that things came to such a pass that she very easily seduced him and that then, of course, she had to reckon with his remorse. True genius can get an idea across even to an inferior mind. She imagined that she took his remorse in hand and changed it into a deeper understanding of life. She took all his shame away and turned it into something useful.

She set off for the gate at exactly ten o'clock, escaping without drawing Mrs. Hopewell's attention. She didn't take anything to eat, forgetting that food is usually taken on a picnic. She wore a pair of slacks and a dirty white shirt, and as an afterthought, she had put some Vapex on the collar of it since she did not own any perfume. When she reached the gate no one was there.

She looked up and down the empty highway and had the furious feeling that she had been tricked, that he had only meant to make her walk to the gate after the idea of him. Then suddenly he stood up, very tall, from behind a bush on the opposite embankment. Smiling, he lifted his hat which was new and wide-brimmed. He had not worn it yesterday and she wondered if he had bought it for the occasion. It was toast-colored with a red and white band around it and was slightly too large for him. He stepped from behind the bush still carrying the black valise. He had on the same suit and the same yellow socks sucked down in his shoes from walking. He crossed the highway and said, "I knew you'd come!"

The girl wondered acidly how he had known this. She pointed to the valise and asked, "Why did you bring your Bibles?"

He took her elbow, smiling down on her as if he could not stop. "You can never tell when you'll need the word of God, Hulga," he said. She had a moment in which she doubted that this was actually happening and then they began to climb the embankment. They went down into the pasture toward the woods. The boy walked lightly by her side, bouncing on his toes. The valise did not seem to be heavy today; he even swung it. They crossed half the pasture without saying anything and then, putting his hand easily on the small of her back, he asked softly, "Where does your wooden leg join on?"

She turned an ugly red and glared at him and for an instant the boy looked abashed. "I didn't mean you no harm," he said. "I only meant you're so brave and all. I guess God takes care of you."

"No," she said, looking forward and walking fast, "I don't even believe in God."

At this he stopped and whistled. "No!" he exclaimed as if he were too astonished to say anything else.

She walked on and in a second he was bouncing at her side, fanning with his hat. "That's very unusual for a girl," he remarked, watching her out of the corner of his eye. When they reached the edge of the wood, he put his hand on her back again and drew her against him without a word and kissed her heavily.

The kiss, which had more pressure than feeling behind it, produced that extra surge of adrenaline in the girl that enables one to carry a packed trunk out of a burning house, but in her, the power went at once to the brain. Even before he released her, her mind, clear and detached and ironic anyway, was regarding him from a great distance, with amusement but with pity. She had never been kissed before and she was pleased to discover that it was an unexceptional experience and all a matter of the mind's control. Some people might enjoy drain water if they were told it was vodka. When the boy, looking expectant but uncertain, pushed her gently away, she turned and walked on, saying nothing as if such business, for her, were common enough.

He came along panting at her side, trying to help her when he saw a root that she might trip over. He caught and held back the long swaying blades of thorn vine until she had passed beyond them. She led the way and he came breathing heavily behind her. Then they came out on a sunlit hillside, sloping softly into another one a little smaller. Beyond, they could see the rusted top of the old barn where the extra hay was stored.

The hill was sprinkled with small pink weeds. "Then you ain't saved?" he asked suddenly, stopping.

The girl smiled. It was the first time she had smiled at him at all. "In my economy," she said, "I'm saved and you are damned but I told you I didn't believe in God."

Nothing seemed to destroy the boy's look of admiration. He gazed at her now as if the fantastic animal at the zoo had put its paw through the bars and given him a loving poke. She thought he looked as if he wanted to kiss her again and she walked on before he had the chance.

"Ain't there somewheres we can sit down sometime?" he murmured, his voice softening toward the end of the sentence.

"In that barn," she said.

They made for it rapidly as if it might slide away like a train. It was a large two-story barn, cool and dark inside. The boy pointed up the ladder that led into the loft and said, "It's too bad we can't go up there."

"Why can't we?" she asked.

"Yer leg," he said reverently.

The girl gave him a contemptuous look and putting both hands on the ladder, she climbed it while he stood below, apparently awestruck. She pulled herself expertly through the opening and then looked down at him and said, "Well, come on if you're coming," and he began to climb the ladder, awkwardly bringing the suitcase with him.

"We won't need the Bible," she observed.

"You never can tell," he said, panting. After he had got into the loft, he was a few seconds catching his breath. She had sat down in a pile of straw. A wide sheath of sunlight, filled with dust particles, slanted over her. She lay back against a bale, her face turned away, looking out the front opening of the barn where hay was thrown from a wagon into the loft. The two pink-speckled hillsides lay back against a dark ridge of woods. The sky was cloudless and cold blue. The boy dropped down by her side and put one arm under her and the other over her and began methodically kissing her face, making little noises like a fish. He did not remove his hat but it was pushed far enough back not to interfere. When her glasses got in his way, he took them off of her and slipped them into his pocket.

The girl at first did not return any of the kisses but presently she began to and after she had put several on his cheek, she reached his lips and remained there, kissing him again and again as if she were trying to draw all the breath out of him. His breath was clear and sweet like a child's and the kisses were sticky like a child's. He mumbled about loving her and about knowing when he first seen her that he loved her, but the mumbling was like the sleepy fretting of a child being put to sleep by his mother. Her mind, throughout this, never stopped or lost itself for a second to her feelings. "You ain't said you loved me none," he whispered finally, pulling back from her. "You got to say that."

She looked away from him off into the hollow sky and then down at a black ridge and then down farther into what appeared to be two green swelling lakes. She didn't realize he had taken her glasses but this landscape could not seem exceptional to her for she seldom paid any close attention to her surroundings.

"You got to say it," he repeated. "You got to say you love me."

She was always careful how she committed herself. "In a sense," she began, "if you use the word loosely, you might say that. But it's not a word I use. I don't have illusions. I'm one of those people who see *through* to nothing."

The boy was frowning. "You got to say it. I said it and you got to say it," he said.

The girl looked at him almost tenderly. "You poor baby," she murmured. "It's just as well you don't understand," and she pulled him by the neck, face-down, against her. "We are all damned," she said, "but some of us have taken off our blindfolds and see that there's nothing to see. It's a kind of salvation."

The boy's astonished eyes looked blankly through the ends of her hair. "Okay," he almost whined, "but do you love me or don'tcher?"

"Yes," she said and added, "in a sense. But I must tell you something. There mustn't be anything dishonest between us." She lifted his head and looked him in the eye. "I am thirty years old," she said. "I have a number of degrees."

The boy's look was irritated but dogged. "I don't care," he said. "I don't care a thing about what all you done. I just want to know if you love me or don'tcher?" and he caught her to him and wildly planted her face with kisses until she said, "Yes, yes."

"Okay then," he said, letting her go. "Prove it."

She smiled, looking dreamily out on the shifty landscape. She had seduced him without even making up her mind to try. "How?" she asked, feeling that he should be delayed a little.

He leaned over and put his lips to her ear. "Show me where your wooden leg joins on," he whispered.

The girl uttered a sharp little cry and her face instantly drained of color. The obscenity of the suggestion was not what shocked her. As a child she had sometimes been subject to feelings of shame but education had removed the last traces of that as a good surgeon scrapes for cancer; she would no more have felt it over what he was asking than she would have believed in his Bible. But she was as sensitive about the artificial leg as a peacock about his tail. No one ever touched it but her. She took care of it as someone else would his soul, in private and almost with her own eyes turned away. "No," she said.

"I known it," he muttered, sitting up. "You're just playing me for a sucker."

"Oh no no!" she cried. "It joins on at the knee. Only at the knee. Why do you want to see it?"

The boy gave her a long penetrating look. "Because," he said, "it's what makes you different. You ain't like anybody else."

She sat staring at him. There was nothing about her face or her round freezing-blue eyes to indicate that this had moved her; but she felt as if her heart had stopped and left her mind to pump her blood. She decided that for the first time in her life she was face to face with real innocence. This boy, with an instinct that came from beyond wisdom, had touched the truth about her. When after a minute, she said in a hoarse high voice, "All right," it was like surrendering to him completely. It was like losing her own life and finding it again, miraculously, in his.

Very gently he began to roll the slack leg up. The artificial limb, in a white sock and brown flat shoe, was bound in a heavy material like canvas and ended in an ugly jointure where it was attached to the stump. The boy's face and his voice were entirely reverent as he uncovered it and said, "Now show me how to take it off and on."

She took it off for him and put it back on again and then he took it off himself, handling it as tenderly as if it were a real one. "See!" he said with a delighted child's face. "Now I can do it myself!"

"Put it back on," she said. She was thinking that she would run away with him and that every night he would take the leg off and every morning put it back on again. "Put it back on," she said.

"Not yet," he murmured, setting it on its foot out of her reach. "Leave it off for a while. You got me instead."

She gave a little cry of alarm but he pushed her down and began to kiss her again. Without the leg she felt entirely dependent on him. Her brain seemed to have stopped thinking altogether and to be about some other function that it was not very good at. Different expressions raced back and forth over her face. Every now and then the boy, his eyes like two steel spikes, would glance behind him where the leg stood.

Finally she pushed him off and said, "Put it back on me now."

"Wait," he said. He leaned the other way and pulled the valise toward him and opened it. It had a pale blue spotted lining and there were only two Bibles in it. He took one of these out and opened the cover of it. It was hollow and contained a pocket flask of whiskey, a pack of cards, and a small blue box with printing on it. He laid these out in front of her one at a time in an evenly-spaced row, like one presenting offerings at the shrine of a goddess. He put the blue box in her hand. THIS PRODUCT TO BE USED ONLY FOR THE PREVENTION OF DISEASE, she read, and dropped it. The boy was unscrewing the top of the flask. He stopped and pointed, with a smile, to the deck of cards. It was not an ordinary deck but one with an obscene picture on the back of each card. "Take a swig," he said, offering her the bottle first. He held it in front of her, but like one mesmerized, she did not move.

Her voice when she spoke had an almost pleading sound. "Aren't you," she murmured, "aren't you just good country people?"

The boy cocked his head. He looked as if he were just beginning to understand that she might be trying to insult him. "Yeah," he said, curling his lip slightly, "but it ain't held me back none. I'm as good as you any day in the week."

"Give me my leg," she said.

He pushed it farther away with his foot. "Come on now, let's begin to have us a good time," he said coaxingly. "We ain't got to know one another good yet."

"Give me my leg!" she screamed and tried to lunge for it but he pushed her down easily.

"What's the matter with you all of a sudden?" he asked, frowning as he screwed the top on the flask and put it quickly back inside the Bible. "You just a while ago said you didn't believe in nothing. I thought you was some girl!"

Her face was almost purple. "You're a Christian!" she hissed. "You're a fine Christian! You're just like them all—say one thing and do another. You're a perfect Christian, you're . . ."

The boy's mouth was set angrily. "I hope you don't think," he said in a lofty indignant tone, "that I believe in that crap!

I may sell Bibles but I know which end is up and I wasn't born yesterday and I know where I'm going!''

"Give me my leg!" she screeched. He jumped up so quickly that she barely saw him sweep the cards and the blue box back into the Bible and throw the Bible into the valise. She saw him grab the leg and then she saw it for an instant slanted forlornly across the inside of the suitcase with a Bible at either side of its opposite ends. He slammed the lid shut and snatched up the valise and swung it down the hole and then stepped through himself.

When all of him had passed but his head, he turned and regarded her with a look that no longer had any admiration in it. "I've gotten a lot of interesting things," he said. "One time I got a woman's glass eye this way. And you needn't to think you'll catch me because Pointer ain't really my name. I use a different name at every house I call at and don't stay nowhere long. And I'll tell you another thing, Hulga," he said, using the name as if he didn't think much of it, "you ain't so smart. I been believing in nothing ever since I was born!" and then the toast-colored hat disappeared down the hole and the girl was left, sitting on the straw in the dusty sunlight. When she turned her churning face toward the opening, she saw his blue figure struggling successfully over the green speckled lake.

Mrs. Hopewell and Mrs. Freeman, who were in the back pasture, digging up onions, saw him emerge a little later from the woods and head across the meadow toward the highway. "Why, that looks like that nice dull young man that tried to sell me a Bible yesterday," Mrs. Hopewell said, squinting. "He must have been selling them to the Negroes back in there. He was so simple," she said, "but I guess the world would be better off if we were all that simple."

Mrs. Freeman's gaze drove forward and just touched him before he disappeared under the hill. Then she returned her attention to the evil-smelling onion shoot she was lifting from the ground. "Some can't be that simple," she said. "I know I never could."

Ramsey Campbell

MACKINTOSH WILLY

Ramsey Campbell is perhaps the most important living writer in the horror fiction field. Jack Sullivan (in his excellent scholarly anthology, *Lost Souls*) calls Campbell "the most sophisticated stylist in current supernatural fiction," and goes on to praise his images, "which dwell on the disorderliness of middle- and lower-class life, have a jagged, contemporary edge," and continues on to credit him with "bringing the supernatural tale up to date without sacrificing the literary standards." He works consciously in the horror tradition and has consistently experimented with all the varied modes of the contemporary horror story, from the Lovecraftian to the Aickmanesque. He is in addition a devotee of pop culture horror in films, comics, and is an acute critic. Campbell is one of the leading figures in the development of the long form horror novel, along with Peter Straub and Stephen King and others. His novel, *The Face That Must Die*, is one of the contemporary masterpieces of the long form, and he is constantly working to extend his range. "Mackintosh Willy" is among his finest efforts in the psychological mode, a disturbing story of male sexual innocence comparable in effect to Robert Aickman's "The Swords." It won the World Fantasy Award for best short fiction in 1980.

To start with, he wasn't called Mackintosh Willy. I never knew who gave him that name. Was it one of those nicknames that seem to proceed from a group subconscious, names recognized by every member of the group yet apparently originated by none? One has to call one's fears something, if only to gain the illusion of control. Still, sometimes I wonder how much of his monstrousness we created. Wondering helps me not to ponder my responsibility for what happened at the end.

When I was ten I thought his name was written inside the shelter in the park. I saw it only from a distance; I wasn't one of those who made a game of braving the shelter. At ten I wasn't afraid to be timid—that came later, with adolescence.

Yet if you had walked past Newsham Park you might have wondered what there was to fear: why were children advancing, bold but wary, on the red-brick shelter by the twilit pool? Surely there could be no danger in the shallow shed, which might have held a couple of dozen bicycles. By now the fishermen and the model boats would have left the pool alone and still; lamps on the park road would have begun to dangle luminous tails in the water. The only sounds would be the whispering of children, the murmur of the trees around the pool, perhaps a savage incomprehensible muttering whose source you would be unable to locate. Only a game, you might reassure yourself.

And of course it was: a game to conquer fear. If you had waited long enough you might have heard shapeless movement in the shelter, and a snarling. You might have glimpsed him as he came scuttling lopsidedly out of the shelter, like an injured spider from its lair. In the gathering darkness, how much of your glimpse would you believe? The unnerving swiftness of the obese limping shape? The head which seemed to belong to another, far smaller, body, and which was almost invisible within a gray balaclava cap, except for the small eyes which glared through the loose hole?

All of that made us hate him. We were too young for tolerance—and besides, he was intolerant of us. Ever since we could remember he had been there, guarding his territory and his bottle of red biddy. If anyone ventured too close he would start muttering. Sometimes you could hear some of the words: "Damn bastard prying interfering snooper . . . thieving bastard layabout . . . think you're clever, eh? . . . I'll give you something clever . . .''

We never saw him until it was growing dark: that was what made him into a monster. Perhaps during the day he joined his cronies elsewhere—on the steps of ruined churches in the center of Liverpool, or lying on the grass in St. John's Gardens, or crowding the benches opposite Edge Hill Public Library, whose stopped clock no doubt helped their draining of time. But if anything of this occurred to us, we dismissed it as irrelevant. He was a creature of the dark.

Shouldn't this have meant that the first time I saw him in daylight was the end? In fact, it was only the beginning.

It was a blazing day at the height of summer, my tenth. It was too hot to think of games to while away my school holidays. All I could do was walk errands for my parents, grumbling a little.

They owned a small newsagent's on West Derby Road. That day they were expecting promised copies of the *Tuebrook Bugle*. Even when he disagreed with them, my father always supported the independent newspapers—the *Bugle*, the *Liverpool Free Press*: at least they hadn't been swallowed or destroyed by a monopoly. The lateness of the *Bugle* worried him; had the paper given in? He sent me to find out.

I ran across West Derby Road just as the traffic lights at the top of the hill released a flood of cars. Only girls used the pedestrian subway so far as I was concerned; besides, it was flooded again. I strolled past the concrete police station into the park, to take the long way round. It was too hot to go anywhere quickly or even directly.

The park was crowded with games of football, parked prams, sunbathers draped over the greens. Patients sat outside the hospital on Orphan Drive beside the park. Around the lake, fishermen sat by transistor radios and whipped the air with hooks. Beyond the lake, model boats snarled across the shallow circular pool. I stopped to watch their patterns on the water, and caught sight of an object in the shelter.

At first I thought it was an old gray sack that someone had dumped on the bench. Perhaps it held rubbish—sticks which gave parts of it an angular look. Then I saw that the sack was an indeterminate stained garment, which might have been a mackintosh or raincoat of some kind. What I had vaguely assumed to be an ancient shopping bag, resting next to the sack, displayed a ragged patch of flesh and the dull gleam of an eye.

Exposed to daylight, he looked even more dismaying: so huge and still, less stupefied than dormant. The presence of the boatmen with their remote-control boxes reassured me. I ambled past the allotments to Pringle Street, where a terraced house was the editorial office of the *Bugle*.

Our copies were on the way, said Chrissie Maher the editor, and insisted on making me a cup of tea. She seemed a little upset when, having gulped the tea, I hurried out into the sudden rain. Perhaps it was rude of me not to wait until the rain had stopped—but on this parched day I wanted to make the most of it, to bathe my face and my bare arms in the onslaught, gasping almost hysterically.

By the time I had passed the allotments, where cabbages rattled like toy machine-guns, the downpour was too heavy even for me. The park provided little cover; the trees let fall their own belated storms, miniature but drenching. The nearest shelter was by the pool, which had been abandoned to its web of ripples. I ran down the slippery tarmac hill, splashing through puddles, trying to blink away rain, hoping there would be room in the shelter.

There was plenty of room, both because the rain reached easily into the depths of the brick shed and because the shelter was not entirely empty. He lay as I had seen him, face upturned within the sodden balaclava. Had the boatmen avoided looking closely at him? Raindrops struck his unblinking eyes and trickled over the patch of flesh.

I hadn't seen death before. I stood shivering and fascinated in the rain. I needn't be scared of him now. He'd stuffed himself into the gray coat until it split in several places; through the rents I glimpsed what might have been dark cloth or discolored hairy flesh. Above him, on the shelter, were graffiti which at last I saw were not his name at all, but the names of three boys: MACK TOSH WILLY. They were partly erased, which no doubt was why one's mind tended to fill the gap.

I had to keep glancing at him. He grew more and more

difficult to ignore; his presence was intensifying. His shape-
lessness, the rents in his coat, made me think of an old bag
of washing, decayed and moldy. His hand lurked in his sleeve;
beside it, amid a scattering of Coca-Cola caps, lay fragments
of the bottle whose contents had perhaps killed him. Rain
roared on the dull green roof of the shelter; his staring eyes
glistened and dripped. Suddenly I was frightened. I ran
blindly home.

"There's someone dead in the park," I gasped. "The man
who chases everyone."

"Look at you!" my mother cried. "Do you want pneu-
monia? Just you get out of those wet things this instant!"

Eventually I had a chance to repeat my news. By this time
the rain had stopped. "Well, don't be telling us," my father
said. "Tell the police. They're just across the road."

Did he think I had exaggerated a drunk into a corpse? He
looked surprised when I hurried to the police station. But I
couldn't miss the chance to venture in there—I believed that
elder brothers of some of my schoolmates had been taken
into the station and hadn't come out for years.

Beside a window which might have belonged to a ticket
office was a bell which you rang to make the window's partition slide back and display a policeman. He frowned down
at me. What was my name? What had I been doing in the
park? Who had I been with? When a second head appeared
beside him he said reluctantly, "He thinks someone's passed
out in the park."

A blue-and-white Mini called for me at the police station,
like a taxi; on the roof a red sign said POLICE. People glanced
in at me as though I were on the way to prison. Perhaps I
was: suppose Mackintosh Willy had woken up and gone?
How long a sentence did you get for lying? False diamonds
sparkled on the grass and in the trees. I wished I'd persuaded
my father to tell the police.

As the car halted, I saw the gray bulk in the shelter. The
driver strode, stiff with dignity, to peer at it. "My God," I
heard him say in disgust.

Did he know Mackintosh Willy? Perhaps, but that wasn't
the point. "Look at this," he said to his colleague. "Ever

see a corpse with pennies on the eyes? Just look at this, then. See what someone thought was a joke.''

He looked shocked, sickened. He was blocking my view as he demanded, ''Did you do this?''

His white-faced anger, and my incomprehension, made me speechless. But his colleague said, ''It wouldn't be him. He wouldn't come and tell us afterward, would he?''

As I tried to peer past them he said, ''Go on home, now. Go on.'' His gentleness seemed threatening. Suddenly frightened, I ran home through the park.

For a while I avoided the shelter. I had no reason to go near, except on the way home from school. Sometimes I'd used to see schoolmates tormenting Mackintosh Willy; sometimes, at a distance, I had joined them. Now the shelter yawned emptily, baring its dim bench. The dark pool stirred, disturbing the green beards of the stone margin. My main reason for avoiding the park was that there was nobody with whom to go.

Living on a main road was the trouble. I belonged to none of the side streets, where they played football among parked cars or chased through the back alleys. I was never invited to street parties. I felt like an outsider, particularly when I had to pass the groups of teenagers who sat on the railings above the pedestrian subway, lazily swinging their legs, waiting to pounce. I stayed at home, in the flat above the newsagent's, when I could, and read everything in the shop. But I grew frustrated: I did enough reading at school. All this was why I welcomed Mark. He could save me from my isolation.

Not that we became friends immediately. He was my parents' latest paper boy. For several days we examined each other warily. He was taller than me, which was intimidating, but seemed unsure how to arrange his lankiness. Eventually he said, ''What're you reading?''

He sounded as though reading was a waste of time. ''A book,'' I retorted.

At last, when I'd let him see that it was Mickey Spillane, he said, ''Can I read it after you?''

''It isn't mine. It's the shop's.''

''All right, so I'll buy it.'' He did so at once, paying my father. He was certainly wealthier than me. When my re-sentiment of his gesture had cooled somewhat, I realized that he was letting me finish what was now his book. I dawdled over it to make him complain, but he never did. Perhaps he might be worth knowing.

My instinct was accurate: he proved to be generous—not only with money, though his father made plenty of that in home improvements, but also in introducing me to his friends. Quite soon I had my place in the tribe at the top of the pedestrian subway, though secretly I was glad that we never exchanged more than ritual insults with the other gangs. Perhaps the police station, looming in the background, restrained hostilities.

Mark was generous too with his ideas. Although Ben, a burly lad, was nominal leader of the gang, it was Mark who suggested most of our activities. Had he taken to delivering papers to save himself from boredom—or, as I wondered afterward, to distract himself from his thoughts? It was Mark who brought his skates so that we could brave the slope of the pedestrian subway, who let us ride his bicycle around the side streets, who found ways into derelict houses, who brought his transistor radio so that we could hear the first Beatles records as the traffic passed unheeding on West Derby Road. But was all this a means of distracting us from the park?

No doubt it was inevitable that Ben resented his supremacy. Perhaps he deduced, in his slow and stolid way, that Mark disliked the park. Certainly he hit upon the ideal method to challenge him.

It was a hot summer evening. By then I was thirteen. Dust and fumes drifted in the wakes of cars; wagons clattered repetitively across the railway bridge. We lolled about the pavement, kicking Coca-Cola caps. Suddenly Ben said, ''I know something we can do.''

We trooped after him, dodging an aggressive gang of taxis, toward the police station. He might have meant us to play some trick there; when he swaggered past, I'm sure everyone was relieved—everyone except Mark, for Ben was leading us onto Orphan Drive.

Heat shivered above the tarmac. Beside us in the park, twilight gathered beneath the trees, which stirred stealthily.

The island in the lake creaked with ducks; swollen litter drifted sluggishly, or tried to climb the bank. I could sense Mark's nervousness. He had turned his radio louder; a misshapen Elvis Presley blundered out of the static, then sank back into incoherence as a neighboring wave band seeped into his voice. Why was Mark on edge? I could see only the dimming sky, trees on the far side of the lake diluted by haze, the gleam of bottle caps like eyes atop a floating mound of litter, the glittering of broken bottles in the lawns.

We passed the locked ice-cream kiosk. Ben was heading for the circular pool, whose margin was surrounded by a fluorescent orange tape tied between iron poles, a makeshift fence. I felt Mark's hesitation, as though he were a scared dog dragged by a lead. The lead was pride: he couldn't show fear, especially when none of us knew Ben's plan.

A new concrete path had been laid around the pool. "We'll write our names in that," Ben said.

The dark pool swayed, as though trying to douse reflected lights. Black clouds spread over the sky and loomed in the pool; the threat of a storm lurked behind us. The brick shelter was very dim, and looked cavernous. I strode to the orange fence, not wanting to be last, and poked the concrete with my toe. "We can't," I said; for some reason, I felt relieved. "It's set."

Someone had been there before us, before the concrete had hardened. Footprints led from the dark shelter toward us. As they advanced, they faded, no doubt because the concrete had been setting. They looked as though the man had suffered from a limp.

When I pointed them out, Mark flinched, for we heard the radio swing wide of comprehensibility. "What's up with you?" Ben demanded.

"Nothing."

"It's getting dark," I said, not as an answer but to coax everyone back toward the main road. But my remark inspired Ben; contempt grew in his eyes. "I know what it is," he said, gesturing at Mark. "This is where he used to be scared."

"Who was scared? I wasn't bloody scared."

"Not much you weren't. You didn't look it," Ben scoffed,

and told us, "Old Willy used to chase him all round the pool. He used to hate him, did old Willy. Mark used to run away from him. I never. *I* wasn't scared."

"You watch who you're calling scared. If you'd seen what I did to that old bastard—"

Perhaps the movements around us silenced him. Our surroundings were crowded with dark shifting: the sky unfurled darkness, muddy shapes rushed at us in the pool, a shadow huddles restlessly in one corner of the shelter. But Ben wasn't impressed by the drooping boast. "Go on," he sneered. "You're scared now. Bet you wouldn't dare go in his shelter."

"Who wouldn't? You watch it, you!"

"Go on, then. Let's see you do it."

We must all have been aware of Mark's fear. His whole body was stiff as a puppet's. I was ready to intervene—to say, lying, that I thought the police were near—when he gave a shrug of despair and stepped forward. Climbing gingerly over the tape as though it were electrified, he advanced onto the concrete.

He strode toward the shelter. He had turned the radio full on; I could hear nothing else, only watch the shifting of dim shapes deep in the reflected sky, watch Mark stepping in the footprints for bravado. They swallowed his feet. He was nearly at the shelter when I saw him glance at the radio.

The song had slipped awry again; another wave band seeped in, a blurred muttering. I thought it must be Mark's infectious nervousness which made me hear it forming into words. "Come on, son. Let's have a look at you." But why shouldn't the words have been real, fragments of a radio play?

Mark was still walking, his gaze held by the radio. He seemed almost hypnotized; otherwise he would surely have flinched back from the huddled shadow which surged forward from the corner by the bench, even though it must have been the shadow of a cloud.

As his foot touched the shelter I called nervously, "Come on, Mark. Let's go and skate." I felt as though I'd saved him. But when he came hurrying back, he refused to look at me or at anyone else.

For the next few days he hardly spoke to me. Perhaps he

thought of avoiding my parents' shop. Certainly he stayed away from the gang—which turned out to be all to the good, for Ben, robbed of Mark's ideas, could think only of shoplifting. They were soon caught, for they weren't very skillful. After that my father had doubts about Mark, but Mark had always been scrupulously honest in deliveries; after some reflection, my father kept him on. Eventually Mark began to talk to me again, though not about the park.

That was frustrating: I wanted to tell him how the shelter looked now. I still passed it on my way home, though from a different school. Someone had been scrawling on the shelter. That was hardly unusual—graffiti filled the pedestrian subway, and even claimed the ends of streets—but the words were odd, to say the least: like the scribbles on the walls of a psychotic's cell, or the gibberish of an invocation. DO THE BASTARD. BOTTLE UP HIS EYES. HOOK THEM OUT. PUSH HIS HEAD IN. Tangled amid them, like chewed bones, gleamed the eroded slashes of MACK TOSH WILLY.

I wasn't as frustrated by the conversational taboo as I might have been, for I'd met my first girl friend. Kim was her name; she lived in a flat on my block, and because of her parents' trade, seemed always to smell of fish and chips. She obviously looked up to me—for one thing, I'd begun to read for pleasure again, which few of her friends could be bothered attempting. She told me her secrets, which was a new experience for me, strange and rather exciting—as was being seen on West Derby Road with a girl on my arm, any girl. I was happy to ignore the jeers of Ben and cronies.

She loved the park. Often we strolled through, scattering charitable crumbs to ducks. Most of all she loved to watch the model yachts, when the snarling model motorboats left them alone to glide over the pool. I enjoyed watching too, while holding her warm, if rather clammy, hand. The breeze carried away her culinary scent. But I couldn't help noticing that the shelter now displayed screaming faces with red bursts for eyes. I have never seen drawings of violence on walls elsewhere.

My relationship with Kim was short-lived. Like most such teenage experiences, our parting was not romantic and poignant, if partings ever are, but harsh and hysterical. It happened one evening as we made our way to the fair which visited Newsham Park each summer.

Across the lake we could hear shrieks that mingled panic and delight as cars on metal poles swung girls into the air, and the blurred roaring of an ancient pop song, like the voice of an enormous radio. On the Ferris wheel, colored lights sailed up, painting airborne faces. The twilight shone like a Christmas tree; the lights swam in the pool. That was why Kim said, "Let's sit and look first."

The only bench was in the shelter. Tangles of letters dripped trails of dried paint, like blood; mutilated faces shrieked soundlessly. Still, I thought I could bear the shelter. Sitting with Kim gave me the chance to touch her breasts, such as they were, through the collapsing deceptively large cups of her bra. Tonight she smelled of newspapers, as though she had been wrapped in them for me to take out; she must have been serving at the counter. Nevertheless I kissed her, and ignored the fact that one corner of the shelter was dark as a spider's crevice.

But she had noticed; I felt her shrink away from the corner. Had she noticed more than I? Or was it her infectious wariness which made the dark beside us look more solid, about to shuffle toward us along the bench? I was uneasy, but the din and the lights of the fairground were reassuring. I determined to make the most of Kim's need for protection, but she pushed my hand away. "Don't," she said irritably, and made to stand up.

At that moment I heard a blurred voice. "Popeye," it muttered as if to itself; it sounded gleeful. "Popeye." Was it part of the fair? It might have been a stallholder's voice, distorted by the uproar, for it said, "I've got something for you."

The struggles of Kim's hand in mine excited me. "Let me go," she was wailing. Because I managed not to be afraid, I was more pleased than dismayed by her fear—and I was eager to let my imagination flourish, for it was better than reading a ghost story. I peered into the dark corner to see what horrors I could imagine.

Then Kim wrentched herself free and ran around the pool. Disappointed and angry, I pursued her. "Go away," she cried. "You're horrible. I never want to speak to you again." For a while I chased her along the dim paths, but once I began to plead I grew furious with myself. She wasn't worth the embarrassment. I let her go, and returned to the fair, to wander desultorily for a while. When I'd stayed long enough to prevent my parents from wondering why I was home early, I walked home.

I meant to sit in the shelter for a while, to see if anything happened, but someone was already there. I couldn't make out much about him, and didn't like to go closer. He must have been wearing spectacles, for his eyes seemed perfectly circular and gleamed like metal, not like eyes at all.

I quickly forgot that glimpse, for I discovered Kim hadn't been exaggerating: she refused to speak to me. I stalked off to buy fish and chips elsewhere. I decided that I hadn't liked her anyway. My one lingering disappointment, I found glumly, was that I had nobody with whom to go to the fairground. Eventually, when the fair and the school holidays were approaching their end, I said to Mark, "Shall we go to the fair tonight?"

He hesitated, but didn't seem especially wary. "All right," he said with the indifference we were beginning to affect about everything.

At sunset the horizon looked like a furnace, and that was how the park felt. Couples rambled sluggishly along the paths; panting dogs splashed in the lake. Between the trees the lights of the fairground shimmered and twinkled, cheap multicolored stars. As we passed the pool, I noticed that the air was quivering above the footprints in the concrete, and looked darkened, perhaps by dust. Impulsively I said, "What did you do to old Willy?"

"Shut up." I'd never heard Mark so savage or withdrawn. "I wish I hadn't done it."

I might have retorted to his rudeness, but instead I let myself be captured by the fairground, by the glade of light amid the balding rutted green. Couples and gangs roamed, harangued a shade halfheartedly by stallholders. Young children hid their faces in pink candy floss. A siren thin as a Christmas party hooter set the Dodgems running. Mark and I rode a tilting bucket above the fuzzy clamor of music, the splashes of glaring light, the cramped crowd. Secretly I felt a little sick, but the ride seemed to help Mark regain his confidence. Shortly, as we were playing a pinball machine with senile flippers, he said, "Look, there's Lorna and what's-her-name."

It took me a while to be sure where he was pointing: at a tall, bosomy girl, who probably looked several years older than she was, and a girl of about my height and age, her small bright face sketched with makeup. By this time I was following him eagerly.

The tall girl was Lorna; her friend's name was Carol. We strolled for a while, picking our way over power cables, and Carol and I began to like each other; her scent was sweet, if rather overpowering. As the fair began to close, Mark easily won trinkets at a shooting gallery and presented them to the girls, which helped us persuade them to meet us on Saturday night. By now Mark never looked toward the shelter—I think not from wariness but because it had ceased to worry him, at least for the moment. I glanced across, and could just distinguish someone pacing unevenly round the pool, as if impatient for a delayed meeting.

If Mark had noticed, would it have made any difference? Not in the long run, I try to believe. But however I rationalize, I know that some of the blame was mine.

We were to meet Lorna and Carol on our side of the park in order to take them to the Carlton cinema, nearby. We arrived late, having taken our time over sprucing ourselves; we didn't want to seem too eager to meet them. Beside the police station, at the entrance to the park, a triangular island of pavement, large enough to contain a spinney of trees, divided the road. The girls were meant to be waiting at the nearest point of the triangle. But the island was deserted except for the caged darkness beneath the trees.

We waited. Shop windows on West Derby Road glared fluorescent green. Behind us trees whispered, creaking. We kept glancing into the park, but the only figure I could distinguish on the dark paths was alone. Eventually, for something to do, we strolled desultorily around the island.

It was I who saw the message first, large letters scrawled on the corner nearest the park. Was it Lorna's or Carol's handwriting? It rather shocked me, for it looked semiliterate. But she must have had to use a stone as a pencil, which couldn't have helped; indeed, some letters had had to be dug out of the moss which coated stretches of the pavement. MARK SEE YOU AT SHELTER, the message said.

I felt him withdraw a little, "Which shelter?" he muttered.

"I expect they mean the one near the kiosk," I said, to reassure him.

We hurried along Orphan Drive. Above the lamps, patches of foliage shone harshly. Before we reached the pool we crossed the bridge, from which in daylight manna rained down to the ducks, and entered the park. The fair had gone into hibernation; the paths, and the mazes of tree trunks, were silent and very dark. Occasional dim movements made me think that we were passing the girls, but the figure that was wandering a nearby path looked far too bulky.

The shelter was at the edge of the main green, near the football pitch. Beyond the green, tower blocks loomed in glaring auras. Each of the four sides of the shelter was an alcove housing a bench. As we peered into each, jeers or curses challenged us.

"I know where they'll be," Mark said. "In the one by the bowling green. That's near where they live."

But we were closer to the shelter by the pool. Nevertheless I followed him onto the park road. As we turned toward the bowling green I glanced toward the pool, but the streetlamps dazzled me. I followed him along a narrow path between hedges to the green, and almost tripped over his ankles as he stopped short. The shelter was empty, alone with its view of the decaying Georgian houses on the far side of the bowling green.

To my surprise and annoyance, he still didn't head for the pool. Instead, we made for the disused bandstand hidden in a ring of bushes. Its only tune now was the clink of broken bricks. I was sure that the girls wouldn't have called it a shelter, and of course it was deserted. Obese dim bushes hemmed us in. "Come on," I said, "or we'll miss them. They must be by the pool."

"They won't be there," he said—stupidly, I thought.

Did I realize how nervous he suddenly was? Perhaps, but

it only annoyed me. After all, how else could I meet Carol again? I didn't know her address. "Oh, all right," I scoffed, "if you want us to miss them."

I saw him stiffen. Perhaps my contempt hurt him more than Ben's had; for one thing, he was older. Before I knew what he intended he was striding toward the pool, so rapidly that I would have had to run to keep up with him—which, given the hostility that had flared between us, I refused to do. I strolled after him rather disdainfully. That was how I came to glimpse movement in one of the islands of dimness between the lamps of the park road. I glanced toward it and saw, several hundred yards away, the girls.

After a pause they responded to my waving—somewhat timidly, I thought. "There they are," I called to Mark. He must have been at the pool by now, but I had difficulty in glimpsing him beyond the glare of the lamps. I was beckoning the girls to hurry when I heard his radio blur into speech.

At first I was reminded of a sailor's parrot. "Aye aye," it was croaking. The distorted voice sounded cracked, uneven, almost too old to speak. "You know what I mean, son?" it grated triumphantly. "Aye aye." I was growing uneasy, for my mind had begun to interpret the words as "Eye eye"—when suddenly, dreadfully, I realized Mark hadn't brought his radio.

There might be someone in the shelter with a radio. But I was terrified, I wasn't sure why. I ran toward the pool, calling, "Come on, Mark, they're here!" The lamps dazzled me; everything swayed with my running—which was why I couldn't be sure what I saw.

I know I saw Mark at the shelter. He stood just within, confronting darkness. Before I could discern whether anyone else was there, Mark staggered out blindly, hands covering his face, and collapsed into the pool.

Did he drag something with him? Certainly by the time I reached the margin of the light he appeared to be tangled in something, and to be struggling feebly. He was drifting, or being dragged, toward the center of the pool by a half-submerged heap of litter. At the end of the heap nearest Mark's face was a pale ragged patch in which gleamed two round objects—bottle caps? I could see all this because I was standing helpless, screaming at the girls, "Quick, for Christ's sake! He's drowning!" He was drowning, and I couldn't swim.

"Don't be stupid," I heard Lorna say. That enraged me so much that I turned from the pool. "What do you mean?" I cried. "What do you mean, you stupid bitch?"

"Oh, be like that," she said haughtily, and refused to say more. But Carol took pity on my hysteria, and explained, "It's only three feet deep. He'll never drown in there."

I wasn't sure that she knew what she was talking about, but that was no excuse for me not to try to rescue him. When I turned to the pool I gasped miserably, for he had vanished—sunk. I could only wade into the muddy water, which engulfed my legs and closed around my waist like ice, ponderously hindering me.

The floor of the pool was fattened with slimy litter. I slithered, terrified of losing my balance. Intuition urged me to head for the center of the pool. And it was there I found him, as my sluggish kick collided with his ribs.

When I tried to raise him, I discovered that he was pinned down. I had to grope blindly over him in the chill water, feeling how still he was. Something like a swollen cloth bag, very large, lay over his face. I couldn't bear to touch it again, for its contents felt soft and fat. Instead I seized Mark's ankles and managed at last to drag him free. Then I struggled toward the edge of the pool, heaving him by his shoulders, lifting his head above the water. His weight was dismaying. Eventually the girls waded out to help me.

But we were too late. When we dumped him on the concrete, his face stayed agape with horror; water lay stagnant in his mouth. I could see nothing wrong with his eyes. Carol grew hysterical, and it was Lorna who ran to the hospital, perhaps in order to get away from the sight of him. I only made Carol worse by demanding why they hadn't waited for us at the shelter; I wanted to feel they were to blame. But she denied they had written the message, and grew more hysterical when I asked why they hadn't waited at the island. The question, or the memory, seemed to frighten her.

I never saw her again. The few newspapers that bothered to report Mark's death gave the verdict "by misadventure."

The police took a dislike to me after I insisted that there might be somebody else in the pool, for the draining revealed nobody. At least, I thought, whatever was there had gone away. Perhaps I could take some credit for that, at least.

But perhaps I was too eager for reassurance. The last time I ventured near the shelter was years ago, one winter night on the way home from school. I had caught sight of a gleam in the depths of the shelter. As I went close, nervously watching both the shelter and the pool, I saw two discs glaring at me from the darkness beside the bench. They were Coca-Cola caps, not eyes at all, and it must have been a wind that set the pool slopping and sent the caps scuttling toward me. What frightened me most as I fled through the dark was that I wouldn't be able to see where I was running if, as I desperately wanted to, I put up my hands to protect my eyes.

Henry James

THE JOLLY CORNER

"The Turn of the Screw" by Henry James is arguably the best of all novellas written to date in the horror mode. It is certainly the most argued-over. James' fiction sits like the tallest skyscraper casting a shadow over all of twentieth-century fiction, fanatically polished and detailed and ultimately unfathomable because it is consistently interpretable on many levels, no one of which exhausts the potential meaning. He is devoted to the inner life of characters of intricate complexity who, in his supernatural stories, are confronted with questions as to the nature of reality. These supernatural tales show a direct line of influence through Walter de la Mare and Edith Wharton to the works of Robert Aickman and others. "The Jolly Corner" is his finest ghost story in the short story form, a masterpiece of delicate horror in which the central character confronts the possibilities of his own ghostly doppelganger, evoking awe and wonder. The story occupies the border territory between the second and third streams of horror.

I

"Every one asks me what I 'think' of everything," said Spencer Brydon; "and I make answer as I can—begging or dodging the question, putting them off with any non-sense. It wouldn't matter to any of them really," he went on, "for, even were it possible to meet in that stand-and-deliver way so silly a demand on so big a subject, my 'thoughts' would still be almost altogether about something that concerns only myself.'' He was talking to Miss Staverton, with whom for a couple of months now he had availed himself of every possible occasion to talk; this disposition and this resource, this comfort and support, as the situation in fact presented itself, having promptly enough taken the first place in the considerable array of rather unattenuated surprises attending his so strangely belated return to America. Everything was somehow a surprise; and that might be natural when one had so long and so consistently neglected everything, taken pains to give surprises so much margin for play. He had given them more than thirty years—thirty-three, to be exact; and they now seemed to him to have organised their performance quite on the scale of that licence. He had been twenty-three on leaving New York—he was fifty-six today: unless indeed he were to reckon as he had sometimes, since his repatriation, found himself feeling; in which case he would have lived longer than is often allotted to man. It would have taken a century, he repeatedly said to himself, and said also to Alice Staverton, it would have taken a longer absence and a more averted mind than those even of which he had been guilty, to pile up the differences, the newnesses, the queernesses, above all the bignesses, for the better or the worse, that at present assaulted his vision wherever he looked.

The great fact all the while however had been the incalculability; since he *had* supposed himself, from decade to decade, to be allowing, and in the most liberal and intelligent manner, for brilliancy of change. He actually saw that he had allowed for nothing; he missed what he would have been sure of finding, he found what he would never have imagined. Proportions and values were upside-down; the ugly things he had expected, the ugly things of his far-away youth, when he had too promptly waked up to a sense of the ugly—these uncanny phenomena placed him rather, as it happened, under the charm; whereas the ''swagger'' things, the modern, the monstrous, the famous things, those he had more particularly, like thousands of ingenuous inquirers every year, come over to see, were exactly his sources of dismay. They were as so many set traps for displeasure, above all for reaction,

of which his restless tread was constantly pressing the spring.
It was interesting, doubtless, the whole show, but it would
have been too disconcerting hadn't a certain finer truth saved
the situation. He had distinctly not, in this steadier light,
come over *all* for the monstrosities; he had come, not only
in the last analysis but quite on the face of the act, under an
impulse with which they had nothing to do. He had come—
putting the thing pompously—to look at his "property,"
which he had thus for a third of a century not been within
four thousand miles of; or, expressing it less sordidly, he had
yielded to the humour of seeing again his house on the jolly
corner, as he usually, and quite fondly, described it—the one
in which he had first seen the light, in which various members of his family had lived and died, in which the holidays
of his overschooled boyhood had been passed and the few
social flowers of his chilled adolescence gathered, and which,
alienated then for so long a period, had, through the successive deaths of his two brothers and the termination of old
arrangements, come wholly into his hands. He was the owner
of another, not quite so "good"—the jolly corner having
been, from far back, superlatively extended and consecrated;
and the value of the pair represented his main capital, with
an income consisting, in these later years, of their respective
rents which (thanks precisely to their original excellent type)
had never been depressingly low. He could live in "Europe,"
as he had been in the habit of living, on the product of these
flourishing New York leases, and all the better since, that of
the second structure, the mere number in its long row, having
within a twelvemonth fallen in, renovation at a high advance
had proved beautifully possible.

These were items of property indeed, but he had found
himself since his arrival distinguishing more than ever between them. The house within the street, two bristling blocks
westward, was already in course of reconstruction as a tall
mass of flats; he had acceded, some time before, to overtures
for this conversion—in which, now that it was going forward,
it had been not the least of his astonishments to find himself
able, on the spot, and though without a previous ounce of
such experience, to participate with a certain intelligence,
almost with a certain authority. He had lived his life with his

back so turned to such concerns and his face addressed to
those of so different an order that he scarce knew what to
make of this lively stir, in a compartment of his mind never
yet penetrated, of a capacity for business and a sense for
construction. These virtues, so common all round him now,
had been dormant in his own organism—where it might be
said of them perhaps that they had slept of the just. At present, in the splendid autumn weather—the autumn at least was
a pure boon in the terrible place—he loafed about his "work"
undeterred, secretly agitated; not in the least "minding" that
the whole proposition, as they said, was vulgar and sordid,
and ready to climb ladders, to walk the plank, to handle
materials and look wise about them, to ask questions, in fine,
and challenge explanations and really "go into" figures.

It amused, it verily quite charmed him; and, by the same
stroke, it amused, and even more, Alice Staverton, though
perhaps charming her perceptibly less. She wasn't however
going to be better-off for it, as *he* was—and so astonishingly
much: nothing was now likely, he knew, ever to make her
better-off than she found herself, in the afternoon of life, as
the delicately frugal possessor and tenant of the small house
in Irving Place to which she had subtly managed to cling
through her almost unbroken New York career. If he knew
the way to it now better than to any other address among the
dreadful multiplied numberings which seemed to him to reduce the whole place to some vast ledger-page, overgrown,
fantastic, of ruled and criss-crossed lines and figures—if he
had formed, for his consolation, that habit, it was really not
a little because of the charm of his having encountered and
recognised, in the vast wilderness of the wholesale, breaking
through the mere gross generalisation of wealth and force and
success, a small still scene where items and shades, all delicate things, kept the sharpness of the notes of a high voice
perfectly trained, and where economy hung about like the
scent of a garden. His old friend lived with one maid and
herself dusted her relics and trimmed her lamps and polished
her silver; she stood off, in the awful modern crush, when
she could, but she sallied forth and did battle when the challenge was really to "spirit," the spirit she after all confessed
to, proudly and a little shyly, as to that of the better time,

that of *their* common, their quite far-away and antediluvian social period and order. She made use of the streetcars when need be, the terrible things that people scrambled for as the panic-stricken at sea scramble for the boats; she affronted, inscrutably, under stress, all the public concussions and ordeals; and yet, with that slim mystifying grace of her appearance, which defied you to say if she were a fair young woman who looked older through trouble, or a fine smooth older one who looked young through successful indifference; with her precious reference, above all, to memories and histories into which he could enter, she was as exquisite for him as some pale pressed flower (a rarity to begin with), and, failing other sweetnesses, she was a sufficient reward of his effort. They had communities of knowledge, "their" knowledge (this discriminating possessive was always on her lips) of presences of the other age, presences all overlaid, in his case, by the experience of a man and the freedom of a wanderer, overlaid by pleasure, by infidelity, by passages of life that were strange and dim to her, just by "Europe" in short, but still unobscured, still exposed and cherished, under that pious visitation of the spirit from which she had never been diverted.

She had come with him one day to see how his "apartment-house" was rising; he had helped her over gaps and explained to her plans, and while they were there had happened to have, before her, a brief but lively discussion with the man in charge, the representative of the building-firm that had undertaken his work. He had found himself quite "standing-up" to this personage over a failure on the latter's part to observe some detail of one of their noted conditions, and had so lucidly argued his case that, besides ever so prettily flushing, at the time, for sympathy in his triumph, she had afterwards said to him (though to a slightly greater effect of irony) that he had clearly for too many years neglected a real gift. If he had but stayed at home he would have anticipated the inventor of the sky-scraper. If he had but stayed at home he would have discovered his genius in time really to start some new variety of awful architectural hare and run it till it burrowed in a gold-mine. He was to remember these words, while the weeks elapsed, for the small silver ring they had sounded over the queerest and deepest of his own lately most disguised and most muffled vibrations.

It had begun to be present to him after the first fortnight, it had broken out with the oddest abruptness, this particular wanton wonderment: it met him there—and this was the image under which he himself judged the matter, or at least, not a little, thrilled and flushed with it—very much as he might have been met by some strange figure, some unexpected occupant, at a turn of one of the dim passages of an empty house. The quaint analogy quite hauntingly remained with him, when he didn't indeed rather improve it by a still intenser form: that of his opening a door behind which he would have made sure of finding nothing, a door into a room shuttered and void, and yet so coming, with a great suppressed start, on some quite erect confronting presence, something planted in the middle of the place and facing him through the dusk. After that visit to the house in construction he walked with his companion to see the other and always so much the better one, which in the eastward direction formed one of the corners, the "jolly" one precisely, of the street now so generally dishonoured and disfigured in its westward reaches, and of the comparatively conservative Avenue. The Avenue still had pretensions, as Miss Staverton said, to decency; the old people had mostly gone, the old names were unknown, and here and there an old association seemed to stray, all vaguely, like some very aged person, out too late, whom you might meet and feel the impulse to watch or follow, in kindness, for safe restoration to shelter.

They went in together, our friends; he admitted himself with his key, as he kept no one there,. he explained, preferring, for his reasons, to leave the place empty, under a simple arrangement with a good woman living in the neighborhood and who came for a daily hour to open windows and dust and sweep. Spencer Brydon had his reasons and was growingly aware of them; they seemed to him better each time he was there, though he didn't name them all to his companion, any more than he told her as yet how often, how quite absurdly often, he himself. came. He only let her see for the present, while they walked through the great blank rooms, that absolute vacancy reigned and that, from top to bottom, there was nothing but Mrs. Muldoon's broomstick, in a corner, to tempt the burglar. Mrs. Muldoon was then on the premises, and she loquaciously attended the visitors, preceding them from room to room and pushing back shutters and throwing up sashes—all to show them, as she remarked, how little there was to see. There was little indeed to see in the great gaunt shell where the main dispositions and the general apportionment of space, the style of an age of ampler allowances, had nevertheless for its master their honest pleading message, affecting him as some good old servant's, some lifelong retainer's appeal for a character, or even for a retiring-pension; yet it was also a remark of Mrs. Muldoon's that, glad as she was to oblige him by her noonday round, there was a request she greatly hoped he would never make of her. If he should wish her for any reason to come in after dark she would just tell him, if he "plased," that he must ask it of somebody else.

The fact that there was nothing to see didn't militate for the worthy woman against what one *might* see, and she put it frankly to Miss Staverton that no lady could be expected to like, could she? "craping up to thim top storeys in the ayvil hours." The gas and the electric light were off the house, and she fairly evoked a gruesome vision of her march through the great grey rooms—so many of them as there were too!—with her glimmering taper. Miss Staverton met her honest glare with a smile and the profession that she herself certainly would recoil from such an adventure. Spencer Brydon meanwhile held his peace—for the moment; the question of the "evil" hours in his old home had already become too grave for him. He had begun some time since to "crape," and he knew just why a packet of candles addressed to that pursuit had been stowed by his own hand, three weeks before, at the back of a drawer of the fine old sideboard that occupied, as a "fixture," the deep recess in the dining-room. Just now he laughed at his companions—quickly however changing the subject; for the reason that, in the first place, his laugh struck him even at that moment as starting the odd echo, the conscious human resonance (he scarce knew how to qualify it) that sounds made while he was there alone sent back to his ear or his fancy; and that, in the second, he imagined Alice

Staverton for the instant on the point of asking him, with a divination, if he ever so prowled. There were divinations he was unprepared for, and he had at all events averted inquiry by the time Mrs. Muldoon had left them, passing on to other parts.

There was happily enough to say, on so consecrated a spot, that could be said freely and fairly; so that a whole train of declarations was precipitated by his friend's having herself broken out, after a yearning look round: "But I hope you don't mean they want you to pull *this* to pieces!" His answer came, promptly, with his reawakened wrath: it was of course exactly what they wanted, and what they were "at" him for, daily, with the iteration of people who couldn't for their life understand a man's liability to decent feelings. He had found the place, just as it stood and beyond what he could express, an interest and a joy. There were values other than the beastly rent-values, and in short, in short——! But it was thus Miss Staverton took him up. "In short you're to make so good a thing of your sky-scraper that, living in luxury on *those* ill-gotten gains, you can afford for a while to be sentimental here!" Her smile had for him, with the words, the particular mild irony with which he found half her talk suffused; an irony without bitterness and that came, exactly, from her having so much imagination—not, like the cheap sarcasms with which one heard most people, about the world of "society," bid for the reputation of cleverness, from nobody's really having any. It was agreeable to him at this very moment to be sure that when he had answered, after a brief demur, "Well yes: so, precisely, you may put it!" her imagination would still do him justice. He explained that even if never a dollar were to come to him from the other house he would nevertheless cherish this one; and he dwelt, further, while they lingered and wandered, on the fact of the stupefaction he was already exciting, the positive mystification he felt himself create.

He spoke of the value of all he read into it, into the mere sight of the walls, mere shapes of the rooms, mere sound of the floors, mere feel, in his hand, of the old silver-plated knobs of the several mahogany doors, which suggested the pressure of the palms of the dead; the seventy years of the past in fine that these things represented, the annals of nearly three generations, counting his grandfather's, the one that had ended there, and the impalpable ashes of his long-extinct youth, afloat in the very air like microscopic motes. She listened to everything; she was a woman who answered intimately but who utterly didn't chatter. She scattered abroad therefore no cloud of words; she could assent, she could agree, above all she could encourage, without doing that. Only at the last she went a little further than he had done himself. "And then how do you know? You may still, after all, want to live here." It rather indeed pulled him up, for it wasn't what he had been thinking, at least in her sense of the words. "You mean I may decide to stay on for the sake of it?"

"Well, *with* such a home——!" But, quite beautifully, she had too much tact to dot so monstrous an *i*, and it was precisely an illustration of the way she didn't rattle. How could any one—of any wit—insist on any one else's "wanting" to live in New York?

"Oh," he said, "I *might* have lived here (since I had my opportunity early in life); I might have put in here all these years. Then everything would have been different enough—and, I daresay, 'funny' enough. But that's another matter. And then the beauty of it—I mean of my perversity, of my refusal to agree to a 'deal'—is just in the total absence of a reason. Don't you see that if I had a reason about the matter at all it would *have* to be the other way, and would then be inevitably a reason of dollars? There are no reasons here *but* of dollars. Let us therefore have none whatever—not the ghost of one."

They were back in the hall then for departure, but from where they stood the vista was large, through an open door, into the great square main saloon, with its almost antique felicity of brave spaces between windows. Her eyes came back from that reach and met his own a moment. "Are you very sure the 'ghost' of one doesn't, much rather, serve——?"

He had a positive sense of turning pale. But it was as near as they were then to come. For he made answer, he believed, between a glare and a grin: "Oh ghosts—of course the place must swarm with them! I should be ashamed of it if it didn't.

Poor Mrs. Muldoon's right, and it's why I haven't asked her to do more than look in.''

Miss Staverton's gaze again lost itself; and things she didn't utter, it was clear, came and went in her mind. She might even for the minute, off there in the fine room, have imagined some element dimly gathering. Simplified like the death-mask of a hand, some face, it perhaps produced for her just then an effect akin to the stir of an expression in the ''set'' commemorative plaster. Yet whatever her impression may have been she produced instead a vague platitude. ''Well, if it were only furnished and lived in——!''

She appeared to imply that in case of its being still furnished he might have been a little less opposed to the idea of a return. But she passed straight into the vestibule, as if to leave her words behind her, and the next moment he had opened the house-door and was standing with her on the steps. He closed the door and, while he re-pocketed his key, looking up and down, they took in the comparatively harsh actuality of the Avenue, which reminded him of the assault of the outer light of the Desert on the traveller emerging from an Egyptian tomb. But he risked before they stepped into the street his gathered answer to her speech. ''For me it *is* lived in. For me it *is* furnished.'' At which it was easy for her to sigh ''Ah yes——!'' all vaguely and discreetly; since his parents and his favourite sister, to say nothing of other kin, in numbers, had run their course and met their end there. That represented, within the walls, ineffaceable life.

It was a few days after this that, during an hour passed with her again, he had expressed his impatience of the too flattering curiosity—among the people he met—about his appreciation of New York. He had arrived at none at all that was socially producible, and as for that matter of his ''thinking'' (thinking the better or the worse of anything there) he has wholly taken up with one subject of thought. It was mere vain egoism, and it was moreover, if she liked, a morbid obsession. He found all things come back to the question of what he personally might have been, how he might have led his life and ''turned out,'' if he had not so, at the outset, given it up. And confessing for the first time to the intensity within him of his absurd speculation—which but proved also, no doubt, the habit of too selfishly thinking—he affirmed the impotence there of any other source of interest, any other native appeal. "What would it have made of me, what would it have made of me? I keep for ever wondering, all idiotically; as if I could possibly know! I see what it has made of dozens of others, those I meet, and it positively aches within me, to the point of exasperation, that it would have made something of me as well. Only I can't make our *what*, and the worry of it, the small rage of curiosity never to be satisfied, brings back what I remember to have felt, once or twice, after judging best, for reasons, to burn some important letter unopened. I've been sorry, I've hated it—I've never known what was in the letter. You may of course say it's a trifle——!''

"I don't say it's a trifle," Miss Staverton gravely interrupted.

She was seated by her fire, and before her, on his feet and restless, he turned to and fro between this intensity of his idea and a fitful and unseeing inspection, through his single eye-glass, of the dear little old objects on her chimney-piece. Her interruption made him for an instant look at her harder. "I shouldn't care if you did!" he laughed, however; "and it's only a figure, at any rate, for the way I now feel. *Not* to have followed my perverse young course—and almost in the teeth of my father's curse, as I may say; not to have kept it up, so, 'over there,' from that day to this, without a doubt or a pang; not, above all, to have liked it, to have loved it, so much, loved it, no doubt, with such an abysmal conceit of my own preference: some variation from *that*, I say, must have produced some different effect for my life and for my 'form.' I should have stuck here—if it had been possible; and I was too young, at twenty-three, to judge, *pour deux sons*, whether it *were* possible. If I had waited I might have seen it was, and then I might have been, by staying here, something nearer to one of these types who have been hammered so hard and made so keen by their conditions. It isn't that I admire them so much—the question of any charm in them, or of any charm, beyond that of the rank money-passion, exerted by their conditions *for* them, has nothing to do with the matter: it's only a question of what fantastic, yet perfectly possible, development of my own nature I mayn't have missed. It comes over me that I had then a strange *alter ego* deep down somewhere within me, as the full-blown flower is in the small tight bud, and that I just took the course, I just transferred him to the climate, that blighted him for once and for ever.''

"And you wonder about the flower," Miss Staverton said. "So do I, if you want to know; and so I've been wondering these several weeks. I believe in the flower," she continued, "I feel it would have been quite splendid, quite huge and monstrous."

"Monstrous above all!" her visitor echoed; "and I imagine, by the same stroke, quite hideous and offensive."

"You don't believe that," she returned; "if you did you wouldn't wonder. You'd know, and that would be enough for you. What you feel—and what I feel *for* you—is that you'd have had power."

"You'd have liked me that way?" he asked.

She barely hung fire. "How should I not have liked you?"

"I see. You'd have liked me, have preferred me, a billionaire!"

"How should I have not liked you?" she simply again asked.

He stood before her still—her question kept him motionless. He took it in, so much there was of it; and indeed his not otherwise meeting it testified to that. "I know at least what I am," he simply went on; "the other side of the medal's clear enough. I've not been edifying—I believe I'm thought in a hundred quarters to have been barely decent. I've followed strange paths and worshipped strange gods; it must have come to you again and again—in fact you've admitted to me as much—that I was leading, at any time these thirty years, a selfish frivolous scandalous life. And you see what it has made of me."

She just waited, smiling at him. "You see what it has made of *me*."

"Oh you're a person whom nothing can have altered. You were born to be what you are, anywhere, anyway: you've the perfection nothing else could have blighted. And don't you see how, without my exile, I shouldn't have been waiting till now——?" But he pulled up for the strange pang.

"The great thing to see," she presently said, "seems to me to be that it has spoiled nothing. It hasn't spoiled your being here at last. It hasn't spoiled this. It hasn't spoiled your speaking——" She also however faltered.

He wondered at everything her controlled emotion might mean. "Do you believe then—too dreadfully!—that I *am* as good as I might ever have been?"

"Oh no! Far from it!" With which she got up from her chair and was nearer to him. "But I don't care," she smiled.

"You mean I'm good enough?"

She considered a little. "Will you believe it if I say so? I mean will you let that settle your question for you?" And then as if making out in his face that he drew back from this, that he had some idea which, however absurd, he couldn't yet bargain away: "Oh you don't care either—but very differently: you don't care for anything but yourself."

Spencer Brydon recognized it—it was in fact what he had absolutely professed. Yet he importantly qualified. "*He* isn't myself. He's the just so totally other person. But I do want to see him," he added. "And I can. And I shall."

Their eyes met for a minute while he guessed from something in hers that she divined his strange sense. But neither of them otherwise expressed it, and her apparent understanding, with no protesting shock, no easy derision, touched him more deeply than anything yet, constituting for his stifled perversity, on the spot, an element that was like breatheable air. What she said however was unexpected. "Well, *I've* seen him."

"You——?"

"I've seen him in a dream."

"Oh a 'dream'——!" It let him down.

"But twice over," she continued. "I saw him as I see you now."

"You've dreamed the same dream——?"

"Twice over," she repeated. "The very same."

This did somehow a little speak to him, as it also gratified him. "You dream about me at that rate?"

"Ah about *him*!" she smiled.

His eyes again sounded her. "Then you know all about

him.'' And as she said nothing more: ''What's the wretch like?''

She hesitated, and it was as if he were pressing her so hard that, resisting for reasons of her own, she had to turn away. ''I'll tell you some other time!''

II

It was after this that there was most of a virtue for him, most of a cultivated charm, most of a preposterous secret thrill, in the particular form of surrender to his obsession and of address to what he more and more believed to be his privilege. It was what in these weeks he was living for—since he really felt life to begin but after Mrs. Muldoon had retired from the scene and, visiting the ample house from attic to cellar, making sure he was alone, he knew himself in safe possession and, as he tacitly expressed it, let himself go. He sometimes came twice in the twenty-four hours; the moments he liked best were those of gathering dusk, of the short autumn twilight; this was the time of which, again and again, he found himself hoping most. Then he could, as seemed to him, most intimately wander and wait, linger and listen, feel his fine attention, never in his life before so fine, on the pulse of the great vague place: he preferred the lampless hour and only wished he might have prolonged each day the deep crepuscular spell. Later—rarely much before midnight, but then for a considerable vigil—he watched with his glimmering light; moving slowly, holding it high, playing it far, rejoicing above all, as much as he might, in open vistas, reaches of communication between rooms and by passages; the long straight chance or show, as he would have called it, for the revelation he pretended to invite. It was a practice he found he could perfectly ''work'' without exciting remark; no one was in the least the wiser for it; even Alice Staverton, who was moreover a well of discretion, didn't quite fully imagine.

He let himself in and let himself out with the assurance of calm proprietorship; and accident so far favoured him that, if a fat Avenue ''officer'' had happened on occasion to see him entering at eleven-thirty, he had never yet, to the best of his belief, been noticed as emerging at two. He walked there on the crisp November nights, arrived regularly at the evening's end; it was as easy to do this after dining out as to take his way to a club or to his hotel. When he left his club, if he hadn't been dining out, it was ostensibly to go to his hotel; and when he left his hotel, if he had spent a part of the evening there, it was ostensibly to go to his club. Everything was easy in fine; everything conspired and promoted: there was truly even in the strain of his experience something that glossed over, something that salved and simplified, all the rest of consciousness. He circulated, talked, renewed, loosely and pleasantly, old relations—met indeed, so far as he could, new expectations and seemed to make out on the whole that in spite of the career, of such different contacts, which he had spoken of to Miss Staverton as ministering so little, for those who might have watched it, to edification, he was positively rather liked than not. He was a dim secondary social success—and all with people who had truly not an idea of him. It was all mere surface sound, this murmur of their welcome, this popping of their corks—just as his gestures of response were the extravagant shadows, emphatic in proportion as they meant little, of some game of *ombres chinoises*. He projected himself all day, in thought, straight over the bristling line of hard unconscious heads and into the other, the real, the waiting life; the life that, as soon as he had heard behind him the click of his great house-door, began for him, on the jolly corner, as beguilingly as the slow opening bars of some rich music follows the tap of the conductor's wand.

He always caught the first effect of the steel point of his stick on the old marble of the hall pavement, large black-and-white squares that he remembered as the admiration of his childhood and that had then made in him, as he now saw, for the growth of an early conception of style. This effect was the dim reverberating tinkle as of some far-off bell hung who should say where?—in the depths of the house, of the past, of that mystical other world that might have flourished for him had he not, for weal or woe, abandoned it. On this impression he did ever the same thing; he put his stick noiselessly away in a corner—feeling the place once more in the likeness of some great glass bowl, all precious concave crystal, set delicately humming by the play of a moist finger round its edge. The concave crystal held, as it were, this mystical other world, and the indescribably fine murmur of its rim was the sigh there, the scarce audible pathetic wail to his strained ear, of all the old baffled forsworn possibilities. What he did therefore by this appeal of his hushed presence was to wake them into such measure of ghostly life as they might still enjoy. They were shy, all but unappeasably shy, but they weren't really sinister; at least they weren't as he had hitherto felt them—before they had taken the Form he so yearned to make them take, the Form he at moments saw himself in the light of fairly hunting on tiptoe, the points of his evening-shoes, from room to room and from storey to storey.

That was the essence of his vision—which was all rank folly, if one would, while he was out of the house and otherwise occupied, but which took on the last verisimilitude as soon as he was placed and posted. He knew what he meant and what he wanted; it was as clear as the figure on a cheque presented in demand for cash. His *alter ego* "walked"—that was the note of his image of him, while his image of his motive for his own odd pastime was the desire to waylay him and meet him. He roamed, slowly, warily, but all restlessly, he himself did—Mrs. Muldoon had been right, absolutely, with her figure of their "craping"; and the presence he watched for would roam restlessly too. But it would be as cautious and as shifty; the conviction of its probable, in fact its already quite sensible, quite audible evasion of pursuit grew for him from night to night, laying on him finally a rigour to which nothing in his life had been comparable. It had been the theory of many superficially-judging persons, he knew, that he was wasting that life in a surrender to sensations, but he had tasted of no pleasure so fine as his actual tension, had been introduced to no sport that demanded at once the patience and the nerve of this stalking of a creature more subtle, yet at bay perhaps more formidable, than any beast of the forest. The terms, the comparisons, the very practices of the chase positively came again into play; there were even moments when passages of his occasional experience as a sportsman, stirred memories, from his younger time, of moor and mountain and desert, revived for him—

and to the increase of his keenness—by the tremendous force of analogy. He found himself at moments—once he had placed his single light on some mantel-shelf or in some recess—stepping back into shelter or shade, effacing himself behind a door or in an embrasure, as he had sought of old the vantage of rock and tree; he found himself holding his breath and living in the joy of the instant, the supreme suspense created by big game alone.

He wasn't afraid (though putting himself the question as he believed gentlemen on Bengal tiger-shoots or in close quarters with the great bear of the Rockies had been known to confess to having put it); and this indeed—since here at least he might be frank!—because of the impression, so intimate and so strange, that he himself produced as yet a dread, produced certainly a strain, beyond the liveliest he was likely to feel. They fell for him into categories, they fairly became familiar, the signs, for his own perception, of the alarm his presence and his vigilance created; though leaving him always to remark, portentously, on his probably having formed a relation, his probably enjoying a consciousness, unique in the experience of man. People enough, first and last, had been in terror of apparitions, but who had ever before so turned the tables and become himself, in the apparitional world, an incalculable terror? He might have found this sublime had he quite dared to think of it; but he didn't too much insist, truly, on that side of his privilege. With habit and repetition he gained to an extraordinary degree the power to penetrate the dusk of distances and the darkness of corners, to resolve back into their innocence the treacheries of uncertain light, the evil-looking forms taken in the gloom by mere shadows, by accidents of the air, by shifting effects of perspective; putting down his dim luminary he could still wander on without it, pass into other rooms and, only knowing it was there behind him in case of need, see his way about, visually project for his purpose a comparative clearness. It made him feel, this acquired faculty, like some monstrous stealthy cat; he wondered if he would have glared at these moments with large shining yellow eyes, and what it mightn't verily be, for the poor hard-pressed *alter ego*, to be confronted with such a type.

He liked however the open shutters; he opened everywhere those Mrs. Muldoon had closed, closing them as carefully afterwards, so that she shouldn't notice: he liked—oh this he did like, and above all in the upper rooms!—the sense of the hard silver of the autumn stars through the window-panes, and scarcely less the flare of the street-lamps below, the white electric lustre which it would have taken curtains to keep out. This was human actual social; this was of the world he had lived in, and he was more at his ease certainly for the countenance, coldly general and impersonal, that all the while and in spite of his detachment it seemed to give him. He had support of course mostly in the rooms at the wide front and the prolonged side; it failed him considerably in the central shades and the parts at the back. But if he sometimes, on his rounds, was glad of his optical reach, so none the less often the rear of the house affected him as the very jungle of his prey. The place was there more subdivided; a large "extension" in particular, where small rooms for servants had been multiplied, abounded in nooks and corners, in closets and passages, in the ramifications especially of an ample back staircase over which he leaned, many a time, to look far down—not deterred from his gravity even while aware that he might, for a spectator, have figured some solemn simpleton playing at hide-and-seek. Outside in fact he might himself make that ironic *rapprochement*; but within the walls, and in spite of the clear windows, his consistency was proof against the cynical light of New York.

It had belonged to that idea of the exasperated consciousness of his victim to become a real test for him; since he had quite put it to himself from the first that, oh distinctly! he could "cultivate" his whole perception. He had felt it as above all open to cultivation—which indeed was but another name for his manner of spending his time. He was bringing it on, bringing it to perfection, by practice; in consequence of which it had grown so fine that he was now aware of impressions, attestations of his general postulate, that couldn't have broken upon him at once. This was the case more specifically with a phenomenon at last quite frequent for him in the upper rooms, the recognition—absolutely unmistakable, and by a turn dating from a particular hour, his resumption

of his campaign after a diplomatic drop, a calculated absence
of three nights—of his being definitely followed, tracked at a
distance carefully taken and to the express end that he should
the less confidently, less arrogantly, appear to himself merely
to pursue. It worried, it finally broke him up, for it proved,
of all the conceivable impressions, the one least suited to his
book. He was kept in sight while remaining himself—as re-
gards the essence of his position—sightless, and his only re-
course then was in abrupt turns, rapid recoveries of ground.
He wheeled about, retracing his steps, as if he might so catch
in his face at least the stirred air of some other quick revo-
lution. It was indeed true that his fully dislocalised thought
of these manoeuvres recalled to him Pantaloon, at the Christmas farce, buffeted and tricked from behind by ubiquitous
Harlequin; but it left intact the influence of the conditions
themselves each time he was re-exposed to them, so that in
fact this association, had he suffered it to become constant,
would on a certain side have but ministered to his intenser
gravity. He had made, as I have said, to create on the premises the baseless sense of a reprieve, his three absences; and
the result of the third was to confirm the after-effect of the
second.

On his return, that night—the night succeeding his last in-
termission—he stood in the hall and looked up the staircase
with a certainty more intimate than any he had yet known.
"He's *there*, at the top, and waiting—not, as in general, falling back for disappearance. He's holding his ground, and it's
the first time—which is a proof, isn't it? that something has
happened for him." So Brydon argued with his hand on the
banister and his foot on the lowest stair; in which position he
felt as never before the air chilled by his logic. He himself
turned cold in it, for he seemed of a sudden to know what
now was involved. "Harder pressed?—yes, he takes it in,
with its thus making clear to him that I've come, as they say,
'to stay.' He finally doesn't like and can't bear it, in the
sense, I mean, that his wrath, his menaced interest, now bal-
ances with his dread. I've hunted him till he has 'turned':
that, up there, is what has happened—he's the fanged or the
antlered animal brought at last to bay." There came to him,
as I say—but determined by an influence beyond my nota-

tion!—the acuteness of this certainty; under which, however, the next moment he had broken into a sweat that he would as little have consented to attribute to fear as he would have dared immediately to act upon it for enterprise. It marked none the less a prodigious thrill, a thrill that represented sudden dismay, no doubt, but also represented, and with the selfsame throb, the strangest, the most joyous, possibly the next minute almost the proudest, duplication of consciousness.

"He has been dodging, retreating, hiding, but now, worked up to anger, he'll fight!"—this intense impression made a single mouthful, as it were, of terror and applause. But what was wondrous was that the applause, for the felt fact, was so eager, since, if it was his other self he was running to earth, this ineffable identity was thus in the last resort not unworthy of him. It bristled there—somewhere near at hand, however unseen still—as the hunted thing, even as the trodden worm of the adage *must* at last bristle; and Brydon at this instant tasted probably of a sensation more complex than had ever before found itself consistent with sanity. It was as if it would have shamed him that a character so associated with his own should triumphantly succeed in just skulking, should to the end not risk the open; so that the drop of this danger was, on the spot, a great lift of the whole situation. Yet with another rare shift of the same subtlety he was already trying to measure by how much more he himself might now be in peril of fear; so rejoicing that he could, in another form, actively inspire that fear, and simultaneously quaking for the form in which he might passively know it.

The apprehension of knowing it must after a little have grown in him, and the strangest moment of his adventure perhaps, the most memorable or really most interesting, afterwards, of his crisis, was the lapse of certain instants of concentrated conscious *combat*, the sense of a need to hold on to something, even after the manner of a man slipping and slipping on some awful incline; the vivid impulse, above all, to move, to act, to charge, somehow and upon something— to show himself, in a word, that he wasn't afraid. The state of "holding-on" was thus the state to which he was momentarily reduced; if there had been anything, in the great vacancy, to seize, he would presently have been aware of having clutched it as he might under a shock at home have clutched the nearest chair-back. He had been surprised at any rate— of this he *was* aware—into something unprecedented since his original appropriation of the place; he had closed his eyes, held them tight, for a long minute, as with that instinct of dismay and that terror of vision. When he opened them the room, the other contiguous rooms, extraordinarily, seemed lighter—so light, almost, that at first he took the change for day. He stood firm, however that might be, just where he had paused; his resistance had helped him—it was as if there were something he had tided over. He knew after a little what this was—it had been in the imminent danger of flight. He had stiffened his will against going; without this he would have made for the stairs, and it seemed to him that, still with his eyes closed, he would have descended them, would have known how, straight and swiftly, to the bottom.

Well, as he had held out, here he was—still at the top, among the more intricate upper rooms and with the gauntlet of the others, of all the rest of the house, still to run when it should be his time to go. He would go at his time—only at his time: didn't he go every night very much at the same hour? He took out his watch—there was light for that: it was scarcely a quarter past one, and he had never withdrawn so soon. He reached his lodgings for the most part at two—with his walk of a quarter of an hour. He would wait for the last quarter—he wouldn't stir till then; and he kept his watch there with his eyes on it, reflecting while he held it that this delib- erate wait, a wait with an effort, which he recognised, would serve perfectly for the attestation he desired to make. It would prove his courage—unless indeed the latter might most be proved by his budging at last from his place. What he mainly felt now was that, since he hadn't originally scuttled, he had his dignities—which had never in his life seemed so many— all to preserve and to carry aloft. This was before him in truth as a physical image, an image almost worthy of an age of greater romance. That remark indeed glimmered for him only to glow the next instant with a finer light; since what age of romance, after all, could have matched either the state of his mind or, "objectively," as they said, the wonder of

his situation? The only difference would have been that, bran-
dishing his dignities over his head as in a parchment scroll,
he might then—that is in the heroic time—have proceeded
downstairs with a drawn sword in his other grasp.

At present, really, the light he had set down on the mantel
of the next room would have to figure his sword; which uten-
sil, in the course of a minute, he had taken the requisite
number of steps to possess himself of. The door between the
rooms was open, and from the second another door opened
to a third. These rooms, as he remembered, gave all three
upon a common corridor as well, but there was a fourth,
beyond them, without issue save through the preceding. To
have moved, to have heard his step again, was appreciably a
help; though even in recognising this he lingered once more
a little by the chimney-piece on which his light had rested.
When he next moved, just hesitating where to turn, he found
himself considering a circumstance that, after his first and
comparatively vague apprehension of it, produced in him the
start that often attends some pang of recollection, the violent
shock of having ceased happily to forget. He had come into
sight of the door in which the brief chain of communication
ended and which he now surveyed from the nearer threshold,
the one not directly facing it. Placed at some distance to the
left of this point, it would have admitted him to the last room
of the four, the room without other approach or egress, had
it not, to his intimate conviction, been closed *since* his former visitation, the matter probably of a quarter of an hour
before. He stared with all his eyes at the wonder of the fact,
arrested again where he stood and again holding his breath
while he sounded its sense. Surely it had been *subsequently*
closed—that is it had been on his previous passage indubitably open!

He took it full in the face that something had happened
between—that he couldn't not have noticed before (by which
he meant on his original tour of all the rooms that evening)
that such a barrier had exceptionally presented itself. He had
indeed since that moment undergone an agitation so extraordinary that it might have muddled for him any earlier view;
and he tried to convince himself that he might perhaps then
have gone into the room and, inadvertently, automatically, on

coming out, have drawn the door after him. The difficulty was that this exactly was what he never did; it was against his whole policy, as he might have said, the essence of which was to keep vistas clear. He had them from the first, as he was well aware, quite on the brain: the strange apparition, at the far end of one of them, of his baffled "prey" (which had become by so sharp an irony so little the term now to apply!) was the form of success his imagination had most cherished, projecting into it always a refinement of beauty. He had known fifty times the start of perception that had afterwards dropped; had fifty times gasped to himself "There!" under some fond brief hallucination. The house, as the case stood, admirably lent itself; he might wonder at the taste, the native architecture of the particular time, which could rejoice so in the multiplication of doors—the opposite extreme to the modern, the actual almost complete proscription of them; but it had fairly contributed to provoke this obsession of the presence encountered telescopically, as he might say, focussed and studied in diminishing perspective and as by a rest for the elbow.

It was with these considerations that his present attention was charged—they perfectly availed to make what he saw portentous. He *couldn't*, by any lapse, have blocked that aperture; and if he hadn't, if it was unthinkable, why what else was clear but that there had been another agent? Another agent?—he had been catching, as he felt, a moment back, the very breath of him; but when he had been so close as in this simple, this logical, this completely personal act? It was so logical, that is, that one might have *taken* it for personal; yet for what did Brydon take it, he asked himself, while, softly panting, he felt his eyes almost leave their sockets. Ah this time at last they *were*, the two, the opposed projections of him, in presence; and this time, as much as one would, the question of danger loomed. With it rose, as not before, the question of courage—for what he knew the blank face of the door to say to him was "Show us how much you have!" It stared, it glared back at him with that challenge; it put to him the two alternatives: should he just push it open or not? Oh to have this consciousness was to *think*—and to think, Brydon knew, as he stood there, was, with the lapsing moments, not to have acted! Not to have acted—that was the misery and the pang—was even still not to act; was in fact *all* to feel the thing in another, in a new and terrible way. How long did he pause and how long did he debate? There was presently nothing to measure it; for his vibration had already changed—as just by the effect of its intensity. Shut up there, at bay, defiant, and with the prodigy of the thing palpably, provably *done*, thus giving notice like some stark signboard—under that accession of accent the situation itself had turned; and Brydon at last remarkably made up his mind on what it had turned to.

It had turned altogether to a different admonition; to a supreme hint, for him, of the value of Discretion! This slowly dawned, no doubt—for it could take its time; so perfectly, on his threshold, had he been stayed, so little as yet had he either advanced or retreated. It was the strangest of all things that now when, by his taking ten steps and applying his hand to a latch, or even his shoulder and his knee, if necessary, to a panel, all the hunger of his prime need might have been met, his high curiosity crowned, his unrest assuaged—it was amazing, but it was also exquisite and rare, that insistence should have, at a touch, quite dropped from him. Discretion—he jumped at that; and yet not, verily, at such a pitch, because it saved his nerves or his skin, but because, much more valuably, it saved the situation. When I say he "jumped" at it I feel the consonance of this term with the fact that—at the end indeed of I know not how long—he did move again, he crossed straight to the door. He wouldn't touch it—it seemed now that he might *if* he would: he would only just wait there a little, to show, to prove, that he wouldn't. He had thus another station, close to the thin partition by which revelation was denied him; but with his eyes bent and his hands held off in a mere intensity of stillness. He listened as if there had been something to hear, but this attitude, while it lasted, was his own communication. "If you won't then—good: I spare you and I give up. You affect me as by the appeal positively for pity: you convince me that for reasons rigid and sublime—what do I know?—we both of us should have suffered. I respect them then, and, though moved and privileged as, I believe, it has never been given to man,

I retire, I renounce—never, on my honour, to try again. So rest for ever—and let *me*!''

That, for Brydon was the deep sense of this last demonstration—solemn, measured, directed, as he felt it to be. He brought it to a close, he turned away; and now verily he knew how deeply he had been stirred. He retraced his steps, taking up his candle, burnt, he observed, well-nigh to the socket, and marking again, lighten it as he would, the distinctness of his footfall; after which, in a moment, he knew himself at the other side of the house. He did here what he had not yet done at these hours—he opened half a casement, one of those in the front, and let in the air of the night; a thing he would have taken at any time previous for a sharp rupture of his spell. His spell was broken now, and it didn't matter—broken by his concession and his surrender, which made it idle henceforth that he should ever come back. The empty street—its other life so marked even by the great lamplit vacancy—was within call, within touch; he stayed there as to be in it again, high above it though he was still perched; he watched as for some comforting common fact, some vulgar human note, the passage of a scavenger or a thief, some night-bird however base. He would have blessed that sign of life; he would have welcomed positively the slow approach of his friend the policeman, whom he had hitherto only sought to avoid, and was not sure that if the patrol had come into sight he mightn't have felt the impulse to get into relation with it, to hail it, on some pretext, from his fourth floor.

The pretext that wouldn't have been too silly or too compromising, the explanation that would have saved his dignity and kept his name, in such a case, out of the papers, was not definite to him: he was so occupied with the thought of recording his Discretion—as an effect of the vow he had just uttered to his intimate adversary—that the importance of this loomed large and something had overtaken all ironically his sense of proportion. If there had been a ladder applied to the front of the house, even one of the vertiginous perpendiculars employed by painters and roofers and sometimes left standing overnight, he would have managed somehow, astride of the window-sill, to compass by outstretched leg and arm that mode of descent. If there had been some such uncanny thing as he had found in his room at hotels, a workable fire-escape in the form of notched cable or a canvas shoot, he would have availed himself of it as a proof—well, of his present delicacy. He nursed that sentiment, as the question stood, a little in vain, and even—at the end of he scarce knew, once more, how long—found it, as by the action on his mind of the failure of response of the outer world, sinking back to vague anguish. It seemed to him he had waited an age for some stir of the great grim hush; the life of the town was itself under a spell—so unnaturally, up and down the whole prospect of known and rather ugly objects, the blankness and the silence lasted. Had they ever, he asked himself, the hard-faced houses, which had begun to look livid in the dim dawn, had they ever spoken so little to any need of his spirit? Great builded voids, great crowded stillnesses put on, often, in the heart of cities, for the small hours, a sort of sinister mask, and it was of this large collective negation that Brydon presently became conscious—all the more that the break of day was, almost incredibly, now at hand, proving to him what a night he had made of it.

He looked again at his watch, saw what had become of his time-values (he had taken hours for minutes—not, as in other tense situations, minutes for hours) and the strange air of the streets was but the weak, the sullen flush of a dawn in which everything was still locked up. His choked appeal from his own open window had been the sole note of life, and he could but break off at last as for a worse despair. Yet while so deeply demoralised he was capable again of an impulse denoting—at least by his present measure—extraordinary resolution; of retracing his steps to the spot where he had turned cold with the extinction of his last pulse of doubt as to there being in the place another presence than his own. This required an effort strong enough to sicken him; but he had his reason, which overmastered for the moment everything else. There was the whole of the rest of the house to traverse, and how should he screw himself to that if the door he had seen closed were at present open? He could hold to the idea that the closing had practically been for him an act of mercy, a chance offered him to descend, depart, get off the ground and never again profane it. This conception held together, it worked; but what it meant for him depended now clearly on the amount of forbearance his recent action, or rather his recent inaction, had engendered. The image of the "presence," whatever it was, waiting there for him to go—this image had not yet been so concrete for his nerves as when he stopped short of the point at which certainty would have come to him. For, with all his resolution, or more exactly with all his dread, he did stop short—he hung back from really seeing. The risk was too great and his fear too definite: it took at this moment an awful specific form.

He knew—yes, as he had never known anything—that, *should* he see the door open, it would all too abjectly be the end of him. It would mean that the agent of his shame—for his shame was the deep abjection—was once more at large and in general possession; and what glared him thus in the face was the act that this would determine for him. It would send him straight about to the window he had left open, and by that window, be long ladder and dangling rope as absent as they would, he saw himself uncontrollably insanely fatally take his way to the street. The hideous chance of this he at least could avert; but he could only avert it by recoiling in time from assurance. He had the whole house to deal with, this fact was still there; only he now knew that uncertainty alone could start him. He stole back from where he had checked himself—merely to do so was suddenly like safety—and, making blindly for the greater staircase, left gaping rooms and sounding passages behind. Here was the top of the stairs, with a fine large dim descent and three spacious landings to mark off. His instinct was all for mildness, but his feet were harsh on the floors, and, strangely, when he had in a couple of minutes become aware of this, it counted somehow for help. He couldn't have spoken, the tone of his voice would have scared him, and the common conceit or resource of "whistling in the dark" (whether literally or figuratively) have appeared basely vulgar; yet he liked none the less to hear himself go, and when he had reached his first landing—taking it all with no rush, but quite steadily—that stage of success drew from him a gasp of relief.

The house, withal, seemed immense, the scale of space again inordinate; the open rooms, to no one of which his

eyes deflected, gloomed in their shuttered state like mouths
of caverns; only the high skylight that formed the crown of
the deep well created for him a medium in which he could
advance, but which might have been, for queerness of colour,
some watery underworld. He tried to think of something no-
ble, as that his property was really grand, a splendid possession; but this nobleness took the form too of the clear delight
with which he was finally to sacrifice it. They might come in
now, the builders, the destroyers—they might come as soon
as they would. At the end of two flights he had dropped to
another zone, and from the middle of the third, with only
one more left, he recognised the influence of the lower windows, of half-drawn blinds, of the occasional gleam of street-
lamps, of the glazed spaces of the vestibule. This was the
bottom of the sea, which showed an illumination of its own
and which he even saw paved—when at a given moment he
drew up to sink a long look over the banisters—with the marble squares of his childhood. By that time indubitably he felt,
as he might have said in a commoner cause, better; it had
allowed him to stop and draw breath, and the ease increased
with the sight of the old black-and-white slabs. But what he
most felt was that now surely, with the element of impunity
pulling him as by hard firm hands, the case was settled for
what he might have seen above had he dared that last look.
The closed door, blessedly remote now, was still closed—
and he had only in short to reach that of the house.

He came down further, he crossed the passage forming the
access to the last flight; and if here again he stopped an instant it was almost for the sharpness of the thrill of assured
escape. It made him shut his eyes—which opened again to
the straight slope of the remainder of the stairs. Here was
impunity still, but impunity almost excessive; inasmuch as
the sidelights and the high fan-tracery of the entrance were
glimmering straight into the hall; an appearance produced,
he the next instant saw, by the fact that the vestibule gaped
wide, that the hinged halves of the inner door had been thrown
far back. Out of that again the *question* sprang at him, making his eyes, as he felt, half-start from his head, as they had
done, at the top of the house, before the sign of the other
door. If he had left that one open, hadn't he left this one

closed, and wasn't he now in *most* immediate presence of some inconceivable occult activity? It was as sharp, the question, as a knife in his side, but the answer hung fire still and seemed to lose itself in the vague darkness to which the thin admitted dawn, glimmering archwise over the whole outer door, made a semicircular margin, a cold silvery nimbus that seemed to play a little as he looked—to shift and expand and contract.

It was as if there had been something within it, protected by indistinctness and corresponding in extent with the opaque surface behind, the painted panels of the last barrier to his escape, of which the key was in his pocket. The indistinctness mocked him even while he stared, affected him as somehow shrouding or challenging certitude, so that after faltering an instant on his step he let himself go with the sense that here *was* at last something to meet, to touch, to take, to know—something all unnatural and dreadful, but to advance upon which was the condition for him either of liberation or of supreme defeat. The penumbra, dense and dark, was the virtual screen of a figure which stood in it as still as some image erect in a niche or as some black-vizored sentinel guarding a treasure. Brydon was to know afterwards, was to recall and make out, the particular thing he had believed during the rest of his descent. He saw, in its great grey glimmering margin, the central vagueness diminish, and he felt it to be taking the very form toward which, for so many days, the passion of his curiosity had yearned. It gloomed, it loomed, it was something, it was somebody, the prodigy of a personal presence.

Rigid and conscious, spectral yet human, a man of his own substance and stature waited there to measure himself with his power to dismay. This only could it be—this only till he recognised, with his advance, that what made the face dim was the pair of raised hands that covered it and in which, so far from being offered in defiance, it was buried as for dark deprecation. So Brydon, before him, took him in; with every fact of him now, in the higher light, hard and acute—his planted stillness, his vivid truth, his grizzled bent head and white masking hands, his queer actuality of evening-dress, of dangling double eye-glass, of gleaming silk lappet and white linen, of pearl button and gold watch-guard and polished shoe. No portrait by a great modern master could have presented him with more intensity, thrust him out of his frame with more art, as if there had been "treatment," of the consummate sort, in his every shade and salience. The revulsion, for our friend, had become, before he knew it, immense—this drop, in the act of apprehension, to the sense of his adversary's inscrutable manoeuvre. That meaning at least, while he gaped, it offered him; for he could but gape at his other self in this other anguish, gape as a proof that *he*, standing there for the achieved, the enjoyed, the triumphant life, couldn't be faced in his triumph. Wasn't the proof in the splendid covering hands, strong and completely spread?—so spread and so intentional that, in spite of a special verity that surpassed every other, the fact that one of these hands had lost two fingers, which were reduced to stumps, as if accidentally shot away, the face was effectually guarded and saved.

"Saved," though, *would* it be?—Brydon breathed his wonder till the very impunity of his attitude and the very insistence of his eyes produced, as he felt, a sudden stir which showed the next instant as a deeper portent, while the head raised itself, the betrayal of a braver purpose. The hands, as he looked, began to move, to open; then, as if deciding in a flash, dropped from the face and left it uncovered and presented. Horror, with the sight, had leaped into Brydon's throat, gasping there in a sound he couldn't utter; for the bared identity was too hideous as *his*, and his glare was the passion of his protest. The face, *that* face, Spencer Brydon's?—he searched it still, but looking away from it in dismay and denial, falling straight from his height of sublimity. It was unknown, inconceivable, awful, disconnected from any possibility——! He had been "sold," he inwardly moaned, stalking such game as this: the presence before him was a presence, the horror within him a horror, but the waste of his nights had been only grotesque and the success of his adventure an irony. Such an identity fitted his at *no* point, made its alternative monstrous. A thousand times yes, as it came upon him nearer now—the face was the face of a stranger. It came upon him nearer now, quite as one of those expanding fantastic images projected by the magic lantern of childhood; for the stranger, whoever he might be, evil, odious, blatant, vulgar, had advanced as for aggression, and he knew himself give ground. Then harder pressed still, sick with the force of his shock, and falling back as under the hot breath and the roused passion of a life larger than his own, a rage of personality before which his own collapsed, he felt the whole vision turn to darkness and his very feet give way. His head went round; he was going; he had gone.

III

What had next brought him back, clearly—though after how long?—was Mrs. Muldoon's voice, coming to him from quite near, from so near that he seemed presently to see her as kneeling on the ground before him while he lay looking up at her; himself not wholly on the ground, but half-raised and upheld—conscious, yes, of tenderness of support and, more particularly, of a head pillowed in extraordinary softness and faintly refreshing fragrance. He considered, he wondered, his wit but half at his service; then another face intervened, bending more directly over him, and he finally knew that Alice Staverton had made her lap an ample and perfect cushion to him, and that she had to this end seated herself on the lowest degree of the staircase, the rest of his long person remaining stretched on his old black-and-white slabs. They were cold, these marble squares of his youth; but *he* somehow was not, in this rich return of consciousness—the most wonderful hour, little by little, that he had ever known, leaving him, as it did, so gratefully, so abysmally passive, and yet as with a treasure of intelligence waiting all round him for quiet appropriation; dissolved, he might call it, in the air of the place and producing the golden glow of a late autumn afternoon. He had come back, yes—come back from further away than any man but himself had ever travelled; but it was strange how with this sense what he had come back *to* seemed really the great thing, and as if his prodigious journey had been all for the sake of it. Slowly but surely his consciousness grew, his vision of his state thus completing itself: he had been miraculously *carried* back—lifted and carefully borne as from where he had been picked up, the uttermost end of an interminable grey passage. Even with this he was suffered to rest, and what had now brought him to knowledge was the break in the long mild motion.

It had brought him to knowledge, to knowledge—yes, this was the beauty of his state; which came to resemble more and more that of a man who has gone to sleep on some news of a great inheritance, and then, after dreaming it away, after profaning it with matters strange to it, has waked up again to serenity of certitude and has only to lie and watch it grow. This was the drift of his patience—that he had only to let it shine on him. He must moreover, with intermissions, still have been lifted and borne; since why and how else should he have known himself, later on, with the afternoon glow intenser, no longer at the foot of his stairs—situated as these now seemed at that dark other end of his tunnel—but on a deep window-bench of his high saloon, over which had been spread, couch-fashion, a mantle of soft stuff lined with grey fur that was familiar to his eyes and that one of his hands kept fondly feeling as for its pledge of truth. Mrs. Muldoon's face had gone, but the other, the second he had recognised, hung over him in a way that showed how he was still propped and pillowed. He took it all in, and the more he took it the more it seemed to suffice: he was as much at peace as if he had had food and drink. It was the two women who had found him, on Mrs. Muldoon's having plied, at her usual hour, her latch-key—and on her having above all arrived while Miss Staverton still lingered near the house. She had been turning away, all anxiety, from worrying the vain bell-handle—her calculation having been of the hour of the good woman's visit; but the latter, blessedly, had come up while she was still there, and they had entered together. He had then lain, beyond the vestibule, very much as he was lying now—quite, that is, as he appeared to have fallen, but all so wondrously without bruise or gash; only in a depth of stupor. What he most took in, however, at present, with the steadier clearance, was that Alice Staverton had for a long unspeakable moment not doubted he was dead.

"It must have been that I *was*." He made it out as she

held him. "Yes—I can only have died. You brought me literally to life. Only," he wondered, his eyes rising to her,
"only, in the name of all the benedictions, how?"

It took her but an instant to bend her face and kiss him,
and something in the manner of it, and in the way her hands
clasped and locked his head while he felt the cool charity and
virtue of her lips, something in all this beatitude somehow
answered everything. "And now I keep you," she said.

"Oh keep me, keep me!" he pleaded while her face still hung
over him: in response to which it dropped again and stayed
close, clingingly close. It was the seal of their situation—of
which he tasted the impress for a long blissful moment in silence. But he came back. "Yet how did you know——?"

"I was uneasy. You were to have come, you remember—
and you had sent no word."

"Yes, I remember—I was to have gone to you at one today." It caught on to their "old" life and relation—which
were so near and so far. "I was still out there in my strange
darkness—where was it, what was it? I must have stayed there
so long." He could but wonder at the depth and the duration
of his swoon.

"Since last night?" she asked with a shade of fear for her
possible indiscretion.

"Since this morning—it must have been: the cold dim dawn
of to-day. Where have I been," he vaguely wailed, "where
have I been?" He felt her hold him close, and it was as if
this helped him now to make in all security his mild moan.
"What a long dark day!"

All in her tenderness she had waited a moment. "In the
cold dim dawn?" she quavered.

But he had already gone on piercing together the parts of the
whole prodigy. "As I didn't turn up you came straight——?"

She barely cast about. "I went first to your hotel—where
they told me of your absence. You had dined out last evening
and hadn't been back since. But they appeared to know you
had been at your club."

"So you had the idea of *this*——?"

"Of what?" she asked in a moment.

"Well—of what has happened."

"I believed at least you'd have been here. I've known, all along," she said, "that you've been coming."

" 'Known' it——?"

"Well, I've believed it. I said nothing to you after that talk we had a month ago—but I felt sure. I knew you *would*," she declared.

"That I'd persist, you mean?"

"That you'd see him."

"Ah but I didn't!" cried Brydon with his long wail. "There's somebody—an awful beast; whom I brought, too horribly, to bay. But it's not me."

At this she bent over him again, and her eyes were in his eyes. "No—it's not you." And it was as if, while her face hovered, he might have made out in it, hadn't it been so near, some particular meaning blurred by a smile. "No, thank heaven," she repeated—"it's not you! Of course it wasn't to have been."

"Ah but it *was*," he gently insisted. And he stared before him now as he had been staring for so many weeks. "I was to have known myself."

"You couldn't!" she returned consolingly. And then reverting, and as if to account further for what she had herself done, "But it wasn't only *that*, that you hadn't been at home," she went on. "I waited till the hour at which we had found Mrs. Muldoon that day of my going with you; and she arrived, as I've told you, while, failing to bring any one to the door, I lingered in my despair on the steps. After a little, if she hadn't come, by such a mercy, I should have found means to hunt her up. But it wasn't," said Alice Staverton, as if once more with her fine intention—"it wasn't only that."

His eyes, as he lay, turned back to her. "What more then?"

She met it, the wonder she had stirred. "In the cold dim dawn, you say? Well, in the cold dim dawn of this morning I too saw you."

"Saw *me*——?"

"Saw *him*," said Alice Staverton. "It must have been at the same moment."

He lay an instant taking it in—as if he wished to be quite reasonable. "At the same moment?"

"Yes—in my dream again, the same one I've named to

you. He came back to me. Then I knew it for a sign. He had come to you.''

At this Brydon raised himself; he had to see her better. She helped him when she understood his movement, and he sat up, steadying himself beside her there on the window-bench and with his right hand grasping her left. ''*He* didn't come to me.''

''You came to yourself,'' she beautifully smiled.

''Ah I've come to myself now—thanks to you, dearest. But this brute, with his awful face—this brute's a black stranger. He's none of *me*, even as I *might* have been,'' Brydon sturdily declared.

But she kept the clearness that was like the breath of infallibility. ''Isn't the whole point that you'd have been different?''

He almost scowled for it. ''As different as *that*——?''

Her look again was more beautiful to him than the things of this world. ''Haven't you exactly wanted to know *how* different? So this morning,'' she said, ''you appeared to me.''

''Like *him*?''

''A black stranger!''

''Then how did you know it was I?''

''Because, as I told you weeks ago, my mind, my imagination, had worked so over what you might, what you mightn't have been—to show you, you see, how I've thought of you. In the midst of that you came to me—that my wonder might be answered. So I knew,'' she went on; ''and believed that, since the question held you too so fast, as you told me that day, you too would see for yourself. And when this morning I again saw I knew it would be because you had—and also then, from the first moment, because you somehow wanted me. *He* seemed to tell me of that. So why,'' she strangely smiled, ''shouldn't I like him?''

It brought Spencer Brydon to his feet. ''You 'like' that horror—?''

''I *could* have liked him. And to me,'' she said, ''he was no horror. I had accepted him.''

'' 'Accepted'——?'' Brydon oddly sounded.

''Before, for the interest of his difference—yes. And as *I* didn't disown him, as *I* knew him—which you at last, confronted with him in his difference, so cruelly didn't, my dear—well, he must have been, you see, less dreadful to me. And it may have pleased him that I pitied him.''

She was beside him on her feet, but still holding his hand— still with her arm supporting him. But though it all brought for him thus a dim light, "You 'pitied' him?" he grudgingly, resentfully asked.

"He has been unhappy, he has been ravaged," she said.

"And haven't I been unhappy? Am not I—you've only to look at me!—ravaged?"

"Ah I don't say I like him *better*," she granted after a thought. "But he's grim, he's worn—and things have happened to him. He doesn't make shift, for sight, with your charming monocle.''

"No"—it struck Brydon: "I couldn't have sported mine 'downtown.' They'd have guyed me there."

"His great convex pince-nez—I saw it, I recognised the kind—is for his poor ruined sight. And his poor right hand——!''

"Ah!" Brydon winced—whether for his proved identity or for his lost fingers. Then, "He has a million a year," he lucidly added. "But he hasn't you."

"And he isn't—no, he isn't—*you*!" she murmured as he drew her to his breast.